WRONG WAY HOME

WRONG WAY HOME

KEVIN PETTWAY

<u>The Kin</u> by Ethan A. Cooper

All Hail the Kin

Gullhome
Oldain's Tempe...
Norrik
Raiders Sea
Icebite
Spiny Oyster River
Summervatn
Vikkan
Krysuvik
Badiron
Majien
Disn...
Turran
Knarrax
Summer Trades
Gradrean
Mirrik
Green
Brainland River
Sheaf
Low
Rousea
Wood
Rousland
The Arlean
Dalud
Arlea
Sleed
Sejent
Sedrios
Whene
Southen
The Paradisals
Banrgut
Rumfish
Port Placid
Pelf
N
W
E
S

Full-color map at KevinPettway.com

Thank you, Eric Flint. I wish we could have had a little more time together, and I would love for you to see what has come of your efforts. The world was made poorer the day you left it.

CHAPTER
ONE

Masika's descent through the darkness of death ended when her butt landed hard against the stone with a splash through a few inches of warm and stinking water. Darkness covered the world.

"Old King Oldam's crusty cracked buttplug! Get out of there. You're sitting in acid."

Strange noises hopped and skittered through the dark. Rumbles shook her spine. While terrifying under most circumstances, the blackness covered her nakedness, and she welcomed that, at least a little bit.

But in fact, her world was not covered in a muddy murk, Masika had simply forgotten how to open her eyes. She covered herself as best she could with her arms, blinked, looked around, and immediately wished for her vision to fail for real.

A miles-wide valley floor crumbled beneath an angry green sky; flashes of lightning thrown by distant horned giants laced billowing clouds above them. High cliffs surrounded the plain on three sides, rock jutting upward into thick stone thorns as if trying to murder any passing birds. Pulled by monsters, ugly barred wagons dotted the landscape. And everywhere wailing people fell out of the sky, nude bodies splashing down into heavy pools of viscous gray—

"Oh, did you just say this is acid?" Masika reached toward the young man who leaned out over the rancid-smelling pool and grabbed at his arm.

The hand at the end of that arm was Andosh pale, and dirty yellow hair poked out from beneath a broad leather hat shoved down tight on his head. His attire covered his skin in dusky hides, haphazardly stitched together with dark leather cording. He pulled her up and out and wiped at her rear and legs with a torn bit of animal fur that smelled, if possible, even worse than the acid.

"Uh, thanks. I'll do that." She took the bit of fur, still wet on the other side from the innards of whatever creature it most recently belonged to, and tried to clean herself, though mostly she just smeared the muck around. Her dark skin pinked up and stung where the acid touched it.

Masika decided to pretend not to be bothered by her own nakedness. After all, hundreds or more unclothed bodies surrounded her in the broad, stinking valley. Maybe nudity was normal here?

"Suit yourself, cutie. But if you want—" the rest of whatever the young man said fell beneath a fresh round of screams from somewhere to Masika's back. She refused to turn around and look.

Over his shoulder she saw one of the far-off giants lance a mountainside with a bright bolt of lightning, causing a massive rockslide that carried two of his fellows tumbling out of sight. He laughed so hard he nearly fell himself.

The man before her frowned and tried again. "You should get in the cart. It's my job to collect dead folks before the acid or the demons get them, and take them where they're supposed to go. And that's you, right? So, upsy-daisy."

"Hey, it's our mighty leader," said a familiar man's voice. "Remember her? The one who got us killed?"

Behind the young Andosh man, a tall wagon with barred sides and a black leather top sat creaking on the weathered stone. And inside the wagon's corroded bars stood Rainn, god of the Alir and Masika's friend. Beside him a willowy Andosh woman shivered against the bars, a hopeless expression on her delicately chiseled features. They were both nude, although the woman's long hair, a soft gray despite her obvious youth, covered most of her.

"Rainn!" Masika bounded to the wagon and clutched the pitted iron bars. "You made it. *We* made it. We're in the Undergates. Where is . . .?" Forgetting not to be embarrassed at the sight of her friend, Masika turned sideways to hide her nakedness, but Rainn gave no indication of noticing. Perhaps gods did not think of humans in such terms? She lowered her arms and turned to him again.

Something about the frightened woman caught Masika's eye. The color of her hair reminded Masika of someone. "Is that Heron?"

Heron extended a trembling hand through the bars and traced the side of Masika's jaw. This trip to the Undergates and the harrowing journey that led to it was all for the benefit of these two godlings. A thousand years ago they had both been captured by Angrim, the mighty Anger Under the Mountain, who ruled the despotic nation of Tyrrane back in Andos, in the world of the living. He had chained them beneath his mountain and carved runes deep into their bodies, breaking their power and reducing them to little more than humans.

Or birds, in Heron's case.

But those runes were gone from them both. Heron was herself again! The goddess Denari once told them that dying would restore them to their proper forms and abilities. Perhaps High King Oldam, lord of the Alir, would finally allow the pair of gods to return to their home.

"Rainn, Heron." Masika gripped them both by the arms. "The runes are gone. You're proper gods again. Use your god-powers to find Glauth and let's get out of here."

The two Alir exchanged a long look. Rainn broke first and faced Masika, expression tight. "Can't. Neither of us. I dunno if we ever had that kinda push, but we certainly don't now."

"But the runes." Masika ran her hand over Rainn's forearm, freckled and smooth and unscarred.

"I can't even remember how to be a god." Rainn shook his head. "I remember I could fuck up a town in seconds, but no clue how I did it." At Masika's horrified expression, he added, "Not that I wanna shit on anyone's day, god style." His gaze narrowed as it fell on the hapless victims wailing from the acidic pools. "Someone else already beat us to the punch anyway."

The young man who'd helped Masika out of the acid pointed into the sky. *He* had clothes. "There's another wave coming. You want to get out of here as more than just a skeleton with a pretty little skull, you're going to want to hop in that wagon." At Masika's obvious confusion, he sighed and went on. "Pools are filled with acid, right? Acid comes from waves. Waves fall out of the sky. You get caught out here without anything over your head, you're just bones and pink goo."

He opened the back of the wagon and pointed again, this time at the dark hide stretched over the top of the bars that made a sagging roof for the rear compartment. "It's a lot, uh, acidier when it's fresh out of the sky."

With a whaddya-gonna-do-about-it shrug, Rainn reached down and helped Masika into the wagon. She clambered up and sat on the rough wooden boards, leaning forward against her knees with her feet crossed.

"I figure wherever this damn thing's headed has gotta be better than here." Rainn stared off into the distance at the shrieking people who continued to plummet from the sky. "I mean, *fuck*."

Rescuing the outcast gods was not the only reason they'd ended up in the Undergates. Masika needed to start looking for a dead woman named Glauth. She was key to saving the lives of dozens of heroes in Andos who were slated for death unless Masika returned her to a powerful magical imp. Of course, the imp, an abandoned creation of Glauth's who wanted revenge for his "mother's" lack of affection, only wanted to be able to say that he'd killed her himself.

But Glauth wouldn't really be any worse off after that, would she?

"Can we talk to someone in charge?" Masika asked the Andosh man as he bounced into the driver's seat. A huge gray-green lizard-like creature, the size of an ox but much thicker, snorted in front of him. The hide roof extended in a sort of awning over the young man's head.

"Probably not," he said. "And I doubt you'd want to anyway. From here you're either going toward the capital to be food for demons or to the front to fight the Hiimrykers. You might get a spear if you can fight, but clothes aren't really necessary either way."

Masika did not know what a Hiimryker was, but she hoped it was not one of the lightning-wielding giants. Armed with a spear and attacking in the nude was no way to go to war against something like that.

"I stand corrected." Rainn shook his head. "Wherever we're headed can certainly be worse than here."

Heron curled into a ball on the boards, and Masika moved to her, placing a hand on her shoulder. Truth be told, she felt little better than Heron did, but the goddess had only just been stuck in the form of a, well, heron. Dying, being returned to her godly body, and finding herself in a place like this must be taking a toll.

The young man whipped the reins and the wagon lurched ahead. Those thick leather straps were tied to either end of a long iron bar which had been driven through the lizard creature's neck, just behind its head. The monster sped up, and the wagon cracked over the stony ground with painful jolts. They made poor time, as their driver rode wide circles around other acidic pools filled with wailing people. A few diligent souls like him cajoled them to hurry against the oncoming wave.

The misery of the place actively sought to overwhelm Masika.

"Wonder what your Sarah Hill Fury would do with *this* situation?" Rainn asked.

"Don't make fun," Masika chided him, pushing her dark thoughts away. Sarah was Masika's hero, and Rainn knew it. "You're the god of doing-things-out-of-doors-in-poor-weather. Not the god of making-people-who-already-feel-bad-even-more-depressed. I bet if you really gave it some thought, you'd come up with some brilliant plan to get us out of here."

Rainn's cheeks puffed out with his half-hearted chuckle. "The depressed god's Lavitrykk. And plans are your thing. I'm just here to kill people and look pretty."

"Hey, I knew the Hill Fury." The young driver cast a glance back over his shoulder as he spoke. "She was crazy. She'd have just told the acid to go away and all the demons to go shove their own dicks up themselves. And they'd have done it too. No one screwed with that woman."

Despite herself, Masika raised her head to stare at the driver. "You knew Sarah?" Masika was allowed to call Sarah by her real name. One of Sarah's best friends told her so. "Who *are* you?"

"Name's Boridan." This time a grin accompanied his quick look. "I was a Capital Guard. One of Tyrrane's best fighters. But I was an asshole. I was there when the Hill Fury attacked the Citadel, and she really cleared my head, y'know? Me and my two best mates. She made us better people. People you and your gray-haired friend might like to get to know a bit better before you go and end up on a demon's dinner plate." He waggled his eyebrows over his shoulder.

While Boridan's being a better person brought up serious questions, there had to be something there she could use. Some way to connect with the man.

Some way other than the way he just suggested, that was.

"Now I just drive the wagon and fish out the slaves." Boridan shrugged and snapped the reins. The wagon rumbled to infinitesimally greater speed.

"What's that?" Rainn asked.

Masika followed Rainn's gaze out the rear bars to a small, fast-moving shape, low to the ground, that ran on all fours after the wagon.

"It's catching up." Rainn cast about the interior, flexing his fingers, but came up empty. "Guess I shouldn't be shocked there's no weapons in a damn prison cart." He moved between the back bars to where Masika sat with Heron and crouched, fists raised.

At once, the tiny monster whipped into focus for Masika. Weathered blue fur, upthrust tusks, a long, thick tail, and a generally apelike build, the whole of it could not have stood more than eighteen inches tall on its hind legs. But that was not what brought a bright smile to her face. Inlittan's sight resolved, showing Masika the truth of the tiny monster.

"Rainn. That's Forbryttan! That little monkey-thing is your sword."

"What?" Fists still in the air, Rainn twisted to look at her. "How can you . . . You don't have your looky-thing."

With a laugh, Masika shook her head "Inlittan. And apparently, I still do."

Rainn and Masika had been gifted with an indestructible sword and a piece of magical jewelry, respectively. The sword, Forbryttan, was even now chasing them down in the borrowed body of a feral demon, a fact Masika only knew because she somehow still possessed the extraordinary sight bestowed on her by Inlittan, the bangle and ring combination her deceased body doubtlessly still wore. Amazing.

No less than twenty feet from the jouncing wagon, the little beast flung itself into the air and hurtled through the bars, rolled between Rainn's legs, and hopped to its feet beside Masika and Heron.

"Isn't this amazing?" It lifted one of its feet in its right hand and pointed to it with its left. A wide grin displayed an intimidating array of fangs and a pair of upturned tusks. "Look at me. I can run. I can jump. I can see stuff. We're going to have such a great time together!"

"Ugh." Rainn turned and slumped to the wagon floor. "This is exactly what he sounded like in my head. Kill me now."

Forbryttan danced a fuzzy blue dance, enjoying himself though he obviously knew nothing about dancing.

"Is it getting darker?" Leaning to one side, Masika stared up into the bilious green sky. The lightning giants fled, and the clouds indeed grew ever more ominous.

"Wave's coming." Boridan shouted over the din of the crying dead. "Hold onto your asses and keep your dicks under the tarp, or you'll likely lose both."

CHAPTER
TWO

Humans in the Undergates. How did that happen? Of course, the souls of humans sink this far, to serve as slaves, fodder for war, or even a delightful snack, but how did entire nations of living humans end up here? Was this some vast cosmic joke by the Dead God, who created the realms? Doubtful, as humans were formed by my Oldam and his opposite in the P'tak, Mother Love, far after the Dead God's fall.

More likely their presence is intended as no more than a thorn in my side. The Undergates, after all, is hell for everyone.

Queen Issta, Ruler of the Reaves and ex-wife of High King Oldam

The wave roared through the valley and over Masika's head, a dark gray breaker in reverse, bulging from the bottom of the clouds and sweeping across the terrified souls. They ran and tried to leap into wagons of their own, though most did not make it.

To Masika's relief, the falling acid blocked Inlittan's sight, protecting her from seeing the sources of the terrified screams.

Heron shivered in Masika's arms, and even Rainn slid beside her, a comforting presence holding them both. The stench was horrifying, and the heavy hide roof suddenly seemed thin protection from the deluge.

The shrieks outside increased—and abruptly fell off.

Only Forbryttan remained uncowed at the apocalyptic display, clawed fingers clinging to the bars, and a huge smile showing bright, sharp fangs. The acid soaked his fur to no effect.

As fast as it began, the wave ended. Rainn scowled up at the clouds. He leaned toward the bars, unwilling to step any closer. "That's not weather. What is that?"

"Just Issta's way of saying hi." With a flick of the reins, Boridan got the wagon clattering up the rocky path again. The broad creature pulling it, faded green and wrinkled skin slick with viscous acid, plodded along, unfazed by the event. "I don't really know for sure, but I think she does it to keep the value on human souls high. Her waves are just one of the ways to permanently kill a human soul. Don't want to flood the market, and she trades them to Murden sometimes. Either way, she's sort of a bitch."

They needed to survive. Get somewhere safe. How could Masika keep everyone alive when terrors pressed in from every side and she knew none of the rules?

Oh, right. They were already dead. But Boridan just said they could they die again? Masika squeezed her eyes shut in frustration. She should have listened closer to her brother Kohmose's lectures. He was the religious scholar.

Heron gripped Masika and pulled herself up until she could whisper into the younger woman's ear. Her fingers dug into Masika's shoulder.

Masika winced. "Ow. You're hurting me. And I can't hear what you're saying. Whisper louder."

Being brought back to her true form had done nothing for Heron's anxiety. Her second attempt was no more intelligible than the first.

Masika leaned back to get a better look at Heron's wide-eyed face. What could she say to allay the fears of a goddess? In the end Masika simply held Heron tighter—and shifted her grasp.

"Hey, Masika." Rainn stared ahead of the wagon. They approached the end of the valley. "Take a look ahead and tell me what you see."

"That's the end of the line," Boridan offered. "You'll be sorted for slaves, fighters, or food, and hauled away. Then I'll go back for another batch. Forever and ever, just like all the other wagon drivers out here. We're all just shiny little beads on Old King Oldam's great stone ampallang." He held out an arm, encompassing the wide valley full of similar wagons, bones, and misery.

"That sounds amazing!" Forbryttan hopped from his perch on the side bars to the front for a better view. "I love this place."

Squinting, Masika peered ahead past Boridan's hunched form. She saw huge humanoid figures, pebbled skin the color of bruised brick, wide-shouldered with big toothy maws where a neck ought to have begun. They plucked humans half their height from the backs of wagons and flung them into piles. She wracked her brains to think of a plan, any plan, to get them out of this.

"It's not amazing." Masika stared harder. A ship with no sails rested on a wooden frame of thick timbers, and a net filled with flailing men was hauled up onto its decks. As Masika watched, the bow of the ship tilted toward the sky, and the rest of the massive vessel followed suit. "Denari clear the fog, it's flying!"

The ship, easily the size of their old vessel, the *Ocean Krait*, rose higher still, and gossamer netting billowed outward from its sides. It resembled a duck, neck stretched forward in front of a rounded, streamlined body. The nets refracted the greenish light into shimmering rainbows and caught an unseen, and unfelt, wind. As the airborne craft gained forward speed, the figure of a man, tiny in the distance, leaped from the deck. He hit the stone far below, and did not move again.

The demons reacted with amusement, or so Masika thought. It was hard to tell, what with their mouths facing the sky.

Rainn needed no runecraft-enhanced sight to watch the ship become skyborne. "Thunder and blood. What kind of place is this?"

"It's the Undergates," Boridan responded with a shrug. "Bet you wish you worshipped the Pavinn gods now. You'd be on a beach in the

Untamed Paradise instead of about to get your head staved in by maniac northmen or your balls chewed on by demons who don't even appreciate the taste. I assume. Never died a Pavinn, so I guess I don't really know."

Beyond the now-empty support frame left behind by the dwindling skyship, Masika spotted another half-dozen much smaller hulls of similar design, skiffs to the first vessel's galleon. As she watched, a smaller load of women was loaded aboard one of them. A sickening suspicion formed in her gut. Soldiers or food—either way, the people she watched were being herded to their deaths.

"Boridan?" Masika knew her next ploy held little hope, but she had to try something.

"What's that, cutie?"

"I never met Sarah myself, but I've met a few of her friends. She would never allow something like this to go on. She'd fight to rescue as many as she could, or at least to escape so she could come back and stop it for good."

"I imagine you're right about that." Without turning around, Boridan nodded into the distance. "She sure shoved Angrim's head up his ass good and tight. She and Queen Jasmayre, bless her soul. Unfortunately, the Hill Fury's not here, and what she might or might not do doesn't do either of us much good, except for a fascinating bit of conversation for the next, oh, six minutes."

Six minutes left. The terrible smell of the acid wave pummeled her nose a little less horrifically, and the opaque green clouds thinned above them. Though they escaped the pits, they faced equally terrifying deaths.

"Heron?" Masika brushed the goddess's long hair aside to stare into her wide, emerald eyes. "Do you remember how you and Ameli turned us all into birds to fly up the mountain? Think you could do that again?"

The goddess shook her head and pushed it against Masika. "Need Ameli. She had the magic." She spoke as if only dimly recalling how to make the words.

Damn. What else did they have?

"Omigosh." As he clung to the corroded iron bars, Forbryttan bounced up and down, his blue-furred tail whipping excitedly. "Are we going to get to ride on one of those? Are we going to *fly*? This is the best day ever!"

Rainn let his arms drop from the bars and released a long sigh. "Glad you're happy, Forby. Maybe they won't eat you."

A spring carried Forbryttan into Rainn's surprised arms, and he buried his face in Rainn's chest. A tusked smile gazed up into the god's face. "I love you. You smell so interesting. Oh, I do hope they eat me. I've never been eaten before."

The wagon creaked along the worn and wet stone, shiny and black, past a few of the ten-foot horrors, even broader and more powerful-looking closer up. They chittered at each other in unnerving high-pitched voices, making no discernable language. Their dusky red skins gave off a dead odor. Not quite rot and not quite abandonment, but someplace depressingly in between.

Masika adjusted on the wagon floor, wishing less for clothes than for a desert hunting bow. The heat from Heron's tight grip brought out a sheen of sweat on her skin.

Experimentally, Rainn pushed at the bars, but as pitted and rusted as they were, they did not give. The typical boost in power and aggression that foul weather brought him failed to manifest during the wave. What did actual bad weather look like here?

"Hey, Rainn. Are you stronger without Angrim's tattoos?" Masika nodded to the unblemished backs of his legs. "Even if you don't remember any magic, you told me that they made you weaker. Maybe you can just decide to be stronger now?"

"I don't"—his brow furrowed—"remember. Doesn't ring any bells. I think I used to be able to fly, but I have no idea how." He slumped. "A thousand years or more is a long fucking time."

No luck there either.

"You're a god? Really?" Boridan sat sideways, one elbow on the back of his seat. "You probably shouldn't mention it to anyone else. I can't imagine how many bits they'll want to chop you into for that. *Everyone'll* want a taste of a real god."

"Your world is a real sack of crap, you know that?" Rainn asked Boridan.

"Yeah, I do."

In much too short a time, they arrived at their destination. The sky shone a clear, if sickly, yellow, with no sun in sight. The path led them up and out of the valley, leaving the cliff walls behind, and the high-pitched snuffling snorts of massive demons surrounded them.

Masika thought she might pass out from Heron's heat, but there was no way she would let the scared goddess go. Not here. Not now. Not when holding her was the only thing she could do to make anything better.

Boridan set the brake and hopped down, crossed behind the wagon, and unlocked the back gate. "For what it's worth I'm sorry you lot ended up here. You were entertaining, and I don't think I ever carted any group that knew each other, much less had a friend in common with me. For your sakes I hope they start eating you from the top instead of the bottom. I hear it's quicker that way."

Out of the corner of her eye, Masika saw Rainn crouch, setting himself to charge the door the instant it opened. She held her breath, wishing for him to do something unexpected and fierce.

But he never got the chance.

One of the huge demons, squeaking in glee, lifted the back of the wagon, sending Rainn tumbling backward. It reached in and grabbed Heron by one long leg, and shaking Masika off, lifted her out.

"No!" Masika shouted.

Heron screamed as the monster dropped the wagon, and Masika lost sight of her. Unexpectedly, the demon detonated in an intense flare of white light that blew the hide roof from the wagon top, sending Masika and a laughing Forbryttan rolling into Rainn at the wagon's front.

The monster fell to the ground in three pieces, both its arms torn from it and its upper torso obliterated.

"Heron!" Rainn shouted.

Rainn shoved the dazed Masika and giddy Forbryttan aside and ran out of the wagon. He dropped to the ground and lifted Heron to him.

Following, Masika stumbled out of the wagon. "Allz's wounds, Rainn. How did she do that?"

"Ohfuckohfuckohfuck." Boridan had his hands on his cheeks, and his glance darted between Heron, the dismembered demon, and the dozen or so others now taking an interest. "Old King Oldam shit a bag of sand, this isn't my fault. This isn't my fault!"

Giggling, Forbryttan jumped onto Rainn's shoulder and patted Heron on the head, imitating Rainn's care. "Is Heron a bomb? That's pretty neat if she is. Boom!"

"Somehow I don't think they give a crap whose fault it is, Boridan." Rainn wrapped his arms tighter around Heron and inclined his head toward the oncoming demons. "You wanna live as much as we do, then you're with us. How do we get the hell outta here?"

They were free. They could run!

Without another instant's delay, Boridan spun and ran toward the closest of the grounded skiffs.

The others followed, Forbryttan braying laughter the whole way.

CHAPTER

THREE

Masika found herself bothered by Boridan's lack of calm, though she tried not to show it. Flying boats never made an appearance in her schooling back home, sickly yellow skies or not.

"Are they still getting closer? They look like they're still getting closer." Boridan pulled a line tight and tied it off, allowing the starboard net to swell with imaginary air.

Blasts of wind alternated hot and cold across the bow of the skiff as they fled four more flying vessels filled with angry, howling demons. The nets shone in jeweled rainbow hues and billowed from behind, though the winds blew from the front, and up close Masika saw they were knotted not into squares as an ordinary net but strange runes and symbols. It was one more mystery than Masika knew what to do with in the moment. There were so many things she did not understand here, any one of which could kill them all.

Deep blue claws on the end of thick fingers buried in the cabin roof, Forbryttan clung and grinned, his pointed teeth gleaming. "This is very exciting. I wonder if they're going to catch us?"

"Yeah, they're a little closer." Masika's narrowed eyes picked out details from the following skiffs. They manipulated their nets forward and back, up and down, in response to some unseen provocation. At the thought, Inlittan shifted her sight to show her what currents they flew on.

Aha.

Masika went to port and studied the mechanism that operated the boom over the nets. Yeah, that would work. She looked ahead and watched flows of something that was not air and moved in response to their boat: clear rushing down, swimmy and translucent roaring up. Without Inlittan's help, these currents were invisible. Even the demons behind them navigated by feel rather than sight. And they only did so to stay straight.

The mechanism required two people to operate. Masika moved to the port handle.

"Boridan, you go to the other side. There. Right. When I say, tilt the nets down and be ready to tilt up again."

His pale face went even whiter, and his voice jumped an octave. But he gripped the long handle in both fists. "What? I don't know what I'm doing here. I just drive the cart!"

"Calm down," Masika said. Rainn had taken Heron into the boat's cabin, otherwise she would have asked him to help instead. "Just do what I do, when I do it." Her sight pulled to a locking mechanism attached to the boom. A series of holes in a thick wooden wheel begged for her attention. Mother Love's fortune, she was happy not to be in that cursed cart anymore. She had something to do again, something positive to help them escape.

"You just got here." A frantic edge overtook Boridan's voice. "How do *you* know what to do?"

"Pull the big metal pin, shove the lever forward two spaces, replace the pin."

Together, they both pulled, shoved, and pinned their respective sides, Boridan screaming the entire way through.

The skiff hit a clear downdraft, and its nose turned down into it. They accelerated.

They pulled away from their pursuers, who continued flying in a straight line.

The boat canted to starboard.

"Whee!" Forbryttan shouted.

From behind the cabin door, Heron screamed. Rainn's voice followed, calm and reassuring.

"Boridan, did you shove the lever two spaces or three?"

The skiff continued to turn on its side as they zoomed away.

"Two. I moved it two." Boridan gripped the post that rose out of the decking with the lever and metal pins and frantically counted. "Stuff my head up Old King Oldam's colon and call it a stone hat, I moved it four!"

A harpoon penetrated the decking just beside Masika's right foot and held fast. Above them in their own skiff, demons gibbered happily and tied off the rope.

She ignored them.

Forbryttan bounded over and licked the harpoon experimentally, long tongue flitting out between pointed tusks. His claws allowed him perfect purchase on the tilting deck.

"Move it back all the way. Four places." Masika smiled and injected as much calm as she could into her voice. "Count it out this time."

He counted and pinned the hefty iron rod into the levered wheel, and Masika corrected their twist on her end with the motions Inlittan showed her.

Even before, when Inlittan was merely a runecrafted piece of jewelry, Masika wondered if it had agency of its own. But now, from inside her own mind, the presence actively directed her toward the correct places to put her hands, showed her how far to pull and where to place the pin. The possibilities flew so much further than simply seeing into the distance.

There, above them and to port, a gigantic swirling of clear and swimmy something spun at vast speed. Masika pulled a long lever situated out over the boom and folded her net slightly, resulting in the skiff turning toward port. She snapped the net out full and shouted.

"Count six spaces up—that's back toward you—and pin . . . now!"

Together they did as Masika commanded. The skiff scudded into an upward stream of translucent ether that strained the nets and shot them upward as if flung from a ballista. They zipped up and past their howling pursuers, and the harpoon cracked in half, snapping back along the line to narrowly miss a demon's headish place.

"Back to home, two spaces. Now!"

The pins entered the broad disks just as the skiff slid into an outer arm of a great and unseen spinning wheel of currents in the sky, and their vessel zoomed away, an arrow shot by an invisible bow. Creaks vibrated from the booms through the decking under their feet as they shot through the yellow sky, black stone whizzing past beneath them.

Boridan screamed in terror.

The demons screamed in frustration.

Forbryttan screamed in delight.

Behind, the demons lifted their boats into the undetectable maelstrom. But without the ability to directly perceive it, their angles were wrong. Three of them spun in circles, one of which lost its nets and plummeted, while the other two bounced off one another before following. The final two vessels peeled away in time, their dark red occupants shrilly bellowing rage and venom.

With Inlittan's help, Masika scanned the booms, nets, and control mechanisms for strain and damage. Surprisingly, there was none.

"Do it again! Do it again!" Bouncing on the decking, tail swinging in the air above his furry blue head, Forbryttan's furry little body shook with excitement. "That was the best thing I ever did."

Boridan threw up on the deck.

At Masika's request, Rainn found big sacks made of a thick linen-like material and asked Forbryttan to slice arm and head holes in them so the naked people could wear them as clothes. The purplish melons that had been inside rolled around on the cabin floor.

The melons were quite tasty, sweet and tart, like a huge stumple-berry that thought it might rather be a lemon.

With a small sigh, Masika stuck her arms through the sack. She wanted to be the kind of hero who did not care about such things as being naked in a life-threatening situation, but she was not quite there yet. Sarah would not have cared.

"Felt like a pair of rabbit's balls bouncing around in that cabin," Rainn said, "but I'm happy to still be in the sky. Too bad we didn't get to fight any demons though." He held Heron tight to his side. Even dirty, scared, and disheveled as she was, the goddess glowed with radiant perfection. "Other than the one Heron here murdered."

"Oo! Can we fight the demons next time? That sounds like fun." Eager hope lit Forbryttan's face. The creature obviously wanted to experience everything—all at once if possible.

"Ask me again when we find some more demons." As ridiculous as Rainn's former sword sounded, Masika could not bring herself to step on its anticipation. "For now, we need to figure out where we are and where we want to be. Boridan, any thoughts?"

"Yeah. I think you've murked me." He sat on the deck, legs crossed, and body slumped forward in glum resignation. "No slave, no fighter, and no food is allowed to escape the Reaves. Those're Issta's orders. They'll follow us wherever we go, and no one will help us. Those're the Standards of Rule. I helped, so I'm murked too."

"Murked?" Although Masika had a pretty clear idea what he meant, she needed to know everything about this place she could.

Boridan canted his head to one side, glancing sidelong at Masika. "When a mirrored person gets killed, they usually come back the next day. Because of souls or whatever. That's called getting broken. It's not so bad."

"Wait. Mirrored?" This sounded more complicated than Masika imagined.

He nodded. "Dead people. Like you or me. Not native humans. Their soul mirrors what they were in life. Got it? Anyway, murked is when a mirrored person goes dark forever, usually because a demon ate them. But really anything that eats you does the same thing. Don't get eaten."

Native humans?

"Then as I understand it, you have nothing to lose by continuing to help us." Masika went to him and put a hand on his shoulder. "You've already shown us how resourceful you are. I could never have piloted this flying boat without you. Maybe it's time for you to leave the demons behind and come back to people again. I promise we won't eat you, and you might even enjoy making some new friends."

Unbelieving, Boridan shook his head. "You don't . . ." He raised his hands and let them drop. Inhaling and letting out a big sigh, he gave Masika a grim smile. "It's a skomp. The boat we're in. It's called a skomp."

"What should we name it?" Heron asked. Rainn jumped and whipped his head around at her question. Hearing Heron's human voice, now that she had a second to think about it, caught the breath in Masika's throat. It sounded older than she had thought it would. Calmer than her squawks and honks as an actual heron. "Every boat should have a name."

"What would you name it?" Masika asked. Her friend was talking. To *her*. No interpreter needed. Masika did not even try to keep the smile off her face.

Heron stepped out of Rainn's embrace and let a delicate hand trail along the starboard wale.

"She's a bird, but she's never been happy. She's been made to do terrible things, and she's angry about it. Her name is the *Bitter Goose*. She will be a solid ally against the demons of this realm."

"That's a wonderful name, Heron." In all honesty, Masika thought the name sounded bleak, but arguing with Heron just seemed like bad form. "Uh, what terrible things did she do?"

Hauling himself to his feet, Boridan slapped dirt from the dark hides he wore—his hat had flown away in all the excitement—and peered over the side. "The big ship you saw hauled fighters to the front, which is where we're headed now. The skomps were for taking food-humans all over the Reaves."

Rainn snorted his displeasure. "That's fucked up. What kinda asshole helps these monsters do that to his own kind?"

Not all that long ago, Rainn had not held much more use for humans himself. But Masika witnessed him become a real hero against a remnant piece of creation when a village of innocents had been on the line.

They needed a distraction.

"Rainn," Masika said, "how do you feel now that your scars are gone? Now that we're not running for our lives. Any more godly yet?"

"I feel angry." He swung his arms front and back, flexing his hands as he did so. "I feel like tearing the heads off the first fuckers I find *with* heads. So yeah. I think I do feel like my old self again."

Heron's voice was as soft as her hair. A faint smile caressed her lips. "We are restored in body. But I don't remember how . . . I don't remember how to *be* a god. Still, I suppose that is a start."

CHAPTER

FOUR

I overheard my housemaid accuse me of being unable to handle losing this morning. She was instructing a lesser servant to be careful never to contradict anything I might say, given that I am incapable of being wrong in any capacity, even losing an argument on the meaning of a certain word or the name of a certain place. In part, she was correct. I am assuredly incapable of being incorrect about anything, due to my superior godly nature, something I am certain provided my housemaid with great reassurance as she was being devoured by my orgars.

The fact that I so conclusively won the point amply illustrates her error.

Queen Issta, Ruler of the Reaves and ex-wife of High King Oldam

---

Masika squinted ahead and tried to concentrate on seeing the invisible currents swirling through something that was not quite air.

This proved more easily imagined than accomplished.

"So, we're headed for a front? An honest war front?" Rainn asked.

"Yes." Boridan's mouth twisted in distaste at Rainn's enthusiasm. "How can you be so happy about it? People are dying there."

"I know." A tight grin turned Rainn's face feral. "Dead people don't need their swords. Or armor or spears."

"Or pants? I think your sack's a little . . . short." Boridan twirled his finger at Rainn's legs. Masika studiously kept her eyes on the horizon.

"It's not my fault this itchy bag doesn't fit," Rainn answered. "No one makes melon sacks in my size."

Turning further away, Masika stared down off the *Bitter Goose*'s bow. Scree and jagged stone passed beneath them, while in the distance she picked out signs of battle. Temporary fortifications, ragged lines of troops, and other flying vessels dotted the horizon.

It was the latter that concerned her most. There were certainly enough ships and skomps there to surround them and bring them down, no matter how cleverly she flew. They would have to find a better way across the front.

Her dinner of tart purple melon settled in her stomach, a stone that dragged down her speed and her mood. What if no way out of the Undergates presented itself? Romi and Catlia both swore to her that their ex, Morholt, was not only from here, but capable of traveling freely back and forth. But what if he lied to them about it? How many women had he married before growing bored and moving on? Was that the behavior of an honest person?

The sky here alternated between wide, fuzzy strips of yellow and blue. If she pretended as hard as she could, it was almost possible to convince herself she was home instead of the realm of the dead.

Almost.

She needed more than this. "All right, Boridan. We're leaving the Reaves, right? Land of demons and evil and ruled by Issta, who used to be married to the king of the Andosh gods."

Boridan left Rainn to join Masika in the bow. "That's right. And we're headed for Hiimryk. That's where the war is."

"And who lives there?" Masika fervently hoped it would be someone who wanted to help them.

"The Andosh dead." He leaned on his elbows against a half-filled barrel of sour water, no doubt for the prisoners the *Bitter Goose* had been intended to ferry. "Old King Oldam's loyal soldiers. That's why the war. No one gets along with their exes."

That brought another thought of Romi and Catlia to Masika's mind.

"Will they help us?" she asked Boridan. "Enemy of my enemy and all that?"

"No. They're mirrored. Barely more than animals. I hear they can't die. They just keep getting stronger and uglier the longer they fight. If it weren't for Issta's demons and all the souls we push to the front, the Reaves would've been overrun ages ago."

"And would that be such a bad thing?" So far, Masika had not seen much to recommend the Reaves over anywhere else.

Boridan shrugged. "I really couldn't say."

"So." Masika blew out her cheeks in a loud sigh. "Assuming it's better than 'all the monsters want to eat us,' how do we get there? How do we get past the front?"

"I don't know that either." His mouth turned down, giving his face a despondent air. "I've never left the acid pits."

"Let's lose some altitude." So far this conversation netted no useful information, and Masika needed to make some decisions. "We're too visible up here." She returned to the port mechanism, but this time Inlittan drew her eye to an empty cable housing.

"Ready when you are." Starboard, Boridan held the pin in one hand and the lever in the other.

"Hang on." Masika followed the narrow housing aft, where she found two pairs of metal cables attached to one another. They ended in loops and ran above the cabin. She climbed a narrow ladder to see some sort of steering bars on an iron column in front of an oversized padded leather chair. Straps hung from the chair, assumably to protect the pilot in the event of the sort of maneuvering they had just been forced to endure.

With Inlittan's help, Masika and Boridan reattached the cables to the port and starboard nets, and Masika strapped herself in.

She pushed the bar forward, and the entire column moved with it. The *Bitter Goose* leaned her neck forward, and gracefully sank toward the blasted ground.

"Hey, this is *way* easier. Thanks, Boridan. You've been a huge help."

From the deck, Rainn laughed at her. "Leave it to Masika to find the one guy on the boat who almost fucking killed us all and make him feel good about it."

Boridan crossed his arms. "Sorry. I don't remember you popping out to help. Or were you waiting for us to need someone to stand around in some fog?"

"Thank the mist. I didn't think I was gonna get to kill anyone until we landed." A wide grin crossed Rainn's rugged features. "C'mere, you little shit. I'm gonna throw half'a you off that side into the Reaves, and the other off that side into Hiimryk. You'll be a dual citizen."

The chair straps prevented Masika from getting to the two men circling one another. Instead, she jerked the steering bar sideways, sending both rolling against the starboard railing.

Heron screamed and fell flat onto the deck. Masika winced, feeling bad for that.

"Sorry." Masika forced a bright smile to her face. "That was my fault. I get so distracted when people needlessly attack each other that I'm likely to kill us all."

"Ow." Heron stood and inspected her hands. She cast about the deck, pointedly ignoring the two men. "Do you think there are any frogs to eat on this boat? Those melons upset my stomach."

Rainn and Boridan untangled from each other, the merely human-strength Boridan getting the worst of the angry exchange. He climbed the ladder and sat next to Masika on the top deck over the cabin.

For the third time, Forbryttan threw himself from the deck, sailing through the air, only to be caught up short by the line Rainn had tied firmly around his thick neck. He giggled and snorted and swung back and forth before scampering back up the rope to look for an even better place to leap overboard from.

"Let's see what we can see." It struck Masika that she might try and look, with Inlittan's help, for a route through the sky where no one would notice them. Or no one with the desire or capability to murder them, at any rate. But Inlittan showed her nothing.

Death flew everywhere.

No better direction suggested itself to Masika. She needed more information. "Boridan, we're looking for a runecrafter named Glauth, and after that, we'll need to find Morholt. He's also a runecrafter. I know it's not much to go on, but do you have any ideas of how to start?"

She chose not to say that they needed Glauth as a bargaining chip back in the living world to return Rainn and Heron to their godly home, and that Morholt was everyone's only way to get out of the Undergates. Secrecy was not her nature, but nothing about this place engendered trust. Her papa the diplomat would have been proud.

Boridan frowned at the decking and concentrated. "Well, I've never heard of Glauth, but there's a runecrafter in Savach named Morholt. Some kind of royalty. That's pretty far away though. We'll need the Crying Road if we're going to have any sort of chance of that."

"Is that an actual road?" Masika hated the idea of abandoning the *Bitter Goose*. Maybe Heron should not have named it.

Mouth open to speak, Boridan hesitated. "I don't know for sure. All my information comes from the orgars, and I don't think they knew what they were talking about half the time. It's supposed to start here in the Reaves somewhere, but I don't think we'd be safe on it, even though demons aren't supposed to be able to hurt humans there. Queen Issta has other humans working for her too, and they're not bound by all that stuff."

"So where do we go to find the road? I assume we can get on it after it exits the Reaves."

Boridan pointed ahead, through the approaching war front. "That way."

"How do we get around them?" Masika wanted to avoid all this mess if she could.

With a shrug, Boridan pointed behind them and answered her. "I don't think we can. Look. There's another flotilla of Reaves ships coming. They'll have seen us by now, and if we turn they'll chase us down as deserters."

"Guess we're not getting out of here without a fight." She tapped her fingers against the steering bar. As much as Masika tried to concentrate on the problem at hand, her mind continued to drift to her father. She left him behind in the hands of an assassin, but that assassin worked for her uncle, the Holy Emperor of Egren. She had to trust the assassin knew better than to harm the emperor's brother. There was nothing to be done about it now anyway.

"Hiimryk's airships are slower than the Reaves's." Boridan poked his legs between the railings of the top deck and stared out at the distant front. "They steer with their peckers." He smirked over his shoulder at Masika. "When they get hard, they can only turn to port."

Even as she tried not to picture Boridan's imagery, another thought occurred to Masika. "Are they really slower?"

He held out his hands. "That's what I was told. Skomps are the fastest things in the sky, but the demons riding in them are the weapons. Same for all the Reaves ships. The Hiimrykers'll shoot you from across the sky. We get too close to them and . . ." Boridan whistled a descending note and arced his hand downward.

"I have an idea." Masika pointed the *Bitter Goose*'s nose further down and looked ahead. Instead of trying to find a path where no one would see them, she looked for someplace where they were certain to be spotted.

There were a lot of those.

"Hey, what are you doing? That's the wrong way."

Masika mirrored Boridan's wicked smirk back at him. "I said I had an idea. If we live through it, you can have all the credit."

He scowled. "We get murked, I'm blaming you."

The nose of their skomp turned toward the thickest region of ships in the air, and they accelerated in a smooth—and alarming—dive. The invisible current filling their nets billowed them out, causing the rainbow-hued runes to stretch far past the vessel's bow, and pulled them at ever increasing speeds.

Curious, Masika inched the steering bar to starboard. Though stiffer, it moved easily, and they flew to the side before she reoriented them. This had a chance of working.

Rainn shouted to Heron over the rushing wind. "We're being stupid again! Time to take you below."

"I'm not going anywhere." Heron gripped the port boom and jerked her other arm away from Rainn. A wild grin overtook her face, and her blue-gray hair streamed behind her. "I want to *fly*."

Was this the same woman who awoke shivering and terrified such a short time ago? Even as a bird, Heron had always been skittish. Or perhaps because she had been a bird?

Rainn stood and watched her for several heartbeats before moving to the opposite boom and taking hold of it. "Suits me. No fights belowdecks I wanna have anyway. Hey, Masika, see if you can pick us up some demons for me to kill as we go." He wrapped a knotted line around his wrist and forearm. Behind him, Heron did the same with hers, and Boridan sat at the port slave bench and encircled both arms in the lines attached there. The bench was intended to keep captives from leaping to their deaths, as Masika saw one do earlier.

It ought to keep Boridan from falling out just as well.

Though Masika very much hoped to steer the *Bitter Goose* far enough away from anything that might want to jump aboard that it would not be an issue, the number of vessels in the sky forced her to concede the possibility.

Then again, at the speed they were moving, it might not matter.

Much sooner than Masika felt comfortable with, they dove through the enemy. Orgars chittered in their shrill, horrible voices, bulky bodies covered in brick-red skin the texture of rain-worn cliffs. The sight of them filled her with revulsion, cavernous mouths ringed with slashing teeth set deep in their shoulders. Not just unnatural, but the lack of a face left her with no way to read them, no way to predict them.

She shifted in the chair, its leather straps preventing her from finding comfort and rotted padding sticking to the undersides of her legs. What if she found herself distracted by the digging into her shoulders and thighs and failed to react in time to some split-second threat? Sweat broke out under the straps, causing them to chafe.

Maybe better not to think about what else might go wrong.

In front of her, Forbryttan chewed on a railing, trying to push his tusks into the wood and see if he could hang by them.

Apparently, he could.

Ahead of Masika's skomp, ever-larger ships moved together to cut them off. One turned in a majestic slide, its multihued nets poofing out to one side.

Half a dozen orgars leaped from its decks.

"Hang on!"

Masika pushed the steering bar forward and dove, turning the *Bitter Goose* in a tight barrel roll. Yellow sky became dark ground, and flying vessels wheeled in wild arcs around her head. Forbryttan howled in delight while Heron laughed, and Boridan turned white as crushed bone.

Rainn simply crouched and held on, face grim.

Thuds came from the hull as the orgars bounced off the curving planks and rained over the sides around them, deep red squeals of outrage following them to the ground. The skomp righted, and a final demon landed with a thunderous crash against the edge of the top deck between Heron and Rainn.

Before Rainn could react, Boridan shook off his lines and flung himself off the deck at the monster, but they were too close to the edge of the higher deck for Masika to see what was going on.

Heron screamed, and Rainn dove in under Masika's view.

A one-and-a-half-foot tall, faded-blue streak followed him in, and chittering squeals erupted beneath the deck's edge.

Through the grunts and thuds and shrieks of fighting, Masika pulled the steering bar back and shot over the decks of a pair of Reaves ships. For an instant they were free, and then they plunged into Hiimryk's fleet.

Wider and flatter by comparison, maybe three hundred feet long, eighty wide, and covered in raging northmen, the hulking stone ships of Hiimryk ponderously soared in every direction about their tiny craft. Inlittan lit Masika's brain, showing her the twists and turns to keep them alive instants before she needed them.

This was her plan. If she could just keep out of range of the north-men's weapons, then the *Bitter Goose* would fly through the Hiim-rykers like an arrow through a window, and the bulky vessels would provide a barrier against the faster-moving demon—

Before she finished the thought, the top deck filled with arrow shafts, and Masika screamed in pain. A pair of arrows pinned her to the padded seat through her right knee, and her vision swam.

There were too many of them. Nowhere to dodge.

Another flight of arrows thunked into the hull from below, a few flying up over both the deck and Masika's head.

Forbryttan's grinning face came up over the edge of the top deck, fur coated in dark red blood. He spat, and a ragged lump of stony flesh flew over the side. The little demon dove back in, eyes wide and fanged mouth wider.

Inlittan's sight vanished as pain turned Masika's world white. She fought for consciousness, and the aerial battle slowed. With pain-fueled detail, Masika watched the Hiimryk vessels flinging themselves through the sky on hulls of stone, gray rock hewn into the shapes of ships, with enormous runes carved into huge square blocks set along the edges of the decking. The runes burned with the violent heat of gargantuan forges and radiated both a shimmering light and a low roaring sound.

One of these runes grew massive, and belatedly Masika recognized why.

She fell unconscious just before the crash.

CHAPTER

FIVE

A warrior serving the Alir in Hiimryk is the most stupendous of honors. The false death's just a door to eternity and glorious battle on the fields of the Undergates. Here any Andosh can find courage and strength and enemies aplenty to whet their blade against, not to mention the richest of ales and fatty fish to feed their fighter's heart. The never-ending chance to prove yourself in combat's the favorite thing about this land in the heart of every Andosh warrior.

My personal second favorite thing about Hiimryk is the creamed spine-fish salad. Long as you can get past all the thorns inside, it's just like herring and almost as good as killing demons.

Be even better if there were potatoes in the afterlife.

Jarl Refur the Bent

The sounds of revelry awakened Masika to cold and to hunger. She opened her eyes.

She lay on a stone bed in an alcove scooped out of solid rock, covered in a coarse fur pelt that stank of mildew and dead animal. Open to the sky, wan light entered the alcove from one side, where music played and rough voices laughed and sang.

Strewn clothes lay in a haphazard bundle on the foot of the bed. Masika exchanged her melon sack for a sleeveless gray tunic and baggy pants held up with a ratty cord. The abrasive cloth scratched her skin, but it was very nearly an improvement over the sack.

As she pulled on the pants, she drew in a breath at the sight of her leg. Where the arrows once ran her knee clean through, a pair of metal rods held a curved leather clamp tight around it. The assemblage was not comfortable but in the manner of a dull ache rather than a sharp, screaming pain. Who had done this? What did it mean?

She bent the knee and felt, rather than heard, an internal clicking. Damn this place. The Undergates was horrible, and none of them could get out fast enough.

Where were Heron and Rainn?

One thing at a time. Sandals hid beneath the clothes, and Masika considered that none of this left her any warmer. Her wellbeing clearly sank far below the consideration of whoever left them, and her, here. The care given to her leg suddenly loomed ominous in her mind. Why mend her injuries only to clothe her so that she froze?

She gingerly stepped to the open wall.

Her alcove was sunk into the side of a mountain, one of untold numbers. Stairs cut into the dark stone ran between all the openings and to the ground, with hundreds of pale-skinned Andosh climbing up and down.

A dim blue sky, with only a hint of yellow directly above, forced Masika to squint at the scene. What had she expected to find in the afterlife of the Andosh? She could not recall having given the matter any thought, but it would not have been this.

The men and women traversing the mountain slope laughed and sang, throwing jests, cups, and gnawed-on bones at one another. Unlike her, they wore faded colors and bits of armor tied together with rope and leather straps. However, what caught Masika's attention, and alarm, was the state of their bodies.

Every man, woman, and child of these people sported horrifying, fatal-seeming injuries, repaired in much the same manner as Masika's leg: arms held on with oversized iron staples or replaced entirely with working wooden and metal prosthetics, legs with the meat chopped out of them and filled with rusted and steaming pipes, and one laughing warrior with a head half cleaved away, who peered through a rounded steel bowl affixed to his skull with protruding screws.

Were they even all made of the same people, or were they put back together piecemeal from whatever recoverable parts lay scattered on the battlefield after yet another clash with the Reaves's demons?

Unlike Masika, these Andosh carried a variety of frightening weaponry. Serrated swords, big-bladed spears, and bows as thick as Masika's wrist decorated the cobbled-together warriors. Where did they get all of this makeshift weaponry?

Not the time to worry about such things, Masika allowed Inlittan to cast further down the mountainside and into the astonishing revel taking place there. She passed over the dances, roasting creatures on gigantic spits, and individual combats, looking for anyone she knew.

In a wide circle surrounded by laughing northmen, Rainn battled a truly enormous man.

Well, *that* figured.

The two collided and shoved apart. More metal and wood than flesh, the bigger man, easily twice Rainn's size, pinwheeled his arms to keep from falling over backward. Even under a cloudless sky, the god's true and unfettered strength showed itself to much laughter and applause.

Masika lowered her head and made as straight a line as she could for the spot. She winced in anticipation of the pain her injured knee would cause her. But other than the strange clicking, it was as if she'd never taken an arrow to the knee. She recalled Boridan's words about everyone here being reflections of the bodies they had while alive. Mirrors. Perhaps the rules for repairing mirrored souls were different than for fixing living bodies.

In the time it took her to arrive, Rainn defeated his opponent and moved on to a pair of northerners, one tall and rangy and the other squat and thick. The taller of the two stood erect, as a corroded iron pole ran up out of his back and kept his head upright, and the more heavily muscled man's right forearm had been replaced with a thick-hafted spiked hammer. Both were covered in scars.

Cheers filled her head, and the smell of the roasting animals became harder to ignore. The field at the foot of the mountain crowded close with happy Andosh. A spinning pitcher sailed over her head, dumping a sour and frothy beer all over her.

"Hey! You made it." Leaning in to make himself heard over the shouting mass, Boridan smiled at her. Like Masika and Rainn, he wore the same gray tunic, pants, and sandals. "I worried about you when the war barge's nets tore you off the chair and those arrows through your leg, but one thing these people seem to know is patching folks up. Hey, you hungry?" He lifted a tray mounded with sliced meats, pink, steaming, and aromatic.

Masika pursed her lips to keep from drooling on herself. By way of answer, she grabbed the thickest slice she saw and took a big bite.

Amazing. Crusted with delicious char, the meat itself proved tender and luxuriant, fatty and flavorful. She had never tasted the like.

"Pretty good, right?" Boridan grinned at her. Insistent Andosh hands reached over his shoulder and grabbed at the meat, and Boridan lifted the tray and lowered his head to make it easier for them.

Instants later the greasy tray was empty.

"Oh yeah, we're also slaves here. I guess I already was, but this seems better than working for Issta's demons. The food is, anyway."

The crowd roared, and Masika flinched. She peered through the excited audience to see Rainn yank on his shorter assailant's arm, foot in the man's armpit, and tear the prosthetic limb bodily from him. He ducked below the rangy fighter's swing and came up behind him, banging down on his head with the hammer at the end of the dismembered arm. The pole erupted up through the top of the taller man's skull.

Rainn lifted the bodies one by one and threw them onto a pile of torn corpses, a wide smirk on his face.

"At least someone's having fun." Masika finished off her meal and looked around. "Do you know where Heron or Forbryttan are?"

A dreamy expression flitted over Boridan's face at the goddess's name. "Heron's with the Jarls' Council. The war barge that caught us got swarmed with demons right after you tried to run into it. Heron murked one with her hand. Just *foof* and he was gone in a white flash. Apparently, the sheepfuckers here think she might be a special new weapon they can use."

Was Heron regaining her abilities? It certainly appeared that way.

Boridan pointed to the pile of Rainn's destroyed opponents. "Your demon's over there."

Forbryttan stood with one clawed foot on a fallen Hiimryker's face, the other on her chest, and yanked at the hand axe embedded in the woman's throat. He said something to Rainn, who chuckled and pulled it free for him.

Masika asked, "So these jarls run things around here?"

"Seem to." Boridan ducked a metal elbow as he spoke. "I have to say, it felt like High King Oldam had his big old granite pecker so far up my ass I could taste rock in the back of my throat the whole time I was in the Reaves. I'm glad you and your two friends showed up and ruined everything for me there. Thanks."

"You're welcome?" Masika shrugged and grabbed Boridan's arm. "Follow me. Stay close."

They entered the fighting ring as another four combatants, swords banging on shields, came in from the opposite side to have their go at murdering Rainn. The god flicked gore from his empty hands and passed a blood-chilling grin over the four fighters.

Their banging skipped a beat, and they glanced at one another nervously.

"Fight's over!" Masika shouted into the brief quiet. "The jarls want this one. He's important to the war. Go have some beer or something. You've all been really great fighting the demons."

"Fuck the jarls!" came a man's bellow from behind Masika to general laughter. The screamer shoved her from behind, and Masika went down on her hands and knees in the bloody circle. "They wanna take our toys they can come—"

The voice cut off mid-shout. Masika had not seen Rainn move, but she saw him back away with a crimson chunk of what might have been a throat in his hand.

The northmen erupted in glee, and a path opened in the crowd.

"That's our cue." Boridan herded Masika and Rainn away from the bloodthirsty celebrants and toward a massive series of stone longhouses. "I hope no one holds a grudge for Rainn killing all their friends."

"That's the best fucking time I've had in a thousand years." Rainn could not keep the grin off his face, and his teeth shone white and straight in his blood-soaked countenance. "We gotta come back here after we find the imp's maker and drag her back to Andos. These crazies know how to enjoy themselves."

Masika patted Rainn on the wrist. "We'll talk about it. I'm glad you had a good time."

"Where's Heron?" Rainn craned his neck looking for her. His muscles tightened.

"She's fine," Masika said. "We're going to get her right now."

"Good." Rainn flicked his hand, and a line of Hiimryker blood decorated the dirt. "I'm not against revenge or anything, I'd just prefer avenging someone I didn't like so much. Like Boridan."

Boridan winked and pointed back at Rainn. "I think that's the first thing we've agreed on."

CHAPTER
SIX

Queen Issta shat the bed with High King Oldam when she decided to fuck around with Angrim, the Son of the Serpent. The king whacked her head right off and sent her here to think about what she'd done for the rest of forever. But even though she was mirrored, she was still a god, you know, so she crowned herself queen of all the Undergates.

Bitch couldn't keep it all though, could she? And any real Andosh, even us mirrored ones, just laughed at her anyways.

Point is, if a god ends up down here, it's because they done fucked up something righteous and they deserve whatever they get. Someone oughta write a poem about that.

Jarl Refur the Bent

S o these people worship the Alir, don't they?" Masika waited in a large stone antechamber with Rainn and Boridan. Clusters of warriors murmured amongst themselves under the guttering torch sconces in the high-ceilinged room. "Why don't we just tell them you and Heron *are* Alir and order them to help us?"

"Did." Rainn leaned his head back and belched. "They said they'd never heard of us. Fuckers. Way to make a guy feel like shit."

"I'm sorry." Reaching over, Masika squeezed Rainn's hand, again marveling at the lack of glowing blue scars. "It's not their fault Angrim godnapped you before people got to know who you were. And if they did know you, I bet they'd be lining up on their knees to—"

She stopped talking at Boridan's wicked leer.

"Stop that. You know that's not what I meant."

"Don't be an asshole to Masika." Rainn scowled down at Boridan. "You haven't earned it yet."

As Rainn and Boridan squabbled, Masika stepped toward the huge wooden door, framed in rusted iron with spiked rivets forming diamond shapes in the cracked and gouged surface. Her leg reminded her of her injury with a dull throb, and she stopped to rub at it.

The leather and steel contraption somehow kept the majority of the pain away, though Masika could not work out the manner of it. She brushed her fingers along the leather, smooth and tight over her skin. The ends of metal posts that held the assemblage in place ran through the holes in her leg left by the arrow shafts.

The thing represented an apology of sorts to Masika. *Sorry we shot your leg, here's a big, weird bandage that you'll never be able to take off. We good here?* Except Masika was not good. While she knew appreciation to be the correct response, the feeling of violation refused to leave her. The Undergates had marked her. Claimed her as its own and branded her with this device. But even the thought of belonging here caused grief to clench in her middle.

Would she be allowed to return home, even if Morholt and Glauth sat waiting in the next room?

Would Masika ever see her papa again?

The giant door rattled, and the two men joined Masika in front of it. She buried her fears and smiled brightly at Rainn. "You ready? Let's just try to get Heron and leave. I don't want to complicate our lives here." *If* the Hiimrykers were willing to let them go. If any of them could ever leave the Undergates at all.

Of course, being a prisoner was not all that complicated.

"We should see if these bloodthirsty northmen have any information we can use." As he spoke, Boridan stepped in front of Rainn. "You know, I take that back. Them being bloodthirsty, anyway. It's kinda nice to talk to people who don't want to eat me." He brushed at his shapeless gray shirt, baggy and stained with the fluids of previous owners. "How do I look? Heron likes gray, doesn't she?"

"She loves it." Rainn shoved Boridan aside. "She just hates idiots."

The double doors creaked open, and a pair of battle-scarred Hiimrykers stepped out, corroded spears in hand. The pair glared at each visitor in turn as everyone shuffled in. On the right side, the guard gazed through one icy blue eye and one pale green gemstone that reflected too much light.

Inside, the hall stretched out enough that the far end only just drifted into view through the smoky haze of peat cauldrons. Light came from a huge open hole in the roof, allowing most of the smoke to float away. The noise of laughter, shouting, and arguments washed over her.

The crowd meandered into the central floorspace, wide, round, and surrounded by tiers, four feet high and continuing up to the ceiling, upon which stood hundreds, if not thousands, of Hiimryk warriors in various stages of bodily completeness.

Anxious, Masika looked about for Heron. Is this where the jarls and kings of old held council? Is this where they would bring a prisoner from the Reaves?

Almost instantly, Inlittan guided Masika's sight to her friend at the leftmost "corner" of the huge, rounded room. Masika pointed. "She's that way. She's not hurt. It looks like she's being entertaining?"

With Rainn leading the way, it took less than ten minutes to get to the stairs that led up into the tiers closest to Heron. Above, the tall goddess spoke to a circle of broad-shouldered fighters, their rapt attention punctuated with bouts of uproarious laughter.

Alarmed, Masika spotted Forbryttan as the little demon crawled up Rainn's shoulder and prepared to launch himself at an impressive-looking Hiimryker with the corpse of a hawk nailed into his skull. Rainn grabbed him and held him still.

"You want a dead hawk, Forby? I'll get you a dead hawk. That dead hawk belongs to him."

Forbryttan squirmed in Rainn's grip. "But I want *that* one!"

Chuckling, Rainn leaned over to Masika. "Just can't take some swords anywhere."

"Don't worry. We'll be leaving soon enough." Or so Masika hoped. But the dark look that Boridan cast up at the burly northmen surrounding Heron signaled potential trouble, and letting that jealousy fester could only hinder their moving on.

Heron likely would never reciprocate Boridan's attraction, but slamming that door in his face, now, here, felt needlessly cruel.

His eyes took a moment to refocus on Masika, and Boridan grinned as though nothing had ever been wrong. "Sure! I'm just happy we found her. Let's go." And he climbed the staircase between the tiers.

Masika followed.

Eyes on Boridan, Rainn scowled.

Each tier rode ten feet deep, supporting a vast number of big men and women, each heavily armed and at least partially made of metal, leather, and wooden bits. As she climbed and clicked, Masika realized from snatches of conversation that each of these individuals was once at least a jarl, and a great many of them had been kings among the living.

With a start, she also noticed that the leg with the leather-and-pin assembly did not tire as she went up the stairs like her other leg did. This did not seem like a good thing.

"Masika. Rainn." Heron's graceful gesture collected the gazes of her attendant kings and focused it on her friends. "These are the people I was telling you about. The ones who brought me to you. Masika, tell High King Ivarr here about how you rescued me from the Reaves and brought me here, where I belong."

Heron's knowing eyes held their secrets and beckoned Masika to do the same. Still, the word *belong* hurt.

"I'm sure I didn't do anything the rest of you wouldn't have," Masika said noncommittally. "I didn't want to be in the Reaves either."

This provoked another burst of loud laughter, briefly over-whelming the riotous sound of the rest of the room.

"Masika, meet High King Ivarr, of Coldspine." Heron nodded toward a huge man to her right. "His son sits on the throne in Brit-tlepin today. A fine young lad from what I hear."

The king's name vibrated in the back of Masika's skull. She knew exactly who he was.

The man, bigger than anyone Masika had seen thus far, with a bushy blond beard starting to go gray and covered in thick furs, shone her a dazzling smile of straight white teeth. Masika found herself so taken aback by the force of his attention that she barely noticed the curving steel plate that wrapped the back of his skull or the metal hand and lower leg on High King Ivarr's right side.

"And how did you come to be here, tiny Darrish?" High King Ivarr fairly boomed. His voice rattled Masika—and at the same time made her feel safe. "Wouldn't you rather have gone ahead to Damah, the afterlife of your people?"

The king made Masika feel the same tiny insignificance that Mount P'takkin did, though he did so with a rich smile. Even his belly, rounded as it was, only increased the overall presence of the man.

"No, sire." Masika forced herself to be heard over the din. "I'm here on a mission for my friends. But didn't you know Sarah the Hill Fury?"

A subtle quirk of the lips crossed Heron's face, while Rainn sighed loudly and rolled his eyes with his whole head.

If anything, High King Ivarr's grin grew, though his regard pinned Masika to the floorboards beneath her.

"I did and do, Darrish. Why? What news do you bring of the world above? Did you know my Sarah?"

"Um . . ." A shiver of quite a different nature ran up Masika's spine. It never occurred to her that she might come face-to-face with Sarah's dead lover here in the Undergates. What should she say?

"*Your* Sarah?" Rainn's question came with a chuckle. "You were fucking little Masika's grand hero? Hah! Was she as epic in the sheets as she apparently was on the battlefield?"

Masika's mouth hung open. Other than being world-endingly embarrassing, Rainn's outburst threatened to get them all killed where they stood. High King Ivarr enjoyed a larger-than-life reputation for impulsivity and brash violence, even among the barbaric north. How likely was it that a few years of death would diminish that reputation?

An oversized iron and wood hand shot out to grasp a surprised Rainn by the shirtfront and dragged him close to High King Ivarr, who leaned down into the god's face. The king's brows drew down, and his white teeth filled his tight grin in a suddenly menacing fashion.

"She still is."

Both Rainn and High King Ivarr burst into laughter as Masika tried to melt between the boards beneath their feet and flow away. She thought she might have done so if not for Heron's steadying hand on her shoulder.

To the far side of Heron, Boridan watched that hand with longing.

"Really now, Your Majesty." Heron shook her head and tutted at High King Ivarr. "Is that proper behavior for a king? You know the Darrish have more delicate sensitivities. This young girl is the niece of Holy Emperor Khasek the Fifth. She is due some measure of respect."

"As Lady Heron commands." High King Ivarr released Rainn and faced Masika. "Masika, was it? Or Princess Masika. Do you know Prince Tennat? He's a diplomat."

"I'm his daughter. Youngest daughter."

"Ho!" High King Ivarr clapped Masika on the shoulder, threatening to send her to her knees. "Your father is the only man born on Darrish dirt worth a sheep's butthole. I'm sorry for him that I'm meeting you here. Still, small afterlife, eh?"

Unsure what to say, Masika merely nodded.

The heat of High King Ivarr's regard softened a little, and he leaned forward, that he might speak more directly. "Sarah visits me still, when the mood strikes her. Do you think she knows you?"

"Oh, no. I don't think so." But did this mean Masika might meet Sarah here? As far as she knew, Sarah was simply dead, although

Heron once told her that she spoke to Sarah when no one else could see.

Wait.

"Heron," Masika asked, "that time on the path to the Alireon. You saw Sarah?"

"I did."

"And you, Your Majesty," Masika said to the high king, "Sarah visits you here? Is that right?"

"It is," High King Ivarr replied.

"Sarah can travel between the realms." The depth of the revelation shook Masika's bones. Would Sarah return them to the living world if Morholt would or could not? For that matter, would Sarah prevent Ild the imp from fulfilling his threat to kill the heroes Masika first met at the Jolly Chicken tavern if they failed to produce Glauth?

Could Sarah return Heron and Rainn to the Alireon?

A brilliant grin spread itself across Masika's face. She gripped Heron and Rainn. "Don't you see? We don't need to find Glauth and sacrifice her to the stupid imp. We only need to find Sarah. She'll help us. And when she does, all our problems will disappear. Sarah is the answer, and all we have to do to find her is wait here with High King Ivarr."

"Oldam's muddy turds." Boridan's sudden grin matched Masika's own. "You think Sarah would carry me back with you? I did help her out there at the end."

Heron and Rainn exchanged glances, and Rainn shrugged.

"Can't go back." High King Ivarr put a gigantic hand on Boridan's shoulder. "Your body's dead, same as the rest of us. Nothing to go back to."

But Denari Clear Eyed sent Masika and the two Alir here with a divine poison. She said they would be able to return. Masika racked her memories. That was what she said, right?

A fight broke out among the kings and jarls on the tier beneath them, one of many since the conversation began, though closer and louder than the others.

"Quiet!" bellowed High King Ivarr, so loud Masika swayed back on her heels. The overall cacophony remained, though it grew a little quieter in the immediate area. "That's better." A thoughtful expression wrinkled High King Ivarr's forehead, and he rubbed his fingers across his lips. "I do not think you could get the help you desire. My Sarah has passed beyond the needs and cares of people like us."

"Except when she's feeling moist?" Rainn leered at High King Ivarr.

"I am glad none of my actual wives have made their way to me as of yet," High King Ivarr admitted. "But Sarah either knows of you, in which case she's doing everything she wishes to help you already, or she doesn't, in which case you're not important enough for her to bother with. Sarah didn't die when she defeated the Anger Under the Mountain. She *transcended*."

"What does that mean?" Heron asked.

"Don't truly know." High King Ivarr's huge shoulders rose and fell, a pair of rounded boulders that considered abandoning gravity but changed their minds. "Sometimes she's a ghost, and other times she's as solid and warm as any other person, mirrored or alive. But I do know her concerns are a fair flight from ours."

To Masika, the conversation felt like a series of blows. She lost her place in it. What had she intended to say?

"Well, Ivarr, I appreciate the lack of help, but it's time for us to move along." Rainn put his hands on his hips and stared up at the high king. "We'll require weapons and armor and our flying duck boat back. I'll mention you to Oldam when I see him."

A faint hint of a smile returned to High King Ivarr's face at that. "You're on your way to the runecrafter Morholt, is that right?"

"Yes?" Suspicious confusion bloomed on Rainn's face. "How do you know that? I haven't told anyone that."

"Duke Morholt is something of a big deal in Savach." Even High King Ivarr's quiet voice rumbled in Masika's chest. "And that's at the far end of the Undergates from here. It's a formidable journey. You would have to travel the entire length of the Crying Road to get there."

"Maybe you could throw in some provisions too then." Rainn's voice went lower, gravelly.

It was at this point Masika noticed the crowd around them had stopped talking and were staring at the king and the god. In fits and starts, the circle of quiet expanded, lowering the volume in the area. A cold feeling settled in her stomach.

"Heron here has told me about the two of you." Behind the smile, High King Ivarr's gaze glinted cold steel. "You are gods of the Alir, captured centuries ago by the Anger Under the Mountain?"

"Millenia, but yeah." Rainn returned High King Ivarr's stare with no less force. "We're Alir, and you're Andosh. So do as you're told and no one has to get all smited over it."

"I bet we can take 'em," Forbryttan said, smiling face staring out over the thousands of grim-looking Andosh warriors.

"Mm-hm." Despite his reputation, High King Ivarr failed both to fall to Rainn's threat or rise to his bait.

Masika hated the way the Andosh negotiated.

"High King Ivarr," Masika said, "you told us that if Sarah did know about us then she might already have done something to help us. Is that a guess, or has she said something to you?"

A flash of discomfort crossed High King Ivarr's expression. His brow smoothed, and he spoke low and clear. "Yes, child, she has. No, calm yourself. I'd hoped to spare you this, given your feelings for her, but Sarah asked me to take you captive and hold you here in Hiimryk for the next thousand years. Give or take."

"What?" Boridan exclaimed. "I'm not with these people. I'm a loyal Andosh. Let's go fight some demons. Yeah? Or I guess I could just go away if you don't want to."

Masika was in freefall. First, Sarah, if not exactly alive, remained ahead of death's clutches. She might even have helped. But to discover that her hero not only knew who she was but had ordered her capture . . . Masika gasped, and her eyes went wide. This was no different from her sister Meritities. But this time they had already been to the summit of Mount P'takkin and their captor was the most powerful sorceress in the world.

Or the ghost of one.

Knees and elbows bent, hands flexing, Rainn prepared to attack the sympathetic High King Ivarr. Until Heron slid her tapered fingers around his wrist and pointed.

The entire chamber, tens of thousands of deceased northern rulers, watched them, silent as a stone. There was no hate on the multitude of faces, but the tension in the smoky haze left no doubt of the outcome should Rainn choose violence.

"It is not up to me, tiny godling," High King Ivarr's voice rumbled. "Gods or not, you are to be treated as nothing more than captives from the Reaves. In that thousand years or so, you may earn your way out of slavery. *If* you show value. That's what Sarah's asked of me, and it's what I intend to do for her. She's earned it."

Before Rainn could articulate a response, Heron stepped in front of him.

"That's fair, High King Ivarr. A thousand years is meaningless to us. And perhaps in the interim we can help you win your war against the Reaves."

Forbryttan bounced up and down on Rainn's shoulder. "That's even better! I've never fought a whole war before."

One horn, followed by others, broke the silence throughout the grand hall. Boridan's head jerked this way and that, trying to ascertain the source of whatever threat was being warned against. The assembled northmen cheered, a wall of sound that rattled the stone and timbers of the huge chamber.

Bits of sand and crumbling masonry fell through the peat smoke from the ceiling.

"We're under attack," High King Ivarr boomed. "More skyships from the Reaves. You'll be jailed until we figure out what you're good for." He cast about the excited warrior kings. "Jarl Refur! Yes, old man, you." He gestured with his human hand, and an ancient fighter, thin white hair blowing up and away from his scarred and patched skull, stumped over on legs of stone bound in steel. More reconstruction than man, Jarl Refur must have doubled High King Ivarr's weight, though the king had a foot of height on him.

The sight of the crusty warrior made Masika's leg "bandage" itch.

"You're staying behind. Take these four and put them in a cell." High King Ivarr ignored Jarl Refur's bitter frown, the old man's face being the only part of him not made of hardness. "Those two're gods, so keep an eye on them. The lady god killed an orgar without a weapon. Don't let her near your cock."

"I'd have to know where it was," Jarl Refur said with a shrug.

Taking that as assent, High King Ivarr lumbered away after his howling Andosh warriors.

In minutes, they stood nearly alone in the massive hall. Only Jarl Refur and a half-dozen of his fighters remained, along with a few here and there too battered to be of use in an aerial battle.

The silence rang in Masika's ears.

She did not want to be here forever. Why would Sarah do this?

Rainn cracked his knuckles, and Boridan crouched behind him The two stood back-to-back, facing their enemies.

A happy laugh flew from Forbryttan's furry blue throat. "Is this how the war starts?"

"How it ends, maybe. Two against six is a lot better odds than one against a zillion," Rainn observed.

"I'd feel a little better about it if we were the ones with the swords," Boridan added.

A quick shake of Heron's head put an end to that. "Play along for now," she whispered. "We'll escape later. These are our people. We should strive not to harm them."

"Hmph." Rainn lowered his fists. "I dunno when you got all thoughtful instead of scared, but I don't like it."

"Follow me, grays." Jarl Refur thumped down the thick wooden stairs while his men surrounded Masika's friends. A wide-headed axe bounced against the bone-and-iron back of the jarl, much too heavy for a normal person to wield.

"Learn to like it," Heron responded to Rainn. "I may not remember how to *be* a goddess yet, but I am beginning to recall how to act like one."

In Masika's opinion, that was the less useful of the two.

CHAPTER

SEVEN

Protecting the Andosh afterlife's what we do here in the contested zone between Hiimryk and the Reaves. While most consider this foreverish fight to be a waste of fighters and resources, I got a different take on it, if you'll gimme a minute to explain.

Up above, every Andosh nation's been at war with every other one at some point or another. But down here we're together. United, is what you'd say. Past the contested zone, Hiimryk is a paradise of snowcapped mountains, tall woodlands, and lush farms, and we're all together on protecting it. That kinda peace is worth an eternity of war, if you ask me.

Jarl Refur the Bent

Bars fronted three walls of solid rock. Unless Boridan learned to burrow through stone, he and his new friends would all be here a while.

Though not thrilled with the danger behind his new accommodations, Boridan admitted to himself that this stood a good leg up over fishing damned souls out of pools of acid. Perhaps he would not have been so quick to leave if they had shown him even a bit of gratitude?

Or not been trying to murk him.

Jarl Refur clicked shut the barred gate that served as the cell's only door. "This's the best prison cell we got, so you all might should consider that whilst you make your plans for escaping. You too, Darrish girl. I've seen the way you go around eyeballing everything."

"What?" Boridan gave Jarl Refur a winning smile and leaned up against rust-stained iron bars, not coincidentally stepping between the jarl and his line of sight to Masika and the others. No less than three inches thick, they did not notice his weight. "Why would we run? Free food, an honest job slaving away once the high king gets back, this place is great. Way better'n a military spear shaft up my ass like I had when I was alive. Tyrraneans know how to kill all the fun in killing other people." Of course, if Boridan had the spear, this conversation would take an entirely different shape.

No. Don't think that way.

Behind Boridan, a single room some thirty feet wide and twenty deep housed the rest of his new companions. The space, carved into a high cliff face and accessible only by a series of rickety ladders outside, was filled with furs, water buckets with ladles for drinking, and empty buckets for shitting. There was even a large loaf of gritty-looking black bread. Mirrored souls did not technically require food to survive, but without it they fast became useless skeletons of their former selves.

Jarl Refur fixed Boridan with a rheumy old eye. Something in his iron and wood shoulder made a series of clicks. "I know you're just trying to get my guard down, son, but I don't take no worry from it. How long you been dead? Less'n a year, right? You still think that the life you left is what forever gets measured by. But it ain't. Forever lasts a *lot* longer'n that did, and you measure it by itself. Don't worry. You can't get out. Rant and rail all you like, you'll come around eventually. Forever makes its own in the end." He rubbed his aged pink chin with a clunky hand of bone and steel rivets. "Someone oughtta write a poem about that."

So saying, he turned and stumped off, a pair of hard-eyed fighters with far too many weapons remaining behind.

"I said I don't know how I did it. Stop asking." Heron tied her hair back behind her head with a bit of twine. The woman, a literal goddess, stole Boridan's breath away every time he looked at her. He had witnessed perfect women in his life before. Even fell in love with one once. But since finding Heron, his memories of the others evaporated, steam from a kettle on a windy day.

But who felt such affection for her? Was it him or the other one?

"Is there anything I can do to help?" Boridan asked.

Heron glanced at him, saying nothing, while Rainn ignored him altogether. Masika smiled in a sort of shocked way, her jittery gaze clearly displaying a brain trying to catch up to its circumstances.

It was a look he recognized, and he felt bad for her.

"I'm just saying," Rainn whispered, "if you could remember how you did your demon-frying trick, it might work on metal bars too."

"No, we can't escape." Masika's hushed comment came out harsh and crackly. "We have to stay here."

The two gods stared at her, neither speaking.

"Why's that, Masika?" Boridan asked. He moved closer and gripped her shoulder in what he hoped was a reassuring manner. He used to do that, didn't he? Try as he might, he could not remember ever being supportive to anyone. That hand on Masika's shoulder belonged to Keane.

She reached up and grabbed his wrist, holding him fast. "Didn't you hear King Ivarr? Sarah wanted us put here. She must have a plan. A *reason* for us to be here. Sarah's not Meritities. She'll show up soon, and then she'll tell us why we're here."

Uncomfortable, Boridan pulled away.

"Thunder and blood, this shit again." Rainn rubbed at his forehead and sighed. "Masika, I know hearing that about Sarah was hard. And I feel for you, I really do. But we gotta get the fuck outta here, and fast. We don't know how long it'll take us to get to this Morholt guy, and if we wait 'til Giant King Ivarr thunders his way back from the front, there's no telling when we'll be able to get away."

Pale, graceful fingers floated out and brushed the hair from Masika's face. Boridan watched it, jealous of Heron's touch but grateful for her presence. He did not know Masika very well, but a crying teenaged girl was rarely a help in prison breaks.

"You have given so much, Princess." Heron continued to brush tightly curled ringlets of hair out of Masika's face. "We have no right to ask more. I would only offer a question to you. If Sarah is what you say she is, as far thinking as you believe, then how do we know that she didn't request our detention to keep us out of the fighting? So that we might then escape while the Hiimrykers were occupied against the Reaves?"

It made sense to Boridan. Everything Heron said made sense to him. He thought it was him.

"But there's no way out. Inlittan can't see anything." Masika's voice sounded like a little girl's to Boridan.

And who was Inlittan?

"Where's your trimpet?" Boridan kept one eye on the guards while he spoke, but other than mean looks, they seemed disinclined to do much about all the secret conversation.

"What's a trimpet?" Rainn asked.

How did they not know all the members of their own party? "The blue-furred demon you showed up with? It talked, which was weird. You were going to get him a dead hawk? No great loss, I guess. They're not usually very friendly."

"Forbryttan?" Masika said.

"Forby! I've gotten too used to this place shitting on my head to even think about him." Rainn scowled and crossed his arms. "Damn. Where the fuck'd he get off to? I need to tie a cowbell around his neck. With the cow still attached."

Masika stared around the cell before her gaze lit once more on Rainn's face. "Inlittan thinks you can do it. You can contact Forbryttan somehow."

"He can?" Heron looked between Masika and Rainn.

"I can?" Rainn's eyebrows rose. "How? How do you talk to Inlittan? And how are you doing it when Inlittan didn't even come with you?"

"I don't know," Masika admitted. "It's like she's part of me now. Like she left the jewelry behind when we all died."

None of this made any sense to Boridan, so he stayed quiet and listened.

"For that matter," interjected Heron, "why is Forbryttan a demon now? I understand why the sword didn't come with us, but why is he a—a trimpet?"

Boridan nodded to Heron, glad to be given an excuse to speak to her. "Trimpet. Yeah. They're pretty common in the Reaves. Scavengers. But they're not all that strong individually. He basked in the goddess's attention.

"Try talking to him, Rainn. What have we got to lose?" Heron put an elegant arm around Masika's shoulders as she spoke.

Rainn frowned while he considered the question. He shrugged and walked away from them, facing the back wall of the brown stone cell. His fingers went up to his temples.

"Forby? You there?"

A moment passed while everyone held their breath.

"Shadows of the Alir! Forby? Is that you?"

Stealing a glance at the guards, Boridan saw them exchange grim looks before unlimbering axes and advancing on the cell door. "Rainn, cut it out," he hissed. "The guards. Stop it."

Worried Keane fretted in Boridan's body. Except that as a mirror, this body was his *soul*. It was everything Boridan was, and it wasn't even his.

For the first time Boridan considered the violence done to him when Sarah crushed him with Keane's personality. Somehow, the fact that such a thing would never have occurred to him without Keane made it all the worse.

"No shit. You are?" Rainn turned back to face them, a broad smile on his rugged face. "Sure. Why not?"

The first guard reached for the barred door. Boridan realized in that instant why these two guards in particular had been chosen. They were tall, broad, and their upper bodies were mostly made of steel cable. How powerful must they be?

Well, Boridan might not be a gigantic dead raider made of steel and ox bone, but he had spent most of his life training as a professional soldier and Keane was a mercenary. He would not allow these two to reach Heron without a fight. As the first of the warriors unlocked the gate, Boridan reflected on two further facts.

First, they had axes; he had a dirty shirt. Second, they weren't after Heron; they were after Rainn, who Boridan did not particularly like.

He stepped aside.

Or rather, he tried to. As Boridan went to get out of the way, the big Hiimryker in front of him stumbled forward. Boridan jumped to one side, narrowly missing the tumbling form, who sported the bottom half of a blue-furred trimpet bloodily burrowing into the middle of his back.

The warrior's axe fell as he did, and Boridan neatly caught the weapon in his right hand.

Behind the falling Hiimryker, his fellow roared and slashed down at the trimpet's rear with his own axe, burying it in blue fur and overextending his reach through the barred door. In return, Boridan swung the first axe in a wide, double-handed arc that ended in a splattering crunch in the bridge of the second guard's nose, chopping across both his eyes.

The axe haft yanked out of Boridan's hands as the guard jerked backward, staggering, open hands flung wide. He reached up to pull the axe out of his face, which Boridan found both disquieting and rude.

The first pull failed to extract the axe blade, but it did wrench the guard's head forward. Boridan ignored the sounds of Rainn's approach and ran out the door to kick the guard in the side of the knee, one of the few places made entirely of flesh. The kneecap popped, the guard tipped forward, and Boridan grabbed him by the hair and rode him down, putting all his weight on the man's head and cracking the axe the rest of the way into the burly guard's brain.

He stopped moving altogether.

"Huh." Rainn stood in the open doorway, the first guard between his legs. He looked down and grabbed Forbryttan by the wriggling tail and pulled. A long *shlorp* accompanied the blood-soaked demon as he was extracted from the man's back. "I think he's dead now."

"Well sure he's dead." Forbryttan hung upside down and dripped crimson all over the guard's back. "But I've never been all the way inside someone before. I wanted to see if I could make the arms and legs go."

"Next time, Forby." Masika strode forward to take her place beside Rainn. Confidence returned to her bearing, and the jittery little girl voice left her. Whatever issues she was dealing with were off the fire for the moment. "We need to get out of here. If us being out of danger was the reason we were in this cell, I'm pretty sure that burned down the instant these two died."

Boridan considered reminding her that they were all dead here, and these two men would only be down until the other Hiimrykers patched them up. But he really wanted to leave, and he could explain all that later anyway.

Who he really was and whether he could ever return to himself would have to wait too.

Oldam fart a sandstorm.

CHAPTER

EIGHT

Hierarchy in Hiimryk is sorta complicated. Most Andosh culture ain't all that respectful to its kings to begin with, and having near a thousand of 'em around at once don't help. Even the Alir don't get a pass if a proud warrior thinks their god's full of shit. As noble as that independence is, it's also probably the reason Norrik hasn't conquered the whole of Andos by now.

Nobody can agree who to kill first.

Used to be easier, back in the beginning. The hardest bastard ran things, and if you didn't like it, you got your teeth pushed down your throat. But being hard and being smart ain't always the same thing, and eventually Hiimryk got big enough that brains started getting more worth'n a solid sword arm.

Course, some of us got both.

Jarl Refur the Bent

O utside, Boridan had discovered the location of their skomp. A palisade of sharpened trunks guarded by Andosh skjold maidens, surrounded a huge yard full of sky craft.

56

No one paid Boridan's little group much attention as they navigated the settlement. Slaves were invisible here.

Mostly.

He bowed again and stared at the dirt as he spoke to the scowling Andosh woman. "No ma'am. I don't think she meant anything by it when she called you a lazy, cat-holing dust-crotch. She was certainly smiling when she said it."

He prostrated himself in front of the pair of skjold maidens guarding the tall palisade of thick timbers. Behind them, the slightly ajar gate showed a sliver of bare earthen ground, trampled by thousands and thousands of northern warriors.

The burly woman smacked her palm with the flat head of a war hammer and snarled. "That shit-talking sack of bees has had it coming for years now." A frightening grin spread across her ruddy round face. "I'ma smash her head into so many fucking pieces they'll hafta make her a new skull outta that damn flowerpot she loves so much."

So saying, the woman squared her shoulders and stomped off, hauberk jingling with each shuddering step.

Boridan smiled up at her no less fearsome companion, who elected to remain behind to watch the gate. "Flowerpot's friend thought it was funny too. I think they're planning to jump your girl next time they see her."

The second woman took a quick glance over her shoulder at the gate and pulled a long-handled axe off her back. "You stay here and watch the gate," she ordered Boridan before running after her mate. "Hang on!" she shouted. "I wanna piece of that slag too."

Crossing his arms, Boridan leaned against the palisade and watched the angry pair charge around a round stone building.

"I gotta admit, I did not figure that'd work." Rainn stepped around a pile of shattered stone and past Boridan. He pushed the gate open, revealing a mostly empty shipyard.

"Then why'd you let me do it?" Boridan pushed himself off the palisade as Masika and Heron approached.

"'Cause even if they decided to kill you, it'd still be a distraction, and I could knock their stupid heads together while they did it." He grinned back over his shoulder. "Plus it would've been funny."

Heron lay a delicate hand on Boridan's shoulder. "Well done, soldier of Tyrrane."

There was some more conversation after that, but Boridan could not recall any of it. He did remember the feeling of Heron's hand on him long after it departed though.

On him.

On *him*. Not on Keane.

"There's the *Bitter Goose*." Masika pointed to their vessel; its damage already repaired by the industrious Hiimrykers. While functional, the repairs left the sky boat's clean lines cluttered with steel plates and rivets. "Let's get out of here before anyone notices us."

They strode with purpose toward their boat, and the few northerners in the huge yard ignored them, not raising alarms until the *Bitter Goose* pointed its nose toward the sky.

An invisible wind bellied their nets and vaulted them into the air. Below, warriors ran and shouted, loosing occasional arrows after them to no effect. By the time they flew over the far end of the shipyard, several smaller stone boats lifted groggily up after them, only to be left far behind by the speedier demon-made craft.

"That's Jarl Refur on the lead boat following us," Masika said, spinning her chair to glance behind. "Something tells me he isn't going to want to go back without his prisoners in hand."

"Fuck him." Rainn leaned out over the side of the boat, one hand gripping a boom and Forbryttan clinging to his shoulder. "I'd like to see him try and take us back without the whole of Hiimryk backing his rusted ass up."

Boridan ran to the aft wale and stared at the flat stone shapes lifting upward and sliding in their direction. He knew Hiimrykers manned the craft, but at this distance they shrank to invisibility. And Masika identified them individually with a single glimpse.

"He's got two dozen fighters with him." Masika stared into the empty air in front of the *Bitter Goose*, making small adjustments in the controls. "A quarter of them are at least ten feet of stone and iron. And all of them're covered in weapons."

She cut a grin at Rainn. "If anyone could take 'em, you could. I'm just not sure anyone should try."

"Especially when we can just outrun them," Boridan offered. In that, both pieces of himself agreed.

This was met with a scowl from Rainn and an approving nod from Heron that left Boridan floating above the deck.

"Oldam's sandstone stiffy," he whispered. "I love her. I'm in love. *Fuck me.*"

Rainn grabbed at a railing as Masika shifted the skiff, and a new current shoved them forward at even greater speed. "Woah. Warn a guy next time. So Heron, what were you and King Bigbeard talking about when we showed up? The two of you looked pretty cozy."

An arrow of disappointment pierced Boridan's chest and pinned his lungs tight. Love squeezed the hope right out of him. Every time he met a woman who caught his eye, this happened. He made a fool of himself, and she found someone else while he watched. Someone who spoke with confidence and intelligence and a lack of desperation.

"High King Ivarr spoke to me about Arso." Heron's posture spoke of longing. The tight shoulders, leaning forward. Not just longing but longing long abandoned and now recovered. "He's here. In Hiimryk."

"Who?" Rainn's head cocked to one side.

A wistful smile stole across Heron's elegant features. "Tall Mirrik boy. Blond. He was pretty. You hated him."

"Oh." Rainn stroked his chin. "Oh! Blood and thunder, Heron. How long ago was that?"

"I don't know." Her smile faded. "A very long time."

Masika asked the question Boridan desperately wanted to yet found himself too terrified to voice.

"Was Arso your lover?"

"He was." Heron's words grew dreamlike. "My beautiful Arso. We were abed when Angrim found me. The monster slaughtered him while I watched, helpless. Or near enough to it not to matter."

Pain refused to recede as Boridan shoved at it, pushing the

damnable feeling down into the darkest corners of his soul, unseen and stinking. But at least his breath returned.

Sort of.

"Did High King Ivarr know where Arso went?" Masika sounded concerned. Concerned and unaware how much Boridan hated her for asking what his frozen heart could not.

"He did." Heron smiled. "He's headman of a village not too far from here. Has a huge family of his own. I'm glad to hear it. I thought I wanted to see him, but I've found what I really wanted was to hear he was good. And it certainly sounds as if he is that."

A grin broke across Boridan's face. He turned away to hide it but listened with a fierce need.

"Plus, they've probably replaced his cock with an oil lamp or some stupid shit like that." Rainn chuckled and winked at Heron. "Sex isn't really the same after a good dick-lamping."

"Well, maybe we *could* spare a few days." Heron's coy smile was of little comfort to Boridan.

"Time isn't something we have a lot of, Heron." Masika's concern washed over Boridan. He discovered himself uncommonly at the whims of this conversation, awash in whatever emotions it carried him in. "A lot of people will die if we don't get Glauth back to the imp in time. Good people. Heroes. They're depending on us."

"That's right." Boridan finally found his voice. "I mean, I'm sure if Masika thinks it's important."

"People dying's a human worry," Rainn said. "Not that I'm not sympathetic." He raised his hands at Masika's open disappointment. Apparently, this point caused some contention between the two. "All I'm saying is those heroes'll be down here a damn sight longer than they'll be up there, no matter how long they live. But uh"—he paused, looking uncomfortable at Masika's glare—"as a god the human stuff's what's important to me. To us. Heron and me. We gotta take care of all our, uh, flock and whatnot. I never liked Arso anyway."

Heron's angry stare doubled Masika's heat.

"Ah, fuck." Rainn threw up his hands. "He was fine for a human that just wanted up your tailfeathers. Good enough?" He pointed past the bow. "Hey, look, mountains. Maybe I'll get lucky, and we'll crash into one and all die. Or at least me."

Maybe Boridan did have reason to hope. The chances of them getting all the way across the Undergates to Savach and Morholt were pretty distant anyway. Better that they all die than Boridan be forced to watch Heron embracing a former lover.

This, at least, was still the same since Sarah's hideous act. He had never been good with women.

"When, dear Rainn," Heron said, ice dripping from her words, "have we ever had that kind of luck?"

No. Boridan's viewpoint shifted on the unfelt breeze. Heron left Arso behind, happily. The man's threat to Boridan evaporated with every swift mile they flew away from him. But Arso meant more than that. He meant that Heron had taken human lovers in the past for whom she still held affection.

He had a chance. And Keane was clever. That meant Boridan was now clever, did it not?

"This is a wonderful new experience," Forbryttan chirped, hopping from foot to furry foot. "What a dull conversation. I've never been bored before."

Boridan leaned over and scratched Forbryttan at the back of the apelike creature's skull. Despite its unbelievable toughness, the tiny neck felt delicate.

"If you like this, you'll love getting your heart broken. Unless you're immune to that too?"

"I dunno." Forbryttan crawled up Boridan's leg and clung to his shoulder. Its hands and feet were hot, and the little demon's breath smelled of sugar and blood. "But I can't wait to find out!"

CHAPTER
NINE

It is harder than most realize to run a kingdom in Hell. Demons may be more reliable than humans, generally speaking, but the politics are beyond tiresome. I could almost be persuaded to believe they were meant as a punishment. Heh.

It is not so difficult to turn a demon's hidebound nature against it. They love nothing more than rules and rigidity. I think it's why they hate the idea of the Eldermurk so. Danger of the unknown and all. Preposterous legends of enormous silver-clawed monstrosities, malevolently intelligent gasses, hate-filled stars, cold in the black.

I wonder if it's too late to build a summer home there?

Queen Issta, Ruler of the Reaves and ex-wife of High King Oldam

The Emissary inclined his silver-haired head to Queen Issta, former mother goddess of the Alir, ruler of the demon nation of the Reaves. Behind her a huge, curved opening cut out of the cliffside palace looked out over her domain, roiling clouds of green wearing away jutting mountains with wind and acid during the day, while at night those same peaks stretched higher to stab back at the malicious sky.

He smiled benignly, hiding a mental sigh. She liked that sort of thing.

"Don't you have more important things to be doing than chasing escaped slaves, Emissary? Diplomatic whatnots and wherefores? Why are you even here in the Reaves at all?" Queen Issta's brilliant gaze flashed upward from her breakfast table, delicate brows pulling together dangerously.

A servant's claws clicked on the white marble floor as it hurried to refill her narrow glass with sweet wine.

The Emissary considered his options. He owed the goddess his fealty, sworn to her untold centuries past. And the Undergates enforced that fealty. But Issta's vision never extended quite as far as he wished, and she could sometimes become truculent or even lazy.

"My queen." Wisdom dictated an assumption of responsible rulership first, no matter how many times that assumption proved itself false in the past. "Reports from the acid pits put the escapees fleeing toward Hiimryk. If they are allowed to flee without even a token effort of retrieval, the simpleminded northmen will see it as weakness on our part, just as they have in the past. That means more raiding by the northmen into the Reaves for slaves and treasure." He caught her deepening frown. "Respectfully."

Issta's gently working jaw crunched down on a blue-green fruit between her teeth, and it squirted thick juice out of her mouth. The juice suspended in the air in front of her, as if afraid to despoil her chin or gleaming golden tunic.

Even honeybloods were scared of Issta. Did the fruit have more sense than he did?

"Aren't you supposed to be putting together a delegation to Murden?" Issta opened her mouth and leaned forward, capturing the floating and intensely sweet juice out of the air. The laws of the world operated differently for gods than they did more common life. "General Dammer is eager to visit his counterpart there. Exchange soft foal recipes and the latest threats of life and limb. That sort of thing."

"I am at that," rumbled a basso voice from the Emissary's right.

The Emissary jumped and twisted to look up into the grinning granite face of General Dammer, a fifteen-foot-tall craggy demon of hard stone angles and bitter smoke. His shoulders as wide as his imposing height, Dammer projected power and cunning. He also enjoyed blending with his surroundings to startle people and put them off-guard.

The form the Emissary wore served a more practical purpose. Six feet tall, thin, a permanently amused lift to his brow, with noble garb and pale skin, he faded beneath the giant's smirk. Physically, anyway.

Time to change tactics.

With a short bow, the Emissary acknowledged General Dammer's presence. "Always nice to see you, General. You're looking . . . huge."

The enormous stony face folded into a sharp-edged scowl, showcasing the surrounding spikes and spines menacingly.

A brief smile was the Emissary's only response. He turned to Queen Issta. "As always, I serve the wishes of my queen. I will continue my preparations." So saying, he backed toward the door behind him.

General Dammer hardly required the Emissary to be there to waste the week drinking and reminiscing with General Kolos of Murden Fell. But the Standards of Rule required that the Emissary obey his queen's dictates, so he would go regardless.

No sooner had the Emissary shut the ornately carved door to the audience chamber behind him than General Dammer opened it again and followed him through it, the rocky smirk once more affixed to his face. The Emissary sighed quietly. Some demons could not miss the opportunity to twist the knife, even when so doing was not in their best interests.

"Escaped slaves." General Dammer stepped close to loom over the Emissary. He flexed, raining bits of broken rock with a grinding crunch. The smell of scorched metal stung the Emissary's nose. "You ought to know by now the way of things around here, *Emissary*. Or did you think you were the most important diplomat in the Reaves?" An abrasive chuckle escaped him. "You're not even the most important diplomat in this room."

Other than a pair of guardians staring firmly into the vaulted ceiling, the antechamber was empty.

"And here I thought you were a warrior, General. I'd have guessed diplomacy to be beneath you."

"Warfare is the only real diplomacy, *Emissary*. My relationship with Kolos represents more to our queen than a thousand years of your putterings." General Dammer punctuated his points by stabbing a hardened finger into the Emissary's shoulder. The long stone nail bit through the red and blue silks and into flesh. "The queen has placed you at my disposal. My words carry her authority, and your expedition for a few slaves will wait for such a matter of vital national interest. You were an idiot to think otherwise."

Did the coarse general actually believed himself to be in the superior position here? It was like him to think that. Dammer never understood why the Emissary's importance to the Reaves eclipsed his own, and now he sought to step out of its shade. But the Emissary's shadow spread everywhere, and the time to remind General Dammer of that arrived with immediate and bloody bells.

"I suppose I should thank you on behalf of the Reaves then, General." The Emissary smiled through his distaste for the brutish demon. "Given that I am now at ends until our departure tomorrow, perhaps I'll come visit you tonight. Your wives and broodlings will be excited to greet your newly loyal servant in the quiet dark, won't they?"

Anger replaced the smirk on the general's gray face. Seconds later, as the full meaning of the Emissary's question penetrated his skull, that anger turned to fear.

"No. That's not . . . I spoke in haste, Emissary. I—"

The Emissary pulled General Dammer's nail out of his shoulder between forefinger and thumb and released it to hover motionless in the air, dripping dark blood onto the elaborate rug.

"Maybe it's a good idea anyway." The Emissary reached up and patted the general on the forearm. "Be certain everyone understands where you and I truly sit in the hierarchy of Issta's house."

General Dammer's flinty, uncertain eyes gazed toward the door of Queen Issta's chamber and back to the Emissary's genial face. Personal power struggles amongst her advisors bored the queen to violence. She would be no help to General Dammer in this matter. He pushed too far, and he knew it.

"Perhaps, this once, the Standards of Rule might not be needed." General Dammer's gaze fell to the carpet as he spoke, his voice sand on a faint wind. "I would be honored for a visit from the Emissary, as perhaps you would avail yourself of the portal web there? No one would ever need know you had used it. I would leave before dawn and be gone a week. Two if needed. No reason for anyone to think you were anywhere but with me."

"Well, that's a *very* generous offer, General Dammer. I imagine you and Kolos would have a better time without me in Murden Fell anyway. I heard the news about his wife, and it sounds like a situation that could require a dedicated period of intense drunkenness." The Emissary leaned forward so as to be in Dammer's sightline. "You know what? You should take a few months in Murden Fell. Make certain that Kolos is recovered before you return here."

"But I . . ." General Dammer fell silent. He nodded.

"I'll be by your palace just after dark. Have your newest wife cook one of her children for my supper before I leave. A young one." The Emissary's smile spread into a grin. The general would be a long time before pressing his luck like this again, and the portal web would be invaluable for running the escapees down in Hiimryk.

"How would you like it prepared?" General Dammer's tone indicated complete surrender but also immense relief. Though short-sighted and brutish, he attained his stature through incisive canniness. He could read a room, even if a little late.

He probably already had a child picked out.

The Emissary fingered the hole in the dark blue and red garment he wore. Blood soaked the silk, though the wound beneath was already healed.

"Oh, surprise me."

CHAPTER

TEN

The devout in the living world think all who die go to their carefully assigned places here in the Undergates. But this is not so, no? Most of the people don't believe in anything enough to go where they are supposed to. Darrish, Andosh, or Pavinn, they die and land somewhere else. The Reaves, Murden, Savach, or even here in the Firefields. They are very much surprised to discover their priests were right and they are not pious enough to go to where they should.

It is very funny to see the surprise on their faces, I tell you that!
Sharp Jonn

The speedier *Bitter Goose* left the pursuing stone boats of Hiimryk far behind, and Masika flew low into the mountains bordering the Andosh afterlife's eastern edge. Her ability to see the invisible currents that caught in the craft's runebound nets and propelled them along gave her a distinct advantage in both swiftness and maneuverability, and she used it to weave a confusing trail among the lower peaks. She caught an occasional glimpse of a

Hiimryk pursuer, but Jarl Refur's stone boats were scattered among the peaks and falling ever further behind.

"Yes, Rainn, I do see the mountain." Masika rolled her eyes and sighed. "And no, I don't intend to crash us all into it and die."

"I wouldn't mind," Forbryttan said, a bright grin on his small face.

The wind whipped at Masika's hair, and she smiled back at the long-armed blue demon. "Thanks, Forby. You're sweet. I think."

Every time she saw one of the great stone ships chasing them, Masika felt an ache where her trusty desert bow would have rested against her side. It likely would have done little good, but she hated being without it.

"We need to head south if we're going to hit the Crying Road," Boridan said. He spoke to Masika but as ever, his gaze followed Heron. "Technically that'll take us back through the contested zone between Hiimryk and the Reaves, but only for a bit. And we'll be more protected here in the mountains if we do run into anyone."

"Uh-huh." Masika ought to pay attention to Boridan's instructions but felt a more pressing need to pay attention instead to the towering spires of hard rock they sped past. "Contested zone. Got it."

"Don't distract her, you fuckwit." Rainn's scowl at Boridan shrunk the former Tyrranean soldier against a stack of crates. "And stop following Heron around like a bonewheel on a carcass. Just don't talk. To anyone."

Heron straightened from her inspection of the rune nets. "Rainn, if you can take some time away from berating our guide on whom we are depending to find Glauth and then Savach so we can all go home, would you mind coming over here and looking at this?"

The craft angled to port and curved around a gigantic outcropping of rock. Masika was very truly getting the hang of this thing. She continued to try and ignore the others on deck, but the whooshing wind failed to drown them out.

"What?" Rainn stomped over to the thick timber boom that held the nets aloft. "I was busy. How's the human supposed to know how stupid he is without someone like me to tell him?" He stared at the nets. "What am I looking at?"

"Runes." Heron extended a hand and let her fingertips brush the gossamer netting. "The Reaves is ruled by Issta, and it seems as if the first queen of the Alir has given her magical secrets to the Undergates. This must be how Morholt learned runecrafting. How extensive is this knowledge?"

"I understand the basics, but I never bothered much with the runes." Rainn stumbled to one side and grabbed a line to maintain his footing. He frowned at Masika.

"Sorry." Masika's breath caught as she dived the *Bitter Goose* beneath a huge arch of stone. She really was not trying to pitch Rainn over the side. She grinned. "Yeah. Right. We're all good here. No need to be worried. Almost certainly not gonna crash."

"Anyway," Rainn continued, "godsblood plus runes makes god magic, right? You don't have to have runes to be a god, or to be *amazing*." He wiggled his eyebrows. "But that's how all the heavy hitters do it. Issta, Hagrim and Magda, Dorastros, even Oldam."

Heron nodded, silent in her contemplation.

"Goddess." Boridan raised a timid hand to Heron. "I don't imagine it matters, but Issta isn't the one who brought runecrafting to the Undergates. It was already here when King Oldam threw her down from the Alireon."

"Fascinating." Heron stroked her flawless chin. "Do you know how that came to be then?"

With a slight bend in his knees, Boridan held himself erect despite Masika's swift swerves. "The Dead God brought runes here when it arrived, according to the orgars anyway. It's the legend of the land. Probably. The orgars lie a lot. They think it's funny."

Somewhere nearby an eagle screeched, and Boridan cast his gaze about to see it. "Um, anyway, the story goes that everything before that was either pitch black or on fire. Even worse than it is now. So the Dead God taught runecrafting to the humans who already lived here, and they used it to build the lands of the Undergates. That went fine until the Eldermurk—that's the part that was left over after all the new lands were made—started expanding and the—"

"No one cares, Tyrranean." Rainn tossed his head away from Boridan. "You can go back to being shutted the hell up now."

When Heron said nothing, Boridan thumped down against the crates and stayed quiet. Masika tried to catch his gaze and give him a quick smile. But the next cliff face looked up first, and the steering bar took her attention away.

Ahead of them, past the peaks of narrowly stacked mountains, the sky blazed bright orange. Less as if silver-edged clouds reflected a brilliant sunset and more like the air caught fire.

"Are we sure this is the right way?" Masika asked. Already the wind dried her face, hotter and more arid by the moment. The smell of rocks in a flame washed over her.

Boridan nodded.

"I'd have thought being able to find runecrafters'd make you happy," Rainn said to Heron. "Oughtta make it easier to get back if more people have magic here. So why the look?"

Shaking out of her reverie, Heron glanced up and gave Rainn a half-hearted smile. "The runes make me think of what Angrim did to us. What he carved into our bodies." Despite the warming currents, Heron shivered. "And that made me think of how none of our family came to our rescue."

"Scared pucker-holed, I guess." Rainn shrugged and smiled back. "Worried the Dead God'd get 'em if they stepped a toe out the door."

"Maybe." Heron wrapped her long gray hair in a length of twine to keep it from slapping into her face. "But how likely is it that none of them actually knew the Dead God was here instead of abroad in the living world? They're gods. Hagrim would have known, and that means Oldam knew too."

"What's it matter?" Rainn asked. "If you're still curious, you can ask when we get back."

"Because the gods were scared to save us, and I don't understand what of." Heron's face went bleak. "I don't think it truly was the Dead God. Especially not after Issta arrived here and would have carried word of its whereabouts back to her allies among the Alir. That leaves

Angrim, but he was weak compared to most other gods. Why be afraid of him? And if they were, why not retrieve us after Masika's Hill Fury dispatched him? For that matter, why keep us out of the Alireon? Denari Clear-Eyed said we were corrupted. But what does that mean?"

As Masika listened to her friends, she tracked Forbryttan with the corner of one eye. He ran at the cabin door and flung himself into it, endeavoring to smash against the wood with a different part of his body each time, eliciting giggles and sage nods as he continued his grand experiment.

Rainn straightened, concern drawing lines across his face. "You think they were scared of us?"

"I don't know," Heron answered, staring into the distant conflagration. "And that means that even if everything we do is successful, and the imp is able to get us home, how do we know what our reception will be? How do we know our family would not rather kill us than embrace us?"

"They are kinda assholes." Rainn winked as he said it.

"If the imp can remove Angrim's corruption, will it matter?" Masika felt she needed to steer this conversation in a happier direction. They entered a lengthy straightaway that required more speed than fancy piloting. "Afraid of the Dead God, Angrim, or what Angrim did to you, none of it makes any difference if the Dead God is here, Angrim is gone, and you're back to normal. Right?" She punctuated the statement with her biggest smile.

"This is going to work. We're going to get you home," Masika said. Heron might be human again, but she was still a worrier.

"Shadows of the Alir." As the *Bitter Goose* passed around the final mountainside, the Firefields finally came into view, and Rainn went to the bow for a better look.

At least a thousand feet above ground, their craft flew toward a solid wall of flame. It started far below, perhaps a hundred feet off the valley floor, consuming nothing for fuel as far as Masika could see.

It simply burned.

On the ground, a wide stone road ran straight into the blaze, traversed by the occasional wagon or cart, and pulled by strange beasts of burden. Above that thoroughfare, the empty air made a vaulted ceiling of flame up another hundred feet or so, creating a tunnel of heated wind down the road's length.

"Hang on." Masika pointed the skyboat's nose down and they dove toward the tunnel. Beneath it, people walked in and out of the burning land without harm. It seemed a reasonable inference to assume they would be fine as long as they did not fly into the actual fire.

"This seems unsafe," Boridan observed.

"If you've got a better idea . . ." Once again, piloting their craft subsumed all of Masika's attention.

The wall of fire ran across the horizon and up until it occluded half the sky. Half the world. And it only grew bigger the closer they came. Strangely it produced no sound, only heat and wind.

"Are those people yelling at us?" Rainn peered over the side at the travelers on the road, past where Masika could see.

"Omigosh! We're gonna burn to crisps." Forbryttan leaped from boom to boom above everyone's heads, his happy expression showing off gleaming tusks in his furry apelike face. "Aren't you thrilled?"

The *Bitter Goose* shot into the tunnel of broiling air, surrounded by flame.

Instantly the runed nets evaporated with a sparking rainbow glow. Masika lurched backward as the tension in the steering bar vanished, and only leather straps kept her in the chair. The world became heat and roaring fire. And screams.

The *Bitter Goose* pointed toward the road, some hundred and fifty feet below, and fell.

"Whee!" shouted Forbryttan.

Masika clapped both hands over her face and held her breath to keep the heat away from her eyes and out of her lungs, and the skin of her knuckles burned in agony. Her stomach lurched in freefall, and she smelled burning hair.

Their plummet slowed, then stopped.

The wind, while not cool, no longer threatened to peel the flesh from her blackened bones.

She opened her eyes.

Rivulets of blinding white light extended from the walls of the tunnel above toward the craft's underside, where they turned upward and blew past, a brilliant fountain pushing them aloft, but without heat of its own. In the center of the smoldering decking, over the heads of a cowering Boridan and an incredulous Rainn, floated Heron, her arms outstretched, head flung back, and her hair glowing too bright to look at.

"Hey, watch where you're putting that thing" came an irate male voice from below. An instant later the hull bumped down on a solid surface and came to rest.

Picking at the burning patches in his faded blue fur, Forbryttan grinned and licked his tusks. "Can we do that again?"

Rainn jumped up and caught Heron as she fell, limp, out of the air and into his arms. He pulled her to him and brushed her hair back out of her slack face. The twine she tied it back with had burned away.

"Fire! We're on fire," Boridan shouted. He ran up the stairs and yanked on the straps holding Masika down, though his eyes never left Heron. In fact, the main structure of the skyboat *was* aflame, and beginning to become a problem.

Masika shoved Boridan away and worked the straps herself. "Sorry. I've got it. Are you all right?"

"You can't put that in the middle of the damn road." A different voice, a woman this time, shouted from somewhere nearby. "It's against the Standards."

"And it's in the damn way," yet a third voice called out.

Hopping around the bits of the *Bitter Goose* actively aflame, Masika peered off the side. They rested and burned on a fifty-foot-wide flagstone road, mostly empty except for a few travelers. Further out, a rocky countryside filled with sharp boulders of red, brown, and pink glowered at them, daring them to try stepping off the road. She gripped the railing and swung down, careful to avoid further burns, and landed alongside Rainn and Heron.

"Is she . . ." Masika stopped herself before she said *alive*, finding herself afraid of the word.

"She's fine," Rainn answered, a scowl drawing down his face. "She'll be fine." He brushed a knuckle gently along one side of her face.

"Ow!" Boridan landed heavily beside Masika on the flagstones. He straightened and waved his arm in a wide arc at the cluster of dusty people congregating behind the calmly burning boat. "Oldam's volcanic climax, how thick are you people? Walk. Around. The. Fire."

An older woman in the lead, face creased with displeasure, harrumphed and led the group right of Masika and what was rapidly becoming the remains of the *Bitter Goose*. "Against the Standards," she muttered as she passed.

Above them the sky raged in flames as far as Masika could see in every direction save the one they'd come from.

"Boridan?" Masika put a hand on his shoulder. "What's going on with these Standards? Do we need to run?"

"I don't know." He glanced about, nervously. "This is the Crying Road I told you about. Goes from one end of the Undergates to the other. Demons aren't supposed to take humans off it. That's all I really know. I've never been here before."

The boat creaked and cracked and sent up a plume of sparks as something fell inward atop it, and the closest boom crashed to the ground.

"I think it's time to get out of here," Masika said. So far no one had thought to blame her for flying into what now appeared to be the hottest part of the sky, and she wanted to forestall that as long as she could.

"Leaving your trash in the road?" A wiry man of average height toyed with a metal-shod club as he stepped from behind a rough boulder and into the road. He was shirtless, and his ruddy skin stretched tight over rangy muscles festooned with scars. A matching woman, also thin and scarred, followed him in a leather brassiere and pants. A desert sword swung easily at her hip, and an extended version of the man's metal and wooden club hung over her back on a shoulder strap.

An uncomfortable thought occurred to Masika that these clubs might represent some further threat than the obvious. They were too similar and too deliberate in their make.

Inlittan showed her what they were for. Masika's eyes went wide.

"That's against the Standards of Rule," the man's gravelly voice said as another thirty people, fighters all, filtered out of the rocks behind him. "That'll getcha in some real trouble there."

CHAPTER

ELEVEN

Has anyone ever wondered where all the dead trolls and giants are?

I have. But I also have a thought, do you see? I don't believe as many do that big folk have no souls. I've known too many of them to think that. It's stupid. I think the trolls and the giants when they die, they say "No thank you!" to the Undergates and they go someplace better instead. Someplace with snow and ships and fat seals to eat. Doesn't that sound nice? Better than a sky full of fire and demons wanting to eat the asshole out of your legs?

I'd want to say "No thank you" too. I like my asshole.

Sharp Jonn

Panic rose in Masika as Rainn stepped in front of her. Her fingers flexed with the need for a bow that was not there.

"Get us in trouble with who exactly?"

Rainn and Heron might have regained what godlike abilities they remembered how to use, which was precious little, but Masika's enhanced glimpse at the wiry couple's weapons left her certain that even the two Alir could not survive a violent altercation here.

A strange expression flickered across the thin man's scarred face: part distaste, part pain, but mostly wicked intent. He raised the hollow club and clicked a tiny lever on the side of it with one finger.

"Hey. It's fine. We'll move our boat out of the road." Masika jumped around a surprised Rainn as she said it, her arms protectively wide. "We don't want to be an inconvenience."

"Too late for that, love." The woman smirked and crossed her arms, making no move for either sword or strange club. Behind her, the hard-bitten men and women gripped knives or bladed hooks in their hands, though none carried the odd hollow clubs.

Masika did not need Inlittan's vision to tell her they moved with the light surety of deadly fighters.

"I assume something else is going on I can't see here?" Rainn whispered.

"Uh-huh." Masika gave a slight nod toward Rainn. To the other side, Boridan slunk away to the rear, half-carrying Heron with him.

With a shrug, Rainn held out his hands before jerking a thumb toward the flaming skyboat. "Where d'you want it?"

Reacting to Inlittan's warning faster than she had ever moved, Masika ducked, spun, and swept Rainn's legs out from beneath him. He shouted and fell backward at the same instant the wiry man's club popped and jumped in his hand. A streak of intense pink fzzzed over Rainn's face and struck the side of the *Bitter Goose*.

For the space of half an instant, nothing happened.

Then the skyboat detonated, throwing Heron and Boridan to the stones and sending an unprepared Rainn and Masika rolling. Forbryttan flew like an arrow from the center of the explosion, a delighted scream on his apelike lips, and collided with one of the couple's men with a horrifying crunch.

"You missed, Ducky," said the woman to her partner. She favored him with an evil leer. "Toldja last night you weren't a perfect shot."

The pained part of his expression returned. "It went in exactly the hole I wanted it to. I didn't miss!"

"And this time you was aiming at the skomp?" She swept an arm at the burning detritus that used to be the *Bitter Goose* covering the flagstones.

Behind them a battle erupted, half-dressed warriors descending on a laughing Forbryttan, knives flashing.

"Can we just walk away from this?" whispered Boridan. Grime coated him head to toe, mixed with streaks of his own blood. He held Heron's hand while she patted out embers in her hair with the other. "Looks like they're paying more attention to each other than they are us. They can't hurt the trimpet anyway. Can we just go back for it after they've realized they can't eat it?"

The foursome crept away beneath the cover of anger and smoke, retreating along the Crying Road in the direction they had come.

Masika, of course, saw it first. "Damn."

"What is it?" Heron asked her. Smoky tears streaked down her soot-covered face.

Masika pointed above the wide road. "I thought we were farther ahead of them. They must've cut through a faster path than we did to get this close."

At the speed of a falling brick, a wide stone craft plummeted toward them. Two dozen howling northmen, each steaming and smoking from metal and wooden limbs, waved axes and spears above their heads, working themselves into a red-faced lather.

"Firebug," said the scarred man. He shoved the weapon through his belt and pointed at the oncoming Hiimrykers. "You want to take care of that? I wouldn't want to *miss* anything."

The woman snorted and pulled her longer version of his metal-shod club from her back. She sighted along its hollow length and pointed it over Masika's head. "I make my own holes."

The club went *click*, and the end of it spouted smoke, kicking up into the air. Inlittan showed Masika a thin, pointed, pink projectile that flew faster than any crossbow bolt at the Hiimryker's craft. It connected with a massive explosion that sundered the stone into large irregular pieces and sent the warriors flying.

Everything crashed to the road below. Even the stone burned.

A hand grabbed Masika by the shoulder. She stopped, turned, and

Boridan pointed her toward the couple and their force of warriors. Firebug and Ducky pointed their weapons at Masika. Behind them, one of the taller men held a gleeful Forbryttan aloft by the tail.

The rest spread out to cut off any lines of retreat.

"Sorry I didn't introduce myself before," said the thin man over his pointing club. "I'm Sharp Jonn. This is my wife January. We're probably still going to eat you all, but I can't help but wonder, why are the Hiimrykers so eager to get you back that they've left their mountaintops? It's most unlike them. Yes?"

Firebug and Ducky must have been the couple's pet names for one another. The nicknames seemed frighteningly inadequate at capturing their brutal nature.

"You can't eat us, you goat-humping savages." Boridan stepped forward, chest out. "We're travelers on the Crying Road. We're protected by the rules."

"But you broke the Standards of Rule." Sharp Jonn's response felt oily in Masika's ears, slick with grime. "You left your broken vessel in the road, do you see? The road's protection no longer extends to you."

"I think you broke that same rule," Boridan answered with a nervous smile. He cast a meaningful glance at the shattered Hiimryk craft and its equally broken passengers who lay burning on the stones. "Maybe everyone should leave before the real demons start showing up."

"*We're* human, Tyrranean." January's weapon ca-clicked in her grip as she prepared it to fire again. "Well, mirrors. But the road only protects from—"

"Firebug," Sharp Jonn interrupted her. "Let's make these fine people our guests, do you see? And if they can say why the Hiimrykers want them so badly, maybe we won't even eat them."

"Don't tell these fuckers anything." Rainn crossed his arms. The sleeveless gray slave tunic he wore showed off his godly physique. "If they want to know something from us, I've got a few things I want first."

"The northmen were chasing us because I am of the Alir," Heron stated. Rainn and Boridan both whirled to stare at her. She straightened and continued, "They believe I belong to them. I do not. I am here on my own business. You have my gratitude for dispatching them. We will now be on our way."

Masika needed to have a conversation with Heron about telling everyone they met who they were. Is this what she had been like before she became a frightened waterfowl?

A canny frown flickered over Sharp Jonn. "And we would know you as?"

"I am Heron. Daughter of Bastük, who is first son to High King Oldam and his favored wife, Hedra."

The full-throated admission caught Masika's breath and froze it solid beneath the burning sky. She had no idea who these horrible people were or where they came from, but how much more danger could they be in now that Sharp Jonn and his clan knew Heron was of value? At least the goddess had not revealed Rainn as well.

Sharp Jonn cast an inquisitive glance over his shoulder at January. She responded with a tight nod.

"Your idiot guide was not wrong." Sharp Jonn's gaze roved around him at the surrounding rock, the endless road, even the burning sky. "The demons will be on their way, and the Crying Road will make you vulnerable to them now the Standards are broken, do you see? You must come with us. We will take you by safer paths until you are out of their sight. We won't even eat any of you."

"Ow!" From off the road, one of Sharp Jonn's fighters shouted and threw Forbryttan to the ground.

"What?" the tiny demon shouted. "You bit me first." He licked the blood from his bluish lips. "Hey. You taste *good*."

"Apparently we can't make the same promise," Rainn replied.

"Hey. Wait up."

Masika paused on the barren ground and waited for Rainn to catch up to her. She pitched her voice low so that their saviors—or possibly captors, she had not decided which yet—could not overhear.

"What's wrong? Do you think we're about to be attacked by these people?"

"Huh?" Wary confusion settled on Rainn's rugged features. "No. I mean, I don't think so. Maybe? That wasn't what I wanted to talk about." He eyed one of Sharp Jonn's fighters. "We haven't had a chance to talk in a while. Not really. Felt like we were due."

"I don't trust these people." Masika stared into the crisscrossing network of scars that ran over Sharp Jonn's back and shoulders.

"Yeah." Rainn's face twitched in the barest glimmer of a smile, there and gone. "I'm getting that. But I wanted to ask you about you. I don't like it, but I guess I care now. About you. So . . . how are you holding up? What're you thinking, or seeing, or what-the-fuck ever?"

At this Masika glanced sidelong at Rainn. The god was no good at hiding his emotions, which typically ran hot. His eyebrows went up on his forehead, which Masika realized meant he thought he was disguising the true depth of his concern.

She almost laughed.

Almost.

"Other than being pretty sure these desert wastrels mean to eat us, I'm worried about my dad. We left him without him having any idea where we were or what happened to us. What if he tried to follow? What if that assassin the emperor sent caught up to him?" Of course she caught up to him. Her dad was a diplomat, not some trained covert agent.

Rainn nodded along. "Well, despite everything, we did exactly what we said we were gonna do, so he probably does know where we are. And while we both know he'd have followed if he could've, we also know he couldn't." Rainn's jaw worked in silence for a second as he considered his next words. "And he and that assassin seemed to have some sort of relationship or whatever. If she did catch him, which seems likely, I can't imagine she'd have hurt him. Just dragged him back to your uncle. The emperor, I mean."

Though everything Rainn said made perfect sense, her anxieties continued to flare, a darker reflection of the blazing sky above them. Her gaze darted among the faces of the hard-sinewed fighters surrounding them, searching for signs of treachery. She had trusted too much of late, and their situation continued to worsen for it.

"I didn't see Refur on the Hiimryker's boat." Masika gripped Rainn's powerful forearm and pulled him closer. "That cussed old goat won't stop looking for us until he's dead. If he even *can* die." She twisted to stare up into Rainn's dark eyes. He was taller here in the Undergates too. "I wonder what'd happen to us if we die. Will we come back like the mirrored souls, or do we get murked like Boridan said happens to unmirrored people?" Another thought occurred to her. "Are we mirrored? Does that mean we're really dead or not?"

He placed a strong hand between her shoulder blades and kept her moving along the invisible track that Sharp Jonn and January picked out for them. "Heron says that we're only, what did she call it? Sorta dead. Our bodies are in"—he fumbled for the word—"*stasis*. Like dead, except we can go back. They'll be there waiting for us. That was the point of Denari's poison that she tricked us into drinking."

Yet another betrayal for Masika to feel guilty over. Another way she led her friends into danger.

"The rest of everyone here, like these Troll Coast fucks, are just dead-dead." Rainn frowned at the unusual weapon on January's back. "Mirrors, I guess. Fine as long as they don't get eaten. The fucked-up thing, though, is that if you live forever and can only be killed or murked or whatever by being eaten, that means that eventually you *will* get eaten. That's the way forever works." He frowned. "Shitty way to build an afterlife, if you ask me."

"Troll Coast, uh, people?" She wanted to talk about something else. Anything else. "I figured they were desert people. Like the mercenaries who live in the Yellow Sea."

"Nah." Rainn waved a hand dismissively. "They may look like normals with all the fat rendered off, but that accent is pure Troll Coast. Demon worshippers. But don't tell them that. They think their Salt Gods are really gods. It's probably why they're always so cranky."

"Now I feel safe," Masika whispered.

"You do?" One eyebrow shot up on Rainn's face. "Well, weird, but good. I mean, I want you to feel safe."

"When did you start caring how I felt?" The question was not entirely fair, but Rainn's assertion still threw Masika.

"I . . ." Rainn started and stopped. "Don't make that face. It makes you look as bad as you smell. Look, you've done more for Heron and me than anyone ever has. That includes worshippers, which you aren't, and family, which you, uh, aren't too."

Masika's almost-smile almost returned. "Yeah. Gods kind of suck."

For his part, Rainn's frown only deepened. "You're a ray of sunshine. And I mean that in the worst possible way." He collected himself. "All I'm saying is that you stuck yourself to the shittiest pair of gods there were, and you stayed stuck no matter what it cost you. I don't know anyone who does that. I never did. You lost a sister, maybe a whole family. Maybe fucking everything. And you're still here with us. Trying. Caring. Can't really imagine that kind of strength." He walked in silence for a few paces before finishing his thought.

"The least I can do is care back."

Stunned, Masika said nothing.

"Darrish, you have a name?" January sidled up beside Masika on the opposite side, and Rainn faded back a few steps, doubtlessly so he could keep a close eye on everyone.

"Masika."

"Why the Hiimrykers want you so bad, Masika the Darrish?" January stalked rather than strode, her rangy frame gliding over the rough and rocky terrain. "High kings get a taste for brown girls all of a sudden?"

"I don't know for sure," Masika answered, dismissing the picture January's words summoned. "We landed in the Reaves and fled into Hiimryk. Boridan says that the goddess Issta doesn't permit escapees from the Reaves, so her demons tried to capture us. Maybe the Hiimrykers only want us because Issta's demons did."

Eyes narrowed, January leaned uncomfortably close to Masika. She smelled of warm skin and smoke. "You know what I think? I think you stole something from the Hiimrykers. Something they want back. And the only thing they want bad enough to leave Hiimryk for is weapons. How's that guess, little Darrish? Or maybe *you're* the weapon? That woman is pretty, but she is no more god than I am. Maybe we oughtta take you to pieces and find out what you really stole?"

Between the burning sky and the baking rock, Masika's guts turned to ice water. She turned away from January, not wanting to see anything that Inlittan might show her.

"That's right, troll-hole," Rainn rumbled from behind. "I took Issta's favorite weapon here in my pants, and she's desperate to get ahold of it again. If you're lucky, I'll give you a peek before I choke you on it."

January cast a black look over her shoulder and reached for her slender desert blade, but she stopped when rough laughter erupted around her.

When Masika first made her promise to escort Heron and Rainn home, she thought it would be easy: the result of a few days ride and she would be the hero. Like Sarah. But things had not turned out that easy, and the two gods became far more to her than she ever imagined. She would see them home, but not for the sake of herself.

For the sake of her friends. Her family.

"That was pretty funny, eh, Firebug?" Face beaming, Sharp Jonn held his arms out to his sides. "Maybe if everyone doesn't get eaten long enough, our new friends will be good Longeyes like the rest of us, do you see?"

"Aye," January muttered.

CHAPTER
TWELVE

The Standards of Rule guide the Undergates, allowing commerce, travel, and occasional lapses in violent bloodshed. A pain in the ass for common demons and humans, they provide a tremendous reduction in headaches for those of us who reign. The Standards seem to be a holdover from whatever realm existed here before the Dead God created his new universe over the bones of the old, much like the Eldermurk.

The Standards enforce themselves against demons and gods alike, though royalty can always push their consequences off on an underling or two. Other major demons act as direct extensions of the Standards, beings through which they work their will, so to speak. Which all means a careful planner can arrange executions without ever getting her hands dirty, simply by forcing a deviation of the rules on whoever she wants killed.

Plus, it's a hell of a lot of fun.

Queen Issta, Ruler of the Reaves and ex-wife of High King Oldam

The Emissary gazed at the portal web, appreciating its dense design and unfathomable complexity. The cavern he stood in extended some five hundred feet in length and only slightly less than that in width and height. Rough black walls curved up into the dim reaches, and the whole of it, located some miles beneath General Dammer's palace, smelled of lightning-burned air and dirt.

The web covered the entire far wall, and the Emissary realized with a start that he could not tell how far back it went. Just how intricate *was* this thing?

A play of bluish light illuminated a fractional portion of the strands composing the web's spell to the Emissary's right. It traveled in an expanding circle before fading out. Silvery, multilegged creatures the size of his hand crawled along the spell, checking for breaks and repairing any ruptured threads. It hurt his head to look at them for long; they seemed of the wrong reality to be here.

General Dammer croaked out the instructions to operate the portal just before his neck snapped. The old demon would be up and around again by tomorrow, but the lesson would stick for a while longer.

It usually did.

Approaching the central portion where the dense mass of strands wound tightly together to become a smooth, solid surface, the Emissary pressed his palm down on it. A light tingle excited his fingers, and another glow, this time a pulsing pink, arose to his left. Smaller than before, it retained its size and roundish shape.

He unbuttoned his silk robes and stepped into the glow. Dammer said—well, spat out along with a few stone teeth—that the web would give him a piece of itself so that he could return when needed and travel to other places. The glowing pink disk of webbing pulled free easily, and the Emissary wrapped it tight across his chest, where it adhered. Not as fragile as it seemed, but it would require some amount of care to keep whole.

He refastened his robes.

As he did so, the Emissary noticed one of the silvery insect-like creatures, motionless, observing him from only a few feet away. Or he thought it observed him. Five thin legs and a pair of antennae protruded from a smooth metallic body, with no obvious joints and absolutely no eyes, mouth, or asshole. He saw no essence there, no core to this creature. It showed only a reflection of what existed around it.

It was not of the Undergates. The whole web came from a different when. But why, and to what purpose?

The bit of webbing across his chest itched a bit, not reassuring him in the least.

"The things we do for duty," the Emissary spoke aloud to no one.

At his thought, a shimmery oval grew in front of him against the portal web's surface, fracturing the dim light like the surface of an agitated pond or the air above a distant lava flow.

He stepped through.

"I wondered if you'd be showing up," Jarl Refur said, setting aside his whetstone and dagger. A small plume of white steam escaped the gearing in his grinding iron shoulder, momentarily indistinguishable from the cloud of white hair that surrounded his balding skull. He did not stand from the stone table in the hide-covered cottage. "Drink?"

The Emissary sat across from Jarl Refur on a cold bench and lifted the clay bottle to his lips. Most Hiimrykers drank fermented yaks' milk mixed with blood, which he did not care for, but Refur always kept berry-tree wine on his table. It tasted sweet and light and was all but impossible to obtain in the Reaves, even if the acid in the air there did not immediately destroy it.

"Thanks," the Emissary said. "Sounds like you already know why I'm here. You have my slaves?"

"Wonder how many actually consider themselves to be your slaves?" Jarl Refur answered.

One of a vanishingly few demons whom the Standards worked through instead of on, the Emissary could not be lied directly to. That did not mean he had to be answered though, a fact Refur knew very well.

It was one of the more irritating features of the ancient northman.

Jarl Refur raised his weathered face and frowned. "What's it like? Not being able use all the faculties you was made with on account of some old set of rules set in place by someone you never met for reasons nobody knows?"

"I imagine it's like whatever you feel when you try to get a hard-on." In truth the situation always struck the Emissary as a bit unfair. For the most part, humans seemed beneath the notice of the Standards.

For the most part.

A mist of a smile chased itself over Jarl Refur's features, only to settle back into his previous grumpy expression. "Thought you weren't allowed to hurt no one while you were on one of these diplomatical excursions."

"I certainly didn't want to." The Emissary raised an elbow to the sheepskin table cover and allowed his chin to fall into his hand. "My intention was an exchange of favors. You scratch my scales, I scratch yours."

A small grunt and some creaking accompanied Jarl Refur's sitting up straight. One wiry-haired eyebrow rose on his mottled head. "What kind of favors?"

"No one's expecting you to give up something for nothing, Refur. You know I've kept your grandkids in one piece for just such a discussion as this. That's an excellent bottle of wine, by the way. Is there more?"

"There's always more. Grows on trees. Over there on the shelf." Jarl Refur adopted a thoughtful stance, though the frown remained.

The Emissary crossed to the one rock wall of the cottage and retrieved another bottle from the half-dozen sitting there. Hiimryk's cold, bitter to his skin, made the drink even more exotic. Picking up a second glass, the Emissary returned to the table.

"What's the matter?" he asked. "I sort of assumed getting your grandkids back would be a no-brainer."

"Normally would be." Jarl Refur's words came sparingly, with care and consideration. "But your slaves ain't all that normal." He quieted, thinking. A hiss came from one of his metal-clad stone legs. "They're more important to Hiimryk than my own grandbabies. Things turn out the way I expect, we won't be long coming to take back all our own outta the Reaves anyway. That'll make quite the poem, I think."

A sigh from the Emissary matched the escaping gasses from Jarl Refur's leg. He pulled the cork on the fresh bottle and poured himself a glass. "You should know that it isn't really true that I *can't* violate the Standards. I just don't want to." Watching the old man's face, he continued, "I like you, Refur. You're a good host and you always keep an extra bottle for me. You're usually pretty easy to work with too. But I'm out on a limb with this, and if I don't bring anything back to show for my time, my life gets difficult and possibly short. And I want that *less*."

Stubby metal fingers rested on the dagger's hilt. Was Jarl Refur actually considering attacking? What was so special about those escapees?

"Wait," the Emissary said. "Is one of those slaves a sorcerer?" Normally immortal, it was rare, but not unheard of, for one of the godsblood to die and end up in the Undergates. That would certainly explain Jarl Refur's stubbornness. To be sure, the Emissary opened his perceptions and allowed the Standards to show him what most troubled the heart of the man—his grandkids. No surprise there, but it upgraded the significance of the escapees.

"No," Jarl Refur answered before he could stop himself. His frown grew pained. "If you're looking for one of them, look somewheres else. In fact, the sooner you're gone, the happier I'll be. Since you like me so much."

"Then what . . ." Realization dawned. It was impossible, was it not? And yet, his own queen was an example of the possibility. *This* would certainly be important enough for Jarl Refur to risk the welfare of his family on. If not sorcerers, could they be gods?

"I'll ask one more time, Refur. Where are the slaves? Before you pick up that dagger, you should know that I am more than capable enough to kill you so completely that no Hiimryker will ever patch you together again. You know what I am."

"Oh, I know." Jarl Refur's fist closed around the pommel and swung the blade quicker than thought. It sliced cleanly through the Emissary's cheek.

At present, the ancient amalgamation of stone, wood, steel, and northman was more than a match for the Emissary. To even the odds would put a timer on his visit here and cause no end of future trouble. It would also destroy the webbed spell tickling his chest, which would mean he would have to walk home.

It occurred to the Emissary that he might not have planned this as well as he thought.

"I do know, you old demon," Jarl Refur said. He stood now, dagger at ease in one hand, the other a solid steel fist. "You need to know I got no idea where your runaways are. And if I did, I wouldn't tell you. Last I saw them they was chatting it up real friendly like with the kings, and if they are what they say they are, you oughtta be fuckin' worried about it. None of them seem to be very fond of you or your kind."

Damn. It was true then. The escaped slaves *were* gods. Where would they go? One of the human nations? It made sense. Easier to rule there. Not a favorable shift in power for a demon nation like the Reaves though.

The Emissary pushed back his stool and stood. The air shimmered behind him.

"Maybe next time we'll just say hi and leave it at that." The Emissary stepped backward. "I'll keep your grandkids safe. I'm sure there'll be an opportunity to trade them for something someday."

"When I show up on your doorstep, Emissary, you can trade them for your own head."

The Emissary backed through the shimmery air and vanished.

CHAPTER
THIRTEEN

When I first came to the Undergates, it was a much bigger place than now. Many more nations cracked the land, and the Eldermurk was no more than a distant dark on the horizon, do you see? But things have a way of wanting to go back to what they used to be, and the Eldermurk eats Hell like we eat clawworms.

Huh. How did I never wonder what the Undergates tastes like before now?

Sharp Jonn

The camp of the Longeyes, where Sharp Jonn and January held court, dipped well below ground level and into a broad declivity in a massive stone hill. Thirty feet high at its tallest, the scoop extended a hundred feet into the rock and close to a thousand in width. Though everything in the Firefields shone in the harsh light of the fiery apocalypse roiling over their heads, the encampment came close enough to shadowed to provide some rest for Masika's aching eyes.

In the rough center of the hollowed-out chamber, Sharp Jonn stood on a six-foot platform of tightly fitted stones, hands outstretched, facing the crowd of his not-so-adoring fighters. Masika failed at first to notice the looks of doubt, suspicion, and occasional hostility they threw his way. Now it was impossible to ignore.

"All right, Heron," Masika said beneath the grumblings of the crowd. "That's twice now. What's your thinking? Why did you tell these—I'm going to say *horrible*—people who you were? Why tell the Hiimrykers? Did you think anyone here was going to fall down and do whatever you said? Because if so, I don't think it's working."

In fact, Heron's admission of identity had resulted in a distinct downturn of reasonable treatment at the hands of their captors. And they were definitively captors.

"I'm not certain." Heron's normally ethereal manner drifted away, opaque to Masika's, or even Inlittan's, vision. Her large emerald eyes glowed with unknowable beauty. She shrugged. "It seemed like the right thing to do."

Eyes squeezed shut and pinching the bridge of her nose between thumb and forefinger, Masika sighed. She preferred human-Heron to heron-Heron, but at least the bird version ratted them out less often.

Behind the tall, gray-haired woman, Sharp Jonn struggled to make himself heard over the dangerous-sounding noises of his people.

Masika shook off her funk and concentrated on a sunny smile. "If we can't get out of here and find Morholt the Runecrafter, I don't suppose it'll matter one way or the other. But I'm sure that we will. We'll find him, and he'll want to help us because we have Sarah's blessing. And Morholt and Sarah were friends. When she was alive."

It would not do to infect her friends with her own growing unease —unease that tipped into hopelessness. She knew neither where they were nor where they were going, and everyone they met seemed determined to attack, enslave, or eat them alive. What Masika *did* know was that she most certainly did not enjoy Sarah's blessing. Not after Sarah asked High King Ivarr back in Hiimryk to hold them captive for a thousand years.

She jerked back when Heron reached out to brush an errant curl out of Masika's face, but the goddess followed the motion effortlessly and tucked the strands behind Masika's ear.

"You have given so much for us. To us." Heron's faint smile held sadness within it. "More than we had any right to expect. And you are tired. When the time comes, remember to let us take care of you in return." Her expression deepened, warmth growing from the retreating edges of a soft gray cloud. "After all, that is a god's purpose."

Masika held that bottomless green gaze for an instant and turned away. She rarely felt so seen, and it unnerved her. Wiping her own eyes, she sniffed and gestured toward Sharp Jonn. "Hey, what's going on over there?"

"No, that's not what I'm . . ." Sharp Jonn hesitated, trying to voice his frantic thoughts. "You're not listening to me. The girl with the gray hair is a *goddess*. She can help us get back everything we lost."

"We been listening to you for near two hundred years now, an' we got shit to show for it." A burly man, taller and broader than Sharp Jonn, stepped out of the crowd and pointed a beefy finger at him. "Yer bugshit crazy, Jonny, and it don't take a genius to see this is yer worst idea ever. Hands up fer everyone wants to run off with Jonny and Jan and get eaten by—"

His voice broke midsentence, and a thin blade, coated in streaked crimson, pushed out between the ribs of his chest. He looked down at it, closed his eyes, and slumped forward.

Behind him stood January, bloodied desert blade in one hand and the long metal-shod club in the other—a weapon Masika learned was called a *graver*. The Longeye gave her people a bone-chilling grin, the force of which pushed even the biggest and most angry warriors back a step.

"Who else here thinks my Ducky is crazy? Don't fear. We can have a nice talk about it while we eat your liver."

"I don't think she's going to get a lot of takers on that one," Boridan muttered. The Tyrranean had been uncharacteristically quiet since their most recent capture, though he was sure to be nearby whenever Heron was around.

"You're not listening," Sharp Jonn complained to the corpse. "Don't you want things to go back to the way they used to be? Before the sky caught fire?" A sad expression stole across his face. "Don't any of you want to be happy again?"

"Well, I don't want to get stabbed," said a severe-looking older woman whose gaze flitted between Sharp Jonn and a predatory January, "but what if we just make it worse? It's not like anyone actually knew what they were doing the first time around."

January leaped on the woman, battering her to the ground and beating her with the hilt of her sword.

Once the splattery crunches stopped, Sharp Jonn raised a finger to the crowd. "That's a very good point, do you see? How do we know we won't make things worse? Well, we have a goddess on our side this time, and if that's not enough, just look around. How could things possibly get worse than this?"

"Do they have a goddess on their side?" Masika whispered to Heron.

"I guess that depends on what they want to do." Heron smiled and shrugged. "Rainn and I haven't helped anyone but ourselves since you freed us, while you try to help everyone we meet. I admire that, and I think maybe I'd like to try it out a little. I think maybe that would make *me* happy."

The admission caught Masika flat-footed, and she swallowed the tears it threatened to bring. A goddess admired her? A goddess wanted to *emulate* her? It was too much to consider.

"These people are all fucking crazy." Rainn's hands opened and closed into fists as he growled his statement. "Whatever they want is going to be fucking crazy too, and it will end in screaming and blood and knives." He cocked his head to one side. "All right. I talked myself into it. Let's help 'em out."

"Where's Forbryttan?" Boridan stood on tiptoe, scanning the crowd. "I haven't seen him since we got here."

Within seconds Inlittan showed Masika a distant crowd of Longeyes gathered around a very large pot, hung over a merrily crackling fire. Several of them held an intense conversation with an amused

Forbryttan, himself inside the pot, who lounged comfortable with one fuzzy arm slung over the side.

One of the Longeyes handed Forbryttan a drink, which he accepted and sipped from. The little demon nodded and smiled at the woman with happy eyes.

"I think he's all right," Masika said. "Forby's better suited to this kind of hospitality than we are anyway."

Outside the cave-like encampment, a horn blared, and a score of Longeyes, spare and leather clad, ran out into the harsh light.

A group of a dozen more came around a spiky hillock carrying a doughy monster on a pair of long poles. The creature, obviously dead with numerous ghastly wounds, somewhat resembled a gigantic hairless mole, with dirty white skin and rolls of fat. Its mouth lolled open where a head should have been as an orgar's might, stuffed full of fearsome triangular teeth. Sharp, curving antler-like horns branched from its back at regular intervals. It took all twelve people to carry the thing, and even then, it dragged on the ground.

"They bagged a soft foal!" came a shout from the crowd.

"Thank the fire. Finally, a decent meal" came another.

"We got any more hot sauce?"

The return of the hunting party elevated the mood of the Longeyes in the camp tremendously, and the interrogation of Sharp Jonn ended when his crowd ran off toward the group.

"Aw, come on, guys." Sharp Jonn put his hands on his hips and stared at his feet. "I was gonna tell you all how amazing everything was gonna be, and you were gonna be excited, and we were gonna go to the Slaughterhouse with—"

"Shut it," January hissed, indicating the listening Masika and her friends.

"Whatever." Sharp Jonn dejectedly kicked at one of the smooth rocks that made the platform he stood on. "You know what? It's fine. It's fine if I'm the only one who cares. It's fine because I care enough for everyone. That's why I'm the leader."

CHAPTER

FOURTEEN

It's important for the common peoples to have someone to look up to, do you see? Normal peoples with all their little problems, they just can't see the world the way someone with vision can. Like me. This is why it's so important to crush the spirit of anyone who asks too many questions and makes other peoples wonder if you really know what you're talking about. It's confusing to normal peoples with their normal brains.

Crush their spirit, crush their ideas, and if that doesn't work, you crush their brains. That's how you keep peoples happy, is it not?

Sharp Jonn

Boridan shifted his gaze away from Heron again. The goddess's attention fell on him less and less, and just looking at her hurt his soul. Since he was a mirror and all that was left *was* his soul, it pretty much hurt his whole him.

Whoever that was.

He walked away from his new friends, if friends they were. Masika's tirade about eating the soft foal, once she found out the delicious creatures were created from the spirits of dead infants, exploded epically, and he felt safer anywhere else.

To be honest, it creeped him out too.

Picking his way amongst clusters of sleeping, chatting, and drinking Longeyes in the open-sided cave, Boridan felt less alone than he had since his death. After the hunting party returned from Hunter's Sweep with their catch, the rest of the tribe decided that Boridan and his group were good luck, and their previously feral suspicions fizzled away, replaced by good-natured acceptance. A few loosely organized fistfights made Rainn an honorary Longeye, and Forbryttan's inability to be killed, along with his boundless enthusiasm for letting them try, turned him into the most popular member of their group by a mile.

At the edge of the cave's shadow, an angry hiss stopped Boridan cold. Outside the sky roiled and baked the hard stone, but fear chilled his guts. Something warned him against another step, but the foot he held suspended in the air remained unsure in which direction to fall.

More hissing—this time from just outside and around the corner—relaxed Boridan, and he eased his foot to the ground. The noise that crept into the cave proved no more than a hushed conversation, nothing to be frightened of.

He padded closer and maneuvered himself against the wall.

"She's not even your real mother. Why do you care so much?" Panic renewed, Boridan realized the voice belonged to January. *High King Oldam's craggy blue butt crack.* The consequences of eavesdropping soared right up into the flames. No cover surrounded him, and running would be certain to attract attention.

Nothing else to do but listen.

"You weren't here." Sharp Jonn's voice this time. "You don't remember how good it was."

"You're saying you was happier with her than with me?" Boridan winced at January's reply. As notoriously bad with women as he had been in life, even he recognized a trap.

"Of course not." The whine in Sharp Jonn's words struck Boridan as out-of-character, given what he knew of the man. "It's different, is all." The trap snapped shut around Sharp Jonn's neck, though he failed to realize it. "You make me feel one way; she makes me feel a different way, do you see? Nothing to be jealous of."

The following silence burned hotter than the bright air outside. Boridan's full stomach gurgled happily, not acknowledging the tense conversation taking place mere feet away. He clutched his middle with both hands, praying no one else heard.

"So, you're choosing her over me." January's reply came flat and deadly. "I don't think you're being honest about the nature of this *friendship*. And you know where that leads."

"Don't you touch her!" Sharp Jonn matched January's intensity with sudden heat. "Don't you *dare*. She is very special to me, as you are, and I won't have you fighting, do you see? I won't have it. I'm the leader here, not you. That means you do what I say. And I say that you will calm down and be contented about this."

Whoops. Seemed like a losing argument to Boridan. But then he had not been dead all that long. Maybe women were different in the Undergates?

"I killed the last woman you tried to three-way with. That's on you, Ducky." January's tone shifted again, now breezy and conversational. "I'll be all calm and contented about it this go-round if it makes things easier on you." A pause. "Your happiness is my *only* concern."

"You killed Sophie? You . . . Argh!"

Boridan pressed himself into the stone wall as a frustrated Sharp Jonn stalked past, less than a foot from Boridan's shoulder. Whether it was because of the relative darkness of the cave or Sharp Jonn's intense frustration or simply because the wiry man did not care, he stormed right by and made straight for the wine barrel.

A slow sigh of relieved air escaped Boridan, and he slumped against the wall. Head down, he raised his gaze just far enough to spy a pair of narrow feet in low, black leather boots standing immediately in front of him.

He yelped. Just a little.

The woman's thin, muscle-wrapped arm slid past Boridan's ear, and she leaned against the stone behind him. Her eyes held his gaze faster than if she gripped it in her fist, and her breath smelled like warm woodsmoke.

A languid smile stole across her face.

"Hello, Tyrranean." January raised one hip and slid closer. Her heat pinked his skin. "You like listening when no one knows you're there? Maybe you like watching even more. That get you hard?"

Uncomfortably aware of January's barely clothed torso—the thin cords and small leather triangles left far too much of her lean frame on display—Boridan turned his head aside and stared at the cave ceiling. "I get hard all the time. Doesn't take that much. Yesterday I popped wood for the honey the Hiimrykers gave me with breakfast, and that still had little bits of bees in it."

Pushing back, January dragged her hand and Boridan's attention back across his chest before resting both on one hip. Tight leather pants hugged her bottom half, leaving no less to the imagination than the top did.

With effort, he raised his regard to her vaguely smiling face. Spare as the rest of her, no kindness resided there, merely curiosity. And cunning.

"No, you don't care about me." Her statement came matter-of-factly, no irritation apparent. "It's Heron's innards you want to slide your cock around in."

Boridan opened his mouth to speak but found no breath for it. What was wrong with him? The merest mention of Heron's name shut down all thought in his head, and he needed to think. Perhaps desperately so.

"I gotta ask," January said, calm as if picking sunblossoms against the back fence, "what makes you think you're worthy of *her*? She's a goddess. You're an idiot what can't even summon the thought to speak in her defense. The idea"—she leaned in and whispered into his ear—"is laughable. I'm laughing at you. Hah. Hah."

At last words fell out of Boridan's mouth, though so low even he could not hear what he'd said.

"Sorry." January's straight teeth shone in the shaded gloom.

"Didn't quite catch that. Were you saying you oughtta stab yourself in the skull with a dagger? Wouldn't blame you." She tapped him on the temple with a long, calloused finger.

"I said I'm not laughable." Boridan's words came so weak they spoke the opposite of his meaning. Damn it all. The only possible thing worse than January knowing he had spied on her was this. Murking seemed a dance through the garden in comparison.

She laughed. The first honest sound from her. "Course you're not. I'm sure Heron ain't laughing. I imagine she's barely noticed you anyway. Whatcha wanna bet she don't know your name, Tyrranean? You do got one, right?"

The thought that January might run him through from behind occurred to Boridan, but it still felt preferable to standing there one instant longer while he listened to her. He shoved past and walked away as fast as he could on the uneven ground, unsuccessfully ignoring her laughter behind him.

The worst part of all of this was Boridan knew January was right. Worthy of a goddess's love? *Him*? How stupid was he? He might as well have tried climbing the tallest peak in the Bitter Heights and putting the whole mountain in his pocket for dinner later. The question of why anyone would want someone as broken as him clogged his thoughts. Who was he, anyway? Cruel soldier or callous mercenary?

Did it really matter?

Why was he even helping these people anyway? If they succeeded, they would be returning to the living world, something Boridan was pretty sure was beyond him. There existed no body for him to return to.

Unless god-magic could make him a new one. But would they bother?

He stopped, wiped his eyes, and cast his glance at the celebrating Longeyes around him. Ahead, Sharp Jonn spoke to a woman with short blonde hair and what passed among these people for a pretty face. Boridan felt a wave of nausea, certain that he would soon watch her die.

Was this any better than being a slave among the Hiimrykers? Was *that* any better than pulling the newly dead out of the acid pools in the Reaves?

What was he doing?

"See you in the morning, Tyrranean." January's mocking voice rang out. "Better stay away from the honey at breakfast. Don't think you'll be needing a stiff pecker anytime soon."

CHAPTER

FIFTEEN

Sometimes a thing gets taken away from you and you can never get it back.
It never seems to happen with things that aren't special. Unique, do you see?
And one way or another, there's always a woman involved.

   A special, and unique, goddamn woman.

   Sharp Jonn

After her sparse meal of stewed barks and insects the foragers from Hunter's Sweep gathered along with the soft foal, Masika just knew she would be sick for days. But nausea and the squirts soared over the alternative of eating . . .

She couldn't even let herself think it.

Instead, she cast about for anyone to talk to. Inlittan's presence in her head reassured her, but the living spirit of a piece of jewelry sucked as a conversationalist.

Boridan walked past, not seeing her. "Where have you been?" she called out to him. "And if the answer is eating that thing, please make something up instead of telling me the truth. I'd consider it a favor.

Stopping, Boridan glanced up, nodded, and plunked down next to her. He leaned back, hands flat on the ground behind him. "I have been climbing mountains made of chocolate and spun sugar with all my naked young wives. But I lost my mountain shoes, and my feet hurt. Sounds like you're having a shitty night too. As much as this place ever has anything you might consider to be a night."

"I'm trying to figure out how eating something here can make me feel sick to my stomach when I left my stomach behind in the living world." A thin plume of smoke hissed out of the contraption at Masika's knee, punctuating her comment with its putrescent scent.

"Oldam's rotten clay turds, woman! Haven't you been cleaning that thing out?" Boridan's face twisted up tight, and he pushed several feet away. "Ugh. Hold out your hands. No, together. Like that. Now hold still. I'm going to throw up in them."

Masika jerked her hands away from Boridan. "No one told me to clean it out. I don't even know how to get it off." Even worse than the smell was her inability to escape it. "Allz's wounds. Can you die from a smell?"

Over the next few minutes, with their immediate area rapidly clearing out, Masika and Boridan worked out how to open the leather front of the mechanical knee and rinse it out with warm water. Neither of them vomited, though Masika went dizzy from trying to control it.

"How could it have gotten so bad so fast?" Masika shook her head. Sitting on the stone floor, she lifted her knee in front of her.

Turning the knee, Boridan examined his work. "There's no rot in the wound. The arrow holes those metal pins run through are just . . . oozy. That's what went bad and smelled so horrible. You're going to have to clean that out every day if you want to keep that from happening again."

Curved leather piece in place once more, he slid the pins home. The coolness of the smooth metal made Masika inhale sharply. "Boridan, I thought that when a mirrored soul died a normal death, they just came back to life the next day."

"That's right," he answered.

"But that's not what this is, is it?" She tapped on the leather knee.

"Those Andosh fighters aren't falling down and getting back up good as new the next day. They're repairing themselves to keep going. And I don't think the repairs should even work."

He shrugged. "It's a mystery. I hope you weren't planning on everything in the Undergates making sense. Because it doesn't. And a lot of what makes the least sense is the worst of it."

A pained look flashed across his face, but he shook it off and sat upright.

Masika decided to steer the conversation in a less bleak direction. "I can't thank you enough for that, Boridan. I think it was about to fall off."

"Maybe better if it did." He grinned up at her as he spoke. Whatever bothered him when he first approached, the hideous stench and the job of ridding Masika of it turned his mood around. "If my only other choice was to smell like that, I'd rather hop."

They both laughed, and Boridan carried the water away to the Longeyes' latrine. When he returned, he sat down next to her.

"I have a question I want to ask you," Boridan said, "about Heron."

Masika recoiled a bit inwardly. She could not imagine anything he might ask about the goddess that she could answer without upsetting him again. Still, her papa taught her that the best way to deal with bad news was as quickly and frankly as possible so as to move on cleanly to happier matters. And he ought to know.

Where would her papa be right now? she wondered. Was he safe? Happy? In their own home perhaps, or in the cells beneath her uncle's palace?

"What about her?" Masika asked, shoving the other thoughts into a mental sock and tossing it in an old drawer full of disquieting ideas. That drawer in her mind did not close as easily as it did before they all arrived in the Undergates.

Maybe his question was entirely innocuous.

"Do you think she could ever love me?"

Then again, maybe not. Masika did not want to be the one to answer this question for Boridan. He hounded Heron's heels, trailing behind her like a baby duck after its mother, only Heron was not his mother, nor was a mother likely what he truly wanted.

The open grin on Masika's face pulled ever so slightly tighter, transforming without meaning to from an open and happy expression to one of taught anxiety. "We all love you, Boridan. You helped us escape from being slaves to demons. How could she not love you?"

Even as she said it Masika felt how clumsy the words were, but she carried nothing better for him.

"Right." His own grin faded, becoming a faint smile of indeterminant meaning.

She wanted to tell him not to worry. Stay true and be yourself. Even a goddess can learn to love a mere man if his heart is good enough, strong enough. But she had seen the way Rainn behaved around Heron, and she was not even certain if it would be safe for Boridan to pursue his infatuation.

Or maybe Masika was wrong. Certainly those two, with all their history together, should be able to communicate their feelings. If Rainn wanted Heron, then Heron should know. Maybe the best thing would be for Boridan to say his piece and get it out in the open, so Heron could either make him happy or cut him free. That was what Masika should say.

But she did not. The risk of making matters worse loomed too large. Instead, she asked him, "If we can't find this Morholt guy, or if we can and he doesn't want to help us, are there any other ways to get back home?"

Boridan's gaze darted to her face, his eyes narrowing. "I get why that'd be bothering you, but how the fuck do you think I would know?" Real anger pushed around the edges of the question.

Masika raised both her hands. "Hey, don't get upset. I understand you don't know everything about this place. It's huge. Bigger than Andos. I'm not mad at you for not being able to answer every little question."

His eyes wide, Boridan's mouth fell open. He shook his head and snorted. Pulling himself to his feet, he snarled at her over his shoulder. "The whole universe isn't about *you*."

He stalked away.

"I never said it was," Masika said to herself.

What crawled up his pants leg? The only thing Masika was guilty of was trying to protect Boridan's feelings where Heron was—oh. She smacked her palm against the side of her head. She meant to protect him, but in truth she ignored him. No wonder he snapped at her like that.

Only slightly wobbly from the knee cleaning, she stood and looked around for Boridan. Capable of spying anything in her range of vision, Inlittan's abilities stopped at seeing through solid objects unless close and small enough to wrap her hands around, and Boridan did not appear to be in the cave at all. She took off in his direction, hoping for some uncharacteristic luck.

Halfway across the wide cave mouth, Masika found Rainn listening to Sharp Jonn, who spoke intently, even while he pulled a willing young woman with short blonde hair and a comparably pretty face, tight against him.

"Hey, have either of you seen Boridan?" As Masika asked the question, Inlittan showed her, quite without her wanting to see, various autonomic responses that raced through Sharp Jonn's blood, whether for the blonde or for Masika, she neither knew nor wanted to. "I, uh, I need to apologize to him."

"I don't see him even when I do see him," Rainn answered. "Hey, Jonn, you should tell Masika here what you just told me. She's the one makes all the decisions anyway."

I am?

"She is?" One narrow brow rose on Sharp Jonn's scarred forehead. He shrugged. "Never played host to a goddess before. Maybe it's normal they let little girls run things for them?"

The blonde woman snorted and let her regard travel disapprovingly up and down Masika's body.

Masika opened her mouth to say she made the decisions for no one, that she simply tried to help as best she could, when Inlittan focused her gaze on Sharp Jonn's face. Imperceptibly to unenhanced sight, his eyes narrowed as he watched her for signs of weakness.

Stop second-guessing yourself. It doesn't help and you don't understand the stakes here. Don't give anyone a reason to think they need to step on you.

Or that they can.

"Heron follows me because she chooses to, and Rainn follows her." Not untrue, even if it played into their established fiction that Rainn lacked Heron's divine status. "No one is asking you to follow too."

"Sorry!" Sharp Jonn raised the hand that was not holding the woman's waist. "I do not mean it that way, do you see? We are just different, right? Anyway, now I know who is the boss, I have a boon to ask of you."

"A boon?" The Andoshi word evaded Masika's understanding. Like the boom of a ship?

"A big boon," Sharp Jonn admitted. He shrugged and sent the young woman away with a sharp slap to her rump. Nose in the air, she stalked off.

He watched her go. "Ah, yes, we need a favor of you. Of you all, if you will listen to it." He paused and glanced around. "There is a keep two dinners from here where lives a nest of shenwing."

"Shenwing are demons," Rainn helpfully supplied.

"Yes." Sharp Jonn nodded and continued to study Masika, though his searching look no longer held a predatory air. "Demons. Like leather wings with claws. Nasty, nasty things. Nest is in the Slaughterhouse, and that is close to the meadows, where we dig up clawworms, so Longeyes are always in peril, do you see?"

"Slaughterhouse?" Masika thought she did see, but questions rose in her mind.

"It's a castle. Called the Slaughterhouse." Sharp Jonn looked away, as if in search of a missing pipe. "It doesn't mean anything."

"Horseshit." Without moving, Rainn loomed over the shorter man. "Why's it called a fucking slaughterhouse?"

"Hah!" Sharp Jonn patted Rainn on the shoulder. "That was a joke, right? It's the Slaughterhouse because in the olden days before . . . we used the site for a slaughterhouse for soft foal. A long time ago." Witnessing Masika's rising temper, he hurriedly continued, "That place is long gone. The keep was built there after. Now it is the

Slaughterhouse because of the shenwing. We want to clear them out so the Longeyes will be safe in the meadows collecting clawworms."

"And you think we can help you kill the shenwing nest, and then it's clawworms for everybody?" The logic of this place irritated Masika, but she understood it. A land permanently under a sky of flame necessitated a different set of morals than her soft life in the living world. Perhaps if the Longeyes could lay claim to a steady supply of food close by, they would have no need to hunt the souls of fallen infants.

"They've tried before but kept getting their asses handed to them." A note of eager bloodthirst sounded in Rainn's voice. "Maybe if they had a goddess on their side, things might be different." He winked at Masika. Obviously, he knew more than he was letting on. As soon as they enjoyed a little privacy, he could explain himself.

"I'll ask Heron what she thinks." And Rainn what he knew. "If she agrees, too, we'll do it." She wanted to ask Boridan's counsel as well, but he was well gone and would not be back until he cooled off. "Until then, go away. I want to talk to my protector."

Sharp Jonn grinned and glanced between Masika and Rainn. "Good. Good. You two talk and inform the goddess. With her help we cannot fail." Still smiling, he turned and strode away in search of lecherous treats.

Masika waited until he and everyone else were out of earshot. "Spill. What's he not want us to know about all this?"

"Sharp Jonn and January are hanging on to power by their fingernails here," Rainn said, a wicked smile on his face. "I think this is their last chance at impressing the rubes enough to keep from getting tossed on the cookfire themselves. 'Ducky' there needs this Slaughterhouse place to stay on top, and January needs him."

"Fine, but why, and please think of who is asking you this question, do you care? Why do you want to help these people?" In truth, Masika wanted to help just because it seemed like the right thing to do. The more she thought about it, the more she convinced herself that a reliable food supply would make better people of all the

Longeyes, even Sharp Jonn and January. But "the right thing" never appeared to hold much weight with Rainn. What did he want here?

Unexpectedly, Rainn greeted her question with a contented smile. "Heron. She said we should be looking for a way to help these psychopaths, and here it is. I think it's part of her intuitions about how we should be navigating this stupid fucking place. We can't argue with the results so far."

"I really can." Masika hated to be the one arguing against helping anyone, but her papa taught her that forcing someone to directly defend their decisions, even if they agreed with yours, was often the only way to get the truth out of them. "I want to help too, but we don't owe these people anything. I think we could leave if we wanted, but we're only here at all because they thought they might want to eat us."

Rainn simply smiled and opened his hands.

"Ah, right." It was not about saving soft foals. It was about saving everyone the Longeyes might prey on. At least that was a reason, and it made sense if Heron and Rainn wanted to start behaving more like gods were supposed to.

"What about the shenwings? Any idea how tough these things are?" Masika wished Boridan were around. Undergates fauna were his specialty. "Can we take 'em?"

"We took Sedja out, I think we can handle a few shitty little bats."

Rainn's answer failed to reassure Masika as much as she hoped, but the point was well made. When they fought the leftover remnant of creation called Sedja, Rainn's power depended entirely on the weather and Heron held no more strength than a bird. Now both of them commanded the physical might of real gods, even if neither remembered how to wield the magic they should also have.

Surely, they could take a few shitty little bats.

CHAPTER

SIXTEEN

Hatred costs lives in staggering numbers, pushing war on those who can ill afford the loss of family or opportunity. But hatred is merely jealousy's pawn, sprouting and growing tall in the long cold of its shadow. Mankind chooses to hate those it is jealous of, for taking the lives and livelihoods of those you cannot hate is an unbearable burden indeed.

And what of love, you ask? That one's the real *bitch.*

The Great and Terrible Murshida Va

The "meadows" lay behind Masika and the rest of the warband, an area unremarkable save for its flat ground, baked to stone under unrelenting flame. Evidence of claw-worms showed here and there, mounds of churned dirt where the voracious predators burrowed up by the hundreds wherever their prey wandered alone.

With calm gratitude, Masika ran her fingers over the curve of the Longeye bow they gave her. Not as refined as her desert bow, it nevertheless soothed the feelings of some vital part of her being missing.

Sharp Jonn warned them all to stay central to the group. A clawworm may be no more than three feet long, but a single human would not make a decent meal for a pack of them.

The lesson forced Masika to wonder how many shenwings might make up a nest? Boridan, unfortunately, had never heard of them. His experience lay far to the west and limited to pools of acid, as well as those who made their lives in and around pools of acid.

"A whole slaughterhouse for babies." Boridan shook with rage. "Oldam's gritty shits, Masika, we shouldn't be liberating this place, we should be razing it to the ground."

Even if only the keep's name came from the actual slaughterhouse that stood there previously, Masika agreed with Boridan's sentiment. Of course, his opinion arose after his discovery that Heron found the concept distasteful. Before then, he barely cared. Afterward, he cared a lot. Although, curiously, he no longer seemed so intent on catching hidden glances at the goddess, or caring if she could hear his agreements.

Listening in on snippets of conversation among the Longeyes proved Rainn's ideas about Sharp Jonn and January's motivations regarding this expedition. While the whole picture was far from complete, Sharp Jonn reportedly found himself unable to control his worst impulses while in January's grip, and everyone sagely agreed that she was far worse than him. Less out of control perhaps, but far eviler.

For reasons Masika still did not understand, the Longeyes felt that retaking the Slaughterhouse should cure Sharp Jonn's behavior.

No one said anything about how January might feel on the subject.

"Masika?" Sharp Jonn sidled up next to her on what might generously be referred to as a trail. Their path through the jutting boulders and sharp hillocks wound in confusing circles, as if laid by a drunken serpent and with no appreciable evidence of it being there. "If now is not a bad time, I would like to talk with you."

Sweat poured off Masika, and she dipped the bleached yellow cowl the Longeyes provided into a small bucket of water carried by a sturdy warrior and draped it over her head. Where did their water come from? She never asked. With a momentary panic she hoped it sprang from the ground somewhere and wasn't made of all the world's dead dogs or something like that.

"Is it getting hotter?" Masika grew up in Egren, a lush and bountiful nation on the other side of the Little Gods Mountains from the Yellow Sea, the world's largest desert. She knew heat, but this was something else altogether.

"Oh." Sharp Jonn squinted up at the burning sky. "Yes, we are climbing higher, a bit. Makes it hotter. Longeyes don't pay much attention. You won't either after a while here."

"What did you want to talk about?" Masika held no intention of staying long enough to grow used to the hideous clime. Curious, she sought to see if Inlittan could show her how much farther up she would have to go before the heat from the roiling conflagration roasted her alive. Instantly she became aware of a bright layer of superheated air that wanted to boil her brain in its skull and vaporize her hair in a crispy flash.

So, not that far.

"I want to ask you about being a leader," Sharp Jonn said. "You are just a woman. A girl, even. You have no more than a single lifetime of experience to your name. Less, even. Yet warriors follow you. A *goddess* follows you. How do you manage it? What did you do to trick them like that?"

Just a woman? Trick them? Masika inhaled seared air and held it, eyes closed and one hand balled into a fist. She relaxed and smiled. "I mean it when I tell them I want to help. That's all."

A thoughtful frown settled on Sharp Jonn's features, wrinkling the scars that crisscrossed his face. "No, that can't be it. I mean, how do you make them *think* you want to help? So, I want them to be happy, right? But I want more not to have to actually *do* anything about it. For them to be happy without them bothering me with it. That's the kind of leader I want to be."

Masika reminded herself that this trek was to give Sharp Jonn the opportunity to become a better person. Even if the Longeyes' belief that the Slaughterhouse would magically do so was as fanciful as she suspected.

"I wouldn't know anything about that. Must be my single lifetime of experience." Masika wondered if any of her friends had to put up with this kind of thing. A quick glance around showed Boridan carefully trudging, his eyes on the rocky path ahead of him, Heron gracefully flowing up an incline of sharp-edged stone with Rainn just behind her and Sharp Jonn watching her with an amused smirk on his face.

She needed to talk with Heron again. Without Boridan.

Sharp Jonn's frown deepened. He stared at his fellow Longeyes warily. "These people worship me, obviously," he said below his breath. "I mean of course they do. How could they not? But I wonder, do they really *love* me?" His voice dropped again, and Masika strained to hear it. "Because I love them. What kind of leader would I be if I didn't? But I'll kill them if they don't love me back."

All of Masika's will went into maintaining a concerned expression of care. A "broken" mirror would not be killed, or murked, unless the body was then consumed, which the Longeyes did with alarming regularity.

He glanced up, but his gaze slid quickly away from Masika's face. "You know. Because I love them so much."

"You're a fucking nutter, Jonny Boy." Rainn slid into the conversation as easily as he stepped up between Masika and Sharp Jonn, Forbryttan clinging happily to his shoulder.

"*You're* a nut butter," Sharp Jonn replied, a sudden grin on his face. "I have to go up front. Firebug is leading us to the Slaughterhouse, and the Longeyes won't like being led by a woman for long, do you see?"

"I see, crazy pants. Get back up there with your terrifying wife and lead us all to our deaths." Rainn's utter lack of respect for Sharp Jonn chilled Masika's blood, which was not as refreshing as it sounded. "Better you than some girl, right?"

"Right," Sharp Jonn said, and bounded effortlessly over the rocky spikes and hot stone in front of them.

"Please never change," Masika told Rainn. There existed a certain kind of people she would never understand or even be able to talk with, but Rainn handled them perfectly every time.

"Not much chance of that now." He waved to Heron as he said it, who faded back from her position at the front of the party to walk with him and Masika. "Learn anything?"

Heron nodded. "You were right. Sharp Jonn and January are slipping here. They're killing too many of their own, and January makes sure they get eaten so they can't come back." The goddess brushed a long strand of silken gray hair out of her youthful face. Even in ragged and dirty slave clothes from Hiimryk, she radiated perfection and grace. "Whatever this Slaughterhouse place means to them, it's their last chance to stay on top. The Longeyes want it too."

Ensuring another eternity of Sharp Jonn just kicked the Longeyes in the shin with a bladed boot, in Masika's estimation. "Are we sure we should be helping then?"

"I think so." Heron's attention left, wandering above the heads of the carefully marching Longeyes in front of her. "Whatever is there, January doesn't want it. She hates and fears it. That's reason enough to help for me."

A better opportunity seemed unlikely to offer itself before they arrived at their destination, and Masika dived in. "Heron, I just wanted to understand why we're doing this. I mean, I understand why it's a good thing to do, but I want to know why you think we should be doing it. I know it's not just to spite January."

The goddess's long legs ate the miles with cool grace. "Reasonable. But I'm not sure I have an answer that'll make it any easier for you to understand. It's more of a feeling that this is where we should go."

"Like the feeling that inspired you to tell the Hiimrykers who you were and landed us in their prison?" Masika asked. "Or the same thing with the Longeyes that made Sharp Jonn decide we should help him kill a bunch of demons and take back some castle in the middle of all this hell?"

"Yes? I'm not sure what else to tell you, Masika. Other than we're still on our feet, and that doesn't seem like a bad thing, while a little bit of sand in January's leather pants maybe does." Heron's smile grew wicked before vanishing.

"Sounds good to me." Rainn nodded and gave a grim smile. "I'm up for punching that bitch in the tits."

Masika grimaced. "Remember when I said not to change, Rainn? I take it back. You can a little bit."

A gleeful bounce carried Forbryttan from one of Rainn's shoulders to the other. "I've never attacked a castle before. Do you think lots of people are going to die? That'd be fun."

"It's good to know someone'll be having a good time." Rainn reached up and scratched Forbryttan under his blue-furred chin.

Sharp Jonn's hiss from the top of the next rise announced that they had arrived.

The Slaughterhouse was here.

Over the crest Masika saw a slight valley, with a hill larger than any they circumvented on their way here. Atop it, a stone keep stretched up into the flames, walls darkened by centuries of fire licking its flanks. Only the bottom portion left itself to view, the majority lost behind the searing bright.

From time-to-time flying figures winged their way in lazy circles around the structure, sometimes clinging to the individual stones that comprised its walls, but more often than not flying back up into the blaze to land somewhere higher.

"Is the fire not hot there?" If so, Masika saw a dozen ways their job might become easier.

"Oh, it's hot, girlie." January unlimbered her graver as she spoke, sighting along the shaft toward one of the flitting shenwings. "The demons just don't feel it, that's all."

"That doesn't seem fair," Rainn observed.

Heron tensed and frowned. "They don't burn. I don't know what I can do here."

"Do I burn?" Forbryttan held a foot up in the air. "Can someone try?"

In truth, Masika never planned on Heron's newfound ability with blazing light to help them. She had yet to be able to use it when their lives were not in eminent danger.

No, Masika had another idea entirely. "Sharp Jonn, will your Longeyes be ready when it's time?"

"That they will, little leader-lady. You get 'em down here, and we'll take care of the rest."

"Forby?" Masika looked up at Forbryttan. Her mechanical knee gurgled a bubbling wheeze. All this walking in the heat was not helping. "You remember what you're supposed to do?"

"Ohboyohboyohboy!" The little apelike demon leaped off Rainn and hopped up and down, his curved toe claws clicking on the stone. "This is the best thing *ever*." He reached up and grabbed the front of Masika's tunic, and a tear rolled down the weathered blue fur on his cheeks. "I love you for this. I love you *so much*."

"Of course it does." Above them, Sharp Jonn chuckled and shook his head. "I don't know how much your trimpet likes the murk, but it sure likes getting killed, do you see?"

Masika reached down and hugged Forbryttan. He felt solid, hard and unexpectedly light beneath the soft fur, but she also felt his heartbeat hammering in excitement.

At least someone was guaranteed a good time in all this.

She released him, patted the back of his head, and he was off. He jumped some twenty feet out of the rocky outcropping they hid in, and bolted toward the keep on the hill, laughing and shouting all the way.

As Forbryttan bounded along, Masika realized the keep lay farther away than her original estimation told her, which meant it was bigger than she initially thought. And that meant . . .

The first shenwing pushed itself from the rock wall and angled out over the valley floor. It tipped left and dived at Forbryttan, a long, foul note of avarice and hunger staining the air between them. No other sound dared raise itself against that vile challenge, other than the gleeful giggle of the shenwing's bait.

"Get ready." Masika held her bow at the ready, and one of the

Longeye short swords scabbarded at her hip. She felt rather than saw the eagerness of the fighters surrounding her.

Speed increasing, the shenwing continued to drop, causing Masika to reevaluate its size. She willed Inlittan to show her more.

"What's wrong?" Heron asked at Masika's gasp.

A wild cackle accompanied the monster's capture of tiny Forbryttan. The thing resembled some kind of nightmare spider, with long trailing ears and leathery wings between its grasping legs. Its mouth opened and closed around Forbryttan's head, who appeared helpless in the paroxysms of his laughter.

"Woah," breathed Boridan. "Did anyone else know how big that thing was?"

"Go now!" Masika leaped to her feet and churned across the parched land. She waved her borrowed blade above her head and howled.

A thousand shenwings plummeting out of the inferno above, each repeating that sonorous call of greedy famine. The cacophony of sound knocked Masika flat on her ass. Forbryttan vanished beneath the beating of multitudes of gigantic leathern spider wings, which formed a staggering ball of hate and claws. They tore at one another, each vying to be the one to consume the furry morsel beneath.

Even if they ate him, they could not consume him. As Masika understood it, the process of being worn away by another creature's digestion was what made a body unusable for return to life, murked, instead of merely broken. Enough of the Longeyes had tried it. And if Forbryttan could not be digested, he should be fine.

She hoped.

Even as Masika reached her feet to charge forward, Rainn gripped her from behind and ran back the way they had come, the Longeyes already cowering behind the rocky formations.

"Did no one know how many of those things there were?" Boridan shouted above the din.

"We tried not to get closer than the meadows!" Sharp Jonn yelled back. "No one ever saw more than three or four at a time."

The clawing, flapping, bleeding ball began to rise.

The shaft of January's graver rose in the direction of the shenwings, and Masika's hand darted out and yanked it aside.

"Let go!" January yanked at her graver, trying unsuccessfully to wrest it from Masika's grip.

Both hands on the weapon, Masika refused to cede ground. "If you just shoot at them without a plan, they'll see us. We'll all die right here." Permanently. Those things wanted a meal.

A slender arm, moving with divine gracefulness, reached out and took hold of the strange weapon. Heron plucked the long shaft out of January's hands and placed it firmly in Masika's. "See for us, Masika. See with *fire*."

Inlittan bore a hole through the space between Masika and her targets, and she *became* the weapon. She saw how to operate it, saw what it could do. She saw a plan.

And she did it.

The graver popped and jumped in her arms, and an explosion ripped against the fighting ball of shenwings, sending torn sheets of spider cascading from the sky. The tone of the monsters' shrieking changed pitch, rising in anger and horror, and the graver popped again.

While heat could not harm the things, explosive force certainly could.

But the mass of bodies packed itself too densely, and each detonation peeled off fewer than a hundred monsters at a time. The things rose further, faster now as they lost numbers, and disappeared behind the firestorm.

Disappeared to everyone but Inlittan and Masika.

This was not fast enough. The graver would stop operating before Masika got them all, and those shenwings that were knocked out of the hate ball oriented themselves on the Longeye party.

Her stomach knotted as Masika realized she accomplished precisely what she warned January against doing.

"Find a spot and grab your bows," Sharp Jonn bellowed. "Keep 'em off her or we're all smoke!"

As she fired the graver amidst the sounds of the battling Longeyes, Masika walked to the crest of a pointed outcropping. The noises of Rainn's war cries fell away, and only the sound of her breathing filled her skull. Imagined, she knew, there existed no way a mere breath rasped above the unbelievable cacophony, but she heard it all the same. Silent winds buffeted her from the force of Sharp Jonn's hand graver, and black arrows reached out to kiss death to the winged spiders.

She stood still, waiting, as Longeyes and shenwings fought and died around her.

There.

Through the blaze and through the churning mass of winged spiders, Masika spied Forbryttan, covered in spittle and monster blood and clearly having the time of his young life. The plan worked. The shenwings converged on the joyously shouting bit of food that none of them could get a piece of.

Pop.

As the pink projectile entered the cascading ball of evil, Masika lost sight of both it and of Forbryttan. Something heavy and hateful knocked against the side of her skull, bearing her to the ground with claws and manic fury.

But she heard the explosion. Everyone heard the explosion.

The screams invaded her awareness once again, bringing pain and blood. But the pitch altered a second time, now calling out in fear that split stone. The pressure against her head lifted—Masika realized her eyes were shut tight—and fell again, this time unmoving. But even here, beneath a lifeless demon, she knew they had won. The shenwings were in retreat.

She only hoped she had not just murdered Forbryttan.

"Upsy-daisy." The shenwing, now missing the top half of its head, slid off Masika, replaced by a grinning Rainn, his powerful hand outstretched. Happy relief flooded her, and she let him lift her to her feet.

Longeyes lay dying or dead around her, while their family and their friends murdered the remaining shenwings. Masika guessed the merely "broken" Longeyes would be permitted to return to life as they had not been dispatched by a vindictive January.

"Give it back." And January stepped in front of Masika, her open hand reaching for the graver.

"You did not make the best use of the weapon, January." Heron stepped forward, a long series of gashes striping her right arm. She even made bleeding all over herself look beautiful. "Are you certain you deserve it?"

Masika judged that January toed the line on genuine stupidity here. If Masika did not return the weapon, the rangy woman was likely to attack, and then they would be forced to hurt—or even kill—her.

With a forced smile, Masika handed her the graver. "Thanks. Couldn't have done it without you."

January snatched it away.

"Hey, look." Rainn pointed out over the bloody field covered with shenwing corpses. From the fire above it, Forbryttan fell, laughing the whole way, and crashed to the stone.

"Time to move." Sharp Jonn opened a chamber in the side of one of his two hand gravers, inspected it, closed it back, and stuck it through his belt strap. "We've got a slaughterhouse to reclaim."

CHAPTER

SEVENTEEN

Wisdom is not in knowing how best to defeat your enemy. A knife in the armpit or flaming lamp oil in the face. That is knowledge, and it is a lesser form of knowing, even if it is still important.

Wisdom is in the quiet spaces between breaths, where you make the decision to react to the dangers and frustrations of your world with anger and fear, or act to become a source of creativity and change, to improve both it and yourself.

Or not. I'm not the boss of you.

The Great and Terrible Murshida Va

The wounded and broken were left to tend to themselves—Sharp Jonn insisted every able-bodied warrior who could still hold a blade come along—and the now considerably smaller war party of twelve advanced across the corpse-strewn plain.

Boridan, unconscious but bandaged, was one of those remaining behind.

"I know that look," Heron said to Masika as they crept over the flat hard bake. "But Boridan is safer there than here. The shenwings may

121

never return to this place, and what life does exist in this place cannot harm them."

"Hmph." Whatever kind of life survived in such a hard-bitten environment as this must be tougher than she was. More dangerous too. Despite Heron's assurances, Masika had a hard time believing a bunch of wounded people were better off on their own.

A small blue head popped up from behind a rock and grinned, tusks prominent in the furry face. Forbryttan scampered to Rainn and leaped onto his shoulder.

Heron's brows rose. "I thought you saw everything. Can you not see the beauty around us?"

"Beauty?" Masika's gaze wandered over Heron's face. The goddess was beautiful, but that was not what she meant. "Inlittan doesn't just show me everything like that. I have to know what I'm looking for. Mostly. Actually look for it. You know? And I wouldn't know where to start to find beauty out here."

This was not the whole truth though. Inlittan had, on more than one occasion, showed Masika something it thought important in the moment. Briefly, she wondered how many other runecrafted objects would accompany their masters into death the way Inlittan and Forbryttan had.

Now only one brow stayed up on Heron's forehead. The expression of a patient and encouraging parent replaced that of confusion.

"Oh. Right." Masika slowly scanned the surroundings, and politely asked Inlittan to show her the life here or the beauty or whatever.

Instantly, Masika's perception shifted, dropping through layers of sight, seeing differently each instant as she followed it down.

Inside the cracks in the blasted ground, tucked away into the shadows where the sky's heat could not touch, life existed. No, it *teemed.*

Bizarre lizard-like creatures, much too small to be observable to an unaided eye, undulated through waves of air molecules in pursuit of fuzzy balls of tentacles extending long, skinny legs that pushed them through space. Bony, infinitesimal worms wriggled through gigantic grains of sand, and floating dots of pale colors attached themselves to deep red eyeballs that searched under flecks of dust with claws twice the size of their bodies. The simple variety of it overwhelmed. It ate itself. Immortal and self-sufficient. Masika's vision rose back out of the cracks and into her own head. But she kept the new perspective, extending it to everything she saw. Everywhere she saw.

And it was everywhere.

And it was beautiful.

A gentle hand with long, tapered fingers touched Masika on the shoulder. "You see now? There is wonder and delight to be taken wherever we go. Even in a place such as this." Heron squeezed Masika's shoulder and released it. "And this place is really just the worst."

The comment caught Masika as funny, and she involuntarily snorted a laugh. Several Longeyes turned to glare at her for the noise, which made her want to laugh all the more after the catastrophically loud battle that only just ended here.

"Right. Sorry," she said instead.

Ahead, Sharp Jonn and January flanked Rainn in the vanguard as the group closed in on the keep. The stones that composed its walls were not gray, as Masika first assumed, but a bewildering mélange of colors that only appeared that way from a distance.

"The keep's magic," Sharp Jonn explained to Rainn. "It resists the heat of the sky. See where it rises up into the flames? You can go up inside those towers and not die from burning up even a little bit."

"It's not magic." January shook her head firmly. "It's science. The stones are special because they form that way. We have rocks just like that at home. No one ever made a magic spell on them or anything."

"You're young." A dismissive shrug accompanied Sharp Jonn's statement. "Two hundred years here? Maybe not that much. You don't remember when the Slaughterhouse was built. But I do. I remember why."

January's face screwed up in anger. She stalked out ahead of the two men.

"Touchy subject?" Rainn's tone sounded open and friendly, but Masika saw the subterfuge in his gait, in the set of his shoulders. He wanted to know why the Slaughterhouse had been built as well.

Sharp Jonn waved a hand. "Everything is touchy with that one. So, Rainn, my big warrior friend, ready to go in first? Might be more fighting. Will definitely be more fighting."

Holding up his heavier sword, Rainn pointed it at the big double doors just coming around the keep's side. "That's why I'm here, Jonny-boy. That's why I'm here."

The heat bore down on them at the top of this hill, a shimmering fist that sought to push Masika into the sharp ground, and the scent of burnt stone filled her nostrils.

"Then the honor is yours." Sharp Jonn stepped aside at the solid stone doors and bowed to Rainn. "After all, we couldn't have come this far without you."

Masika moved forward, but Rainn intercepted, his rough hand scratchy on Masika's collarbone. "Ducky here's right. I'll go first. Something in there might wanna happen to you. But I'm gonna happen to it first."

"I think that Rainn should go in ahead of us. He is the strongest, do you see? And look how much he wants to go." Sharp Jonn's hands shook in anticipation.

Although irritation rose as her first reaction at being brushed aside, Masika saw the wisdom in sending a god who really liked to fight in ahead. She stopped, smiled, and extended a welcoming arm.

"After you, big guy."

Sword held in front of him, Rainn kicked the doors. Whatever mechanism existed for keeping them closed snapped under the sudden attack, and the stone flew open with a thunderous bang.

Louder than Rainn's snort of laughter, Masika noted.

Following his blade, Rainn entered, Forbryttan clinging eagerly to his shoulder. The interior was dark, and Rainn quickly vanished from sight. "Hey. Oh, heyyy . . . Yeah. C'mon in."

Masika followed Rainn in, Heron and the rest of the remaining Longeyes behind her. The instant she crossed the threshold a swirl of air dropped the temperature.

"Denari clear the fog," Masika gasped. "It's cold in here. It's actually *cold*."

"Magic," Sharp Jonn stated with a pointed nod to January.

"Science," she said.

"I did not believe you would return, Slender Jonn."

What? Masika searched the room. Even Inlittan failed to find the source of that sepulchral voice. She gripped the unfamiliar blade in her hand tight. Something moved unseen in this room. The Longeyes spread out, backs to the wall, casting nervous glances through the dark.

"Don't go by that anymore, Throdd" Sharp Jonn responded with a nervous grin. The other Longeyes smirked at him. "I'm Sharp Jonn now. That's what everyone calls me, and you should call me that too. Because I am sharp and will cut you."

"You have chosen your champion," the voice intoned. "Enter the circle."

The entrance hall brightened to dim relief as Inlittan granted Masika fuller sight in the gloom. The room spread broad and round, with walls of tall stone and a ring of columns around a twenty-foot circle in the center. Rings of slowly rotating runes spun around the walls close to the arched ceiling and decorated the tops of the columns. On the far side, an eight-foot-high door made of stout wood stood barred and closed. Otherwise, all was white stone, stained here and there with yellowed filth.

Within the columned circle, a man stood, one hand resting comfortably on the pommel of the sword sheathed at his hip.

January slipped around behind the columns and tried the tall wooden door. It did not open.

Large, Throdd stood half a head taller than Rainn, and his skin held a golden cast. Long gray hair fell over an unremarkable bronze breastplate.

"What's all this about a champion?" Masika went to the edge of the circle. "We didn't choose anybody. We're not going to fight you, but if we did, we wouldn't do it one at a time. We're a family, and that's just stupid."

"You wouldn't fight an unwilling champion, would you?" Heron stepped up beside Masika. The goddess sounded merely curious, as if no one's lives were at stake.

"Slender Jonn chose his champion when he allowed the godling to enter first. The godling is the only one permitted to enter the circle." Throdd flexed, and an embarrassment of muscle rippled across his neck and arms. "I am but a stopper in your bottle. I separate you from the sweet wine within. It is my purpose here, and I have been far too long without serving it. Enter, champion, that I might be fulfilled." He swallowed and half-smiled. "It's been a while."

"Kinda sounds like he wants to fuck me." Rainn joined Masika at the circle's rim. "But I'm pretty sure this is one of those fight to the death things. Unless he just wants to thumb wrestle." He nodded at Masika. "You wanna come with?"

"No. We're not going in there at all. Our guide here is. But first I want to know," she spun on a surprised Sharp Jonn, "why you decided to nominate one of mine as your champion." Masika pointed the upturned tip of her short sword at his neck. "If you hoped to avoid having to fight, I think your plan might just have fallen through."

"I have to agree." Heron's eyes flashed white in the dark.

"What? No. I didn't do that." Sharp Jonn's gaze flicked between Heron's eyes, Masika's face, and the end of Masika's blade.

Masika shook her head. "That's a lie. You practically shoved Rainn through the door first. Circle guy there said that's how the champion is selected, and you said you know more about this place than anyone else, right?"

"It's Throdd. Not circle guy," Throdd explained helpfully.

Eyes wide, Sharp Jonn tried an ingratiating smile. "He's wrong. It must be random or something. Do you see?"

"The Darrishwoman speaks true," said the warrior. He lifted his big sword and cut the air with it. Strength danced beneath his gold-tinted skin. "That is the arrangement we reached when you left this place, Slender Jonn. I have waited—"

"Stop calling me that!" Sudden anger flitted away, to be replaced on Sharp Jonn by warm conviviality once again. "Yes. I understand what you meant now. How I chose my champion. Of course." He licked his lips. "He has the best chance. Rainn does. Obviously, I knew he was a god, like Heron—"

"*I* knew he was a god," January interrupted. "I'm the one who told you."

Around them, the remaining Longeyes stared at Sharp Jonn and January with flinty expressions, their faces as unimpressed as Masika was.

"Does that really matter right now, dear?" A single drop of sweat fell off the end of Sharp Jonn's chin and spattered against Masika's blade. "Anyway, Throdd there is no ordinary swordsman. Only someone special will beat him. We need Rainn."

"*You* need Rainn," Masika countered. "*We* are only here as a favor. Or we were before you lied to us and tried to get Rainn murked, at any rate. Rainn? Heron? You two ready to move on?"

"You bet." Rainn sheathed his blade. "I'm sure I can find another scrap to get into along the road."

In truth, Masika had no intention of abandoning their purpose here. All the reasons they held before remained true now, some even more so. Sharp Jonn's evil was the result of his desperation, and abating that hopelessness remained the best chance for all the Longeyes, whether his wickedness was pointed at Masika and her friends or not. This was about doing the right thing, not the most satisfying one.

She felt a little bad about keeping Rainn and Heron in the dark though.

Forbryttan spun to face Masika from Rainn's shoulder. "As go my tribe, so go I." He grinned fiercely, sharp tusks and long canines gleaming. "I just gotta say, thanks for that outside. It was so much fun! We need to find some more of those pretty bird things."

Involuntarily Masika shivered at Forbryttan's characterization of the shenwings as *pretty bird things*, but she pushed past it. "You're welcome? What about you, Heron? Ready to find Morholt the Runecrafter and get out of hell?"

"I suppose." Heron breathed out a soft sigh. "It's a shame we'll never find out what drew me to this place though."

"Yeah, I agree. But it doesn't matter now." Masika lowered her blade to the center of Sharp Jonn's chest and pushed him out of her way with it, putting a very literal point on her metaphorical one. "Have fun with your little friend here. We won't be seeing you later." If her papa's lessons held true, this would be Sharp Jonn's moment of truth.

"Please don't go." Sharp Jonn jumped in front of Masika's blade once again. "If anyone walks out that door, Throdd'll murk all of us. He's too strong, do you see? We won't be able to stop him."

"Get out of the way." Irritated, Masika pushed the sword until she saw blood, but Sharp Jonn refused to move.

She had him.

"Slender Jonn speaks true," boomed the gold-skinned warrior. "Single combat or kill everyone. Such was our arrangement."

"That was a stupid arrangement." Rainn scowled down at Sharp Jonn.

"It seemed to make sense at the time," Sharp Jonn answered.

"Can I go first?" Forbryttan asked.

Hands on her hips, Masika stared at Sharp Jonn. "So will you finally tell me why we're really here? What's so special about this place that you'd risk everything for it?"

"Honestly, I'd risk all the Longeyes just for the magic cool air," Rainn said, smiling.

"Science," January repeated.

Hope leached out of Sharp Jonn's face, and his normally tense muscles went slack. "Our salvation. An end to the fire."

Heron raised an elegant gray brow while Rainn scowled.

Masika stalked to the ring of columns, intending to demand answers from Throdd the Big Gold Guy. But she stopped between two of them against a wall she could neither see nor feel. "What is this?" She ran her hand along the invisible wall, but still couldn't feel it under her fingers. What kept her out of there?

"I'll take care of it. C'mon, Goldfucker, let's get it over with." So saying, Rainn strode through the columns to Masika's left. "I'll kill Ducky after you and me're done."

Throdd lifted his long blade at Rainn. "You cheat. The combat must be individual. You may not bring help." He pointed at Rainn's shoulder. "I can see it, you know."

"What're you . . . ?" Rainn looked behind himself, then laughed when he realized he was craning his neck to see around Forbryttan. "You talking about Forby here? He must be the champion, too, otherwise he wouldn't be able to come in here with me, right?"

"I know not how you cheat, only that my eyes reveal that you do." Throdd showed his teeth in anger, and Masika winced against the power of his voice.

"Oh, I'm with my buddy Rainn here," Forbryttan said through smiling teeth. "I'm his goddamn *sword*." With that, Forbryttan leaped across the space between the two combatants, and landed, tusks flashing, on Throdd's face.

Even as Throdd raised his sword and screamed, Rainn charged in and shoved his own blade into the larger man's stomach. Throdd went backward and crunched against a column.

Overconfidence against Rainn had been a bad idea even in the living world, before the god regained his proper divine strength. Now it was just insulting.

Forbryttan spat out Throdd's nose over his furry blue shoulder and went back in. But a huge golden hand punched out, catching Rainn in the chest and shoving him back, and the other one grabbed Forbryttan by the neck and threw him.

The apelike demon bounced off the smooth stone floor and back onto Rainn's shoulder.

An arrow from Masika's bow stopped at the invisible barrier and fell to the floor.

Pinned to the column behind him by Rainn's sword, Throdd reached down, snapped off the hilt of the blade between his thumb and forefinger, and slid himself down the length of it.

Rainn kicked him, sending him against the protruding sword blade again. Throdd slashed out with his own blade and cut Rainn across the chest. Red welled against the gray slave tunic.

"Ow! Fucker. That hurts." Rainn danced back before Throdd gave him a more serious cut.

Masika's hand went to her mouth just ahead of her gasp. Face a wreck and punctured twice through the torso, Throdd spun and slashed around the confined space, cutting into Rainn again and again. Masika kicked against the hidden wall, but it resisted her fully, unmoving, and inviolate.

Beside her, Heron pressed both hands to the barrier and strained. It moved no more for her than it had for Masika.

Unable to do more than watch her friend be slaughtered in front of her, Masika stepped back and gripped her sword in both hands.

Around the perimeter of the room, the other Longeyes did the same.

On one knee, Rainn dripped blood from a dozen wounds, some shallow and some not. Throdd regarded him from the wreckage of his face.

"Your perfidy has availed you not, godling. You will die true death in this place, by my sword. If beings such as you pray to another, now is that time." He whipped his sword to one side and a line of Rainn's blood splattered to the ground. "And also, on a more personal note, thanks for this. You have no idea how dull it is to stand in one spot for centuries waiting for someone to try and steal something no one even knows is there, you know? This has been a treat."

He glowered at Sharp Jonn. "And would it have killed you to leave a book or two?"

"Forby?" Rainn's whisper came out a feathery rasp, only just audible to Masika's ears. He held an arm out to one side and opened his hand.

"Yeah, boss?" Forbryttan's omnipresent grin faded at last. He watched Rainn with sad pride.

"I need my sword."

"Your sword?" Abruptly, the wild grin returned to Forbryttan's face. "Oh, hell yeah you do!"

A streak of weathered blue fur swarmed up Rainn's arm as the god rolled to his feet. Throdd, alert to the danger, jumped in, all his considerable weight behind the sharply pointed tip of his long blade. But Rainn punched at that tip, his fist a ball of blue demon.

"Haaaah!" Forbryttan yelled, the blade fully stopped by his invulnerable hide.

Body tense and eyes wide, Heron helplessly watched the two combatants. She continued to push at the wall beside Masika.

Momentary confusion passed over Throdd's mangled features, before Forbryttan dropped from Rainn's hand, and the god swung Forbryttan by the tail at the golden man's head.

Thud.

Throdd shuffled backward. The same blow that staggered him also left three long claw marks in the side of his neck. Worse, it left him unprepared for the fusillade of blows that followed, each more powerful than the last.

The sudden reversal caught in Masika's throat, and she found herself unable to breath as Rainn went to work.

His bloody task painted the circle in glimmering crimson gold.

From his back, curled up to protect himself, Throdd raised a blood-streaked arm. "I yield!"

Arm raised for the next blow, Forbryttan dripping and grinning manically in his fist, Rainn stopped. "Yield? I thought we were murdering each other here."

"I never said that," Throdd sputtered. "The battle is only to determine your . . . worthiness. It need not be to the death."

"You implied it." Rainn held his next attack high in the air. "I could've fucking yielded? You told me to pray."

"To win." Throdd stopped and grimaced. "Pray to win and enter the keep."

"Oh." Rainn straightened and took a step back. "Well, am I worthy?"

Throdd coughed and spat a mouthful of blood. "Yeah. Totally worthy."

At his words, the wall between Masika and Rainn dissolved. She fell inward and ran to Rainn. "Are you all right?" Covered in red, some bright crimson and some with a metallic golden sheen, Masika found it impossible to gauge Rainn's wounds.

"He's injured," Heron said, suddenly at Rainn and Masika's side, "but he'll heal quickly now that he has his true strength." She held her face in one hand, and Masika saw a taught smile behind it. Some of the wind went out of Heron, and her shoulders shook.

"Hey, uh, it's all fine. No one got murked." Masika's arm around Heron's shuddering shoulders felt too heavy somehow. Awkward. But Heron leaned in, and Masika held her close. For more than a thousand years, chained to stone tables in the torture dungeon of a mad demon-god, the only thing they possessed to stave off despair was each other. "They weren't fighting to the death anyway."

"I thought it *was* supposed to be to the death." January's face settled somewhere between confusion and disappointment. "Didn't we have that conversation, Ducky?"

The flare of anger Sharp Jonn directed at January shut her up, and he jutted his chin in Rainn's direction. "You must've misunderstood, Firebug. What I *said* is everything was perfectly safe, and the god had the best chance of keeping everyone *else* alive."

Murder crossed Masika's mind, but she pushed it away. In the Undergates and surrounded by untrustworthy killers and demons she may be, but she remained herself. And she was no murderer, even if Sharp Jonn was.

"Let's go." Masika put a hand on both Alir. "We'll grab Boridan on the way out and make our way back to the Crying Road. There's nothing left for us here."

"Huh?" Rainn's head spun around. "I get chopped up like a cabbage and you want me to leave before we find out why?" He stuck a finger out at Sharp Jonn. "I knew that little fucker wasn't gonna play fair soon's he got all cagey over what was really in this place. I'm not going until I see whatever it is I fought for."

"I wasn't cagey." Sharp Jonn's voice rose an octave.

Heron squared her shoulders. "I agree with Rainn. We need to know."

With a silent sigh, Masika smiled and nodded. She wanted to be away from these bloodthirsty animals, but she wanted to know why this place was so special too.

"So what's in here then?" Rainn asked him.

"Ah, that's not a . . . We don't . . . Uh."

"See what I mean?" Rainn extended an arm to indicate Sharp Jonn's recalcitrance, and Forbryttan, still at the end of that arm, hissed at the Longeye leader.

Stepping between the two, Heron addressed Sharp Jonn. "There is something I don't understand going on in the Undergates. I feel as if we are being led on a specific path. Knowing what lies here may well give us some idea what it is or what it wants."

That's what Hereon meant before when she told Masika about her intuitions. "Being led. Why haven't you mentioned this before?"

"It was only a feeling," Heron admitted. "I hope to confirm, one way or another."

"Well, I'm definitely leaving." Throdd stood, collected his lengthy blade, and sheathed it. He gasped in pain and leaned against a column. "In just a minute. My cousins will be here soon to collect me. They will have heard my binding break, and you should move on before they arrive. They will not be pleased to know you cheated in our contest."

"More like you?" Rainn's brows rose. "Thanks for letting us know. You heard the man." He shoved against Masika and Heron, urging them toward the now-opened doorway at the back of the entrance hall. "Time to go."

This hardly represented the first time Masika felt the hand of unseen forces guiding their steps. The goddess Denari, back in the living world, brought them here at Masika's request. Perhaps she now watched over her Darrish daughter and prepared the path in front of them. Were gods capable of reaching across the divide between life and death to do such things?

Or could it be Sarah?

"I'm with you, Rainn. Sharp Jonn, what's down here?" Masika stood squarely in the open doorway, and Rainn crossed his arms beside her.

Heron tilted her head back and stared down at Sharp Jonn.

Tongue flicking across his lips, Sharp Jonn held out his hands. "Everyone wants to know what's behind the door, don't they? No sense in keeping secrets now, yes?"

The other Longeyes darted glances among themselves but held their silence.

Heaving a theatrical sigh, Sharp Jonn slumped his head forward. "Deep below the Slaughterhouse, where the rock is cold, is the graverstone mine. It is where the bullets for the graver weapons come from. If we don't get more soon, the demons from the Reaves will come to murk us all." He held his pose, gaze flitting about the faces surrounding him.

"Well, he's lying, but I guess we'll deal with whatever it is when we get there." Masika frowned at Sharp Jonn. Betrayal proved easier to deal with when you knew exactly when and where it was happening.

"I'll deal with whatever it is." Streaked in gore, bare arms bulging in the half-gloom, Rainn cut a terrifying image.

"He'll deal with whatever it is," Masika said to the wide-eyed Sharp Jonn.

Everyone crept into the dark, and Sharp Jonn clicked the door shut behind them. Though black as the inside of an ale cask in a storm cellar, Masika saw with perfect clarity. "Come on, everyone." She moved through Longeyes and Alir. "I'll lead. Keep a hand on the person in front of you."

Through musty storage halls and down narrow stairs cut into the rock, Masika followed Sharp Jonn's dimly recollected instructions toward their apparent objective. Whatever that might actually be.

If it proved to be a weapon he intended to use against them, Masika intended to make him eat it.

At the bottom of a lengthy stair, they arrived at a narrow hall. Rainn turned his shoulders sideways to fit into it. At the end, candlelight filtered in beneath a small door. A smell of baking bread caused Masika's heart to jump for no reason she could think of. *Bread's not scary. Right?*

"I could eat." Rainn slid to the end and shouldered the door open.

CHAPTER

EIGHTEEN

The recovery of things once thought lost is often considered to be joyful, but it can just as easily become frightening, stressful, or even traumatizing. It can be purposeful or entirely accidental. These conflicting ideas hold doubly true when the things we find are not outside ourselves but within. But what does this mean?

Looking for the happy child inside your own mind only to discover a soulless murderer might be the same sort of shock as discovering the cookies you've been waiting all day for are all made of sawdust and raisins.

Well, I guess you'd have to really like cookies, but you know what I mean.

The Great and Terrible Murshida Va

A cheerful glow encompassed the tiny room behind the door, a single candle burning brightly enough to chase off most of the shadows. A tall, smiling woman gestured Masika and the rest into the smallish chamber below the Slaughterhouse and toward a tiny round table with a steaming loaf of light-colored bread and one wooden chair. The warm space, decorated with patterned earth-tone shawls and dried flowers lulled Masika's mind and begged to be cozied up in.

"Hello, my darlings! Come in and sit down. You've all come so far to see me. You need to rest and have something to eat."

"I've come for you, my Murshida Va!" Sharp Jonn bulled past Masika and Rainn and clutched the white-haired woman in a fierce hug. She hugged him back, though Masika felt a sad reserve in the embrace. "We need you so badly."

January sat in the chair and tore off a hunk of bread.

The rest of the Longeyes filtered in around the outer walls and stared at the Murshida Va, reverential awe on their faces.

"Is she the thing we're here for? I knew it wasn't graverstone," Masika whispered to Heron. No reason for things to start making sense now.

Heron replied with a nod, the rest of her attention riveted on the Murshida Va.

"She's so . . ." Rainn said.

Again, Heron simply nodded.

"You realize you've left me down here for the past eight hundred and sixty years, right?" the Murshida Va asked Sharp Jonn. "And you expect me to be happy because you finally need me?"

Stricken, Sharp Jonn stepped back. "But I love you. I only put you here to protect you." He pointed up. "That's why Throdd was here. I made you safe."

A bare arm rose from the Murshida Va's array of flowing silks, the thin muscles moving with surety and compassion to cup Sharp Jonn's jaw. "No, my Slender Jonn, you put me here because of your guilt. And now you return because the heat of your anger and pain threaten to burn you all. Does that sound like truth to you, my boy?"

His *anger* would burn them? Had this woman never seen the sky?

"He doesn't go by Slender Jonn anymore," January said between mouthfuls of bread, butter, and candied apple jam.

A tear traced the scarred contours of Sharp Jonn's cheek. He nodded to the Murshida Va.

"So, there's no graverstone mine under here, is there?" asked Rainn. "Not that I thought there fucking would be."

"Is that the fiction my poor Jonn told you to win your help on his way in here?" Though the truth bared its teeth in her words, the Murshida Va's voice carried none of that aggression. It calmed. It demanded honesty with both her and within one's own mind. Masika found herself wondering why her path led her to this place in this time.

Her path. Could it really be Sarah behind everything?

Rainn wiped his face with a rare clean spot on his tunic. "Yeah. We knew he was lying, but we didn't know why. I was ready to tear his smug little head off his damn shoulders if I didn't like the answer though."

"He lied because he thought you'd murk him if you knew what was really down here, and how it got here." January pushed the chair back from the tiny table and brushed crumbs off her bony chest. "On account of you all having such a hissy fit over the soft foal."

"Sometimes death teaches us how to live," the Murshida Va said, her eyes resigned as she looked at Sharp Jonn. "And other times it teaches us very little. But the lessons themselves are always there, whether we choose to heed them or not."

Randomly, it occurred to Masika that no fireplace heated the warm little room. How had this woman made bread? Where did the ingredients and other bread-things come from?

What even went into bread? Masika had no idea. Potatoes made it brown, right?

"I want to learn." A long sniff followed Sharp Jonn's statement. "I want to be a better leader. I want the Longeyes to love me."

"Like the way you love them?" January asked, a little heat in her voice. "I think maybe you should be careful what you wish for. You want them to murk you if you don't give them your food or your affection or maybe your *wives*?"

The last one about the wives sounded rather pointed to Masika, and she wondered briefly about the origin of Sharp Jonn and January's relationship.

"No!" Sharp Jonn whirled on January, his face shiny and wet. "I mean I want to learn to be worthy of their love."

January leaned an elbow on the table and crossed her legs. "Well, that's the trick then, isn't it? You're too busted for that, aren't you, Ducky? You're not worthy of anyone's love. That's why we work so well. Because I don't care. I'll have you in my bed no matter how much of a ruin you really are. You don't need her." She waved a dismissive hand at the Murshida Va. "You need *me*."

Sharp Jonn's head swiveled between the Murshida Va and January. He wept openly now, great hiccupping sobs that wracked his rangy frame.

"I know I just said I'd tear off his head," Rainn said, jerking a thumb in January's direction, "but I'd be happy to tear hers off instead. Sounds like she deserves it more." He stopped and one brow rose. "And gimme some of that bread. It smells great."

"I think we may be getting off track." The Murshida Va burst forth a glorious grin, bright sunlight shattering the dark, hundreds of feet below the Slaughterhouse and the hill it rested on. "No one needs to kill anyone. My dear Jonn has reached out for help, and I will help him. That's why the Pilgrim Handmaiden bade me come to this place."

Bells went off in Masika's head and her breath caught fast. The Pilgrim Handmaiden was the Arlean name for Sarah.

"As for you, young woman," the Murshida Va turned her attention to January, who shrank from it, "I will be here for you as well, although you will not accept my help and will exile yourself in the end when your bitterness has at last pushed the last of the Longeyes away from you."

"What, now you see the future?" January's defensive tone rang like weakness and fear in Masika's ears.

"No, poor child." The Murshida Va's resigned smile returned. "I don't. It's just an educated guess."

Stunned, January offered no resistance when Rainn swiped the loaf from in front of her and tore off pieces for the other Longeyes watching from the walls.

He kept a generous part for himself and dunked it into the butter and jam. An entertaining game followed, with Forbryttan trying to interpose his face between the bread and Rainn's mouth.

"Fucking stop that." Rainn palmed Forbryttan's skull with his other hand and shoved the bread into his own face.

The little demon reached into Rainn's nose with its clever little fingers and yanked a nostril hair. Rainn's eyes and lips went wide, and Forbryttan snatched the bread out of the god's mouth and scarfed it down.

A stuttering screech accompanied January shoving the chair further from the table. She jumped to her feet and ran out the small door, slamming it shut behind her.

"How does her absence make you feel, my dear?" The Murshida Va put a hand on Sharp Jonn's shoulder and led him to the chair.

He sat, sniffled, and raised a finger. "Relieved, if I'm being honest. But she isn't really gone. Firebug's just on the other side of the door, listening to see what else we might say about her."

An angry shriek from the hall shook the door, and everyone heard January's feet pounding away. Several Longeyes snickered to each other.

Sharp Jonn smiled ruefully. He shrugged. "I've known her for almost two hundred years now."

In response, the Murshida Va gave a great, happy belly laugh that drove away darkness from the corners of the room. The sound brought the image of Masika's papa to her mind. Not that he ever laughed like that, but it was a sound of parental love, of caring and holding and safety.

Where was her papa now? Was he worried for her? Should she worry for him?

"You found a real wildcat with that one, Jonn." The Murshida Va stared at the closed door. "I'm afraid she's beyond my abilities to help. She would prefer being dead to wrong, and there's not much an extended hand can do for someone who'd just cross their arms and stick out their tongue as they fall past it."

"Hi. Sorry. Masika here. Sharp Jonn tricked us into rescuing you, I guess? We need to be on our way, but all of this has left me with more questions than answers, and I think you may be the only one capable of resolving them. Also, I'm glad you're not trapped underneath the weird castle anymore."

"Yeah." Rainn inclined his head. "We can relate to that."

"Masika. Thank you." The warm, maternal voice of the Murshida Va enveloped Masika. "Of course, you are free to leave as you wish, but as for your questions, you might want to stay just a few more minutes. I'm not sure what I know that could be of help, but I do have a message for you."

"They have to stay," Sharp Jonn said, hands on his hips. "They shared meals with the Longeyes to nourish their flesh, now they must provide meals from their flesh to nourish us, do you see?"

The horrified expression the Murshida Va gave him stopped Sharp Jonn cold. "Uh, that is, maybe we made that rule after you were put down here?"

Her face shifted from horror to stern disapproval.

"And maybe we can just dig some clawworms on the way home, right?" Sharp Jonn wrung his hands together as he spoke. "No need to eat anyone, is there? No, not so much."

Well, that made sense. Masika forgot the number of times Sharp Jonn "joked" about eating them when this was all over. She found herself unsurprised that was his plan all along.

"Why was I pulled here? To you?" Heron stepped to the center of the room and stood straight, divine bearing adding unseen weight to her question. "Every shining line of destiny I saw bent to this place. They bent to you. And yet, I can't help the feeling I had nothing to do with it." Confusion and anger warred across her face. "What is so important to you that you would seek to pull the very gods from their divine agendas?"

Woah. Heron never spoke like that. So angrily. And what was that about seeing lines?

Could Inlittan show Masika shining lines of destiny? Would she want to see them even if she could?

As answer to Heron's question, the Murshida Va swept across the distance between her and Heron and enfolded the taller goddess in a wordless hug. At first Heron stood stiff, discomforted by the Murshida Va's grasp. But little by little, she warmed, melting into the embrace.

When Heron finally hugged her in return, the Murshida Va gripped her by the shoulders and held her out at arm's length, staring into Heron's eyes.

Masika thanked Denari it was not her being stared into like that.

"I'm sorry you misunderstood," the Murshida Va whispered to Heron, "but this always was your path. From the moment you saw her on the mountain. Possibly before. We serve the same mistress."

Saw her on the mountain? Of *course*! Masika was right. There really had been someone pulling their strings from the very beginning. Someone uniquely suited to command Masika's loyalty and attention.

Masika gasped. Or was she raised for obedience from birth?

"Sarah," Heron breathed. "This has all been about Sarah."

The Murshida Va nodded, eyes intent on Heron. "I didn't come from Andos," she said. "My life was lived worlds away, in a place that would have considered yours a fantasy, and you would have thought frightening and bleak. But when I died, Sarah appeared to me and made me an offer. I could continue to my reward and become one with my universe, or I could come here and do good for those who needed it most."

"Are you a goddess or a sorceress?" Masika's stomach twisted. According to legend, normal humans could not perceive Sarah. She hated the idea of being at the whim of yet another uncaring and powerful force. Even if she seemed wonderful.

Fear melted away along with the Murshida Va's kind regard. "No, Masika. I'm neither. I'm just a woman who has lived a long life and tried my best to pay attention to it. You'd be surprised how much power that gives you, and all the good you might accomplish with it."

"Wait one minute." Sharp Jonn's affronted attitude struck Masika as wildly out of place. "This Sarah is the one who sent you to us? You are following her orders? Do you even love us at all? Do you even love me?"

"Oh, my dear Slender Jonn." The Murshida Va released one of

Heron's shoulders and collected Sharp Jonn's hand. "My mission for Sarah is this very conversation with these three individuals you brought to me. Nothing more. Any other choices I've made have been my own. Including loving you and your people."

"Sarah died less than a year ago." While it sounded foolish to her own ears, Masika needed to understand before she could accept. "You said you've been down here for eight hundred and sixty years?"

"And another hundred before that," the Murshida Va answered. "Before Jonn imprisoned me."

"I was protecting you!"

"Call it what it is, dear," the Murshida Va admonished. "Hiding from the truth will not help you or your land."

"Yeah, sure." Masika shook her head, trying to dislodge some hidden comprehension. "That's almost a thousand years ago. But Sarah died months ago, and she was only in her forties when she did. I think. She certainly wasn't a thousand years old. So how did she talk to you that long in your past?"

The Murshida Va shrugged. "I don't know. Perhaps time doesn't mean the same to her as it does to us. Perhaps it's always a thousand years ago in my universe. Is it important?"

"I guess not," Masika answered, pretty sure it really was important.

"I don't serve Sarah." Heron's declaration lacked its earlier heat but not its force. "What is it she wants from us?"

"I don't know that either," the Murshida Va admitted. "It wasn't part of our conversation. She did leave me messages for all three of you though. Would you like to hear them?"

A message from Sarah, left a millennium before the woman's birth. Did Masika want to hear it?

Having apparently forgiven him, Rainn scratched Forbryttan under the chin, getting Throdd's sticky blood on his fingers. "Sure, why not? I'll bite."

"Your brethren among the Alir never came to your rescue, because they were afraid." The Murshida Va spoke with calm evenness, neither hiding the barbs in her message nor emphasizing them. "But they were not afraid of your jailor Angrim; they were afraid of you and Heron. If you seek to return home, you must take that into account. They will not fear you less for your release, though they will certainly fear you more."

Not exactly an uplifting observation.

Rainn stood and processed this message. His eyes narrowed, and he glanced at the ceiling. "Khanah's damnable eggs, woman, that's not even a convincing lie. The other Alir treated Heron and me like fucking jokes even before Angrim carved all that nonsense into our 'living bodies' and crippled us. There's no way we're any danger to the least of them."

In return, the Murshida Va merely shrugged. "Heron, would you hear Sarah's message to you?"

A pensive nod was Heron's only reply.

"Be certain of your goal." That intense scrutiny returned, the Murshida Va staring once more into Heron. "The Alir lack compassion, and mercy is unknown to them. Their fear is deadly. No matter your intentions, there is no shame in changing what you want. Remember the truths of your home before deciding it is truly what you're after. You already follow your own destiny, or rather you follow that of three of you. That can't change, no matter what you decide."

If anything, Heron's message scared Masika more than Rainn's.

"Well, that puts a pretty fucking bow on it, doesn't it?" Rainn cast a bitter smile to Heron, who looked at the floor. "This woman thinks we went and got ourselves killed and sent to the Undergates to tuck tail and run here at the end? I imagine we're fairly certain about where we're headed, thanks."

"I'm not sure, Rainn." Heron's gaze never lifted. "I've been thinking about this very thing. The closer we get to our goal, the less certain I am I want it." She raised her head, and Masika saw the conflict there. "Our time in Angrim's chambers, the centuries of torture. Rainn, I think it changed us."

"Obviously it changed us." Rainn spoke as if Sharp Jonn, his Longeyes, and even Masika were nowhere near. "He broke us. Stole our power. Made us less than what we were. How's that news?"

"That's not what I meant." Heron spoke slowly, measured. She weighed each word before choosing it. "That's only *what* we are. All that pain and misery in the dark, with only each other to rely on. It changed *who* we are. This woman is right. Our brethren are not capable of considering anything but themselves. They have no compassion. But we do. We no longer belong among them because we are changed."

"What does that mean?" Rainn by contrast, struggled to air his thoughts. Forbryttan stroked his hair. "They're afraid we might be nice to them? Come on, Heron. How does that make us any kind of threat to anyone?" His volume rose. "Why wouldn't they want us? And stop that!"

Leaving the Murshida Va, Heron crossed to Rainn and held him. Discreetly, she took Forbryttan's arm between thumb and forefinger and pulled it down from Rainn's head.

"I don't know." She held out one arm, away from Rainn's torso and gazed at it. It came away slick with blood. "You're a mess."

He laughed, and she laughed too.

"And you, beautiful child?" The Murshida at last turned her smiling regard on Masika. "Are you ready for Sarah's message to you?"

"Ah, no." Masika's heart thudded. "I mean, I appreciate all the time you've spent waiting to give it to me, but these don't seem to be happy messages, and I don't . . . No. Just no. I don't need to hear it." Of that Masika felt utterly certain.

Questions still burned within her. But they felt like distractions now. Knowing the answer to Sarah's involvement would not help Masika fulfill her obligation to Rainn and Heron, if they even still wanted her to. And it certainly would not help her save the people that Ild the imp intended to kill if she could not bring its creator Glauth home with her.

The idea that she could refuse to hear Sarah's message, a message especially for her, rattled Masika. But as soon as she decided, she felt the relief of it.

"It's your decision." The Murshida Va put her arm around Sharp Jonn's shoulders and favored Masika with a knowing look. "You'll know where to find me should your feelings change. My duty to Sarah is discharged, and my time is my own for the rest of *this* eternity."

"Murshida Va, what is it that you can actually do for Sharp Jonn?" Masika did not want all their efforts to recover the woman to be for naught."

At first, a shrug and a smile appeared to be the only answer. But at length the Murshida Va inhaled deeply and spoke. "I can do nothing for him, my dear. Certainly nothing he might not have done for himself. However, the decision to let go of shame . . . and fear . . . and anger can be easier if there's someone to share it with instead of simply running from it."

An uncomfortable suspicion dawned on Masika that the woman spoke as much to Masika's thoughts as her question.

"This land was not always as you see it now." The Murshida Va squinted up into the shadowy stone above her head. "It was once known as the Shadowwood, a regency of the Forests of Hell. Tall gray heavens, full of rain and life. I taught the Longeyes to grow food and make medicine. But the Undergates is a hard place, and war taught my Slender Jonn to set the clouds aflame with hate, after imprisoning me for my 'protection.' Perhaps together we can make this place what it once was."

She glanced around at the small room and at the waiting Longeyes. "I have a few things to gather here. Would the rest of you be willing to help me?"

They were.

The conversation was over.

Sharp Jonn led Masika, Rainn, and Heron back the way they came, out of the Slaughterhouse and to the resting spot where they left the Longeyes injured in the shenwing battle. Boridan had been tightening a bandage on the arm of the woman with short blonde hair but stood up when they approached.

Two of the Longeyes lay face down, unmoving in the rocky declivity. The rest of the wounded either slept or chatted quietly with each other.

Was it cooler than it had been when Masika last passed through here? She glanced up at the flaming sky above. It seemed quieter than before. More distant. Less angry.

Was this the real prize of the Murshida Va? By healing Sharp Jonn and his Longeyes, could she somehow restore the Firefields to life?

How long had they let things go before deciding to come and rescue her? Of course, Masika knew the answer to that question already. Sharp Jonn waited until Masika and her two Alir came along because Sarah set them in motion to do so.

Or had she? Sarah left this message here for them, but she also ordered the Hiimrykers to keep them for a thousand years. What was the game here?

"We get the treasure?" Boridan asked.

"Yeah, we got it." Or, Masika wondered, did Sharp Jonn's "treasure" get them? "We're heading out. Can you walk? There's probably stuff back in the Slaughterhouse to make a litter."

"I can walk." He hefted himself to his feet. "But I'm not going to. I'm not walking with you, anyway."

Masika's eyes widened, and she shook her head. "What? Why not?"

Rainn shrugged. He barely paid attention to Boridan when the man stood directly in his path.

Heron seemed not to notice. She stared at the blonde woman.

"You don't need me anymore." Boridan limped over and clapped Masika on the arm. "I don't know any more about where you're headed than you do, and I've got some stuff to sort out in my head anyway. Old King Oldam's had my brains clenched in his butt cheeks for a while now, I was just too stupid to see it."

How could he leave them? They all depended on one another. Where would he go?

"Are you sure?" Masika asked. "Maybe Heron—"

"I'm sure," Boridan interrupted before she got any further with the thought. "I'm going to stay with the Longeyes. At least until they tire of me. Violans here told me about what you were after in there, and I'm kinda eager to see what happens next."

"You're Sharp Jonn's sister, aren't you?" Heron directed the question at the woman with the short blonde hair, whom Boridan called Violans.

"Is, was, and always will be," she answered.

"Best sister a man could ask for." Sharp Jonn snapped her a grin as he said it. "You seen Firebug come outta the Slaughterhouse a little while back? She was pretty mad."

"I didn't," Violans answered. "But I figure she's no longer welcome in the Firefields?"

"No." Sharp Jonn heaved a sigh and then smiled once more. "You were right about that too. And you can shut up about it already, thank you."

"Does anyone know what direction we should be walking in to get to our next destination?" Every direction stretched away exactly the same to Masika. Shattered rock below, flames above. "We're looking for Glauth, the ex-wife of Morholt the Runecrafter. Maybe where he lives? Sarrach?"

"Savach," Sharp Jonn said. "It's that way, but you'll never get there unless you're on the Crying Road. Too easy to get lost traveling through the Firefields. I'll send Pepper to show you the way. He's our best scout. Knows every rock and crack of the Firefields."

Masika held up both hands. "No, that's not a good idea. Won't that just put us right back in front of the Hiimrykers? They chased us onto the road before."

"They're that way." Sharp Jonn spun and pointed in the opposite direction. "The road circles part of the Firefields, so we'll take you far away from the borders of Hiimryk. Too far to chase slaves. They probably think you're dead now anyway. Been here too long." He winked at Masika. "Not like you got a lotta choices anyway. Pepper'll make sure you get to the road far away from the flying sheepfuckers."

"You're really staying, Boridan?" His decision hurt Masika more than she thought it would.

He nodded and smiled, though no happiness touched his face. "Yep. Time I stopped chasing things I can't have and started looking for things I can."

"Don't look at me," Violans said.

Heron strode purposefully to Boridan, turned him toward her, and gathered him in. She kissed him fully, deeply, and at embarrassing length. When the kiss ended, she took a step back, one hand still on the nape of his neck.

"Be well, Boridan of Tyrrane." Heron drew a hand across her lips, wet from their kiss. "You've been a most excellent companion, and I'll miss you. When you do find the love you're searching for, grip it with both hands and do whatever you must to keep it. Eternity is a longer time here than it was above."

She released him and walked away.

"Um," Boridan said and fell, dazed, to his butt on the stone ground.

CHAPTER

NINETEEN

Lots of people hate the Undergates, but I think it's pretty terrific, you wanna guess why? All right, I'll just tell you then. I love the Undergates because no one down here can hide who they are like people make believe up in the living world. Up there they lie and act like they're good, but really they're just horrible and you don't know it because they're lying about their face, you know what I mean? I mean, people here can lie about stuff, obviously, but who they are just comes right out on their face, like when you squeeze a zorine really hard and the juice comes out, and that's, like, who they really are all over your chin because that's where it usually hits you, because I guess biting is a lot like squeezing, except you do it with your teeth. I really like zorines.

Pepper

Flames seared the sky above their little party with the heat of boundless rage, though perhaps not quite so boundless as it had been a week ago.

In the intervening time the Longeye scout, Pepper, led them a twisting route to the Crying Road, speaking at great length about the hidden caches of water and plants to be found or the reflectiveness of this type of rock against that one. He explained lizards and insects and a few tiny creatures that seemed somewhere between.

In fact, he rarely seemed to shut up at all.

Masika sighed and squeezed her eyes shut, stopping momentarily on the fire-baked rock path to concentrate on summoning all her reserves of will. The next thing she wanted to do, had to do, was going to be difficult. Perhaps the hardest thing she ever set before herself.

"Pepper," she said, "can you tell me why, exactly, some countries in the Undergates are filled with demons and some with humans? I know they fight, but no one seems all that invested in actually murking each other."

A loud groan escaped Rainn, and he clapped his hands over his ears. Even Heron winced a little. Pepper's non-stop talking out on the baked rock frayed all their nerves, and tempers unraveled further and faster with each step despite the lowering heat and diminishing stink of scorched metal.

Masika held out her hands and shrugged, an apologetic smile lighting her face. "He's not going to shut up anyway. We might as well find out something we *want* to know." At the very least the slender desert bow she received from the Longeyes made Masika feel better, so much like the one she left with her corpse in the P'tak House of the Gods.

"Oh, yes." Pepper clapped and beamed broadly at the request. His bright red hair glowed in the brilliant light of the conflagration above, and the freckles liberally sprinkled across his bare shoulders and chest danced with the movement of wiry muscles beneath.

"Humans were here first, and by *here,* I mean in the Undergates, and then the demons came, and things got scary, but then the Dead God came and taught the humans runecrafting, so that scared the demons right back. All the memoths and saurox and orgars and shaikos and trimpets and—"

"Motherfucker," Rainn whirled on Pepper and stuck a finger into his chest, "if you don't answer the fucking question and stop running off on all these . . . What's the word?"

"Tangents" came Heron's tired reply.

"Fucking tangents," Rainn continued. "I'll shove my fist down your throat, pull out your cock, and make you eat it!"

Wide, blinking blue eyes regarded Rainn. Pepper said nothing for nearly a full second. "What was the question?"

"Hey, aren't I a trimpet?" Forbryttan, cleaned and dry though still with some rusty patches in his weathered blue fur, ran a clawed hand over his tummy.

Still watching Rainn, Pepper nodded.

"Oh. That's cool." Forbryttan gave Pepper a sharp-toothed grin, tusks prominent. "That sure explains some things."

Masika asked again. "Humans and demons?"

"Right!" Pepper opened his mouth and glanced at Rainn. "Like I was saying, the demons were big and had claws and teeth and acid and everything, but the humans got magic and swords and armies, and while a demon might eat a human to murk him, the demons never came back anyway so they got destroyed the first time they died, bang. When the odds evened up, the demons didn't really want to press the issue, and the humans were more than happy to fight quietly among themselves because that's a lot less trouble, I guess. Hey, did I tell you how the Murshida Va taught the Longeyes to talk?"

"What does that even mean?" Rainn kicked a stone as they walked, and it bounced high up into the air. "You crazy jackals didn't know how to talk before she got here?"

"That's not what I mean. I'll show you." Pepper screwed his eyes shut, and his mouth moved silently. "Right. I hear what you're saying." His words came slow and considered. Even Masika could see the effort this cost him. "You're asking if we knew how to talk? I feel like you have some aggression toward me and mean this question as an attack, but I'm going to look past that and answer you honestly."

Rainn cocked his head to one side, and a faint smile played across his lips.

Pepper's speech returned to its normal, breathless pace. "Yes, we could talk to each other before the Murshida Va came, but we weren't any good at communicating, you know what I mean? Lots of yelling, lots of fighting, and a bunch of killing. But she stopped all that just by being there and talking to us and making us talk and listen, and listening was really important, even though I've never been all that good at it, but the Murshida Va said that my gift was helping *other* people learn to listen, so I guess that's pretty great and—"

"Pepper." Masika stepped into the flow without waiting for it to slacken of its own accord. "Did Sharp Jonn really set your sky on fire?"

A weathered blue shape ran in from behind a boulder and leaped atop it. "Hang on. That guy set the sky on fire? Did everyone else already know this? Can he do it again?"

Rainn reached over and lifted Forbryttan to put the little demon on his shoulder. "Yeah, Forby, we knew that already."

Face brightening, Pepper cleared his throat, and Masika's shoulders tensed involuntarily. "Well, the land you live in here in the Undergates doesn't hide your face. Demon lands are all acid and fumes and poky bushes and nasty green lightnings and awful things like that, and Hiimryk is cold and hard and full of bears and their ale grows on trees."

Surprise lifted Rainn's head. "It does?"

Masika felt little surprise. The things Pepper told them about the nature of the Undergates confirmed some already formed suspicions she held. This land shaped itself to the baser emotions of those living here. How had such a catastrophic place ever come to be?

"Wine too." Pepper nodded at the god. "Because they're all foolish and drunk and love to fight, so the land makes that like happen. But Longeyes are hard and hot tempered and fast and clever, and Sharp Jonn—he was Slender Jonn back then—wanted to rule all the Forests of Hell, but the Murshida Va showed us a way we could live with the other regents and trade clothes and boots and food and find wives that we didn't even have to kidnap, and things could be peaceful and nice. She said that war would make the sky burn with hate, but we all kinda figured that was just sorta the way she talked, you know what I mean? Because she did sorta have that way of talking."

"And the Murshida Va's desire for everyone to not kill each other made Sharp Jonn feel bad, so he locked her away." Masika recalled the woman's words beneath the Slaughterhouse. "But she wasn't just talking. The fire in the sky was literal, and once you'd started it, no one knew how to go back."

This brought a vigorous head shake from Pepper. "Oh, we knew. We knew for sure. But Sharp Jonn said that the fire was there to scare all our enemies and show them not to mess with us because that fire meant they'd get burned if they did. But it also meant most of our food died, so pretty soon we only had time for trying to eat, and we couldn't make war anyway. But now no one had time to talk or listen or try to be peaceful, so the sky kept getting hotter and hotter and then January came."

"As the fall of an axe." Heron gazed ahead as she picked her way through the spiky scree. "That woman brings nothing but sorrow and leaves naught but pain."

"What's sorrow?" Forbryttan asked. "Do we have any? What's it taste like?"

Pepper cocked his head to one side before nodding and pointing to Heron. "Right. I told everyone that all the time whenever January or Sharp Jonn couldn't hear, only I didn't say it so nice. More like 'I think January's a bitch, and she's gonna get us all killed if Sharp Jonn doesn't do it first because— '"

"Thank you, Pepper." Masika needed to sit with this. Most of it she either already knew or guessed, but the new information gave cause for worry. "Maybe you could scout ahead for a while?"

"Sure, I can do that." Pepper hopped over a series of sharp, upturned boulders; his narrow frame cut an easy arc through the air. "Just call out if you want to talk about more stuff. You know I'm always ready to talk. My mom used to say—"

"Bye now." Rainn waved in a short, chopping motion.

The rangy Longeye ran until almost out of sight and slowed, moving in a crouched stride, taking advantage of the terrain and stooping often to glance around.

"Was any of that fishshit useful?" Rainn frowned at the distant Pepper's back.

"Now we know not to trust anyone who lives in a horrible hole?"

Masika ventured. "I don't know. Maybe. I'm still wondering what Sarah wants. Why push this on us? Why not just come out and ask us instead of all this chasing around and almost getting killed?" She rubbed her forehead. "Sorry. I meant getting murked."

"Maybe you should've listened to her message for you then." Rainn's statement was simple truth, though it pained Masika no less for that.

Of course, Rainn was right. She should have listened. Even Pepper knew that much. "I was scared. After your and Heron's messages, I just couldn't bear to hear whatever Sarah might have to say to me. What if she said I was a failure? Leading the two of you to something awful?"

"Then she would've been an idiot." Heron took Masika's hand as they crossed the blazing terrain. "Though I doubt very much that was her message. At any rate, it's January that has me more worried."

"How so?" Rainn asked.

Hesitating, Heron pursed her lips. "She does not seem to me to be the sort to allow a slight to pass without comment, and we've done much more than that. Two days ago January enjoyed the highest position she could hold in the Firefields without murdering her husband and taking his. Today she is in exile, and I'm not sure the Firefields will even exist in six month's time. She has ample reason to hate us, and I think she'll see it all as our fault."

Heron's logic left Masika confused. "But it wasn't. January and Sharp Jonn were losing control. If we hadn't helped recover the Murshida Va, the Longeyes would eventually have murked them. Forever. How can that be a bad thing?"

"I keep coming back to something the Murshida Va said." A hot wind blew Heron's beautiful gray hair into a broad mane of smoke. "She admitted that, for all her obvious power and knowledge, she was incapable of helping January. That speaks to a genuine commitment on January's part to being an angry and vindictive woman. She believes she is right. She has faith in her superiority, and that means any fault in her own life must belong to another."

"I guess we're another enough for that," Masika said, blowing out her cheeks. She continued to be impressed by the changes in Heron. The goddess was so much more confident and thoughtful now. Or was she simply the same person she had always been, just not a bird?

"And now she has nothing but time to plot her revenge." Heron finished.

Forbryttan wrapped his tail around Rainn's neck and hung upside down over his chest. "If we see her again, I'll poop in her hair."

"Don't say things like that when your butt's pointed at my face," Rainn groused.

Ahead, Pepper shouted happily and waved to the right of them, only to be replaced with an explosion that threw stone and fire at the blazing sky.

"Nothing but time and that graver we returned to her," Rainn said. "Run!"

CHAPTER

TWENTY

Most folks don't remember how they died because they were asleep or knocked out or whatever, but I do because I was looking right at the guy who plunked a fat crossbow bolt right in my forehead. You don't really think of crossbow bolts being all that fat until one is pushing its way through your brains, and then they seem just crazy giant. I wonder if I'll remember it when I finally get murked here in the Undergates.

Probably. If I forgot, what would I talk about?

Pepper

Masika dived left and felt the whizz of the graver bullet buzz by the side of her face. Before she hit the ground, another explosion from behind lifted and threw her forward, and she rolled hard on the stone.

"Thunder and blood! Where the fuck is she?" Rainn yelled.

Forbryttan was already gone. Presumably stalking January to try and get her to hit him with the graver again.

"Why do you care where I am, god?" Debris rattled to the ground

156

as January shouted from the distance. "Will knowing where the murking comes from make you any less dead?"

There. Inlittan showed Masika a single errant hair blown by the ever-present wind of the Firefields around the edge of an upthrust boulder five hundred feet off. She waved to attract Rainn's attention and pointed.

"This'll make you better people, you know." January's voice carried cruel amusement. "Consider it a lesson against butting into other people's affairs. If not for you three, I'd still be queen of the Longeyes. Someone's got to pay the price for that."

The acrid smoke of the graver explosion held an undercurrent of another, familiar smell. Masika ran her hands over the leather and steel that comprised her knee and pulled out a short blade of stone shrapnel. It must have hit her during January's near miss. If they lived, Masika needed to clean the joint out again and see if she could fix the rent.

"I dunno how that crap makes sense to you, Jan, but I think your head's cracked." Rainn lay back on a sloping rock, a stone the size of his fist in one hand. He craned his neck backward to try and see where Masika pointed. "I've never met anyone who shit the bed as thoroughly as you did here. You been fucking up this place for two hundred years. and you wanna blame someone just got here three days ago?"

"They don't do days here. No night." Masika caught herself whispering, but it really didn't matter. "Allz's wounds! Where's Heron?"

Blood spattered the ground close to the crater from January's attack, but no body lay nearby. Masika stretched to see, but too much cover lay in the area that Heron might have been thrown behind.

That's what Masika hoped, at any rate.

January's slim form jumped out from behind her cover, yanking at Forbryttan, who clung to her scalp. She screamed and pulled him free, flinging him to the ground at her feet.

The trimpet bounced off the rock, headed right back for January's head, but the preternaturally fast woman swung the graver, catching

Forbryttan's skull with a sharp crack and sending him flying amongst the blasted scree.

"What the *fuck*?" January stood in plain sight and lifted her long graver at the boulders Masika and Rainn crouched behind. "You don't know what you're talking about, moron. The Longeyes have always been jealous of what I had with my Duckie because they knew I was the most important thing in his life. Especially his sister, Violans. She sabotaged us every chance she got. After I finish you off for your part in all this, I think I'll go blow her to bits and eat the pieces. The important ones anyway. I bet she tastes like shit."

"Get down," Rainn breathed to Masika. So saying, he whirled around and hurled his stone at January's head.

Just before she ducked aside, January activated the graver. The huge boulder in front of Rainn detonated, flinging him back and over Masika's head, like a damp leaf in a gale. Even so, the mass of the boulder absorbed enough of the force to leave him alive and cursing.

More stones and filth showered down.

"Good arm," January mocked. "I think that would have murked me. Even now you can't stop attacking innocent people. I'm really doing the Undergates a service here."

"I want to murder her *so much*." Rainn spat the words through gritted teeth. Burns and blood covered his neck and shoulder, and one side of his tunic hung in tatters, revealing rage-clenched muscle. "Fuck this."

Rainn gathered an armful of stones, stood, and slung them as fast as he could.

Following suit, Masika crouched down and strung her new bow. She sent an arrow spinning through the hot air, but more to drive January behind cover again and keep her from using the graver.

The second stone Rainn threw hit the boulder January hid behind and shattered it, sending shards of rock into the woman's face.

"Fuck! Ow." January fell backward and shouted, even as Rainn's third throw passed through the space where her head used to be. "You deserve to die permanent for this, godling. You can't just blame other people for the things you've done!"

But Rainn was already in a dead sprint toward January, one rock in each fist. Masika followed, but she could not hope to match Rainn's ground-eating pace. She moved sideways, bow at the ready.

Just before Rainn got there, January popped back up on the other side of her boulder, sighting down the length of her graver at Rainn's head. The god was right in the path of Masika's arrow.

"Surprise," January said, blood from numerous cuts on her forehead running into her grin.

This time, Rainn had nowhere to hide.

From behind, Heron punched January in the skull. The blow sent her to the ground but also caused her to reflexively activate the graver again. A pop of smoke erupted from its end, and the baked rock under Rainn's feet threw itself skyward, him with it. Bits of sharp stone whizzed through the air, slicing bloody lines in Masika's arms and torso.

Dazed from the explosion of rock and scree, Masika pulled herself to her feet. Her ears rang, and her brain felt too large to fit inside her head. No feeling rose above her right shoulder at all, and the arm swung uselessly, dripping blood on the rock next to her fallen bow. Everything swam around her, and she stumbled forward. Rainn was somewhere. Pepper too. But all she could think about was getting to January before she lifted that hellish weapon again.

She need not have worried.

"You're wrong. You don't know what you're doing." January pushed against Heron, who held her just off the ground by the leather straps of her top, in a nearly reclined position. "If you murk me, you'll regret it. You're listening to the wrong people!"

Heron threw a granite fist into January's jaw, shutting her up and audibly cracking several teeth.

"I listen to myself, you vicious scold." Heron's words floated across the rock, all the more chilling for their lack of animus. "That's what *gods* do. What you have done"—she hefted January higher to see into her face—"is wreak destruction on everyone around you, nearly to their deaths. Certainly to yours."

"No." January's head lolled to the side, and she caught sight of

Masika, shambling toward her. "You! You're so pretty and so sweet. You won't let her murk me, will you? You'd never let her murk an innocent woman. You're a good person. Like me."

A good person? Masika's thoughts blew like errant winds. Who was a good person? Masika was?

"Be silent." Heron shook January, and blood flew off her face. "It's much too late for that." Heron took January's chin in her other hand and turned the rangy woman's face to look into her own. "Tell me, January. Does it frighten you to understand that you will never hurt another soul again, living or dead?"

"No. *No!*" January struggled, but Heron's grip was iron. The hand on January's jaw slipped around behind her head, took a firm hold, and squeezed.

There was a crack, and January's eyes widened and lost focus.

She fell to the ground.

"Masika, are you all right?" Heron's expression immediately became one of deep concern.

"I'm um . . ." Was she all right? "I think so. Am I standing?"

A small smile flitted across Heron's lips. "You are. There's something I need to do here, and I think I only have a few moments to do it in. I don't really know. Just that we don't want her coming back again. Can you find Rainn? I'll be right behind you."

"Sure." Masika turned around to where she thought Rainn might have been—hadn't she just walked past him?—crumpled to the ground.

Everything went dark to the sounds of wind and roiling flames and the smell of burning stone.

Consciousness clawed its way out of that dark and into yet more dark. Masika felt cool, and in the distance, she heard the sounds of people talking.

Well, one person talking, at any rate.

"Oh yeah," the voice said as it rose from the depths, "there're a few caves like this one if you know where to look. The Longeyes know them all, and that means I do too, because I'm also a scout, so I have to know where everything is in case I need a refill while I'm out hunting because I'm also a hunter. Did you know I was the one who brought down the soft foal? They all look different, you know what I mean? Some are tall and some are wide and some jump and others fly or run really fast or have antlers, but I think they all have feet because that'd be weird if they didn't, right?"

"Pepper," Heron's voice broke through the noise, "I only asked how fast the reeds worked."

At the sound of Heron's words, Masika pushed with all her strength—and opened her eyelids.

"Hello, Masika." Heron smiled in the gloom and wiped Masika's forehead with a deliciously wet cloth. The water was not just cool, it was positively cold. Masika shuddered in delight. "Glad to have you back."

"Oh yeah, those reeds are real miracles, which is good because it's easy to get hurt bad out here, but it isn't that much of a problem if you know where the caves are like I do because I'm a scout. Of course, you already know that because I just told you, but you probably don't know just how strange it is that we caught those fish in the water, not to mention all those frogs, which tasted great by the way, but there's never been any fish in these caves. Maybe some bugs, which don't taste all that good, but they'll get you through the day if there's nothing else."

"Rainn?" Masika croaked the name, but Heron understood.

"He's sleeping," she said. "He was up a little while ago, cursing January and Sharp Jonn and the Longeyes." Heron's voice faded, and she turned to smile at the snoring lump a few feet away. "Anyway, I think everyone will be all right in a few more days. Thanks to Pepper here."

The Longeye scout opened his mouth to speak, but Heron reached out and placed gentle fingers over his lips.

"Shh," she said.

Beside the wall, Rainn reclined on his back, eyes closed and chest moving in deep and regular rhythm. Atop it, Forbryttan guarded in a faded blue ball, eyes blinking in the gloom.

"Did someone mention fish?" Masika's stomach grumbled out loud at the thought of actual food. "And water? I'm really thirsty." *And I have to pee. How long have I been asleep?*

"Let's get you up against the wall then." Heron lifted Masika and slid her to a sitting position against smooth, sloping stone. Even the stone felt cool. Pain rustled her shoulder, and Masika saw the constriction she felt there was caused by broad reeds, pale in the dim light, bound tightly around her arm.

The cave tunnel inclined up to a small opening, through which bright light from the sky outside shown. At the bottom, it ended in an oddly shaped chamber where Masika and the others rested. In the rear of the modest-sized room, a dip led to an open pool eight feet across.

"Heron, can you see destiny?" Masika had to know. How much more could she help them if she could figure out a way to ask Inlittan to see into the future? To avoid the obstacles in their path and go straight to their goals? "You told the Murshida Va that every line of destiny you had seen led us straight to her."

"Oh. No, Masika. I'm sorry." Confusion settled on Heron's face, only to be chased away by guilt. "I didn't mean to give you that impression. It's a turn of phrase. Something those in the Alireon say. When you can see the shining threads of destiny, it simply means that a particular outcome seems inescapable. That's the way I felt about us ending up there."

That made more sense, though it left Masika deflated.

"Now drink something. Here." Heron put a waterskin fashioned from stiff leather to Masika's lips, and she drank cold, amazing water.

Again, Masika's stomach made itself known.

Heron laughed and fed her a piece of fish, improbably well-cooked.

Opposite Heron, Pepper sat and grinned, his bare chest and face dotted with dozens of tiny puncture wounds, already healing. Again, Masika wondered how long she'd been out, but food kept the question silent.

Before she could ask it, drowsiness pushed her head back down, and she fell into dreamless sleep.

She still had to pee though.

THE NEXT TIME MASIKA AWOKE, Rainn sat up with Heron and Pepper, and the three of them discussed how far it would be to the Crying Road and the likelihood of further danger getting there.

Forbryttan splashed in the small pool, chasing fish. The frustration on his face showed his lack of skill at it.

"Hello, lazybones." Rainn laughed and tousled Masika's curly hair. "You know Heron and I aren't going to finish your mighty quest for you."

"Excuse me." Although sparring with Rainn sounded like just what Masika needed to restore some normalcy, priorities came first, and right now she needed to run outside and find the little girl's rock.

Finished, she returned to the cave. The reeds on her arm and shoulder itched, but that meant her feeling had returned, which seemed a good thing. "Is there any more of that fish left?" she asked.

"An inexhaustible supply," Rainn said, handing her a small platter made of woven reeds. "Pepper here claims that eating it off of this'll help you heal even faster, if you can believe it."

Naturally there would always be more fish as long as Heron was here. The goddess of catching small animals in slow or unmoving water was exactly what you needed in a cave with nothing but a pool of water in it. Masika currently appreciated that more than Forbryttan did.

"The reeds are one of the few plants left from Shadowwood." Pepper's words arrived in an uncharacteristic crawl. He smiled. "Rainn and Heron have been helping me speak slower. So I'm not so—"

"Fucking irritating," Rainn supplied.

Masika covered her mouth and looked away, trying not to laugh. "What's the plan?" she asked as soon as she mastered herself.

"Same as before," Heron answered with but a half-smile to betray her amusement. "Pepper will take us to the Crying Road, and we'll travel it to Savach. There we'll find Morholt, and hopefully he'll know where to uncover Glauth."

"Mm." Masika chewed the fish, savoring its barely perceptible flavors. Her brother, Kohmose, would have loved it. He detested spices of any kind. While her other brother, Djephan, would have hated it, or simply covered it in hot dust. "Oh! What happened to January? Is she still out there?"

"Nope." Rainn chuckled. "Heron here took care of that pretty thoroughly."

"And we have her graver." Heron raised the weapon in the air.

"But won't she come back?" Masika recalled the lesson about dying in the Undergates. Unless something ate your soul, which here was your body, you would always return. "Oh. Ew. Never mind. I didn't ask. Please don't tell me. Crying Road. Savach. That sounds like fun. When do we go?"

CHAPTER

TWENTY-ONE

In general, when chasing fugitives, whether the lowest escaped slave or the loftiest fleeing monarch, the more powerful and dangerous the target, the easier they are to find. Roaches will scuttle into any crack in the dark, sight unseen, and that way avoid your stomping boot. But the powerful can't seem to help rubbing people the wrong way, and that makes them much less problematic, tracking-wise. No one is willing to cover for them.

So what do you do when chasing a truly powerful roach? You think like a roach, you anticipate what the roach wants next, and you show up there before the roach does.

And then you wear your really big boots.

The Emissary of the Reaves

The Emissary stood in front of the shimmery gate beneath General Dammer's palace and pondered. Had he been to the Shadowwood since it caught fire? He did not think so. Nothing existed there but a rough tribe of wild humans, and the Standards never had recognized any of the forest regents anyway. No royalty meant no reason to treat with them. But things had changed.

A report from the Crying Road said the slaves were taken captive by the Longeyes, that very same rough tribe of wild humans with whom the Emissary had no contact.

No way that could go awry.

What the . . .? One of the silver bugs crawled onto his chest and repaired a single strand that floated away from him, causing the whole to glow pink momentarily. It skittered back to the dense webbing that stretched to an unknown depth across the entirety of the cavern and comprised the physical spell that made the gates to any location of the Emissary's choosing.

He only had to know where he was going. Fortunately, this time he did.

On the other side, the Emissary shimmered into being in a wide, shallow cave that extended for hundreds of feet left and right, and to a depth of a hundred at its deepest point. Innumerable weapons greeted him in the hands of barely dressed savages, malnourished beasts with snarling faces and little comprehension.

The Longeyes.

"Hello, everyone." The Emissary put on a wide smile and raised his arms in open greeting. "It's grand to make your acquaintance. Any chance there's someone in charge I could speak to?

A blow from behind struck the backs of the Emissary's legs and drove him to his knees. Dirty laughter erupted among the savages.

"You wanna talk to Sharp Jonn?" A very thin woman with short blonde hair and numerous scars stood in front of him with a solid club slung over one shoulder. She wore torn leather pants and an open leather vest. "Wait here. I'll get him for you."

She caught the Emissary in the jaw with that club on the upswing. He heard a crack in his own face, and everything went dark for the space of several heartbeats. No mistaking the Troll Coast accent. No wonder this tribe was so feral.

Push down the anger, do the job. No one benefited if he destroyed them entirely, even if it made him feel better.

Pain throbbed in his jaw. Angry laughter rolled around him. Feet shuffled on stone. The smell of scorched rock and metal, burning meat, clean water, and his own blood confused his nose.

Blinking, the Emissary healed his jaw and opened his eyes.

The tip of an iron dagger hovered a scant fraction of an inch in front of his eye.

"Might oughtta sit still while Violans gets the boss." The elderly dagger holder squatting in front of him sounded friendly. Conversational. "I figure we oughtta hear what you gotta say afore we eats ya."

Giving his most winning smile, only slightly marred by his bloody mouth and teeth, the Emissary lay still as requested. A gray curl fell into his face, and he left it there. The Standards showed him the thing most troubling the heart of this skinny old man. While there was nothing to aid him immediately, the vision was hardly a waste. The older Longeye feared that the arrival of an outsider might not prove the balm to their leader's broken mind everyone expected. He feared burning as a result.

"I'll just stay right here then," the Emissary said. Even General Dammer had been easier to manage than these people, and he was the commander of all the demonic hosts of the Reaves.

Two minutes passed with the dagger wavering much too close to his eye before another man, wiry and strong, shirtless like the other males but with a canny cast to his eyes, approached. Behind him strode a tall woman in a flowing garment that left her arms uncovered. Her hair glowed silver, and peace radiated from her core. Though he ought not, the Emissary felt nothing but unease in her presence.

"Hey there, I hear you wanna talk? I'm Sharp Jonn. I lead the Longeyes." The canny-eyed man carried the same accent as the blonde woman. Other similarities showed in his face. Siblings? Perhaps he was her father, or her son? Family at any rate.

"I do. If I might be permitted to stand?" The Emissary indicated the dagger holder with a glance. The old man backed away, and the Emissary got himself to his feet.

As he did, another man with dirty yellow hair wearing a Hiimryker slave tunic stepped from behind Sharp Jonn. "Oldam fuck a rock garden, that's the Emissary. He's a demon from the Reaves. A big one."

"That so, Boridan?" Sharp Jonn waved his tribesmen back and stepped closer. The Emissary saw a pair of pistols stuck through his belt—the kind that fired thorn gypsum bullets.

Those could hurt.

"I am." Time for a little tactical honesty. "I am the Emissary from the Reaves. I serve the Standards of Rule through the eternal grace of Queen Issta. I am here to recover our lost property, which seems to have stumbled into your lands at no fault of your own." He pointed at the one in Hiimryk slave garb, Boridan apparently. "He is one of them. The others would have come with him, and Queen Issta would like all of them returned. I'm sure you can think of reasons having the ruler of the Reaves on your side could come in handy?"

"Sounds good to me. You can have that one." Sharp Jonn waved at Boridan. "But the rest are gone. Never even got to find out what they tasted like. I bet the woman tasted like redcrow."

"Jonn." The uneasy-feeling woman put a gentle hand on Sharp Jonn's shoulder and leaned forward to speak into his ear. "Boridan is a person with value. That value is to himself and the universe, it doesn't need to be to you. And we don't throw out things of value."

With an exaggerated sigh, Sharp Jonn raised an arm toward Boridan. "Although I am your superior in every conceivable way, it is your choice whether or not you want to return with this demon-man to the Reaves and get raped in your butthole by demon dicks for eternity." He dropped his arm. "But I'd appreciate it if you did. I'd like to know what Queen Issta could do for me."

"Don't kink-shame, dear," the woman whispered. "We'll work on it." Her tone was maternal, but she did not resemble Sharp Jonn or Violans in the least. She caused the Emissary genuine fear. What was she?

Sharp Jonn rolled his eyes but said nothing.

"I don't mean to give the wrong impression, and it's possible you misunderstood the exact nature of my visit here, so that's on me." The Emissary spoke as calmly and reasonably as he could with that woman-*thing* in the room. "As I mentioned before, I'm a servant of the Standards. The Standards enforce the will of the rulers of the Under-gates. That means I have no choice about taking your delightful boy Boridan back with me because Queen Issta wants it. Everyone following me?"

A nod from Boridan's glum face came just before a narrowing of the silver-haired woman's eyes. The Emissary did not like that look. It promised storms and stones and no end of trouble. He focused his own sight to no avail. She appeared entirely human but raised the hairs on the back of his neck like the most ancient of powers.

Most of diplomacy was confidence. The confidence to walk away in the middle of a difficult negotiation and leave the other party feeling as though they missed out on something valuable. Or if faced with a frightening thing you did not understand, simply pretending confidence could work too.

"What I *do* have is a choice in the manner of that taking." The Emissary spread his arms wide in the most open gesture he could and smiled. "We can be favored of the Reaves, or we can be murdered by a rampaging demon. And by *we* I mean *you*. Murder isn't my first choice; you all seem like wonderful . . . people. But I won't lose any sleep over it either."

"Why do you believe we should fear you?" The woman side-stepped Sharp Jonn and moved in front of him. Her scrutiny caused the Emissary physical pain. "Are you unworthy of our affection? Has the world so broken you that compassion for yourself causes you guilt that crushes your soul? Because if that's your problem"—her eyes said she knew it was, despite the question—"you should know that guilt over caring for people isn't a problem for *me*."

Hot anger flared behind the Emissary's cool demeanor. Some kind of witch then?

"And exactly who are you?" he asked, unable to keep the defensive sneer completely out of his voice.

"Oh," Sharp Jonn said, grinning, "this is the Great and Terrible Murshida Va, soother of the sky, warrior of the soul, and fabulous hugger."

The name struck the Emissary like physical blows. Whatever manner of creature this Murshida Va was, it knew too much. An aspect of himself always resented the narrow existence the Standards forced him into, while humans, the least form of sentience in the Undergates, were allowed free reign of their stupidity.

She read him. She knew his thoughts. He showed his teeth and immediately regretted it. A display of strength now only highlighted his weakness.

"You understand why we can't allow you to take Boridan, don't you?" The Murshida Va spoke with the same calm that fled the Emissary only moments before, and he hated her for it. "That would have to be his decision, and we both know that'll never happen, don't we? He won't go willingly back to a life of pain and abuse, and you can't take him by force. Accept the truth of your world. It will bring you peace."

"Peace has never been in the cards." The Emissary smiled. Inadvertently, she had just provided him with the answer. He looked into the heart of Boridan and saw the thing that troubled him most.

"Boridan," the Emissary said, "I do have to bring you back with me. That's just a constant of the universe, a law, and it's already true. No one, even this very impressive person"—he nodded to the Murshida Va but did not look at her—"can alter that. But you don't have to return in chains." Time for the pitch. "Help me find the others, tell me where they're headed, get me ahead of them, and you go back to the Reaves in splendor instead of chains. You'll have an estate and slaves of your own, be respected by human and demon alike."

And now the kicker.

"And you'll have the gray-haired goddess as your wife." His smile widened. "In the words of the man whose personality you wear, 'If you're gonna fuck a sheep, put it all the way in.' This is as all the way as you're ever going to get, my lad."

Boridan's eyes widened, and the Emissary gloated just a bit in his own head. He had won.

"Oh, Boridan, no." The Murshida Va's sad face gave the Emissary an extra thrill as she stepped over to Boridan and encircled him with her arms. "You poor, poor man. This won't make you happy. It isn't love. It's control, and it's never ever enough."

Gently, Boridan pushed himself out of the Murshida Va's embrace. "I know."

He faced the Emissary. "I'll go with you."

Not wanting to spend one instant more in that woman's presence than he had to, the Emissary willed the webbing affixed to his chest to summon the shimmery portal and held out his hand to Boridan, who took it.

Even at the cusp of getting everything he wanted, bleak gloom hollowed Boridan's features. "They told me everything. Everything. You won't have any trouble finding them."

"Hey, wait just a second there." Sharp Jonn jumped forward and pulled Boridan away from the Emissary with a surprisingly powerful grip. "Before you go anywhere, you need to explain yourself."

The Emissary closed his eyes, clenched his jaw, and reached for a calm that danced, laughing, just out of reach. "Yes?"

"Why don't the Standards ever enforce my will?" Sharp Jonn shoved Boridan aside and set his fists on his hips. "I rule the Fire-fields, and no demons ever showed up to make sure everyone does what I say, do you see what I mean? I think you're lying."

At this, the Emissary chuckled aloud. "You're the chieftain of a dying tribe in a withering regency. You're hardly a ruler. Boridan, come along."

As the pair shimmered away to the spellweb, Sharp Jonn said, "Well, you're a big asshole."

TWENTY-TWO

I have many times now met with the Emissary of the Reaves and found him to be a singularly vexing individual. His power all but guarantees his enslavement to the Standards, yet his intelligence guarantees his resistance and resentment, though he hides it well. I believe that if he could, he would gleefully tear down all the edifices of civilization we have built here, both human and demon, just to ease his conflict.

We should be grateful then, given the Emissary's raw strength and canniness, that the laws that govern the Undergates preclude his acting on his own whims in favor of those of his queen, Issta of the Alir—though perhaps in retrospect, she isn't all that much better.

Regardless, I'm just glad he's only out to tear down our governments, structures, works, and lives and not here to destroy something truly important, like ice cream.

General Kolos of Murden Fell

At last, Masika stepped off the baked stone of the Firefields and onto the cobbled surface of the Crying Road. Behind them, the blazing sky retreated from the edges of the land, its vaulted ceilings stretching off into dim, gray infinity.

To the road's far side, mountains loomed in the distance over flat plains of black rock and occasional farmlands where yellow fields rendered unknown crops. Further along, the deserted road curved into stark hills, occluding the view to either side.

"Guess that's Murden." Masika stopped and rubbed the small of her back with both hands. Walking on level ground seemed a novel treat after their time in the Firelands. "How far does the Crying Road go through it before it curves back up into the Forests?"

"Not long, barely a thousand miles, so that's nothing really. You'll barely even notice it." Pepper stood at the edge of the blasted scree, gazing up and down the wide, cobbled surface. He held himself hunched and tight, ready to spring into flight on an instant's notice.

"Nervous?" Rainn asked, a kindly smile in his voice. Improbably, the god had taken a shine to the fast-talking scout.

"Just remember"—Pepper took a breath—"don't leave the Crying Road and don't talk to anyone along the way because you never know who they really are or who they work for, and some of them won't like you very much, and even the ones who do'll probably still want to eat you, so keep watches, and if you think you've actually attracted anyone's attention . . . run."

"Eat us, huh?" Rainn chuckled at his friend. "You mean like the Longeyes wanted to?"

A fast headshake no, and Pepper drew in another breath. "Not like the Longeyes. That was mostly just Sharp Jonn, but that means it was probably all January's idea and she's gone now, plus the food'll come back now that the Murshida Va's free and the fire is shrinking. So we won't need to eat anyone at all except we'll probably still hunt soft foal because they're delicious. And, by the way, I want you to know that I really appreciate you teaching me to talk slower like this and no one's gonna recognize me now that I'm so different and reserved, hah!"

Masika went to Pepper, hugged him, and laughed herself. "Thanks, Pepper. You've been a gift."

With a minimum of fuss, Pepper made his goodbyes and departed, leaving Masika, Forbryttan, and the Alir to continue on their own. The air, already cooler, blew cold out of Murden's dark hills. It smelled of dust and forgotten joys.

"Cheery." Heron shouldered her pack of provisions, straightened her back, and faced the long road ahead. "Let's go."

Unlike the comparatively crowded stretch of thoroughfare they touched on earlier, this length of the Crying Road went all but deserted for vast lengths, and those that they did see traveling remained huddled and silent, eager to pass them by. The burning sky of the Firefields dwindled to a ruddy glow over the hills to their left, while towering black clouds dominated a slate-gray sky above and to their right.

Forbryttan wanted to explore, and Rainn indulged him with a scouting expedition before Masika had long enough to consider that the diminutive demon would be just as likely to lure something dangerous back to them. She kept her silence. Damage done at this point.

"So, Heron," Rainn said at length, "I guess we oughtta talk about what we're doing out here. You sounded like maybe you don't wanna go home at all anymore."

"I'm not sure I do." Her gait remained serene and peaceful, despite the worried frown on her face. "I'd always been of the idea that the human world was not worth being in. A collection of savage beasts that only just managed to reproduce faster than they murdered each other. No offence."

"None taken." Masika often thought the same, or had come to since this quest began. But Heron's change of heart hit her deeply. Masika had gone through so very much already to get the two gods home, the thought that it might all be for naught left her sad and hollow. She felt like her knee smelled.

As she spoke, Heron carefully trod the road, one deliberate step following the next. "But you and I have only been among humanity a very short time, Rainn, and already we've seen how untrue that is.

People aren't beasts; they *shine* with their love for one another. And the gods we left behind suffer greatly in comparison."

"Hm." Rainn's own frown spoke of deep thought more than disappointment. "I get what you're after, but when we lived in the Alireon, I don't remember it bugging me much."

Heron shrugged. "Me either, but I think that makes it worse. The coarse indifference of the Alir didn't bother us, because we were the same as they were. We didn't care for anything further than our own fingertips, because that was all we knew. It was normal. But we spent a millennium apart from them, learning to care for each other. And then we found Masika—"

"Masika found *us*." Rainn corrected.

For some reason just beyond her grasp, the acknowledgement threatened tears for Masika. She furrowed her brow and forced them back.

"That's right." Heron visited a whisp of a smile toward Masika. "She did. And she showed us the depths of what caring a human being is capable of. She showed us her family and how they love her in return."

"Except for the sister. That one's a fucking waste." Rainn grinned at Masika, who burst into clumsy laughter.

Heron nodded in reply. "Meritities is not exemplary, no. But even still, I have found more joy in the past few months than I believe I ever have before. I don't think I want to leave, and I'm even less certain about returning to the Alireon."

"Well," Rainn said, "if we accomplish what we want to here—bring Glauth back to Ild the imp and he opens the doors to the Alireon for us—we can still spend as long as we want with the humans and go back home when and if we decide to."

So Masika's efforts might not be in vain after all?

"That's not a terrible idea." A gust of cold wind formed a gray cloud of Heron's silken hair. "And at any rate, we need to get Masika here back to her own family. The good ones at any rate."

"Meritities isn't so awful a person." Masika found it harder than she expected to defend her sister. "She's just . . . She followed our mother's example instead of Papa's. Mama works hard to maintain the family's status in the court, and Meri does too. I can't imagine that's easy given a sister like me."

Rainn's mouth dropped open. "After all that she-beast put you through—put *us* through—you're still willing to stand there and defend her? Shadows of the Alir, girl, she's a monster."

Having no other answer, Masika shrugged. "She's my sister. I love her."

"That's just stupid." Rainn shook his head. "Love is stupid."

"It's not stupid, Rainn." A warm smile spread itself on Heron's face. "Masika's just better at it than you."

Time for Masika to change the subject. "How do you two think Boridan'll fare with the Longeyes? It has to be better than pulling people out of acid pits in the Reaves." Another of the curious mists rose, twenty feet high, from a crack in the ground and flitted about as if searching for something. Masika had watched a dozen of them form by now, though she had only seen one dissipate.

"And easier than running with us." Rainn eyed Heron sidelong. "Maybe he'll even find someone there who cares for him back."

Masika winced inwardly when she saw the pained expression from Heron.

The goddess sighed. "I cared for Boridan. But he is dead. A true mirrored soul. Where we're going, even if it's just back to the living world, he won't be able to follow. How is that fair to him?"

"Shoulda told *him* that." Rainn kicked at a loose cobble and sent it skittering along their path. "Poor fucker might not've spent all his time swinging around your ass like a limp turd."

"He helped us a lot." Masika wondered how she really felt about this. Boridan acted as a guide in good faith, but Masika could see even without Inlittan's help that Heron wasn't interested in him. So why didn't *she* tell him so when the goddess did not? Did she simply never really think of him as one of their group?

Is that how Boridan saw himself?

"Kinda thought you were going somewhere with that, Masika."

Rainn shrugged. "I guess we oughtta marry everyone who helps us. Hope whoever gives us a hand next knows how to cook."

Whatever Heron said after that was lost to Masika, as she spied Forbryttan tearing across the closest hillside with all the speed at his command.

Masika sighed to herself. She should have spoken up earlier, even if it was too late to do anything about it. At least then she could have held it over Rainn's head.

"Our scout's coming back." Inlittan showed her more. "And he's bringing a friend."

"A friendly friend?" Rainn toyed with the hilt of his gifted Longeye sword. "Or the other kind?"

"Definitely the other kind." Unlimbering the long weapon Heron took off January's corpse, the surface of the graver felt more like skin than metal and wood. Masika pushed the strange sensation to the back of her mind as her vision narrowed onto her target.

She pushed Inlittan's sight into its ranges. The lumbering monstrosity behind Forbryttan remained too far away as yet. They did not have sufficient food for the next two days, much less the next thousand miles. Would that demon-thing taste good?

"What's it look like?" Heron asked.

"Big, six legs, sorta like a hairless crag lion, but greenish? Allz's wounds." The monster's neck abruptly extended, covering the remaining distance between it and Forbryttan. It crunched down on the fleeing trimpet, tossed back its head, and swallowed him in one go.

"What happened?" Rainn slid his blade out of its sheath. "What's going on?"

The running creature halted, talons digging into black dirt. It swung its head back and forth in increasingly desperate distress, howls of pain barely audible in the distance.

"I think . . ." Masika stared harder, willing Inlittan to show her more.

Neck bulging, the demon pitched its head back. Black fluid

erupted, and Forbryttan hopped out the exit it clawed for itself; glee was obvious on its tiny face.

"Nope," Masika said, turning away, "not going to be able to unsee that."

"I don't see it. Is it still coming?" Heron asked. "Aren't we supposed to be protected here on the Crying Road?"

"No. It's not still coming. And yeah." Masika squeezed her eyes shut. If she closed them tightly enough, she might push Forbryttan's delighted face out of her brain. "We're protected. That's what Pepper said."

"You think they know that?" Rainn tapped Masika on the shoulder and pointed. Opposite Forbryttan, on the left side of the road, four variously horned and fanged demons, powerfully built and half again as tall as Rainn, strode onto the cobblestones, with wicked smirks promising trouble and pain.

"I sure hope so," Masika answered.

CHAPTER

TWENTY-THREE

One genuine soft spot the Emissary of the Reaves has is for happy couples. If he is able, he will always avoid disruption to their lives and is known to be considerate to the married lives of his staff. It is honestly surprising and refreshing to witness a being of his power who lives their life by such a compassionate code of honor.

Strangely he does not extend the same affection to the children of happy couples, who should absolutely be hidden from him at all times.

General Kolos of Murden Fell

H eads down, keep moving." Masika hissed the reminder to the two Alir, who followed her example. A thready height of mist crossed the road, left to right, in front of them, purposefully floating against the breeze.

They ignored it and pressed on.

"Hey, it's not safe for humans to go walking through the Mists of Murden without an escort." Masika did not know which of the demons spoke; she was not looking. But she recognized the tone of the comment.

After all, Meritities had bullied her most of her life.

"Just gonna walk off without saying hi?" This voice pitched lower, more dangerous. "Hey, Feng, these bugs think they're too good for us, yeah? Don't gotta observe the niceties of civilization and whatnot. Makes me kinda angry."

"You're always angry, Grax. It's your most defining trait." Feng's voice sounded calm, almost human, if a bit baritone.

Masika walked faster. She hated this. Her papa taught her to confront her problems head-on, though, admittedly, he likely had not envisioned this precise situation.

"You're running." Rainn leaned down to whisper in Masika's ear. "Don't run. Fucks like these'll have to chase and then you're just prey. Don't turn around and don't stop, but *don't run.*"

"They're runnin'!" shouted Grax.

"Now you can run," Rainn said as he spun, dropped his pack, and drew his sword.

A stony hand from a demon, as wide as he was tall, shot out and batted Rainn's blade away to clatter down the road. "It's usually better if you don't fight back," he said with an apologetic smile across his wide face. The pebbled tan skin wrinkled. "Usually."

"Fuck me!" Rainn shouted and ducked a follow up blow intended to remove his head.

The biggest of the four thundered up to Masika, scaled fist the color of dried blood cocked back for a killing blow. But Inlittan showed her a weakness in the thing's leg, just above its knee, and she plunged a Longeye dagger into it, driving the blade upward to slip between the thick scales.

The demon leaned down and roared in raging pain, and Masika yanked the dagger out and shoved it in the creature's open mouth. It choked and convulsed and spat dark yellow blood on the cobbles, trying to pull the curve-tipped blade out without doing even more damage.

Leaving her combatant behind, Masika jumped away and spun to Rainn, only to catch a blue-black forearm to her throat. She collapsed at the feet of a lithe demonic figure, with tall, spiraling horns and a swishing, muscular tail. It might even have been considered beautiful in its white breeches and blousy shirt had it not been trying to kill them.

With a cry of pain, Rainn connected a solid punch to the stony hide of the demon fighting him. He staggered back, holding his hand.

"Sorry," that demon said and clubbed Rainn in the temple, driving him to the cobbles with a loud crack.

Masika struggled to breathe, and looked past the blue-black legs to see Heron, held in the grip of an eight-foot-tall sneering demon, most of his dark green skin covered with glossy black armored plates.

"Think we're done here," it said. Masika recognized the voice as Feng. He pulled Heron's head up, exposing her long, pale throat and menacing it with the powerful claws of his other hand. "They're no fun dead. Graxat'Flem, you gonna be all right?"

The huge monster Masika disabled nodded, though he remained hunched over and coughing up blood.

How was that thing not murked? Or destroyed? Whatever they called it here when you killed a demon for good.

"Oblique?" Feng addressed the beautiful demon that dropped Masika. "Is yours intact?"

A dark foot at the end of a shapely leg toed Masika in the ribs. "Yes." Oblique's voice slithered into Masika's skull, a poisonous viper nestled in the folds of her brain. Masika felt unclean at its touch.

And pissed. And a little nauseous.

"Mine hurt its paw," said the pebble-skinned monstrosity. It patted its own stomach. "Shouldn't'a tried punching with your own limbs. I'm solid."

"Yer dense. 'S'not the same thing." Graxat'Flem hawked a huge wad of blood and mucus and stood up straight. "Dense also means *stupid.*"

"Hey." Feng's admonition carried the bark of authority. He must be the leader, then. "Stop screwing with Sandy. Sandy, you're dead hard, and no denying it. Grax, *you* wanna punch him in the gut?"

"No." Grax, taller and much more powerfully built than Feng with frightening talons backing it up, stared at his own feet.

So Feng commanded through strength enough to frighten Grax-at'Flem. Hopefully that would prove useful information before all of them got their heads bitten off. Masika's brain kicked into action, visualizing tactic after tactic to free themselves and get away, but nothing she came up was likely to work. These demons kicked them down so fast she had no idea as to their real strengths, other than hard, fast, and mean.

"The Standards forbid what you're doing." Though Feng's claws caressed her throat, Heron remained unbowed. "Release us now, before you're made to pay the price."

Graxat'Flem snorted laughter, while Feng merely smiled.

"Oblique, dear," Feng purred. "As our expert on the Standards, can you tell our victims why they are so very wrong?"

Her scowl indicated that she would rather slice Feng into fish bait than speak unnecessarily, but she answered anyway, pointing at Rainn with a needlelike talon.

"That one drew first. We lawfully responded. Your lives are ours." Again, that voice infected Masika's thoughts. It left her filthy and feverish on the inside.

"And?" Feng asked.

A low growl accompanied Oblique's grim glare. "And you have no escort. Humans unaccompanied by a demon escort are forfeit. Your lives still belong to us."

Eyes wide in excitement, Masika's head popped up, her gaze meeting Heron's. Behind the goddess a tiny blue and black blur raced toward them.

Rainn paid more attention to his broken hand than the conversation.

"Then fuck off, fuckbutts." Forbryttan, covered in black demon blood, stalked onto the cobblestoned road, tiny chest puffed out and elbows wide. He gave his best impersonation of Rainn. "These humans are mine, and I'm a fucking demon. So unless you wanna piece of me, you can all just fuck, uh, I already said fuck off. Just go away. Fuck-fucks."

Masika bit her lip. Laughing at the demons held little chance of improving relations.

"A trimpet? Talking?" Graxat'Flem's great head cocked to one side, his short, stubby horns comically resembling a dog's ears.

Rainn rolled his eyes to Masika. "If only."

"What of it, you hornless shoefucker?" By now Forbryttan stood in front of Graxat'Flem, all foot-and-a-half of him glaring straight up into the enormous demon's confused face. "Gonna do something about it?"

Feng gave Oblique a quizzical glance, and she sighed and nodded. "Yes. That counts. The trimpet has challenged Grax for the humans."

The evil leer Graxat'Flem favored Forbryttan with curdled Masika's blood.

"No way this lasts, trimpet, so I'll just tell you what's gonna happen after I kill ya." Graxat'Flem dipped down and snatched Forbryttan off the ground, held him at face height in one gigantic hand, and squeezed. "First thing, I'll eat your brains and learn what makes you so special you can talk. Not that I care. Then I'll tear you in half and find out which side is the better fuck. Whatever's left I'll feed to Sandy's korgers 'cause he hates it when I make 'em eat my leavings."

"Aw, come on, Grax." Sandy's plaintive tone made it obvious this wasn't the first such conversation. "Don't do that. It's gross. The korgers don't know any better. Feng, don't let him do that."

Feng rolled his eyes. "Just kill the trimpet and let's go. We don't have time for comparison studies."

Despite witnessing it over and over, Masika continued to worry that this time Forbryttan's unbreakable nature would fail. This time she would watch him crack in half and die in front of her, while she stood helpless to stop it.

But not this time.

Biting, chewing, stabbing with his fangs and twisting with both hands, Graxat'Flem only succeeded in eliciting giggles from Forbryttan, who writhed as if being ruthlessly tickled.

"You're kidding me." Feng released Heron and strode to Graxat'Flem's side. "Just let me." Feng reached out to help, and Oblique leaped over and grabbed his arm.

"No." Oblique's hiss vibrated in Masika's soul. "The challenge is for Grax alone."

"He's invulnerable too." Sandy smiled, pleased. "Just like me. Can I keep him, Feng?"

"Garrh!" Graxat'Flem heaved a roar of frustration and flung Forbryttan to the ground so hard he shattered one of the oversized cobbles. "I can't! It ain't a trimpet. It can't be. It's a disguise. What are you, coward?"

Forbryttan only laughed all the harder.

Leaning down for a closer look, Feng's eyes narrowed. "It's a trimpet, all right. But it's got something else in there with it. Something from the living world. Something of value. But they're right. We can't take it, or them"—he glanced up and Masika and the Alir—"without inviting the Standards to fall on our heads."

"Think they can help us with your dad, Feng?" Sandy's open smile withered at Feng's searing glare.

Shaking it off, Feng stood erect and put his dark green hands on his armored hips. "We'll leave for now while we think about it. But we'll see you all again soon. There's more going on here than you're showing, and when I figure out what it is . . ." Feng clapped his hands together with an unnaturally loud boom. "Well, see ya then."

Forbryttan lifted an arm and wiggled his fingers at the retreating demons in a vaguely offensive-looking nonsense gesture. "Whatever, fuckleg."

CHAPTER

TWENTY-FOUR

The wrap on Rainn's hand bound it tight, and though his healing progressed at an incredible pace, that failed to slow his complaints about it. After three days walking, he no longer wore the bandage and appeared none the worse for wear.

By contrast, Masika shambled along, obsessively scanning what little she could make out around them for the return of the demonic quartet. Sleep proved impossible given that her vision so far exceeded any of the others. Merely closing her eyes put them all at risk.

The Crying Road stayed flat and easy to navigate, taking broad curves around huge rocky hills of dark stone, beneath scudding castles of deep cloud and the occasional flash of reddish lightning. More and more those hills butted right up against the road, tall cliffs occluding the landscape.

Although Masika never caught sight of anything, the idea of tremendously powerful entities moving just out of her eyeline never left her brain. Things that could crush them all with but a thought.

For the most part she tried to ignore the feeling, reasoning that maybe the unseen presences might not acknowledge her if she never acknowledged them. It felt like the behavior of a child, hiding her head beneath the covers from some strange sound in the night. But what else could she do?

Feng and his friends were another matter altogether. They had proven themselves all too able and willing to notice her.

She scanned the clifftops for them again. Even Inlittan's sight stopped at the stone hillside.

"I'm worried." Heron cast a concerned look at Masika, her emerald eyes compassionate and knowing. "It's been days."

Masika kept her silence and listened. She did not want to give her location away.

"Yeah." Rainn sighed and pulled the filthy front of his Hiimryker slave tunic away from himself to inspect it. "You'd think we might've thought to ask the Longeyes for better clothes. These are getting kinda ripe."

"Not the clothes, dumbass." This came with an exasperated smile, which from Heron, fell on those around her like dazzling sunlight in a darkened wood. "She won't sleep. She shuffles like a corpse and mumbles her words. Aren't you worried?"

"No," Rainn replied slightly too fast. "She gets tired enough, she'll fall the fuck over. Self-correcting problem." He rolled one shoulder, and Masika realized he used the action to disguise a quick glance at the hilltops. "Just wish we could shake trouble, is all."

"Nothing out there to shake. We've gotten away from Issta in the Reaves, Jarl Refur of Hiimryk, January and Sharp Jonn aren't a bother anymore. We're free and clear." Heron drew her long, straight hair back and tucked it behind an ear. She was doing the same thing! Hiding nervous vigilance in mundane actions despite the calm words. They felt it too. How long had this been going on?

Or was Masika imagining their responses?

How could she be? They were gods. They must feel they were being stalked. Opening her mouth to speak, it occurred to Masika to wonder why her two friends chose not to talk of the looming presence in any kind of straightforward manner, or, in Heron's case, at all. Could the thing Masika could not see hear them? For that matter, why had Masika kept quiet about it?

Yet Masika said nothing. It would be listening. Waiting for anyone to acknowledge its presence openly that it might swoop in and doom them all to an eternity of torment.

"The one you punched when you broke your hand, Sandy, they called him." Heron was trying to change the topic. Pull the ghostly hunter's attention away from thoughts of attack. Clever of her.

"Yeah, what of it?" In response, Rainn played his part well, acting as if nothing was wrong. "I didn't know how fucking solid he was. Next time I'll use a big-ass club to say hello."

It worked. Masika felt the monstrous presence's phantom regard pass over them, extending away into the hills beyond the road. Giddy relief washed over her. The thing would return, she knew. But for now, everyone was safe.

"Good job, Heron." Masika stumbled forward and caught the goddess in an awkward hug. "It's gone for now. You did it. And you were fine, too, Rainn. I was worried it'd see through you and attack, but we got lucky."

The two Alir exchanged a significant look. Heron tilted her head slightly, and Rainn nodded.

The two gods stopped walking and Rainn's expression grew stern. He glanced about the road, and back at Masika. "All right, you. You're laying down right, ah, fucking there. It's out of the way and we'll watch over you. If anything happens, you'll be the first stupid little girl we wake up."

"What? No! I can't go to sleep. What if it comes back? It's been floating over us for days." Frantically Masika clutched at Heron's dirty tunic. "How will I know? How will we run away?"

"You won't know, because you'll be asleep." Rainn pulled at Masika's arm and with Heron's help, led her off to one side of the road. "And when you're asleep, the monster can't see you. It hunts by looking for, uh . . ." He looked at Heron, who just shook her head. "It looks for your feet?" He shrugged and helped Masika to the cobbles. "It can only see when your feet strike the ground. It sees your footfalls. Stop walking and you go invisible."

"But . . ." They refused to understand. They *needed* her. "What about Feng and the others? They can see me if I'm asleep."

Rainn twisted and pointed a thumb at the bundle down the back of his tunic where Forbryttan snored. "We're still escorted, and Forby here isn't going on any more goddamn scouting missions. Let 'em come. We still have those weird Standard things on our side."

"And we're on the alert for them now." Heron gave Masika a secret little smile, full of conspiratorial menace. "If they come back, I'll burn them with light, like I did that orgar in the Reaves."

Even as Masika lay her head on the cobbles, more objections floated to the surface. While Heron certainly had reduced the demon orgar to ash and held up the *Bitter Goose* above the Firelands to prevent their crashing on their first experience with the Crying Road, she also could not reliably call on those powers yet. Maybe she never would.

"No." Masika lifted her arm to pull herself up by Rainn's elbow, but it was far too heavy to get that far. "I don't . . ."

MASIKA AWOKE to Heron shaking her by the shoulder.

"Wha'? How long was I asleep?" She pushed herself up on her elbows and blearily looked around. The cobblestones left her sore and irritable.

"I dunno." Rainn stood in front of her, faced away. "Eight hours? Maybe ten. We'd have let you stay that way except for these fuckers." He stepped aside.

At once fully awake, Masika jumped to her feet. Feng, Sandy, Oblique, and Graxat'Flem all strode down the middle of the Crying Road, laughing at some doubtlessly evil joke between them.

Except for Oblique. She merely rolled her eyes and stared ahead at Masika.

"What's the plan?" Masika pushed all humiliating thoughts of an invisible imaginary monster floating over their heads away. As little as she wanted to deal with Feng, at least she did not have to worry that Rainn might make fun of her about made up monsters floating above their heads. From now on, she would sleep every day.

"We switch up." As Rainn spoke Forbryttan clambered out of his tunic, stretched his little clawed hands above his head, and gave a great yawn. "If they attack us, I'll take Feng, Heron has Oblique, you're on Sandy, and Forby'll keep Grax busy until the rest of us can help."

"But they won't attack." Heron's eyes narrowed and her jawline grew firm. "We still have our escort, and they can't hurt us."

"Fucking right you fucking do," Forbryttan said, chest puffed out.

"Don't do that." Rainn dropped his head and shook it slowly.

"Do fucking what?" Forbryttan asked.

"Don't pretend you're me." Rainn rested a hand on the pommel of the Longeye sword but pointedly did not unsheathe it. "It's embarrassing. Just be you. But meaner."

"Hello again, my friends." Feng waved as he shouted. "You'll be happy to know we've spent some time and effort divining a means to get you off this damned road where we can snatch you up properly."

"And have some fun with you." Graxat'Flem's evil leer was not lost on Masika. She gripped the hilt of the dagger she recently planted in the giant's open mouth but followed Rainn's lead and left it in its sheath.

A shift in perspective showed Masika not what the quartet planned, exactly, but at least where they intended to go. Oblique sidled to the right, headed toward the closest edge of the road while the three others snaked left to line up on the opposite side.

"They're going to try to shove us off the road so Oblique can catch us, one at a time," Masika whispered. "And I don't think we can stop them."

"That's because you're not as mean as me." Forbryttan leaped at Sandy but bounced off the road just in front of him, launching himself at Feng's legs. Grabbing one calf in his arms, the tiny demon wrapped his legs around the other, and Feng fell forward onto his face.

"Ow!" Feng lifted himself to see, and Forbryttan jumped onto his head, wrapping his tail around Feng's eyes. "Flaming shits! Grax, Sandy, just do it. I'll take care of this slug."

Graxat'Flem charged forward, arms outstretched, while Sandy, a sad frown on his wide pebbled face, followed him.

As much as Masika pushed, Inlittan's vision faltered at showing a way out. The demons were bigger, stronger, and faster. A rough stiff-arm shoved Masika backward a dozen steps and Graxat'Flem laughed. He swatted at Heron next and sent her spinning to the cobbles.

"Khanah's damnable eggs, you fish-fucking filth!" Rainn screamed at Graxat'Flem, forgetting to even draw his blade and not noticing when Sandy moved into position. "I'll kill you for touching her. Coward. Fight *me* if you want a fight."

Sandy shoved at Rainn with both of his huge hands, and the god went rolling backward, ass over teakettle and much farther than the shove should have taken him, until he sprang up to his feet right behind Oblique.

The upturned point of Rainn's Longeye sword pressed hard into Oblique's throat, just before the point of entering it and spilling her all over the dirt.

"Damn" was all Oblique said, but the word buzzed like insects in Masika's brain.

"Since we're not playing gentleman's rules," Rainn said, his jaw tight and eyes wild, "I guess everything's fair. Get the fuck back, or I'll happily splash this skinny demon right in your faces. I bet you all deserve that anyway, circle jerks."

"Go ahead and kill the cunt." Graxat'Flem licked his fangs with a long, ropy tongue. "Won't save you."

"Well, hang on there." Sandy stepped in front of Graxat'Flem and held his arms out to either side. "We don't want that. Let's talk about it."

"Out of my way, sand-dick." Graxat'Flem pulled himself to his full height and glared down at Sandy. "Not sayin' it twice."

Masika helped Heron to her feet. The woman weighed next to nothing.

"Get off of me!" To one side, Feng finally managed to extricate Forbryttan from his head and swung the biting trimpet at the end of one arm. "Ow! Stop it. For fuck's sake." He glanced up and took in the situation. Heron and Masika still stood on the road, Graxat'Flem and Sandy were almost at blows, and Rainn gripped Oblique by her tall, tapered horns with a blade shoved into her neck.

"Stop!" Feng shouted. "Everyone just stop."

"You gonna let that smear get away with that?" Graxat'Flem's question held hidden menace. What else was going on here, and could Masika take advantage of it? "Think, Feng. They're *humans*."

Feng ignored Forbryttan, who savagely chewed his hand, to place himself just behind Sandy and stare up into Graxat'Flem's face. He pointed at Oblique with his non-Forbryttaned hand. "I'd miss you a lot less than I would her."

One brow raised, Rainn yanked on Oblique's horns and appraised her, head to toe. He shrugged. "I didn't even know this was a girl demon. How can you tell?"

Mother Love's fortune, Rainn. Just be quiet!

"I won't take that from a damn animal." Graxat'Flem shoved at Sandy, who moved back a half step and replanted his feet.

"Grax, I swear if you don't stop, I'll finish you right here and now. You know I can." Feng sighed and slumped. "I don't want to, but I will."

"You just can't stop being weak, can you?" Graxat'Flem carried a hint of victory in his voice. What was he winning here? "You wanna go back home? Fine by me. Can't wait to spread the news of all your glories."

That was it. Graxat'Flem wanted to disgrace Feng and what? Take his place as gang leader?

"Flaming shits, Grax. This is supposed to be *fun*. That's why we're here." Feng put a hand on Sandy's back and glared at Graxat'Flem over his shoulder. "This isn't a slave hunt, we're just out here shirking work. And I'd much rather be on the farm than watching Sandy or Oblique die."

"What about me?" Graxat'Flem's jaw stuck out as he spoke, flaring the razor-edged scales of his neck.

"I said what I said." Feng crossed his arms. "Now you wanna back the fuck off, or you wanna die here in the road?"

"You guys are all *farmers*?" Rainn's voice rose and a wide grin split his face. "Fuck me. I'm glad we didn't run into anyone scary."

"Rainn, dear." Heron's words floated in the air, relaxed, unhurried, but intensely compelling. "Please shut up and hold the sword still. Bravery isn't helping."

"Hm? Oh. Right." He frowned and readjusted his sword blade.

Good point though. "Forby? Hey, Forby," Masika called to the demon. "Stop biting Feng's hand. I think he's giving up."

Hanging from Feng's torn hand by his teeth, Forbryttan cut his eyes to Masika. He dropped to the road.

Feng shot Masika a black look before returning his attention to Graxat'Flem. "What's it gonna be, big guy? Walk away, or make me kill you?"

"Why should I care?" To Masika's amazement, Graxat'Flem sounded distraught. On the verge of tears. "Do any of you even like me?"

Sandy merely shrugged.

"No," rasped Oblique.

"Well, no, not really." Feng raised his hands. "But when has that ever stopped you? I mean, you're an asshole. No one likes you. But you're Graxat-fucking-Flem. What do you care about anyone else?"

Eyes welling, Graxat'Flem hung his head, dropped his gaze to his feet, and walked away.

"Whew." Feng blew out dark green cheeks and leaned forward, hands on armored knees. He glanced up. "Can we talk now? Let Oblique go, and we'll leave you alone. This shit is just too much trouble."

"No." Masika refused to let them have another go at them so easily. She waved them away. "You three take off. Go home. Forbryttan'll watch you. When he comes back to us, which better be soon, then we'll let Mrs. Creepy-Voice go. And if we see you again, we'll know where to hit you."

Feng's gaze darted between Oblique and Masika. "Fine. But don't you dare hurt her. There're a lot more demons out there than us who'd take it bad." Momentary anger sped across his face. "And no one knocks Oblique where I can hear. Understand? Call her creepy-voice again and—"

"No, it's fair." Oblique's speech slid into Masika's ears, a cold, wet, and dirty slime that corrupted all it touched. "My voice is pretty creepy."

Fists clenched and shoulders tight, Feng spun and, without looking to see if anyone was following, stalked off the Crying Road and ascended the closest hill. Sandy smiled, waved to Masika, and clomped heavily after his two companions.

"Feng's just had a bad day is all," Sandy said as he moved away. "He and his dad had a fight earlier. That's bound to put anyone out of sorts."

"Feng's out of sorts?" Heron shook her head, incredulous. "What about Grax?"

"Oh, he's fine." Sandy gave a chuckle. "You caught him on a good day."

"Go," Rainn prompted Forbryttan.

"Oh! Right. Back soon." And Forbryttan bounded off after them.

After the four demons vanished behind the hills, tension leeched out of Masika's shoulders and back. She let go of the dagger handle, its leather wraps imprinted on her palm.

"What about you?" Masika asked Oblique. "Did you know about Feng's affection for you?"

The demon woman rolled her eyes. "Yes. Why would I care?" But her gaze flickered back over the hills Feng just walked behind.

Despite the squirming in her brain, Masika smiled.

"Tell him." Maybe if Masika helped Oblique, Feng might find better things to do for a while than chase them. "Tell him you want him, too, and then you can both be happy. Wouldn't that be nice?"

From the corner of her eye, Masika caught Heron's glance to Rainn.

"Shut up," Oblique replied, her voice buzzing maggots in Masika's ears. She cast her gaze down and her lower lip poked out. "I'm not doing that. You're stupid."

TWENTY-FIVE

The nation of Murden is a multicultural melting pot of aligned demonic races. Together, we act in accordance with our innate superiority to the human souls that have invaded our realm. It is a land of laws and structure, and functions smoothly and easily and without the wild abandon of places like Hunter's Sweep or the Reaves. The Standards of Rule are enhanced by a rigidly maintained hierarchy, flowing down from the top through every noble demon empowered by our king, Veliel the Fundament.

Some nobles use this authority better than others, but hey, that's demons for you.

General Kolos of Murden Fell

A ny chance that's the last we see of them?" As Rainn asked the question, Oblique passed behind a ridge in a distant hill and disappeared.

Believing it unlikely, Masika used Inlittan to search as far as she could see for likely ambush spots. She spotted a dozen, and that was only as far as the next curve in the Crying Road.

"I doubt it." Heron brushed herself off. "I don't think they're all on the same page about it though. Maybe we can be out of their range before they decide to return and deal with us for good."

"We should keep moving then." Masika glanced through the pack Sharp Jonn provided her on leaving. Not much food left, and water would be a problem soon. "Wasn't there supposed to be a roadhouse somewhere? Pepper said each one was a day's walk from the last, but we haven't seen one yet."

"Looking for some home-cooked hell-bug stew?" Rainn resumed walking and grinned. He loved teasing her, like her brothers did. The banter about what they might eat made her feel at home, even here.

"No, but we're going to be pretty thirsty before too much longer. And I'm worried that if we do find one of those roadhouses, Feng and his friends'll be there waiting for us." Masika's semi-mechanical knee squeaked with every step they took. The next time they stopped she would take another look at it.

"We have more than you think." Heron shifted the pack on her own shoulder. All three of them carried one. At Masika's quizzical glance, the goddess shook a fingertip between herself and Rainn. "Gods. We *can* eat and drink, but we don't have to. We never would've survived Angrim's dungeon if we did. Rainn and I haven't been eating so you'll last longer."

"Oh." The admission caught Masika flat-footed. "That's so sweet!" She pulled Heron close in a one-armed hug. "You never stop surprising me." It was the kind of thing her papa would have done for her.

"You would've done no less for us," Heron responded. "And you have done considerably more. We were happy to."

"*She* was happy too," Rainn said, a gruff haughtiness in his voice. "I was *willing* to. It's totally different. Hey!"

Masika snatched Rainn around the waist in her other arm and pulled him in too. They proceeded this way for another dozen paces before the awkwardness of it forced them back apart. While not the people she grew up with, Heron and Rainn proved themselves family nonetheless.

A group of twenty or so filthy, underfed, and naked humans came into view around the bend, moving closer to the hillside cliff face when they spotted Masika and the Alir. A pair of very large demons, scales the color of dried blood just as Graxat'Flem possessed, strode behind them, snapping their heels with long whips.

"Hey, wake up. We need you." Rainn poked at the bundle in the small of his back and Forbryttan hopped out.

"Wasn't sleeping." The tiny, blue-furred demon shook one of his feet. "What's up? Escort duty? Ah. I see 'em." Forbryttan ran out ahead of their little group, puffed out his chest, and waddled forward on his short hind legs, elbows held high. "Keep it moving. These're my humans. Fuck off, you."

The two huge demons, one possibly female and the other a massively overweight male, scowled mightily at them but continued past. Their humans trudged ahead, having left all dignity and hope far behind.

"I hate this place." Masika craned her neck to see as the last of the other group moved out of sight. "I mean, I appreciate that these weird rules that run the whole thing can occasionally work in our favor, but could we at least see a copy of them? Is there an Undergates library we could stop in for a look?"

"Probably." Rainn drew his sword, twirled it a few times over his head, and sheathed it. "But they'd likely take your dick as a late fee if you missed the return. Besides, I hate to read."

"Well, you're going to have to learn to like it," Masika said with a grin. "You're the only one here with a dick."

Disappointed surprise crossed Rainn's face, and Forbryttan searched frantically between his own legs.

"I don't think I have a dick either." His fingers felt around in the fur. "Wait. What's that? Hang on."

"Please stop," said Heron. "You can be whatever you want to be. No proof required."

"I found it." Forbryttan grinned a needle-toothed grin. "It's really up in there."

"Not looking." Masika stared at the most distant of thunderheads Inlittan could show her. "Don't want to see it."

"Unh. See?" Forbryttan sounded inordinately pleased with himself.

"I don't think that *is* a dick, Forby," Rainn said.

"It's not?" Forbryttan asked. "What is it?"

"I dunno. You should probably put it back though. It doesn't look like it oughtta be out like that." Rainn's observations made Masika's stomach crawl up her spine.

"That does not look good." No matter what Heron saw, Masika refused to look at it. "Masika, dear? Can you look ahead and tell me what I'm seeing? Just there."

Oh. Thank Mother Love's fortune, it was only life-threatening danger.

Heron pointed ahead, where, with Inlittan's help, a bright silver line across the Crying Road resolved into a solid row of a hundred thick-bodied and pebble-skinned demons in a line, shoulder to shoulder, facing them. They wore silver plate armor and carried barbed halberds, and not one spoke or smiled. Heavy helms covered their eyes.

"You're right. It's not good." Cliffs lined the road on either side. At fifty feet they counted as short as far as cliffs went, but as walls they were perfectly adequate. "That's a war party. Or a really intense escort."

Going back might be an option, the demons were a full mile off, but they faced more than a day of backtracking before they could leave the road in any direction except that taken by Feng and pals. And was leaving the road any better an idea?

"Might not be for us." Rainn stared ahead. "They sure don't need a hundred fuckers to take us down. We've already seen what happens when we try to fight four, and I kinda think any one of those coulda taken us if we hadn't got lucky." He bit his lip. "Fuck. Whether it's a trap for us or someone else, I definitely get the feeling we're getting bushwhacked here."

"Hm. I wonder if Boridan would have been any help here?" Heron asked.

A snort of laughter escaped Rainn. "Definitely not."

"'S'not a problem." Forbryttan puffed out his little chest again. "I can escort the crap outta you guys. I escorted you past loads of demons already. That's just one more load."

"I don't think so, little buddy." The strength drained out of Masika. "I don't think these demons are here to kill us anyway. I think they're here to wall us off." Inlittan showed her a break in the cliffs just to the line of demons' right. "Or force a detour."

A detour away from the Crying Road.

THE QUESTION of going back resolved itself when bow-armed demons, smaller than those ahead, with long, rangy muscled shoulders and dull yellow furred arms, loosed a line of oversized arrows across the road behind them with enough force to crack the cobbles.

Masika noticed other cracks indicating this tactic had been used before.

"If we get killed out here, I'm gonna really regret not chopping Oblique's head off when I had the chance," Rainn muttered.

"What would that have helped?" As if not walking to her death at all, Heron continued picking her careful yet graceful way up the road toward the line of demon soldiers.

"Not a fucking thing. I just woulda felt better about it."

"No idea if January's graver would do any more to those soldiers in front of us than make them angry," Masika said, slipping her thumb under the shoulder strap of the weapon, "but I could definitely blow those archers off the clifftop. Maybe even dump the whole thing down into the road."

Heron squinted up at the archers. "If we attack them, they're allowed to attack us back. I think, anyway. Right now no one is killing anyone, and it might be a better idea to keep that going as long as we can." She stared again at the soldier demons. "Masika, can you tell why they're there? I mean, there in that particular place."

Inlittan lit up the scene for Masika. A well-worn path into the hills that the soldiers marched out of, two at a time. Halberds well maintained but not unused. Rigid physical discipline kept the line perfectly still. They refused to so much as turn their gaze.

C'mon, give me something I can use.

As if in answer, Inlittan showed Masika wide stains of dried blood and other fluids across the whole of the road where the soldiers' line stood.

Thanks. I already knew not to attack the overwhelming force in front of us. Masika could almost feel Inlittan shrug helplessly.

"Yeah." Masika let go of the shoulder strap and wiped her palms on the sides of her tunic. "Looks like this is just where they kidnap people. And it doesn't always go well."

When they reached the line of soldiers, the group wordlessly turned to the right toward the break in the cliffs. The soldiers, seen up close, were each considerably more massive than Sandy, showing Feng's friend to be a relative youngster. Were Feng and his gang all just a bunch of disaffected teens?

"They're with me." Forbryttan hooked a thumb at his chest and stalked ahead, a stern attitude in his step.

"In case anyone wasn't aware," Rainn said, "I don't like this."

"Noted." Masika tried to see ahead, but the path twisted and quickly moved out of view. "At least they haven't murdered us. Maybe someone just wants to say hi."

No one answered, and together they proceeded up the comparatively narrow hill pass.

CHAPTER
TWENTY-SIX

A duke close to the throne might find himself in the shadow of such power that he is rendered inert by proximity. A mere country baron, on the other hand, in some far-flung corner of Murden, can be as mighty as any monarch among their own estates, if not as wealthy.

It has ever been thus, and the situation is hardly unique to Murden. But a baron and his family don't have the training or support structure that goes with that level of authority, and they can't be counted on to make the correct decisions, to not muck it all up. But when they inevitably do, they are simply culled, and their lands given to the next crappy baron who deserves a favor from the throne.

The Undergates is a complicated place, and anyone can make a bad choice.

Except me. No culling here.

General Kolos of Murden Fell

At last, the group left the confusing tangle of passes through the dark stone hills into a ten-mile-long valley of green and yellow farmland that terminated in a squat gray palace.

From their vantage on the valley's side wall, Masika observed that all the buildings were of the same dark rock and that thousands of demons made it their home, along with more than a few human slaves.

Farm smells of earth, cut fields, and animals carried on the breeze.

Slavery was considered distasteful by the upper classes back in Masika's home of Egren, something the barbaric Andosh and uncultivated merchant Imars did. The more of it she saw here in the Undergates, the less she approved.

"Fancy." Rainn gave a low whistle.

Two of the broad soldier demons led them, while the remainder followed close behind, halberds at attention. The entire trip they remained stubbornly silent in the face of Masika's many questions.

"I have a theory." Heron tapped her chin as she picked her way down the sloping path. "Whoever it is that lives in that palace found out the Hiimrykers are after us, which we were told was unusual. The northmen rarely leave their borders except on short-distance raids. This demon"—she indicated the palace—"knows that and made an unjustified assumption as to our value. That would explain all this fuss for three escaped slaves."

Although the soldiers held their silence, their ears functioned perfectly. Masika, Rainn, and Heron kept scrupulous track of what they said around them. Mostly.

"Or they found out what an amazing dancer I am and captured me to be someone's concubine." Rainn shrugged. "Wouldn't blame them."

A cool breeze brought spicy flavors on the air, as well as sounds of work—and even song. Whatever Masika's assumptions of demonic life were, this reality was not among them.

They made their way to a broad central road of packed rocks and gravel that led, straight as a falling drop of blood, to the gates of the distant palace.

Better rested, Masika's mind no longer created phantasms in the sky to plague her, and Rainn and Heron thankfully did not mention it either. Abduction by actual demons to an unknown palace for unknowable reasons rose quite naturally to the top of her concerns.

Given time, Masika's thoughts returned to her larger doubts. She led the Alir to the imp, to Mount P'takkin, and eventually to this very spot. But why worry about failure now? None of them would be here at all if she had not already led them to their deaths.

The palace grew as their rapid pace ate the miles, Masika's knee squeaking all the while. Most of the demons in the fields, either overseeing slaves or toiling themselves, were of an as yet unseen race. Smaller and wirier than Feng and his brutes. A few resembled Sandy, as did the soldiers, but none of the other three were represented.

"I have reconsidered and have a second theory," Heron announced. "It occurs to me that since slaves here can't die unless they're murked, they might be worth considerably more in the Undergates than in the living world. It might actually be worth it to send out this kind of welcome to capture three able-bodied humans."

"But we had a demon escort." The idea of slavery soured in Masika's thoughts. She retained her bow, dagger, and short sword, but Inlittan showed her no vulnerabilities in the heavily armored and rock-skinned soldiers to exploit.

"We left the road under our own wind," Rainn answered. "Technically they didn't capture us. We did that to our own fucking selves."

"Can you leave the road if you have an escort?" Heron wondered aloud. "Could we just turn around and go back to the road right now?"

The four of them, Forbryttan included, slowed and looked at one another. The small and huddled homes and shops of a demon village surrounded them, and the gates to the palace, wide and deep gray, stood open less than two hundred feet in front of them.

From behind, a soldier shoved Rainn toward it. "No," he said. The first word any of their chaperons had spoken.

"I am gonna have to read a goddamn book about these goddamn rules, aren't I?" Rainn caught his balance and strode ahead, his posture arrogant and undefeated. "You know, Forby, when you were a sword, you could've chopped these assholes' heads right off. Whack!"

Through the slits in their visors, Inlittan showed Masika several demon brows rise at the notion.

Ahead, an elegant demon of Oblique's race, over eight feet tall, masculine, and immaculately attired in flowing white shirt and trousers, stepped out of the gloom of the palace interior.

"Honored guests," he said. His voice cut a dirty gash into Masika's nerves. "Welcome to the estate of Baron Stolas, hero of the Smoking Lakes and loyal servant to King Veliel the Fundament. Let's, ah, get you all cleaned up, and then we can find something presentable for you to wear. Hm?"

Masika tried to find any hint of condescension in the seneschal's horrifying voice, but none existed. Either that or his acting exceeded Masika's ears.

They entered.

"This way, please," the greasy-voiced demon said. He led them down tall, oppressive corridors of light-eating rock, candle sconces hopelessly outmatched by the sheer volume of shadows.

"Cheery place." Rainn craned his neck, staring up into the dim ceiling. "I bet you guys are super popular during party season."

"It is always party season here at Baron Stolas's palace." The seneschal's face and hands vanished completely whenever he entered an area of fuller dark. His white clothing, not dissimilar to Oblique's, marked him out well enough. "We are a very popular destination." He stopped in front of an open door. "Ah, here we are. Refresh yourselves in here. There are clothes and food. Wait until you are summoned."

"Please stop." Masika leaned against a wall with her hands over her ears. "Talking. Please stop it. I-I can't think. It hurts."

At this, the seneschal smiled, his amusement apparent in the cruel lines of his face.

Until Rainn's fist crashed into his jaw, sending him spinning into the stone wall and to the floor. Rainn took Masika's elbow and led her into the guest hall.

"Thank you," Heron said, stepping over the large figure on the ground. "I think we can manage from here."

AFTER A FEW MINUTES of lighting everything that would burn, the guest hall nearly became tolerable. Though not bright, it danced with pinpricks of light everywhere and assumed an almost festive atmosphere.

They bathed, ate weird food, and dressed in surprisingly familiar attire. Masika found a golden-hued kaftan and robe with red trim befitting a princess of Egren, as well as a slender desert sword similar to her own. The leather wrapped grip felt off, not yet conforming to her hand through years of practice and occasional practical use as had her blade back in the living world, but it was a start.

Rainn discovered black pants and boots, a gray shirt, and a woolen vest the color of a storm-filled night. By stark contrast, Heron's dress glowed in brilliant white and pale blue, and a scalloped cape reminiscent of feathers covered her bare shoulders and plunging neckline. In all, the clothes seemed a reasonable facsimile of what they wore when they died. Just much cleaner.

"I truly hope I'm not forced to flee in these clothes." Heron held out the cape and looked down at herself, every inch the goddess. "It's beautiful but hardly terrain appropriate."

"Hang on there." Forbryttan approached Rainn as he strapped a thick-bladed sword to his waist. "Lemme see that."

Rainn drew the weapon and held it out for the little demon, who recently had been Rainn's sword himself.

Sniffing the blade, Forbryttan shook his head disapprovingly and grimaced. "That'll snap the first time you hit a mountain with it. It's crap. Where can we get a better one?"

"I don't think we can, buddy." Rainn tightened the belt and adjusted the scabbard. "Though I'm not liking that they're leaving us fully armed. These fuckers obviously aren't a bit worried about us."

"Is there any reason we should be?"

Everyone jumped at the intrusive voice. Masika whirled, sword in hand, to see an obviously amused demon of Feng's race, though older, standing in the doorway. Even without the tall, curving horns, he stood a full ten-feet-tall and dressed in glittering jewel-toned raiment.

He glanced down at the point of Masika's blade. "We just gave that to you. Be a shame to dirty it so fast."

"Why are we here?" Masika concentrated on calming her breathing, though she did not lower the weapon. "Why have you abducted us? What's the point of all this?"

"Ah. I see." He crossed his lanky arms and leaned against the doorframe. "You are here because Baron Stolas wishes it. You were *encouraged* to be here—no one was abducted—for the purposes of international relations, and the point is to gain favor for the aforementioned Baron Stolas with King Veliel of Murden by way of returning you to the Reaves. Queen Issta will be delighted. I've no idea why, but she truly has a memoth up her ass for the three of you."

"Four," growled Forbryttan.

The stranger's gaze flickered to the tiny trimpet and one brow rose. "You weren't mentioned. Sorry."

"That's gonna be a problem, asshole." Rainn pulled his own blade but left it hanging loosely at his side. "That's outta our way. *Sorry.*"

"Hm." The demon tapped his lips in thought. "That does sound bothersome. Tell you what. You come with me and meet all the pertinent players, and we'll see if we can figure out a compromise that makes everyone happy."

"We're not going back," Masika said. Whoever this Baron Stolas was, he knew that Queen Issta wanted them, but maybe he did not know why any more than this servant did. For that matter, Masika was not certain how Issta herself knew. She must know Heron and Rainn were gods, mustn't she? Why else go to all this trouble?

"Noted." The finely dressed demon straightened in the doorway. "Coming?"

"I'll come with you"—gathering her cape around herself, Heron raised her head—"*if* you answer a question for me. I understand that Queen Issta is looking for us, but how did you know where we were? *Who* we were?"

"That's two questions, but I'll tell you since both have the same answer." He smiled and showed a mouthful of sharp fangs. "My son Feng told me."

CHAPTER
TWENTY-SEVEN

Forgiveness is as deadly in the Undergates as it is in the Alireon. As soon as you give it to one, everybody thinks they deserve it, and then no one is doing what they're told. After that it's only a matter of time before the Standards deem you unworthy of rule, and you're cast down just to be replaced by the chamber pot cleaner or some other ludicrous individual like that.

Much better to kill the guilty rather than forgive them. No one ever got hurt that way.

Queen Issta, Ruler of the Reaves and ex-wife of High King Oldam

Masika gasped as she walked into the audience chamber. Not because of the lavish finery absent everywhere else in the palace, nor the dizzying height of the unusually well-lit chamber. Nor even because of the bewildering array of demons of every imaginable appearance that all turned to stare, leer, or scowl at them as they entered. No, her surprise came at the sight of two central figures standing in a place of honor before an empty stone chair at the raised far end of the chamber. One was a well-proportioned man with gray curls and a floor-length button up robe she did not recognize.

And the other one was Boridan.

"Shadows of the Alir." A faint grimace passed over Rainn's rugged features. "How'd you get here ahead of us? And who's your friend?"

Masika followed Rainn and Heron to where Boridan stood, his expression both relieved and uncomfortable. Silence swept the rest of the hall, filtering up to the smoke-filled ceiling. The entire situation screamed alarms in her skull, though she could not put her finger on exactly why.

Other than the obvious, of course.

"Hi, guys." Boridan stopped and cleared his throat. "Uh. There were portals involved. Like sliding through High King Oldam's colon if I'm honest." He glanced at the gray-haired man, who looked on impassively. "This is the Emissary. Of the Reaves." He paused as a faint smile flickered across his face only to immediately vanish. "He works for Queen Issta."

At this point Masika noticed Boridan's improved clothing. Unlike theirs, it was not simply a nicer version of what he might have worn while alive, it was some kind of uniform: dark blue jacket with gold piping—military.

"What's going on here, Boridan?" Perhaps everything might still be rescued from sliding into the chamber pot if Boridan had been made central to it. Could he possibly have enough influence to gain their freedom?

"Queen Issta and King Veliel have already agreed on your return. But the Emissary apparently had a tiny amount of wiggle room. In exchange for my service as his personal attaché, whatever that is, I was allowed to keep Heron out of Issta's grasp. I'm sorry, but it's the best we could do."

It made sense that Boridan's efforts concentrated on keeping Heron free, given his affection for her. While not thrilled over her and Rainn's continued predicament, at least Heron would fly.

"Thank you for that at least." Masika clasped Boridan's hand between her own. "I hope your servitude isn't hurtful to you."

At that the Emissary sniffed. "I'm standing right here. Do I look like the kind of person who abuses their servants? Boridan shall always be well treated, as will Heron, for as long as she is with us."

Rainn stepped between Masika and Boridan, knocking their hands apart with a rough slap. "You unbelievable fuck. You made a deal, and Heron's your prize. And you come here looking for our blessings for it? Maybe you think you'll have a sweet little life together after I chop off your head?"

The thick-bladed sword hung easily in Rainn's hand, ready for use the instant he deemed it necessary.

Softly, Masika slid a reassuring hand over Rainn's sword wrist. The watching demons' expressions turned to amusement at the pets fighting one another.

"Would you rather her face whatever Issta has in store for you?" Boridan's obvious fear heightened his belligerence. "She's the evilest creature in the Undergates. Heron wouldn't—"

"Heron is perfectly capable of making up her own mind about where she goes." Heron tilted back her head to look down at Boridan. "You have been a true friend in the past, Boridan of Tyrrane, so I am choosing to believe that you're doing this to protect me. But Issta is Alir, as are Rainn and myself. We're all gods of Andos. She is my, well, step-aunt? Honestly, she didn't leave the family under the best of circumstances. Still, we are the same, and I prefer to take my chances with Rainn and Masika. I hope your servitude is revokable."

"It isn't," the Emissary said, eyes twinkling, "but neither is yours. I'm afraid you aren't being provided with a choice. By the way, that dress is simply stunning on you. Boridan, I believe you chose very well."

Moving fast, Masika hooked her elbow through Rainn's to prevent Boridan's skewering.

Feng's father sidled through the little group. "This has been entertaining, but you'll have to excuse me. Things to do, you know." Once through them all, he went to the huge stone chair, faced the room, and sat.

That was Baron Stolas? Feng was Baron Stolas's son?

The sinking feeling in Masika's stomach sank further.

"I don't suppose anyone remembers any new god magic yet?" Masika whispered to Rainn and Heron.

With a shrug, Heron indicated their doom, while Rainn merely glared at Boridan.

No help there then.

"You know, godling"—the Emissary inclined his head to Rainn as he spoke—"if you break my new attaché here in front of all these Murdens, it'll make me look bad. There are consequences to that sort of thing."

Rainn flicked a glance to Masika, who released his arm and stepped back. Her head hurt, and her irritation at their helplessness since arriving in the Undergates mounted every moment.

"You know what?" Masika waved a hand at Boridan. "No one cares about Boridan, but I bet someone somewhere will miss *you*. What do you think, Mister Emissary?"

"I think it's bad form to go killing people in someone else's court. Especially when they're waiting to speak." The Emissary grinned. "Destroy me when the meeting's over."

"If we're all finished over there," Baron Stolas said, his loud baritone floating effortlessly over the large room, "we're here to witness a new age of cooperation between the Reaves and the great and infernal nation of Murden. These escaped slaves have caught the eye of Mighty Queen Issta, and this very court is about to turn them over to her Emissary. In return, the Reaves has pledged to abandon their rivalry over the Firefields and relinquish those lands to Murden."

Applause went up from every corner of the hall.

"And as the baron of the lands in closest physical proximity to the Firefields, as well as the king's servant brokering the deal, our own King Veliel has announced that I will be made a member of his royal family and granted the Firefields as my official dukedom." Into the stunned silence, Baron Stolas added, "You've all been given a promotion. Congratulations."

This time the joyous shouting and applause shook the walls and clapped Masika's hands over her ears.

"Settle down, settle down." Baron Stolas stood and indicated quiet, shining garments swaying on his lanky frame. "You witness history, Emissary? Are you prepared to take possession of these prisoners as the Reaves's charge, in full completion of Murden's responsibility in this arrangement?"

Heat flushed Masika's face. She felt as if she might explode if she failed to act.

"I do, sir." The Emissary smiled and bowed to Baron Stolas in a gesture that communicated friendship more than outright deference. It was the type of motion that Masika's papa had made many times in his service as ambassador to Egren's emperor.

"That is *it*." Masika shoved the Emissary over mid-bow and stalked to the base of the steps leading to Baron Stolas's grand chair. "Do you know *why* Queen Issta wants us so bad?" She spun to face the room. "Do any of you?"

The Emissary, pushing himself up from his knees, shook his head and drew a line back and forth across his neck, pleading with her for silence. Rainn glared at him, fingering the handguard of his sword.

But Heron merely smiled a secret smile to Masika and widened her eyes ever so slightly.

"Heron and Rainn are Alir." The sudden and complete silence rang in Masika's ears, highlighting the pounding of her own heart. No more second-guessing. No more weakness. "Queen Issta doesn't want the Firefields. She wants Hiimryk. But more than that, she doesn't want *competition*. Competition she knows two of her own kind will bring." Masika projected real strength, just as she had heard her papa do in many an Andosh throne room. No one could speak as long as she held them with her voice.

She knew Papa would be proud of her.

Her voice lowered dramatically, and she turned to Baron Stolas. "And just think what Murden could accomplish. Just imagine what a baron of Murden could do with *two* Queen Isstas in his pocket."

Excited speech broke out across the hall. The Emissary dove forward, interrupting. "Baron, I won't deny what the human child claims but think about your own skin here. If you renege on this deal, you go from a wealthy baron to a bucketful of shaikos bait. Queen Issta will destroy you if King Veliel doesn't do it first. You're talking about war with the Reaves here. Real war. The kind the Undergates hasn't seen since the Dead God came to us."

"If you give us to them," Masika said to Baron Stolas, "Issta will march over Murden and you're dead anyway. This way you have a chance."

Gradually the hubbub died out in the room as Baron Stolas contemplated, his face a frowning mask of deep consideration. He returned to his seat. "The Barony will keep the prisoners in the name of Murden and send them to King Veliel. If this brings war with the Reaves, so be it."

This time the excited demons' conversations escalated to shouts both fearful and challenging. Messengers ran out of the room to bring news to family and soldiery alike.

A firm hand gripped Masika's forearm. "Run," Boridan whispered harshly. "He'll destroy them all."

The Emissary stood in the center of the whirlwind, silent, still, and staring at Masika.

She ran.

A flash of weathered blue fur passed in front of Masika and latched onto a shrieking demon's neck, the rolls of brick-red fat exploding with blood as Forbryttan tore into his throat.

"Forby, stop! We're running away," Masika yelled.

The tiny demon stopped and stood on his victim's quivering chest, casting his gaze to the frantic Masika. "Oh, we're not fighting? All right. That's on me."

As the four of them hit the corridor outside Baron Stolas's audience chamber, a crack of thick stone reverberated through their feet, followed by screams. The floor jumped sideways and flung Masika to the ground.

"Thunder and blood!" shouted Rainn, barely audible above the din of terror and whatever else it was that happened behind them. "Where's the fucking door outta this shithole?"

Rainn and Heron grabbed Masika and pulled her to her feet as a crack pulled apart the ceiling above them and rained debris on their heads. Soldiers poured in from the entryway at the end of the hall, and shrieking demons rushed through doors to either side, uncaring of the safety of the much smaller human and her two gods.

Which way, Inlittan? An instant later, Masika found her attention drawn to an onrushing demon. To her dismay, he was one she knew.

"Follow me!" Feng bellowed, glossy black armored plates clacking in his haste. "We'll get out through my rooms."

Lacking a better plan, Masika changed course and pelted after Feng, Rainn and Heron hot on her heels. Huge sections of the walls and roof came crashing down around them. Inlittan showed her which portions of the palace were about to fall instants before they did, allowing all of them to flee uncrushed.

Masika wanted to stop and ask where they were going, why Feng was helping them, but she did not dare. Wherever they headed, at the very least it represented a few moments more without becoming broken mirrors.

Feng led them through richly appointed rooms where canopied beds and closets full of fine garments went smashing to the ground as they raced past, and several times each of the three of them went sprawling to the stone, only to be hauled back to their feet by the other two.

Ahead, Feng lowered his head and smashed through a door leading outside, but before the rest could reach it, a broad length of exterior wall fell in on itself, trapping them within. As it went, the ceiling directly above them chased it down.

They were trapped, unable to move ahead. Even worse, the floors above continued to crumble down on their heads.

"Aaargh!" Collapsing stone pushed Rainn to one knee as he caught a fifteen-foot section of solid rock and held it over Masika and Heron, both of whom were knocked to the ground. "Get . . . out . . ." he said, grunting the words.

Masika rolled out and helped pull Heron free but could do nothing for Rainn. He could not move without dropping his burden on himself, and soon he would fall beneath it. Above them Masika saw the roof and more of the exterior wall crumbling. Inlittan showed her nothing.

There was no safe place to go.

Watching Rainn lose his battle with the enormous length of stone ceiling, Masika pulled Heron close. The goddess embraced her.

Then the part of the wall that fell in on Feng's getaway door lifted and flew away.

"Come on!" Feng yelled. From beside him, Graxat'Flem rushed in, lifted the ceiling from Rainn's shoulders in one great scaled hand, and tossed it aside.

Everyone ran.

Outside, the screams and crashing reached new levels of terror, and the two demons shouldered and elbowed their way indiscriminately through the panicked crowds. They entered a narrow break in a row of shaking stone outbuildings, and Masika chanced a backward glance.

In the clouds of dust and falling debris, Masika thought she glimpsed a flash of dim gold shimmering in the afterimage of a darkly shifting humanoid figure at least a hundred feet high, standing in the ruin of Baron Stolas's palace.

Before the image fully registered in Masika's brain, it vanished, as if it had never been.

Rainn lifted Masika and ran with her. Her feet swung uselessly below, unwilling to listen to her wishes. Somehow, Masika knew she held the blame for that monster, fully and singly. Her fault.

She pushed against Rainn. That meant she was responsible for Baron Stolas's certain death, and right now the baron's son led them away for some doubtlessly sinister purpose of his own.

"What?" Rainn's breath came short and fast. His own feet stumbled against the irregular ground. He let her down.

"We can't follow them," Masika hissed. "We killed Feng's father!"

But Heron ran ahead and around a corner, unable to hear Masika's warning—or heedless of it—and they both followed anyway. If they were to be murked by Feng and Graxat'Flem, they would do it together.

Behind the lengthy buildings, Rainn and Masika ran out into the edge of a wide cultivated field of purple-black plants that grew far over their heads. In front of the rows of vegetation, Feng and Graxat'Flem ran laughing and waving up to Sandy and Oblique, who held the reins of what could only be described as dragons. Forty feet in length, with glittering velvet scales, one dark green and the other a calm brown, the creatures sat and ignored the noise and excitement, docile as any well-trained horse.

Unsure what to do, Masika went to Sandy's beast.

"What happened?" yelled Sandy. "It sounded like the whole thing went down."

"It did!" Feng's obvious glee even elicited a small smile from Oblique as he slowed beside her. "She made the Emissary fight. I just thought I'd get out of trouble with the baron for turning them in, but this was *so* much better. Flaming *shits* that was beautiful!"

"Um, does this mean Feng doesn't want to kill us for murdering his father?" Masika asked Sandy.

"What? No." Sandy beamed at her. "I told you they had a fight. Baron Stolas wanted to disinherit Feng and cast him out. Make him a full-time farmer or whatever. We would've had to go too, as Feng's official staff. The Baron'd been making all of us do farm work for weeks now. But he never told no one he was going to throw Feng out, and now he's dead! We all owe you bunches."

Menacing delight shown in the bared fangs of Feng's grin. "More than owe you. You provided me a Dreadful Service, without my even asking! I'll be baron after this, and the Standards will have noticed. That means I have to return service to you or let you call on me later for anything you want. We can't have that, so I'm saving your worthless hides instead."

He climbed up onto the long saddle bench between Oblique's dragon's shoulders. "So climb on and let's get out of here while you're still in one piece, hey? Wherever you wanna go. Let's fly!"

TWENTY-EIGHT

Rulership is a top-down affair. Even King Oldam knew that, curse his crusted liver. Inferiors are important but not more so than a firm hand on the tiller. Wisdom in royalty is not a matter of engendering love and loyalty through compassion and support but in understanding your subjects' hatreds and fanning them in the right direction.

Like at each other.

Queen Issta, Ruler of the Reaves and ex-wife of High King Oldam

---

W ow." Boridan brushed stone dust off his fine military jacket, gave up, removed it, and blew on the epaulets instead. "That was an absolute shitshow. You sure you've done this before?"

In the spell hall, with its limitless webs and creepy silver bug-things constantly writing the spells that transported a worthy subject wherever they wished, the Emissary balled his fists and squeezed his eyes shut. "You said that they're headed to Savach to obtain passage back to the living world from Morholt the Red." He opened his eyes and breathed deeply. "But that doesn't explain why they came to the Undergates in the first place. Why're they here? What're they after?"

"Before I answer," Boridan said, his thoughts jumping ahead, "I need to know that whatever I tell you won't affect our arrangement. I still get Heron for eternity, and you'll do whatever it takes to see that through."

She would love him eventually. She loved a mortal man once before. Arso, damn his septic cock.

Since agreeing to be the Emissary's attaché, Boridan had thought a lot about the state of his own mind. A Tyrranean soldier or a mixed-breed mercenary, he decided the difference was negligible. His contemplations were his own, Boridan's, and the personalities that made him completed within him. Keane enjoyed no greater intelligence than he ever had, the mercenary simply grew up learning to use what he possessed in a different way.

A way Boridan now could.

The Emissary frowned and crossed his arms. "Obviously. You're not a trusting sort, are you?"

"Uh, you're a demon. What's there to be trusting about?"

"You're new, so I'll explain it to you. You'll need to understand if you're to serve me effectively anyway." The Emissary's calm reasonableness relaxed Boridan. He would have to watch out for that. The sight of the raging creature this placid diplomat had become haunted his thoughts.

"I operate under certain strictures that other demons do not. The Standards demand more of me. Or through me. In a sense, I *am* the Standards. As such, my word is resolute. I honestly couldn't break it if I wanted to. In point of fact," he warmed to the topic with a bit of rhetorical flair, "I'm also incapable of making a promise I can't keep. How's that for keeping your testicles in the orgar's mouth?"

If all of this proved truthful, which Boridan suspected was the case, he had heard all he needed to. "In that event, I'm not telling you where they're going next."

"You're kidding me." The Emissary's arms dropped to his sides.

His eyes went wide. "You understand I hold your future in the palm of my hand?"

"I understand you've already promised me an eternity of happiness with Heron, which won't happen if you take your vengeance on me here and now." Boridan sighed. He liked the Emissary; he simply maintained his own motivations. "I'm not shoving your head up a bull's butt because I want to, I just don't want to see the others go back to Issta if I can help it, and I think maybe I can."

"*You* want?" A hint of pique rose into the Emissary's words, but he shoved it back down. "May I be privy to exactly how it is you think you're helping anyone here? You're certainly not helping me, and I already gave you my word."

Trust in your own stupidity. It'll take you where you want to go.

"In exchange for which I told you about Morholt." Nerves fluttered in the back of Boridan's throat, but he already knew the rightness of his tactic. "That deal's done. You want to make another, we can talk. But sure. I'm hoping that when it comes down to it, these Standards of yours will weigh your word over Queen Issta's desires, and while you're catching Heron for me, the rest will escape back to the living world. Everybody wins."

The Emissary's expression grew black. "Except for me. And Heron, apparently. And you, when Queen Issta discovers you were the cause of my failure. She's not part of the Standards, you know. They enforce her decrees because she's the queen, but they don't operate through her like they do me. She's Alir. Not really from around here. And once she orders me to revoke my promise to you—"

"But she won't find out." Unlike Keane, Boridan kept the triumphant smirk off his lips. No sense antagonizing the monster further. "Because that would prevent your promise from happening, right? And we both know it can happen, and will, because if it couldn't, you wouldn't have been able to promise it in the first place."

The Emissary rubbed his temples between the thumb and fingers of one hand. "Please be quiet. I need to think. I had no reason to think you so damnably canny."

"Yeah. Sure. Whatever." *I wasn't always. But we can thank Sarah for that. And I will if I ever meet her.* The notion popped into Boridan's head that he should be happy to have gone on long enough without being murked to be able to appreciate the person he had become. He certainly was happy not to be all whiney about it anymore.

The Emissary royally screwed Boridan's chances to have Heron of her own volition with his giant-monster-destroys-everything act. Boridan's notion was to cause Heron to think that he simply wanted to rescue her from a worse fate. Which he did. But now she would be wary of him, and the only way he could have her would be to take her by force, which he needed the Emissary for.

But was he really willing to do that? Keane never would have, but as he just reasoned, he was not Keane. His reasoning held up, but he loved her. He did. And she would love him, too, if he could just get her past the getting of her.

Plenty of time to worry about that later.

"Hello, what's your name?" Across the still chamber, a single silver insect hung from a strand of the infinitely intricate spell. Despite having no eyes—or ears or mouth or anything of the like—the thing somehow managed to convey a serious stare at Boridan. Or else Boridan made it up. Hard to say.

He approached it and leaned over, staring back at its seamless silver hide. Nothing there but his own face. As if he stared into a physical representation of what getting murked actually meant. The thing lacked any form of identity at all. *And how would I know that?*

Perhaps they had that in common.

No. Boridan knew who he was. And he knew to what extents he would go for his love.

Close by, a mute circle of dim blue light erupted along the strands of webbing, expanding and fading from sight. The smell of ancient wars and timeless silences filled his nostrils.

"They could travel through Murden but not without help." The Emissary's muttering voice gave Boridan a touchstone to keep himself grounded in the otherwise silent cave. "But who would help the dears? No one after today. More likely they'll be hunted by Stolas's loyalists. The Forests of Hell are close. If they go there I can't track them. No contacts. In addition to other problems."

The face of Boridan looked back at him in the tiny creature's reflective hide, impassive and inscrutable. Vacant. It pulled at him. Unnerved, Boridan stuck his tongue out at the thing. After a second's delay, his reflection did too.

"Well, that's unsettling." But Boridan did not look away. Perhaps he could not. No way to be sure since he did not try.

"I could sit and watch the Crying Road, but if they simply cross it instead of following it, I'd never find them." The Emissary paced as he talked to himself somewhere in the periphery of Boridan's awareness. "Or I could press an invitation on Morholt the Red, since I know that's their final destination. But he killed the old handük, didn't he? Good on him. So now he takes his father's place—and the boy is not popular with the Sovereign Council. An official visit would signal the Reaves favoring him over them. Can't do that."

Of its own volition, Boridan's hand stretched out toward his other face.

"I could ask the Council, but those old bags'd be a week getting me an answer."

The face was smooth and cool under his fingers. Slightly pliable, like taught silver cloth. Not like Boridan's face at all. Somewhere in the back of his skull, a warning voice shouted. Dim. Far away. Easily ignored.

"So I contact Handük Morholt secretly and offer him what?" The Emissary's voice struggled across to Boridan as if through thick blankets. "What do I offer that doesn't sour the Sovereigns?"

The silver thing's bite lanced painfully through Boridan's fingertips, just as he expected it to. Impressive feat for a creature with no mouth. Cold nothing rushed into his veins, with an ancient eternity of more nothing behind it. It wanted nothing. Boridan maintained control, but his perspective became, for a brief instant, limitless.

He shook his head and stepped away from the web. "Huh. That was a thing." But was it over, or did it continue to be? Nothing remained behind, a reverse whisp where he ought to be. "Oldam's empty granite gonads. What do you want with me?"

"Come away from there." The Emissary's attention snapped up to Boridan. "You'll damage it. That's a delicate . . ." He trailed off, his eyes scanning the glittery web. "You wouldn't understand. Don't screw it up."

But the Emissary was wrong. The web was many things, but delicate was not one of them. It carried redundancies throughout time. If they somehow managed to burn it all away, whole and entire, the spell's threads would simply reach back to a point where it still existed, or forward where it existed once again, and reconnect. Regrow. Be respun? The web transfixed a lynchpin in the architecture of the universe, so much more than the Emissary understood. Using it to jaunt about the Undergates was akin to using an army of unstoppable chromium to butter your toast.

Whatever a chromium was.

Not that Boridan felt the need to share any of his newfound knowledge. "You figured out a plan?"

"It'd be easier if you'd trusted me enough to tell me where our quarry was headed before Morholt, but yes, I believe I have." The Emissary followed Boridan with his calculating gaze. "And in the spirit of that invisible trust, I'll tell you. The problem suggests the answer. While Morholt the Red is a recent addition to the Sovereign Council . . ."

Boridan stopped listening, instead devoting his full attention to his hand and the cool lack of presence there. Empty, like the trust.

Invisible.

CHAPTER

TWENTY-NINE

Want to know about him, *you say? Fine. Morholt the Red might've been a thorn in my side while I was alive, but now that I'm dead, he's the burning coal up my asshole. He fucks demons and serves them the souls of his own parents for supper. He's the wickedest bastard in all of Undergates, I think, and I won't lie down 'til he's in bits under my heels. What'll stop my hand? Not nothing, I tell you. Not nothing at all.*

You think you're funny? No, a burning coal up my asshole wouldn't hurt me. Fire knows better. Wanna see how you'd fare?

Runecrafter Glauth, Mistress of Flame and Regent of the Arrowwilds in the Forests of Hell

Black wind yanked at Masika's hair as she raced through a dark sky full of sickly green clouds. The air stank of stagnant pools and cold rust.

"It may not be as fast as our other boat, but it's a helluva lot more fun!" Rainn gripped the long saddle with his knees and held his arms above his head, laughing as loud as Forbryttan.

While Masika held a deep affinity for the shattered *Bitter Goose*, she understood Rainn's point. She sat behind Feng on the brown-scaled dragon, Rainn, Forbryttan, and Heron behind her, and Oblique at the rear. Sandy and Graxat'Flem rode the green, the two of them outweighing the other six.

Below, a dark gray landscape raced past, farmland, foothills, and ebon rivers where demons in boats traveled and caught wriggling pink creatures with too many limbs and strange squawking sounds. Behind and left of them the distant glow of the Firefields finally winked out, and ahead the sky gradually lit a dim blue-gray over the Forests of Hell.

"I can see the route we need to take!" Masika shouted over the roaring wind. She reached past Feng and pointed slightly right. "Head that way for now and we'll get there soon. A few days at most."

"Oh, sorry." Feng shrugged and held out one hand, palm up. "I'd love to take you all the way, but I only need to save your mirrors, and I've already done that. We can't fly over the forests anyway. There's things in there'll eat up ol' Sanda and Gaira like that." He snapped his fingers and lowered his hand. "But we can drop you off on the Crying Road close as we can to where you're going." He turned as far as he could and grinned a sharp-toothed grin down at Masika. "And no, Sanda and Sandy aren't related. They just look like it."

Dropped off on the Crying Road. Unfortunate, but still more than Masika expected. She could not fault Feng for looking after his own first, just as she was doing. To their left, Masika watched green Gaira soar, carrying Sandy and Graxat'Flem through the air as if weightless.

Oh. Masika smiled. Not related. That was funny.

Leaning down, Masika swept her hands over Sanda. The brown scales felt like satiny metal under her fingertips, and the furry mane and crest that ran down its back surprised her with its softness. Only the acrid chemical smell of the beasts put Masika off.

The demon's sudden reversal on wanting to kill her and the Alir still troubled Masika, but she decided not to examine it too closely. So much about the Undergates and its rules beggared comprehension. Did Feng's actions mean he was a better demon than she thought he was or just more practical? What kind of ruler had she unleashed on his barony? Did it matter? Whether or not the new Baron Feng would be any better than the old Baron Stolas was outside of her purview. "How about the four of you? You told your dad about us. Is anyone going to hold you responsible for what happened?"

"Nah," Feng shouted over his shoulder. "Dad never shared credit for anything unless he had to, and he thought you were his biggest coup yet. He told everyone you were all his idea, and I didn't correct him." He snorted laughter. "Can you believe it? He couldn't have played his part in his own destruction better if I'd written it for him!"

Could Masika be happy for the demons who just days ago tried to capture and "have fun" with them? Maybe. She avoided asking exactly what having fun meant to a quartet of bored adolescent demons, and she intended never to find out.

With a low, hornlike bellow, Gaira lifted a wing and angled sharply toward the ground. Sanda followed her. In minutes, both dragons stood in the midst of the Crying Road, munching contentedly on a horse-sized quadruped while its owner stood by shrieking. Matted white fur, dirty and blood-soaked, fell to the cobbles everywhere.

Feng and his brutes hopped off the dragons.

"Too bad the Standards don't say shit about protecting livestock, eh, stick?" Graxat'Flem flicked the wailing demon—who did bear some resemblance to a skinny stick—in the head, sending him to the ground.

"Thanks for the rescue and the flight," Masika said. She angled herself between Graxat'Flem and his emaciated victim, who turned tail and fled. "I'll be happy to address the new Baron Feng and his retinue on our way back through, and I'm pleased to have made it possible."

Heron bowed to Feng, while Rainn just stood there, one brow raised.

"Oh sure." Feng put his hands on his hips and thrust his chest out. "And good luck on your whatever it is you're about. Killing more nobles, I assume."

"Plenty of regents in the forests, if that's what you're after," Sandy supplied helpfully. "I'm glad we ran across you. I've never met any humans that weren't slaves before." A look of concern showed itself. "You're not slaves, are you?"

"Feel at ease, Sandy." Heron placed a restraining hand on Rainn, who obviously resented the implication. "You've not stolen us away from your brethren. We—"

"I already told you they're mine, fuck-foot." Forbryttan climbed on Rainn's shoulder and scowled up at Sandy. "Now beat it. I'm tired of looking at your ugly fuckbutts."

Laughing, Feng hopped onto Sanda's back, Oblique climbing up behind. "Good enough, lord trimpet. Be well, and good fortune to you. Our debt is paid, and the Standards are satisfied. C'mon you wastes, we got a barony to put back together and have some *fun* with!"

The two dragons and their riders beat their way back into the sky and vanished against the cloudy gloom of Murden.

To the opposite side of the road, the Forests of Hell's gigantic trees brought Masika memories of the pine woodlands of Tyrrane and extended out of sight. Similar, yet somehow more sinister. A slight and voiceless susurration permeated the dense vegetation, as if the enormous trees whispered to one another.

"Lives up to the name," Rainn observed. "We have any idea where we're headed?"

Masika frowned. "Uh, I don't know."

"You can't see Glauth because she's too far away? Or because she's behind trees or a mountain or something like that?" Staring into Masika's eyes, Heron canted her head ever so slightly, like a waterfowl searching for fish beneath the surface of a stream.

The sensation for Masika was of being held in a mother's arms. Not her own mother, but one who actually cared. "I guess? We've never really spoken."

"Then don't look for Glauth. Look for the path that will take us to her."

Aha.

"That way." Masika pointed through the black boles. "That's the path to Glauth."

Everyone took a step forward before Heron raised her hands.

"Masika," she said, "I assume you've asked Inlittan to give you the path to Glauth and she shows it to you? Lights up the way or something similar?"

"There're no lights, and honestly I'm not certain how she draws my attention." Masika considered the question. "But yes. I think of what I want to see, and then I can see it. Sometimes I can even see around corners if I can reach around the thing I'm looking at with my fingers. If not, then solid objects block it."

"And Inlittan says that's the path to Glauth?" Heron's brow knit thoughtfully.

"That's the path she's showing me."

"Which way would we walk if we were to ask for a path that led to Glauth without life-ending danger?" Heron asked.

Masika rolled her eyes. That was silly. Inlittan would never send them into . . . "Oh." A warm flush burned Masika's cheeks. "That way over there." She grinned abashedly. "Yeah. That's a good idea. Let's go that way."

"All this time and we just had to ask where the danger was?" Rainn shook his head, and one corner of his mouth ticked up. "We are so fucking stupid."

As Masika and the two Alir set off in the new direction, Forbryttan stood on his squat hind legs and stared off toward the path of greater peril. At length, he sighed and followed his friends. "Can we go find the big danger after? I just hate missing it."

Travel proved more difficult than Masika imagined. Inexplicably, Inlittan switched their path away from the safer route to one of greater danger every time Masika's attention wandered the smallest bit. And after two days of rough hiking through the woods, Inlittan stopped helping at all.

"I don't understand." Masika felt Inlittan as a part of her that lived in her spirit. "She's there, but she's gone quiet."

"Maybe she's tired," Heron said. "Do you think that some kinds of requests tax her more than others?"

"I don't know." Masika kicked dirt over their tiny campfire. Unlike many places in the Undergates, the Forests of Hell possessed an actual sun, with actual sunlight, though it made one slightly nauseous to look at for too long. "I don't really understand how she works at all, or even where she is, for sure. I can't communicate with her, exactly. But it's more like she's scared of something. Hiding, maybe?"

The trees continued their disturbing whispers, raising Masika's anxiety.

"More scared than certain murking?" Rainn asked. "And it's something that's no threat at all." He shook his head. "I think you broke it."

That thought filled Masika with an empty sadness she possessed no words to express. Rainn and Heron's company buttressed her, supported her both emotionally and physically, but Inlittan's potential loss hit more like losing a limb. The silent voice was part of her.

Unless it no longer was.

"We wouldn't leave Forby behind," Heron combed her graceful fingers through Masika's thick curls. "We won't leave Inlittan either. We'll find a way."

"Yep." From his seat on Rainn's shoulder, Forbryttan plunked his blue-furred chin on top of the god's head. "Getting left isn't near as much fun as getting eaten. It's like the opposite."

"Thank you." Masika wiped her nose. "And you have really weird priorities, Forby. But first let's just keep going. I think this is the right path." It struck Masika just how poorly dressed Heron was for a journey through dense woods in her glowing white dress and cape, and she laughed despite herself. "Yeah, uh, that way."

More than once Masika felt malign eyes on them, but nothing happened. She decided she was jumping at shadows, as she had been traveling the Crying Road through Murden. Even the whispers faded to background noise. At least the phantom impressions took her mind off her stomach. No one grabbed anything to eat on their way out of the Baron's collapsing palace, and occasional pools of green-tinted water proved a poor substitution for any actual food.

Inlittan stubbornly refused to rouse. Every time Masika searched for the correct path and got nothing, she worried more that something dire had happened to her odd friend. As they traveled, Masika's anxiety increased.

This portion of the forests blew cool, pine-scented breezes, undercut with the soft rot of vegetation. Less than a day in, Heron detected the smells of cooking food, and before long Masika and Rainn did too.

"I hear people." Heron stood still, her long neck curved to pluck the sounds from the air. "A village, maybe. They sound"—she paused, and a wistful smile ghosted across her face—"happy."

"I'd be happy here, too, especially if I knew how shitty the Longeyes had it over in the Firefields." Rainn spoke quietly, peering through the trees. He absentmindedly played with the hilt of the much-improved sword Baron Stolas gave him. Decorated him with, more like. "I'll lead, in case they get less happy when visitors show up."

"Fine. But you'll lead with me beside you, not behind." Masika strung her bow and nocked an arrow. "I'm still here to protect the two of you."

"I'd argue," Rainn said as he rolled his eyes, "but I know it'd be quicker to try and kill a saltblood giant by staring him in the eye while I jerk off." He headed through the huge trees. "Whatever. C'mon mirror people. Let's go get broken."

"Yay!" Forbryttan stage whispered.

Ten minutes later they approached a wide opening in the woodland, beyond which a small but ornate wooden home sat facing away from them not more than fifty feet away. Trampled grass made a sort of back yard with a central fire pit, around which close to thirty happy people laughed and ate delicious-smelling meat and roasted root vegetables. They wore simple clothing and carried no weapons other than those also useful for cooking.

A growly rumble escaped Masika's belly. She had not eaten more than scavenged berries in the past two days.

The partiers were both Andosh and Darrish in equal number, as well as a slight smattering of Pavinn. They frequently cast expectant glances into the trees where Masika and the Alir hid.

"You getting the idea we're expected?" Rainn whispered.

"Yeah." Masika craned her neck to take in the scene. "Except it looks like they'd rather feed us than trade us to demons for favors."

"Be careful." Heron hung back, and her large emerald eyes glinted in the shadows. "Even good people in the Undergates have their own realities to deal with. We can't count on anyone for certain but each other."

"Now she wants to be careful meeting new people," Masika said with a grin.

Rainn held her gaze for another moment, then stepped into the clearing before Masika could follow.

Slowly at first, the people looked his way and quieted. They smiled, excitement on their faces. An elder man with frizzy white hair stepped forward and bowed. He rose and waved to someone behind him, who struggled forward with a platter of fire-roasted foods.

"Evening, Radiance." He inclined his head, balding on top, to Rainn. "You've had a long journey. We got food and wine and soft beds for you to recover from your time in the trees. We're hoping you're willing to spend a little time with us before pressing on. Be a right honor, it would."

Hand leaving his sword pommel, Rainn cast a quick smirk over his shoulder at Masika and Heron, and strode forward, one arm raised in an expansive welcome. On his shoulder, Forbryttan repeated the gesture. "Honor's all mine, Mister . . .?"

"Abram," the white-haired man said, an eager smile on his face. "Just Abram. No mister. Your companions coming too? We can just leave some plates close to the trees if they'd rather stay all hidden-like. They like smoked beef?"

Masika stumbled out of the underbrush, and Heron carefully stepped after her. An audible sound of awe from the gathering arose at the sight of the goddess, even with her clothing in disarray from her trip through the trees.

Instinctively, Masika tried to reach out with Inlittan, looking for danger, looking for Glauth. But Inlittan refused to answer.

If she even could.

The Longeye bow was unstrung and put away, along with Masika's arrow. "We like smoked beef. We like that a lot. Can I have some?" The platter came her way, and Masika grabbed a handful of steaming beef, a red ring around the outer edges from the aromatic smoke.

Could they really have beef here in the Forests of Hell?

Cackling, Forbryttan jumped onto the tabletop and shoved food into his face just a bit faster than he could actually eat it.

Her eyes rolled back into her skull as she bit into it. "Ohgflrd, thfizamzng!" Every time Masika swallowed enough to be able to speak, she shoveled more food into her mouth. Finally, she stopped and breathed and glanced up at the circle of warm and amused faces. "Thank you. Thank you so much."

Ever graceful, Heron comported herself with a bit more dignity, though Rainn was an absolute mess. He may not have needed to eat, but he certainly enjoyed it.

Satisfied at last, Masika sat on one of the wooden stools next to Abram. The other people here kept a respectful distance, as if afraid of spooking their guests. It seemed almost reverential.

She tried to ignore Forbryttan, who lay on the table, one arm and one leg hanging off the side, his distended belly stretching toward the sky.

"Who are you, Abram?" Her mind at last off the food, suspicion flared in Masika's brain. "What is all this? Why were you here waiting for us?" She leaned forward, eyes narrow. "How do you know who we are?"

Abram grinned and refilled his wooden cup with wine from a clay jug. Sipping it, he closed his eyes and sighed. He opened them again and stared at Masika. "I'm a carpenter, and this's my house, and we're on the edge of Ring, the only real town in the Old Growth regency of the Forests of Hell worth the name." He swirled a fingertip in his wine. "Our regent and headwoman Taywilah—we just call her Tay— told us you was coming and that you'd be hungry. She said them two was gods." He waved his cup in Rainn and Heron's direction. "And that you was their guide and protector. I expect that makes you some kinda special."

The old man certainly answered Masika's questions, but he left her with even more. There was a town out here? She could neither see nor hear it from where they were, and Inlittan showed her nothing.

"How does Taywilah—Tay—know us?" Masika asked. Abram's open manner threw her. To all appearances he was exactly what he claimed to be. Her father taught her to sniff out liars and prevaricators, and this man showed none of the signs. "Are you allied with the Reaves? Baron Stolas?"

A kindly chuckle accompanied a twinkle in Abram's eye. "No, lass. We don't truck with demons, and your enemies can't reach you here. As for Tay, she was a sorceress when she were alive. A daughter of the Deep Witch over in the Paradisals. She's good people, but she knows things the rest of us don't, you kennit? Tay's took an interest in you three, and your little trimpet too. Whatever you're about, she wants to help. So I wanna help too." He sighed again and set his cup down on their end of a long wooden table. "Beds're this way." Abram hauled himself to his feet and pointed at his house. "All the doors lock, and you'll have the key. I got a room at a friend's to ease your minds. I'll be back in the morning to make breakfast, and Tay'll be by after that. How's that sound?"

Though Masika wanted to object, no reasons came to mind. Inlittan was certainly no help.

"I guess we'll see you tomorrow then," she said. Trusting people had not been a good idea in the Undergates so far, and Heron's newfound caution still rang in Masika's head. But once everyone else left and they had the house to themselves, Masika reasoned that she and the Alir could more intelligently plot their next moves.

Abram clapped her on the shoulder. "Hope you like sweet cheese buns for breakfast. Folks around here murk for 'em."

CHAPTER

THIRTY

Don't let anyone fool you, Undergates or not, marriage is the real hell. So why do I keep doing it? I married twice in the living world and four times here, and one of those was to a demon spy. And she's been the best one so far, if for no other reason than I hate getting beaten up, and she's mean enough not to have to attack me physically.

So what's wrong with me? Why do I keep making the same mistake over and over again?

Raven says it's because I'm stupid. But I think that's only half the story. I'm horny and stupid.

Royal Handük Morholt the Red of Savach, Dan Tura Province, and Keeper of the Cognition Engine

---

Morholt squeezed his eyes shut against the beautiful view from the tower top. Frustration jaded him to the golden sunset over fields mid-harvest, the happy sounds of the villagers at the bottom of the hill, and mostly from the sight of his stunning, maddening, and all-around flaming pinecone up the ass of a demon wife, Venthria.

"No, I am not going, and I'd appreciate it if we could stop discussing it." Venthria spun and leaned against one of the crenellations atop Morholt's broad tower. She crossed her shapely violet arms and shook out a headful of blazing white hair.

She knew what that did to him.

"Yes, you are." Morholt found himself wanting to pitch Venthria from the tower top into the courtyard below. He wasn't even sure it would hurt her, he just felt like making some kind of effort. "War's coming, and we don't know if we can win it. How would it look to your father if I married his eldest daughter and got her killed within the year? He's not really happy we're screwing anyway." He went to lean against one of the oversized war engines that adorned the tower roof and almost sliced his hand open on the smoky glass blades. He should know better. He designed the damn thing.

"My father will send demons to rescue you, Morholt. You only have to ask him."

He breathed, glaring at Venthria's pretty purple face. Sure. Her dad would *love* to station demons in Savach. Murden tolerated the human nation because Savach sold them slaves, but even Morholt's own father knew better than to let them set foot on the land. Something Morholt had already fucked up, if his most recent wife was anything to judge by.

He hated politics.

"Buy you a new dress," he said. Lame and ridiculous. "A pretty one. You can seduce all the dogs down in town with it." Amber light played in her hair, reflecting yellows and oranges through the crystalline sheen, and the dusky floral scent of her filled his head.

Bitch.

Venthria narrowed her eyes. "You're making fun of me, aren't you? Raven's up here, and the two of you are going to laugh at me behind my back as soon as I'm gone."

"No." He opened his arms. "Do you see Raven anywhere up here?" He glanced around as if to prove his assertion. A line of trees in the distance smudged black against the fields of Dan Tura, distracting and giving him pause. He knew what monsters dwelled within the Forests of Hell. He knew very well. If only he could make Venthria understand.

Silent, Venthria stared at him. She made a noise of frustration and gazed at the sky. "You know what? Maybe I *will* go back to Murden. I hate your sun and your nighttime and a sky that can't make up its mind what it's supposed to be. I'll just leave you and Raven to be killed by your past mistakes. You deserve it, you know. How many humans have shown up for you to pull your balls out of that fire? Huh? None is how many. Exactly none."

She stomped to the hatch and kicked it open. Morholt suppressed a wave of desire watching her ass jiggle as she moved.

"He's all yours, Raven!" Venthria shouted. "You're perfect for each other. May you die screaming each other's names."

She slammed the hatch shut after her.

For a full minute, Morholt stood in silence, the drooping sun casting stripes of shadow through the crenellations, the smell of harvested grain and evening fires breezing in to replace the last whisps of her perfume. Fuck her. Who wanted a sky without a sun in it?

Finally, he released his sister's invisibility.

"I'm good with making fun of her if you are," Raven said. As thin and pale as he was, Raven's hair was black as night, while Morholt's shone with sundown reds. She refused to wear typical courtly gowns and frippery in favor of her old black leathers.

"That woman isn't going to stop until my balls are mulch for her daddy's flower bed." Morholt dropped his head into his hands. "How did we bugger this up so bad?"

"We?" Raven's flat expression never changed. "I didn't tell you to follow your dick up a demon's ass. That's all on you."

"Not just Venthria." Morholt looked up and sighed. "All of it. All of them. How did Mom and Dad handle it?"

"Our parents murked the shit outta anyone who got in the way." Raven took out a dagger and held up the blade in the departing sunlight. "Which, as you'll recall, I told you that we should do too."

"Yeah. I know."

"What about the purple bitch?" Raven tossed a glance at the hatch.

"She gonna go running back to daddy? You're kinda fucked there either way."

Morholt picked at the embroidery on the sleeve of his fancy green coat. He wished he had his sister's courage to wear whatever he wanted. "I can probably make her life miserable enough here for her to leave. I do a pretty good job at that even when I'm not trying."

"You're a sack of sunshine today, Holt." Raven sheathed the curving dagger. "There's no contest for saddest red-haired dog turd, you know."

He smiled up at her. "Only because everyone else knows they'd lose."

CHAPTER

THIRTY-ONE

The Forests of Hell. It's not the Grim Pines, but I guess it's home now. At least here everyone is honest about wanting to break you and steal your shit, yes? Demon tribes want to murk you and steal your food, and human tribes want to break you and steal your young ones. Seems like it oughtta be the other way 'round, I think.

Anyways, I gotta run. Time to break some folks and steal their shit.

Runecrafter Glauth, Mistress of Flame and Regent of the Arrowwilds in the Forests of Hell

Somewhere off in the darkening wood, an animal screamed. Masika wondered if it were a victorious predator or its dying prey. Was there any allowance between being broken and returning the next day as the mirrored souls were and being murked forever for the animals everyone here ate?

The queasy off-color sun dipped out of sight, leaving the town of Ring in complete shadow. Only a few other buildings were visible through the massive trunks, and trees obscured the horizon in every direction.

"You like sweet cheese buns?" Rainn stood by the front door of Abram's cottage, frowning through a small-paned window as people outside closed their day.

Sitting upright in the center of a cushioned bench, her arms wrapped tight around her knees, Masika nodded.

"Do *I* like sweet cheese buns?" he asked.

Masika rubbed at her temples and rocked slightly. "Yes, Rainn. You would love sweet cheese buns. But I'd really like to talk about our situation here." After so long being betrayed or hounded by everyone in the Undergates, the idea of anyone acting this nice threw her into a spin. How could she possibly trust anyone outside this very room?

"This *is* about our situation." Rainn's right fist smacked into his left palm. "You know how much I like cheese."

The cozy red wood walls of Abram's cottage fairly screamed aging bachelor but still managed to be homey and welcoming for all that. Neat as a pin, with a single cleaned and dried plate beside a single well-used cook pan on a small but sturdy table, the small dwelling kept a lingering scent of spices, pipe smoke, and gentle consideration.

"Obviously there's no telling about Taywilah"—Heron slid onto the bench beside Masika and placed a hand flat on her back—"but I don't sense any malice in these people. That makes it hard to imagine that their leader could possibly be all that horrible." In slow, calming strokes, Heron moved her hand against Masika's back, as a kind older sister might.

Logic frustrated Masika. "Are you counselling trust? We don't know this woman or what she wants. They say they're not allies with any demons, but how do we know that? Our only guide was . . ." Masika found she could not bring herself to say Boridan's name. "Our only guide wouldn't have known either. Should we risk it and see if this Tay can bring us to Glauth or run off as soon as the light's fully gone and take our own chances? Abram said she wanted to help us, but what if Tay and Glauth are enemies? I just can't see what to do."

"And Inlittan?" Heron asked.

Masika shook her head.

Rainn thumped down on the other side of Masika and patted her on the knee with one rough hand. Warm. Brotherly. "I imagine I'd be worried about it too if one of my eyes just up and went dark. It'd be like half the world fell off. And here's you, the guide and protector to a pair of gods. Whew. That's a tough spot to find yourself in."

He cocked his head and smiled out of one side of his face. "But see, the kinda guide you are doesn't need magic eyeballs. The most important place you took Heron and me wasn't the top of Mount P'takkin or halfway across the fucking Undergates or even to stand in front of old King Oldam on the path to the Alireon. It was here." He poked Masika's shoulder with one finger.

"I took you to my shoulder?"

"No, fucknut." Rainn rolled his eyes. He was getting quite good at the gesture. "In your heart. In ours. You showed us what it looks like when people care about other people. We didn't really have much of that before. You changed us, Masika Oburn, Lahamila to Tennat Oburn, and Featherwind to Mahu and Sabni. And thank the mist you did."

Masika was unable to speak. She stared straight ahead at the cottage floor while sorting out both her feelings and how to ever talk again with a tongue that was suddenly much too large for her throat. *She* changed *them*? She never set out to do anything more than be herself, and now here was Rainn of all people, telling her that he cared enough to see her, to see what she meant as a person when Masika couldn't herself—to see it enough to be profoundly affected by it.

They saw more than she, or Inlittan, ever could.

Wordlessly, Masika reached out to either side of her and pulled the two gods close. She held them there, feeling their warmth and their love for her.

"But what makes them sweet cheese *buns*, exactly? Is the cheese sprinkled over a sweet bun and baked? Is it sweet cheese in the shape of a bun? Oh, that'd be good."

"Shh," Heron said. "Enjoy the moment."

Quiet voices intruded Masika's slumber, not rousing her enough to speak, only to search out through the dark with eyes barely opened. Heron had left Abram's bed where she laid down beside Masika and was talking in the main room with Rainn.

Masika crept to one side of the door, as silent as she could, to hear what the two gods were saying. It occurred to her that she was not being a good friend by spying, but she was sleepy, and announcing herself felt like a lot of bother. Besides, they might stop talking.

"What's that mean?" Rainn asked. His rugged face was open, vulnerable. Whatever conversation Masika had fallen into held real meaning to him.

By contrast, Heron's face was set. Even the hand she left on Rainn's knee showed her determination. "I'm saying that you were right. My perceptions of the world have grown bigger than they were when we lived in the Alireon." Her hand squeezed his knee. "I want more."

Rainn's eyes widened, and his glance flickered between Heron's face and her elegant fingers on his leg. Masika thought to make a noise or even move to close the bedroom door, but it was too late. They would know she had seen more than they were ready to share.

Now she felt like a terrible friend.

Rainn covered her pale and slender hand with his larger one. "I—I want that too. I don't think I knew it until I realized how fucking relieved I was when you decided you didn't want to go find Arso. I even considered pushing Boridan out of the skomp, but he never stood a chance anyway."

The long and tapered fingers of Heron's other hand found Rainn's dark hair and slid through it. Her gaze lingered on his lips. "No, he didn't."

Watching the interaction, Masika almost felt Heron's breath on her ear, down the side of her neck. She really should have closed the door herself at the beginning of all this.

Even as Heron drew Rainn's face closer to her own, he reached up and pulled her hand away. When he spoke, Masika felt the agony and the longing behind his words.

"I think you are everything I want, Heron. I think you have been for a long time. Maybe a really long time. But we need to wait a little longer. Just until we're outta here. Until we know what we're gonna do."

The goddess withdrew her touch, sat back on the loveseat, and stared into Rainn's eyes. "It's all right to be scared, Rainn. I'm scared too."

For a moment Masika thought Rainn would break apart while she watched. Conflicting emotions chased each other across his face and battled behind his eyes. He rallied and gave Heron a resigned smile. "You're right. I *am* scared. There's nothing in all the worlds I love more than you, and here you are in the most dangerous fucking place in all those worlds. I mean, the Undergates? I've never felt so vulnerable."

"Can't we feel vulnerable together?"

"Heron, I . . ." His mouth hung open as he searched for the words.

Tears hung in Masika's slitted gaze. She could not let them free.

"I can't."

Heron's head turned to one side, so slight as to be nearly imperceptible. She glanced at Masika but returned her attention to Rainn without comment. "You can't be vulnerable, or you can't love me?"

Included. With that slight glance, Heron reached out and folded Masika into her conversation with Rainn. Masika was not an intruder. She was family.

"I can't *stop* loving you." Clearly miserable, Rainn bulled ahead. "But this isn't like Angrim's table. No matter what kind of fuckery went on there, I knew it was out of my hands. Nothing I could do. Plus, gods. We couldn't die. But that's not now. Now we can die for real and forever, and it's on me to keep that from happening." He dragged in a ragged breath.

"And I can't, I just can't let myself go the way I want to. I want to love you completely, you know? Fuck the world and fuck the Undergates and fuck all of it except for me and you. But if I let myself do that, there won't be anything left for keeping us alive. I think just trying would break me for real."

For a long moment, Heron did not respond. Masika held her breath until she thought she might pass out. Then the goddess spoke.

"You're quite stupid, Rainn. Of *course* you can love someone and keep them alive. And we also have Masika for that. You know she's the kind of hero real legends are made of. She's already done more for us than Mirrik and Norrik ever did as mortals combined." She stopped, lowered her head, and sighed. "But I can wait, as you say, a little longer. I won't stop loving you, either, and I have faith in you, and in Masika, that we will escape this place and that you'll make good on our conversation here. Yes?"

She leaned over and hugged Rainn, bringing him tight against her body. He remained stiff, his eyes wide and unblinking.

At last Heron stood and patted Rainn on the cheek. She spoke facing Masika, with him just behind her. "I'm off to stare at the ceiling for the rest of the night. The sofa is yours. Good night, Rainn."

Masika flitted back into the bed, and shut her eyes firmly, as Heron returned to Abram's bed and laid down beside her.

Thankfully, the goddess allowed her the subterfuge.

THIRTY-TWO

The first thing I learned in the Undergates was not to trust a fucking sorceress. Well, the second thing, yes? The first thing I learned was not to eat anything handed to you by a giggling Hymrikker.

Runecrafter Glauth, Mistress of Flame and Regent of the Arrowwilds in the Forests of Hell

A polite knock on the front door woke Masika. Swimmy sunlight came through the panes in Abram's bedroom and struck the reddish wooden wall above Masika and Heron's heads.

The world seemed different today.

Carefully, Masika crept out of the bed and made her way through the common room to the door. Rainn's heavy breathing from the loveseat kept her quiet.

She opened the door.

"Morning." Abram carried a large basket made of interwoven wood slats in both hands. "Hope you're hungry."

As Masika stood aside to let Abram back into his own home, her stomach growled angrily. "I could eat."

"Start us a fire and I'll get to work on the cooking," Abram said. "Pot's in the cupboard next to the hearth. Hang it first. We'll want it hot to fry the buns."

"Mfnr." Bleary, Rainn sat up. "Hot cheese buns." He fell back over. Masika could not imagine he had gotten much more sleep than Heron, who tossed and turned most of the night.

"Heh." Abram tilted his head toward the backyard. "We'll set up out there. No place in here for this many people to eat, and Tay'll be joining us too." He set down his basket, opened it, and withdrew a stack of plates, a cloth wrapped around clinking utensils, and several handfuls of raw foodstuffs.

It was clever, Masika had to admit. Giving them a comfy space to settle so that it seemed as if Taywilah was meeting them on their own turf, when the truth was the opposite. No. Thoughts like that only prejudiced her before the meeting. She should judge then, as it went, instead of letting her suspicions rule the encounter.

Probably.

And still, no Inlittan.

The smells of bacon, eggs, and the buns—small chunks of sweetened goat cheese wrapped in thin dough and fried in the cookpot—woke Rainn where noise and conversation failed, and Heron drifted out of the bedroom soon after. Somehow, she had managed to clean the white evening gown and cape she wore, and even repaired the tears and snags from their flight away from Stolas's palace and travel through the woods.

Heron whistled an unfamiliar tune as she picked up the plates and whisked them out the back, something Masika never heard her do before. Was she happier, or was it an act?

Hair sticking in every direction but down, Rainn stood, stretched, and scratched his butt. "Thinks she's a songbird all of a sudden. Hey, we got any browl?"

Another wooden cup hit the cutting board, and Abram lifted the teapot out of the coals. "No, but the tea's strong. Wake you up just fine and tastes a lot better than browl."

Soon the whole group of them were in the backyard at the long table, eating and laughing. As predicted, Rainn loved the sweet cheese buns and even left a few for the rest of them. Forbryttan had moved from the tabletop to the grass beneath it, his snores a comforting buzz in the morning air.

"Remember when you didn't *have* to eat?" Masika asked.

"Don't be cruel, girl." Rainn swallowed and grinned. "This place really would be fucking hell if I had to sit here and watch the rest of you eat this."

If Rainn and Heron could behave as though nothing happened last night, it would certainly make it easier for Masika to pretend she knew nothing about it.

"Any left for me?" An older woman, dressed in a plain brown shirt and mustard-colored pants, her steely gray hair pulled back tight, stepped around the side of Abram's house. "Looks like I'm a little late."

"Not at all, Tay." Abram hopped off the bench and ran inside to return moments later with a cloth-covered plate. "I kept some aside for you, just in case."

The woman was Pavinn, her skin somewhere between pale Andosh and the much darker Darrish. The loose curls that fell from her hair tie lent her an islander cast.

"How do you do?" Masika stood and extended her hand, which Taywilah clasped in greeting. "I understand we have you to thank for all this hospitality."

"Not at all." Taywilah waved the notion away. "Abram here would've set you up without my asking. I just happened to feel you on the road, your shoes pointed to Ring. Seemed ill-mannered not to fix up something for hungry travelers."

"Hey," Rainn said between bites, "Abram here said you were one of the Daughters' Coven, from the Paradisals? We know one of your sisters. Ameli."

"After my time. Anyways, the Deep Witch's daughters only used to be my sisters." Taywilah picked up her cup of hot tea and settled across from Masika. "I got kicked out, which is why I'm here instead of the Untamed Paradise with the rest of my people. Fell in love with the wrong boy."

"He was a rotter," Abram observed, the twinkle back in his eye.

"That he was." She cut a fond glance back at the old man. "But let's talk about you. Ring is a beautiful little town in a whole patch of nasty, but I don't expect you came for the sweet cheese buns."

"We will next time." Rainn tossed the last one in his face and chewed on one side of his mouth. "Our Ameli got kicked outta the Daughters too. You two may have more in common than you thought."

"We're looking for Glauth." Masika thought it time to cut to the point. Heron watched silently, assessing any reaction from either Taywilah or Abram. "We need to borrow her for a bit, and then we'll move on. Does she live here in Ring?"

"Oh no. No, she don't live here." Taywilah took a sip of her tea and smiled, eyes half-lidded. "Perfect, Abram. Anyways, I'm regent here of Old Growth, and Ring is our capital. Or near enough, anyway. Runecrafter Glauth's regency of the Arrowwilds is on the border of the forests and Savach. It's a month's hike on foot, but I suppose we can lend you some mounts and a guide to take you down the right path."

"That's . . ." Masika did not quite know how to respond. "That would be incredible. I only wish there was something we could do in return."

"You could tell me what you're about." Taywilah's eyes narrowed, but her mouth held its genial smile. "Not to pry, but us in Old Growth are kinda standoffish at the best of times, and downright aggressive the rest of the year. My word would likely be enough to get you a meet with the runecrafter, but I'd like to make sure I'm not sending her something'll come back to bite me on the tit."

Rainn shrugged, and Heron gave Masika a nod. At the same time, Masika felt a wash of trust flow over her. A warm feeling of safety that started in her shoulders and ran down her back and chest. Was it a natural feeling? Was it Inlittan? No. Inlittan was gone.

All right. "There's someone in the living world who feels like they need to see Glauth again, and they're going to kill a bunch of people if we can't bring her back." Wasn't Taywilah supposed to have been a sorceress back in the living world? Perhaps that sudden intensity of trust was some sort of magical influence. That seemed a rude thought to think.

Masika tried her best to give enough information to make Taywilah feel no hidden agendas, but not to say anything too revealing at the same time. Her papa had been a master of finding that line.

"People dying above don't hit as hard after a few centuries in the Undergates." Taywilah placed her chin in one hand and tapped the side of her face, elbow on the table. "But that don't explain a pair of gods with you. No offense, but gods've never really gave a pickled shit about murdered humans."

"We're on the Hill Fury's business." At last, Heron broke her silence.

"That so?" Though largely untouched, Taywilah pushed her plate away.

Abram looked slightly crestfallen.

"I've heard of that creature, though I've never seen it myself." Taywilah shrugged. "But that's not good enough anyway. How do I know what some busybody ghost wants? Maybe she wants Runecrafter Glauth to come down here and set me on fire from the inside out. I need more than that."

Masika smiled. The feeling of trust redoubled. This was no spell. How could she even have suspected such a ridiculous thing? "Rainn and Heron were captured by Angrim, the horrible sorcerer-thing that ruled under Tyrrane."

"I know the son of the serpent," Taywilah responded.

"He did something to them, and now King Oldam won't let them back into the Alireon. An imp named Ild told us he would fix it if we brought back Glauth for him to kill again himself, though we're working on that end." She felt so good for having revealed everything to Taywilah. Trust built allies. And they needed allies to accomplish their goals.

"And I suppose him killing all them other people was just to add a little incentive?" the old woman asked.

Happy in her vulnerability, Masika nodded. "I guess so."

"Well, you all sure came to the right place." A big grin rose from Taywilah. "I happen to know where there's a hidden door from here right into the Alireon itself. Bypass all that nonsense with the imp. And High King Oldam too. I imagine he's still a big rock sitting on the road to the front doors? Yeah. He'd never even know you were back."

"A hidden passageway?" Heron leaned forward the tiniest bit. "Have you ever been through it?"

"No, no." Taywilah shook her head. "Didn't figure I'd be welcome. I'm just some dead sorceress, not a god."

"Where did it come from?" As she asked, Heron leaned further over the table, hunting for answers in the kindly water of Taywilah's past. "Do you know who built it?"

"Not directly," Taywilah answered. "But the legend is that Dorastros built it to hide all his lady friends. I hear he was quite the hound dog. Probably from being god of time. He could always make some time for himself if he wanted to get up to something he oughtn't."

Rainn's face darkened, and he stared at Taywilah hard. But his pique vanished as fast as it appeared when Taywilah turned to regard him with a warm wink.

"Could I go through it with you?" Masika asked Heron. "Would it be safe for me if you escorted me out as soon as we arrived?"

"Well, that's sort of a problem," Taywilah said. "I need something from you in exchange for me telling you where the door is."

One brow arched upward on Heron's forehead. "Oh? Certainly, that seems fair. What would that be?"

Taywilah pointed to Masika. "Her."

Something snapped in Masika's brain. Heron pulled away as if bitten, and Rainn's severe frown showed teeth.

"Lady, you're out of your lumpy, wet mind." Rainn slammed a fist down on Abram's table, and the old man winced to hear it crack. "Dorastros did *not* build a fucking tunnel to the Undergates in his goddamn shoe closet, and we wouldn't trade Masika to you for King

Oldam's farted-up throne. So anything you *could* give us isn't worth a runny turd. Do you hear me?"

"Sure. Whatever you want. But you're the only ones can go back anyways. You're gods. Rules are different for you." Taywilah raised her hands. "But a dead human's a dead human. It's not like your friend here can return home."

Another wave of warmth passed over Masika, but this time it found no purchase in her heart. This *was* sorcery. Unfortunately for her, Taywilah had pressed too far, asked too much. Even her magic could not come between Masika, Heron, and Rainn.

"You are fatally out of line, Tay." Heron stood. "This is your one chance to pull this back."

Instead of answering, Taywilah locked gazes with Masika. "Tell me, Darrish princess," her voice rasped, low and harsh, "do you *see* a way out of this where you get to live?"

Unbidden and unexpected, Inlittan sought an escape. Before one became apparent, Taywilah's hand shot out, curled in a quick circle in front of Masika's face, and jerked down to the tabletop. Her knife followed, stabbing through empty air and thunking into wood.

Masika screamed. Though it never touched her, she felt the knife blade punch through the front of her skull and into her mind. She never even had time to be happy that Inlittan was not dead.

With a roar, Rainn came across the table at Taywilah, only to shoot up into the sky as she flicked a finger at him while mumbling words under her breath. Heron tried a faltering spell, but Taywilah only laughed and flicked again, sending Heron flying backward to be held in place by suddenly animated trees.

Rainn shouted and raged, caught fast in nothingness, twenty feet above the table.

An instant later Taywilah grunted and kicked her leg against the underside of the table. Her face went ashen, and her eyes rolled back in her head. An orange flash popped beneath the table, and the sharp smell of ozone stained the air. "Excuse me a sec."

She reached under the table and lifted a dazed Forbryttan up by the tail, his tusks dripping bright red blood. "How are you not a big blue splat? That spell had enough juice to destroy thirty trimpets. And now I gotta heal my leg."

This time Taywilah closed her eyes and held out her hand, palm down. There were no more flashes, but the color returned to her face. She smiled and raised Forbryttan to the level of her eye. "Ah, you're another one. Same craftsman as made the seeing spell. Too bad I don't need an invulnerable trimpet." She flung Forbryttan over her shoulder and extended her healed leg. "That's better."

"What are you doing?" Masika tried to breathe through the piercing pain. "Please. Please stop." Pain paralyzed her. While Inlittan existed as no more than a concept here in the Undergates, that concept lived in Masika's head. Attached. One part of the other.

And now Inlittan extended invisibly from her skull, the other end of her pinned to a tabletop with a knife through it.

"This is an impressive creation." Taywilah lifted and pulled separated strands of air in her fingertips, each touch agony inside Masika's head. "I hope whoever made it dies soon. I'd love to get them on the payroll."

"Tay." Abram's voice cautious and steady. "What are we doing here? I thought these people were honored guests."

"Sure were, sugar." She reached over and plucked a second knife from the tabletop, hesitating only to catch Rainn's hurled sword in her other hand and drop it to the grass beside her. "Then they had to go and get all aggrieved over a simple request. Didn't even try to haggle first. Who does that?"

Abram sighed and lowered his head. "I'm going inside. Please don't murk anyone permanent."

"You know I can't promise things like that." Taywilah grimaced and glanced at Abram sidelong. "You're just trying to make me feel guilty when I do gotta murk someone. Well, it won't work. You already owe me anyways, so I don't gotta do anything for you."

He picked up some of the dishes and returned to his cottage.

Above, Rainn thundered deprecations and threats.

"Thing was trying to hide from me. Can't wanna hide unless you can want, and you can't do that unless you can think. So how's it do that? No brains." Taywilah rubbed her chin, considering the problem while Masika cried. "Oh, yah. It's *in* your mind. It's using your noggin to do its thinking. Ow. I bet this knife really does hurt."

From the trees behind Masika where Heron struggled against her confinement, a blinding white light accompanied the sounds of crackling flame. Taywilah glanced up.

"Looks like I got a timeline. Good for you, this next part won't hurt a bit." She raised the second knife and put it against Masika's skull, just above the point where Inlittan clung to her, body and soul.

"Well, that's a lie now, isn't it?" Taywilah smiled thoughtfully. "This is gonna really kick your brains in. I can't wait to see what you see."

The knife fell, slicing through Inlittan and severing the bond between her and Masika.

In that final, fleeting instant, Inlittan showed Masika one more thing. She placed a light over Masika herself, illuminating the person as she truly existed, stripping away all the self-doubt and recriminations. A strong young woman who stood loyal and true to her friends, and a clear-headed daughter who honored a father that loved and respected her.

Someone smart. Someone capable. Someone right and loving and determined.

Masika's world went dark, spiraling down through her screams.

THIRTY-THREE

Getting to be regent of the Arrowwilds was simple. The previous regent was a hoary old bastard named Figgi, and he'd been here for five hundred years. Long time, I think. That's what he said, anyway. He wanted me as one of his wives. Said I'd improve my station through him. Said a woman couldn't do anything for herself in the Undergates, just like in the living world.

Figgi'd been dead and out of knowing things in the living world a long time, I think. But he was right about one thing. I did improve my station through him. Burned my improvements right through the middle of him, yes? Got rid of all his old bastard friends too. The ones that couldn't stomach taking orders from a woman.

Kept the wives, though.

Runecrafter Glauth, Mistress of Flame and Regent of the Arrowwilds in the Forests of Hell

---

Speech eluded Masika. Only whimpers fell from her, bereft and dead limbed. Her head swelled with pain and blood.

"Is she gonna be all right?" Rainn's deep voice provided a

ground for Masika, a stable place to lie, maybe even stand, if she conjured up the courage.

"I don't know." Heron wrapped her in a scratchy blanket. "I think that . . ." The goddess's voice stalled, uncharacteristic rage choking her throat. "That *creature* somehow cut Inlittan out of her. I've no idea what that might do to a person. I can't even imagine how she did it."

Rainn grunted and rubbed the back of his neck. "Same way she made us all trust her. Magic."

The smell of burned forest trees overwhelmed everything else, an itch across Masika's pain.

A measure of control returned to Heron's voice. "We're fortunate she was one of the Daughters' Coven. Together they're an unstoppable force, but individually, not so much."

"Right. So we can take her. Now if Tay cut Inlittan out of Masika, then we can cut it back outta her, right?" Worry coursed through Rainn's tone. "We can put it back in Masika's head where it belongs?"

"Stop." Masika opened her eyes and squeezed them shut again. The bright world lanced into her fresh mental wound. "Allz's wounds, this hurts." She reached up and found them both. "Help me up."

The Alir lifted Masika into a sitting position, her back against a table leg.

"Thank you." The tears on her face went cold, and the space where Inlittan once lived filled itself with hollow vapors. "She's gone." At last Masika opened her eyes and faced the concern on the faces of her friends. That hurt too. "Allz's wounds, this hurts. I—I don't even know if Inlittan could survive something like that."

I don't truly know if I will.

The three of them held each other, Masika drawing strength from their love and uncompromising affection for her.

"Dry your tears, Masika." Heron lifted from the embrace and guided Masika's hair out of her face. "I can't imagine the pain you're in, but we need to find Tay now and get back what she stole from you. Speed may yet save Inlittan."

And maybe me. Masika left the thought unvoiced.

Smart. Capable.

Rainn helped Masika to her feet and the three of them, Forbryttan once more on Rainn's shoulder, went to the curving dirt road in front of Abram's house. No one said what Masika felt, certain they all thought, that it would be so much easier to find Taywilah with Inlittan guiding them.

"Hey, I, uh, I have something for ya." Abram's voice set Masika's heart racing. She spun to see him standing in the open doorway of his cottage. "Tay's gone. Said she had everything she needed now to murk Glauth once and for good. Took a bunch of fighters with her too. It's kind of a hike where she's going." Abram reached inside and produced three heavy packs. "Everything you'll need for the trip's in there. Yours got a map so you can follow her." He handed Masika the first of the packs.

"Why are you helping us?" Heron asked, somewhere between compassion and anger. "I've seen what Tay means to you."

A sour look came over Abram, and he fidgeted in the doorway, clearly wishing to go inside and shut the door behind him. "Because I'm hoping that me helping you will give you a reason not to murk Tay permanent when you go do what you're intending. Maybe for me?"

As unreadable as Heron's expression appeared, Masika knew she would not kill Taywilah. But without looking, she also knew that Rainn would.

"It was wrong, what Tay did. Horrible. But she's still my Tay. I still love her. And she crossed *two gods* doing it. I just . . ." He held out his hands, words failing him.

"We'll do what we can to keep from killing Tay." Masika's torn heart could not bear more hurt, more anguish from all of this, though she felt Rainn bristle beside her. "But you should know it won't be our first consideration. What she took . . ." How to say it? "She took a friend. Might even have killed her. Either way I'm taking my friend back, whatever that entails. If Tay'll let us do that without killing her, then that's what we'll do. If not, then I'm sorry too."

"I won't be sorry," Rainn said as they walked away.

THEY DREW LOOKS as they worked their way through the streets of Ring, though no one interrupted them. For the most part, the small town felt tidy and bustling, the folk friendly, and the sky more blue than green and slightly less queasy than before.

"Here's the right way out." Masika studied Abram's map, drawn in a clear, simple hand. It gave her mind something to focus on other than the painful wind that blew through her skull where Inlittan used to be.

"They're only a few hours ahead of us." Rainn stared at the trampled ground leading into the woods. "Long as we don't run ourselves up their asses, we can just hold back until they camp and make our plans then. Masika, you good?"

No, I am most certainly not "good." She nodded.

"That-a-girl." Rainn nodded to Masika and then to Heron. "Let's go."

After some effort scrubbing Heron's white gown and cape in dirt and leaves, they dirtied it enough to blend in rather than glow, beaconlike, through the giant trees.

"I think I like this better," Heron observed. "Though I smell like the floor of a horse stall. Are you sure you didn't rub any animal droppings on this thing?"

"You're making it up." Rainn smiled at Heron and winked at Masika. "Totally poop-free. Just grass and crushed leaves, some berries, and a handful of poop."

Heron rolled her eyes and passed her hands over the garments. The rough stains smoothed out to form a beautiful pattern of brown and green, with the occasional splash of soft rust or purple. A subtle scent of lavender wafted off it.

"You're remembering your magic." Masika tried to feel happiness for Heron but none came. She could still fake it though. "We'll get through all of this. I know we will."

Though she knew no such thing, it felt like something the confident young woman Inlittan showed her might say. Masika needed to honor that last vision, no matter how much it hurt.

Loving. Determined.

"Bits here and there," Heron admitted of her forgotten magic. "Not enough to rely on yet, but I'm getting there. It's like trying to read through a blanket."

That first night, they watched Taywilah's camp from a distance. She traveled with thirty-five warriors and made camp in clearings tailored for the purpose. Each of these were marked on the map with a tiny drawing of a campfire, and a dozen lay between Ring and Glauth's village of Ash. Regular changes of guard and scouts kept Rainn distant while he observed their habits.

"Thoughts?" Heron asked him on the second night.

"Yeah." Rainn scratched his stubbled chin thoughtfully. "I got an idea." He grinned to himself. "Heh. This is much better. We're gonna fuck up her whole day."

AS PLANS WENT, it was not terrible.

Masika watched Forbryttan slink off through the underbrush between the three-hundred-foot trees and vanish from view. His stealth hid him from normal eyes, but it wouldn't hide him from Inlittan, if Taywilah were looking. Yet Masika's understanding of her runecrafted ex-companion still fell well short of everything she and Inlittan might have done together, and her hope was that a similar breaking in period would, at least temporarily, hobble Taywilah. It remained possible as well that Inlittan would refuse to help her.

The idea that Inlittan inside Taywilah's head could scuttle Rainn's entire plan had not occurred to him. Once Masika mentioned it, he hoped the same.

As the three of them followed Taywilah and her fighters, Forbryttan would circle around them and run ahead. The trimpet required far less sleep than a human and was their best bet not only for getting to Runecrafter Glauth unseen, but also for surviving entering her camp long enough to talk to her.

They knew little about Glauth, and what knowledge they

possessed indicated a scary individual who burned you alive with magic first and, well, there did not seem to be anything after that.

If Glauth could be persuaded, she would lay a trap for Taywilah in the trees well before the old woman arrived at the village. When the trap sprang, Masika and the Alir would hit them from behind, ensuring Taywilah's forces would be confused and divided and easy to defeat.

Glauth the runecrafter could defeat Taywilah the sorceress, remove a threat, and be grateful to Masika and the Alir for the trouble.

The plan stank of uncertainty, but it also held enough possibilities for on-the-fly pivoting that Masika thought it doable.

"Seven days now?" Rainn's lack of counting ability both entertained and concerned Masika. Should they have followed his strategy after all?

"Nine, dear." Heron stepped through the leaf litter, never crunching one underfoot. "It was seven two days ago, and yesterday, too, by your count. For good or ill, Forbryttan ought to have reached Glauth by now, and she ought to have decided on a response. We should stay prepared."

"What's the matter with you?" Rainn asked Masika. "You been kinda quiet lately."

"Just thinking about when Tay cut . . ." Masika's mouth faltered, not quite able to make the words her brain told it to. "When Tay took . . ." She tried a third time. "Inlittan showed me, well, me. It felt like a final gift. I guess I'm just worried we won't get her back."

"What did you see when she showed you this?" Heron kept her gaze on the ground and glided silently among the trees.

She had not intended to share that part of it. Still, it felt natural that they would be curious. "It's embarrassing. I guess Inlittan thought I was some kind of hero or something. It does make me wonder if everything she showed me was the world as she saw it instead of simple truth."

Heron and Rainn exchanged covert smiles.

"What?" Awkward anxiety crept up Masika's spine. Well, of *course* they would make fun of her for such an idea. Though Heron said something similar herself back in Abram's cabin. "No, don't tell me. I don't want to know."

"That's how we see it, too, ya ninny." Rainn gave a chuckle. "I never met anyone needed a damn mirror more'n you."

"That was a fine gift," Heron said, her voice drifting through the wood. "And a true one. Being a hero isn't a job you do, Masika. It's not an aspiration. It's just who you—"

An explosion and screams cut across the misty woodland. Shouted orders followed, and the sounds of combat.

"That's us!" Rainn charged ahead, Masika and Heron hot on his heels.

While Rainn bulled through the tall trees, Masika cut left, her bow strung and arrow ready, while Heron went right, ready to blend into the brush and strike from concealment.

Strong. Loyal.

Masika lost sight of them both, though running figures ahead dashed among the trees, waving blades and cursing one another. The graver on her back was useless when she did not know where her friends were. It was too indiscriminate, too destructive.

Without Inlittan's help, she was better with the bow anyway.

"Fu—oof!" Rainn's shout cut off, and Masika stopped hearing him at all.

She tried to line up any kind of attack with her bow, but the running figures moved too fast, and she had no way of telling friend from foe.

A dagger pressed into her back and a rough hand removed the graver from her shoulder.

That might become a problem.

"Heya, girlie." A rough voice accompanied foul breath on Masika's shoulder. "Drop the bow so's I don't gotta drop you." He pulled her sword from its sheath from behind. "Your friends are prob'ly already grabbed. Nice sword for a girl like you. And what's this other thing you got? Is this a graver? Wonder if Tay'd let me keep it?"

Ahead, the shouts of combat turned to laughter. The whole thing was a trap.

She dropped the bow but kept the arrow tight in her fist.

Masika stomped on the unseen man's instep with the heel of her boot. He screamed. He stabbed forward, but Masika spun away, whirling and planting her arrow in his hairy neck. Even as he fell, her eyes slipped off his form, unable to track his movements. If his breath had not reeked so badly, she never would have known how close he was or where to stab.

Taywilah's magic made him—not invisible, but unable to be looked at. Denari clear the fog, how could they fight an enemy their eyes refused to see?

Graver, sword, and bow recovered, Masika ran ahead, ranging farther left. People shouted and ran after her, people hidden from Masika's normal, human eyes.

True. Clear-headed.

"Caught your trimpet. Again." Taywilah's whisper thundered in Masika's ear, and she spun, flailed out with her bow at nothing, over-balanced, and fell on her back with a grunt. "He didn't tell us what you were about, and we got tired of trying to destroy him, so I decided it'd be safer if we collected you up before the big fight. You shoulda stayed behind in Ring. Woulda been heaps safer than this."

Regaining her footing, Masika rushed ahead. She flew through scratching brush and grasping roots, but the sounds of pursuit only came closer. Pursuit her sight rejected. Masika dove through a wide bush.

Two dozen hard-bitten spearmen faced her, led by a tall, hatchet-faced woman in dark green furs, an axe in one hand and a shield in the other. Her eyes blazed bright orange.

"They're right behind me!" Masika dove to the ground. Since she could see them, she took the chance that they were not with Taywilah. "But Tay made them invisible. Get ready!"

Behind her, Masika heard Taywilah's forces closing through the brush, but in front, a spinning band of flaming runes encircled a tall woman's outstretched arm, illuminating her severe face and black hair, whipping in the sudden wind.

A blast of heat from behind pressed Masika to the dirt, arms over her head. The air whumped, and the sound of bodies falling to the ground thudded around her.

Black-scorched trunks smoked as high as thirty feet, while what recently had been underbrush floated gently to ground, a fine gray ash that settled over everything. Masika's sight continued to slide over the bodies of Taywilah's men, though the depressions in the ash they lay in, as well as the dusting of gray atop them, remained visible.

They died without time to scream.

"Thanks." Masika jumped to her feet and tore back the way she came, leaving an expanding plume of ash in her wake.

"Oldam's spear," the woman, certainly Glauth, growled as Masika fled. "Swing out" was all Masika heard before she got too far away.

At full speed, Masika stumbled into an unseen elbow and went down hard. Her world spun.

Across a tiny clearing, Heron lay on the grass, a line of blood running across her forehead. Close beside her an open pit welcomed anyone else fool enough to charge in without looking first, and Rainn's wrathful proclamations rumbled up out of it.

"I am gonna have *so* much fun tearing your fucking heads off and shoving them up each other's asses." Rainn bellowed. The heavy sound of falling dirt rose, announcing his determined efforts to free himself. "Hope you're thinking about your last words now. I'll be up there soon."

"Heh, heh," a gravelly voice said from above. "Oughtta watch where you're going. All of you oughtta. I can't believe how good that worked."

"Shut up, Sten," Taywilah said, a hissed command from some-where central to the clearing. "Glauth's out there. They got word to her some other way. The trimpet's a baffle. We need to—"

All the bushes took flame in a ring around the clearing. Masika reached out, grabbed the leg of Sten, Taywilah's fighter that clubbed Masika in the face, and buried her dagger into it, between the shin bones and the kneecap.

He screamed.

Masika dove toward Heron, roughly bumping into several more

unseen opponents, before grabbing the goddess and rolling right to drop into Rainn's pit. She fell on Rainn, who shouted alarm, and Heron fell on them both.

"What the fuck?" Rainn said before the sky turned white hot, and all three of them pushed their faces into the dirt to escape the burning conflagration.

Once again, bodies fell to the ground, and ash fluttered down on top of them.

"Tay?" Glauth's rough voice called from the medium distance. "You still there?"

A harsh cough answered, "I'm still here." Taywilah coughed again. It did not sound good. "Beginning to rethink this notion of attacking you though." More coughing. "Unh. Any chance we might call it a draw? You owe me one."

"Rainn," Masika whispered. The pit walls rose up fifteen feet. One side held rough gouges where Rainn tried to dig himself out. "Lift me up. Quietly."

"I don't think that's likely, old woman," Glauth answered. "The trees tell me you got some new power, I think. I let you go now and how long before you're back again? No, I got to murk you here. No more mercies, yes? I think yes."

The sounds of movement, shuffling and ponderous, halted Masika as she stood on Rainn's shoulders. It stopped, and Masika balanced on Rainn's hands so he could lift her higher.

Taywilah's dozen dead fighters stood in plain view, sorcerously reanimated, their smoking backs to Masika. They held weapons at the ready, and as Masika watched they faded from view. Glauth would be walking into yet another trap.

This was Inlittan. Somehow, Taywilah's magic drew Inlittan's power over sight out and used it against them. How many other things like this was Inlittan capable of that never occurred to Masika?

But where was Taywilah? Masika raised her bow, searching for any hint of an unseen presence. A footprint. A wheeze. Anything.

Near to where Masika stumbled into Sten's forearm, she saw Glauth's men and women creep forward, heedless of the unseen corpses standing in front of them. Behind them, Masika just made out the top of Glauth's dark-haired head.

Taywilah, still invisible, coughed.

Masika's spin threw Rainn's grip off, and she fell even as she released her arrow. She cursed, watching it fly left of her intended target. Masika landed in the soft dirt at the bottom of the pit flat on her back and knocked the wind out of herself. Above, Taywilah grunted, followed by the sounds of bodies falling to the dirt a final time. Masika had missed where she thought Taywilah stood, only to strike where she actually was. If Taywilah had been visible, Masika would have missed her for certain.

Soon, Glauth and two soldiers, similarly dressed in dark furs of brown and green, stared down at them.

Unable to do anything other than try to breathe, Masika watched them back.

"Hi there." Glauth waved but did not smile. "This time you'll hold still for a minute, yes? Although I think maybe I should thank you for this somehow." She held up a finger. "Sit there. I have a thing to do first."

Leaving the edge of the pit, Glauth walked out of sight. "Seems a shame to do this while you're not able to appreciate it, but I've made that mistake before. Last time we do this for a while, I think."

The undersides of the trees lit up in the glare of harsh flame, which immediately died back to a steady flame.

"Oh no. No. You can't." The reality of Glauth's action struck home. "Don't kill her. Not yet. Not while she has Inlittan!"

Smart? Capable? Loving? Determined?

Failure?

"What is that?" Glauth stuck her head back over the side. "She's pretty murked now. She had something of yours?" Glauth cast a quick glance toward the source of the firelight. "I don't think you'll be getting that back now. Sorry. Best to do things like that quick. Never know when a sorceress's gonna hop back up." At that, Glauth did smile. "But she won't be hopping back up now, right?"

CHAPTER

THIRTY-FOUR

Fire doesn't tell between good and bad. It doesn't care if you loved your babies or fed your livestock, yes? Fire just does the only thing it knows how to do. It burns. It cleans away what's in front of it and leaves a mess behind.

But it's a better mess. Complicated messes before fire, with treachery and stealing and threats, but after? Just need a bucket and a broom to clean it all up.

That's why fire is better than talking, I think. Ash doesn't talk back.

Runecrafter Glauth, Mistress of Flame and Regent of the Arrowwilds in the Forests of Hell

The village of Knifewall, seat of the Arrowwilds, nestled among the high trees on a low hill, homes, markets, even two long farms working their way up its gentle slopes. Glauth's keep rested atop the hill's crest, wooden palisades surrounding a two-story fortification that stared down on the village with calm indifference.

How many months had passed since they first entered the Undergates? So much walking, riding, flying, and only now did they finally reach the first of their goals. And how much had that goal cost them?

How much had it cost Masika?

From the top story, she stared down, too, at a lake that extended into the woodland, massive trees growing up out of its depths.

Two days ago, when Masika clambered up out of the pit at the site of the battle, nothing remained of Taywilah but bones and dust. Inlittan was well and truly gone, replaced by numbness. Numbness that left no way out but forward.

Their rooms in Knifewall were small but comfortable. The walls, floor, and ceiling were made of red-hued wood, a cheery fire crackled in a stone fireplace, and warm, worn quilts covered lumpy beds, already contorted into the shape of a human sleeper.

"I understand I owe you my life again." Heron smiled from the bed, but the happiness never reached her voice. She sat up, nestled in pillows, the dark leather pants and brown shirt she had been given to wear muting her natural radiance. "So, thank you. Again."

Masika tried to hide her sigh. The goddess worried for her. She wasn't alone. Masika worried for herself too. Inlittan was dead. How much had Masika come to depend on her, on her unique abilities to guide them? Now she was gone, just as Boridan was gone. No, more than that.

Throughout Masika's young life, someone had always been there to help her, to lift her up and show her the way, Uncle Mahu, her brothers Djephan and Kohmose, and Papa. Especially Papa. But they could not follow her here, and now those that sought to help on this side of death were gone too.

"We're still here for you, Masika," Heron said. "And we're here because of you. What Inlittan showed you about yourself really is true. And no one, sorceress or not, can take that away from you. That piece of Inlittan will be yours forever."

"Do you think we'll really get you and Rainn back to the Alireon?" Masika asked.

A flicker of indecision creased Heron's brow. "No. But not because we'll fail." At Masika's wide-eyed distress Heron raised a hand. "Wait.

Listen to me. Rainn and I have decided not to return to the Alireon. It's not our home anymore. The gods are uncaring and selfish, and we no longer have any wish to live with them."

"I thought you were still thinking of going back after Ild fixed you." Why did this bother Masika so much? Shouldn't she be happy? "Keeping the door open."

"We were." Heron's soft voice brought depths of compassion Masika never thought possible. This was what it was like to be loved by a god. "But why? The Alir have had since the beginning of time to change. To grow. But they haven't, and they won't. Holding our breath for that day doesn't help anyone."

The strength went out of Masika's legs, and she sat on the edge of the bed. "Too bad you didn't think of all that before we got to that bar in Greenshade. The not-so-Jolly Chicken." But she knew that for a falsehood. At the time, Masika only helped Heron and Rainn to show up Merities. No wonder her sister hated her so much.

She needed to change the subject.

"Do we know where Rainn went?" Masika asked.

"Feast hall," Heron answered. "It has its own wing on the ground floor. He heard they had some kind of fried lizard and went sniffing off. You hungry?"

"Mother Love's fortune, yes." Hunger pangs accompanied Masika's admission. Guilt too. Was she being a proper friend to Inlittan's memory if she allowed herself any measure of happiness? Her last vision swam up behind her eyes. Misery was not what Inlittan wanted for her.

"Let's go eat."

The smoky atmosphere of the feast hall transformed from eye-watering to comfortable to outright cozy, a good trick in a space twenty feet wide and twice that long. Rafters hung beneath peaked ceilings, and huge round windows, open to the night, cut into the roof to whisk off some of the thick haze. A roaring fireplace stood at either end, and one of a pair of long tables suffered under the weight of mountains of roasted meats, tubers, and breads. The smells tried to overwhelm Masika, tugging at the more animalistic, and hungry, side of her brain. Fried beasts and charred roots, berries and brines, ales and flame, the scents painted a scene of excess and camaraderie that frayed her restraint.

At the table's head sat Glauth, holding court over her warriors and laughing as Rainn finished some tale of his godly exploits. Masika never heard him speak of his days before his capture by Angrim. He treated that portion of his history as if it happened to another person entirely. Perhaps it had.

In front of Rainn on the tabletop, Forbryttan sat cross-legged, enjoying a plateful of food close to half his size.

"Heron, Masika! Join us." Rainn raised his flagon, and a score of fighters, mixed Andosh and Darrish and a single Pavinn, both men and women as well, joined him. Glauth nodded, and two of the dark fur-clad warriors moved down the table.

The two women sat to one side of Rainn.

"Rainn here explained that you sent your trimpet to warn us of Tay's attack." Glauth's manner was languid, but her gaze glittered beneath those lazily lidded eyes, not unlike Taywilah's. "It was a brave thing to do. I'm glad it didn't all turn out for the worst, yes?"

"And for that we offer our thanks to you." Unbidden, burly smiling fighters piled more food onto Masika's plate than she could eat in a month. "Um, for this too." Her stomach urged her to shut up and eat. "But how did you know where we were? How did you find us to rescue us?"

"Try this one." Rainn pointed at a slab of meat on her plate coated in crunchy fried nuts and flour. "Some kinda lizard monster. Best thing I ever ate."

"We knew nothing about you being there." Glauth's thin hand described a vaguely apologetic gesture. "The trees told me where the invaders were coming for us. Finding you before Tay killed you was just good fortune, I think."

"The trees told you?" Heron cut a piece of pickled fish and onions. Her eyes lit up when she popped it in her mouth. "Oh, this is delightful."

"Aye, yes. The trees." Glauth reclined in her chair, somehow making it seem more thronelike than the other, identical chairs. "Tay managed to evade every one of our scouts, but being regent in the Arrowwilds isn't without benefits, yes? She did not know the trees tell me what walks under their branches. All her new magics did nothing to protect her. Not from Masika's arrow in her head, I am thinking."

In Taywilah's head? Masika loosed blind at an unseen target. She had not known where her arrow hit the woman, only that it had killed her.

Appetite gone, Masika stared at her mounded plate. It had not been Glauth's fire that killed Taywilah. That only ensured she would never return to the Undergates. It had been Masika's arrow. That meant it was Masika who killed Inlittan too.

Quietly, Rainn squeezed her knee under the table, and Heron placed a soft hand on her shoulder. Their support flowed into her, buttressed her.

"So why are you here?" Glauth asked. "What can the rebels of the Arrowwilds offer to pay back your efforts? After all, you fought at our sides and made the killing blow against Taywilah the Bleak, yes? That is deserving of honor."

The other fighters shouted and banged their cups on the table in loud agreement, sloshing everything in sight with strong ale.

"We're looking for Morholt the Red," Rainn answered. "And I guess we'd like for you to come with us."

The warriors met this with even louder banging and shouting, as well as quite a bit of laughing and chest-thumping.

Glauth stood and held out her arms, palms down, until the rowdy table quieted.

"What you say is true?" Glauth asked. "You go to the Runecrafter Morholt and want me to go too?"

"It is." Rainn smiled, only somewhat tipsy.

Once they had Glauth with them, they had only to find Morholt so he could show them the way back to the living world. With so much behind them since arriving in the Undergates, final success waited almost within their grasp.

But Masika sensed a problem in the smoky haze that she could not yet see clearly. At least for the moment, she could be thankful that Taywilah went down before revealing all the secrets her sorcery had pulled from them. What would Glauth do if she knew Heron and Rainn were gods? It was long past time they started guarding their identities more carefully. Thus far trust, magical or not, had not exactly played in their favor.

Raising her cup above her head, Glauth bellowed triumphantly into the hall. "Soldiers of the Arrowwilds, this is the sign we've been waiting for, yes? Tomorrow, we ride to war against the wicked Runecrafter Morholt the Bloody Mouthed, father slayer, demon lover, and persecutor of his own kind. Tomorrow, we ride for vengeance!"

Beneath the thunderous roaring of the table, Masika dropped her head into one hand.

Ah, there it is.

CHAPTER

THIRTY-FIVE

I'm not one for vendettas. By the time a blood feud happens, everyone's already lost anyway, so what's the sense in fighting about it anymore? There's more'n enough excuse to fight for things what actually matter in the Undergates already. Some demon wants to eat all your toes, some new warlord wants to make you kiss his boots, anything involving feet, really. Course, I lost my own feet ages ago. All I got now are these big steel clompers.

But then I'd probably fight over those too.

Jarl Refur the Bent

Wide double doors in the middle of the long wall crashed open, and Jarl Refur of Hiimryk, flanked by a pair of huge northmen, stomped into the feast hall in a cloud of steam and hissing joints. Wolf pelts fluttered on their shoulders as the ancient jarl scanned the room.

"Runecrafter Glauth," he said, his gravelly voice carrying easily over the alarmed sounds of the crowd. "Thanks for looking out for my charges here." He inclined his head toward Masika and the Alir.

"Soon's the feast's done, I'll be returning them to Hiimryk, where they belong."

"Jarl Refur." Glauth slid back into her chair, resembling some great cat eyeing new prey and trying to decide if it was worth running down. "You and yours're invited to eat, as you always are, but these are under my protection. They're allies now. We go to war tomorrow."

"Hey there, buddy." Rainn craned his neck to wave at Jarl Refur. "Glad you weren't in that flying brick when it got exploded at the edge of the Firefields. "That woulda sucked."

"I'm glad too." Jarl Refur bowed to Rainn. "But it was a noble murking in pursuit of a worthy goal. I wrote a wonderful poem about it."

"Please, no poetry at the dinner table," Glauth said, both hands raised to ward away any potential doggerel. "So you gonna sit or we gonna fight? Why do you want these three so bad you'd fly all the way to the Arrowwilds for them?"

From his seat on Rainn's plate, Forbryttan's toothy grin shone at Glauth. "I beat six of his best fighters in a game of punch-my-face. He's still sore about it."

Jarl Refur's bushy gray eyebrows pulled together as he regarded the trimpet. He raised his tired old eyes to Glauth. "You don't know who you're feasting with, do ya?"

Nausea gripped Masika. She should say something, take command of the situation. But what would she say?

"I thought I did." Glauth stared at her three guests. "But maybe we didn't get that far, is what I'm wondering. Maybe you should tell me."

"We just want—" Masika began.

"Them two are Alir." Jarl Refur pointed to Heron and Rainn. "They're gods of the Andosh, and they oughtta be in Hiimryk, where the Andosh got their own afterlife. And you oughtta know I'm willing to fight about it."

"Never met a northman who wasn't." Glauth's gaze never left Rainn's face.

Mother Love's fortune! Must everyone in the Undergates know our story?

"You can't take us." Masika stood and turned to face Jarl Refur. His stone shoulders were almost as wide as he was tall, though no balder than his skull. "We've already agreed to fight alongside Glauth here. If you make us break our word, you bring, uh, dishonor all over your gods." It sounded lame, even to herself. "Sorry. We can't do that."

"Wouldn't want a dishonored god, would you?" Glauth asked.

Jarl Refur rolled his ice-blue eyes. "I accept their dishonor on myself, right? It's on my own head."

"That might work," Glauth admitted, "except a pair of gods're worth a lot more in a war than two lucky travelers, I think. No deal."

"Don't wanna fight you." Jarl Refur slumped, his scarred and whiskered face resolving into a frown. "It won't go well for you, and I've always liked you, Glauth. There's another twenty-five Hiimrykers waiting in the squareboat, and that's twenty-four more'n it'd take to peel Knifewall like an overripe apple."

"Thanks." Glauth sat up and grinned. "But I'm kinda wanting to fight you now, yes? You eaten yet? I hate to burn a man without a proper meal in his belly."

Jarl Refur simply sighed. "As you will."

FRUSTRATION HEATED Masika's cheeks as she watched the preparations for the contest of arms. She had no idea which combatant might emerge the victor, but either way, Masika felt like the loser.

Jarl Refur stepped off the wooden planking onto the tiny island, and his own men withdrew it behind him. Thirty feet away, Glauth waited on the opposite side, short spear in hand.

The island was little more than a packed mound of sand in the center of a moat, surrounded by hundreds of the men and women of Knifewall, and Jarl Refur's twenty-five clanking Hiimryk warriors, plus seven more stone boats' worth that had arrived since dinner. As the rules were explained to Masika, the fight ended when one of the two combatants broke, yielded, or touched the water. If Jarl Refur won, they would return with him to where their journey in the Undergates began. Or close enough, anyway. If Glauth won, on the other hand, Jarl Refur and his rebuilt northmen would accompany Glauth to kill Morholt.

A dozen Hiimryk guards and another dozen Knifewall fighters watched her and the Alir warily. No one was taking any chances that Masika's group might try to flee. Not that they could anyway. Running away from Glauth defeated their purposes for coming to the Undergates to begin with.

"How do you keep getting us into this sorta shit?" Rainn poked Masika with an elbow. As guests of honor, they stood on the moat's edge, able to witness every parry and thrust. "You know, gods never have problems like this. We're whaddyacallit . . . Heron?"

"Perfect," Heron answered with a sly smile. "Never make a mistake, never need rescuing from torture chambers beneath dreary old citadels, and certainly never need a human girl to save us over and over again." She smiled and crossed her arms, watching Jarl Refur cut the air with a wide blade. "Absolutely perfect."

"Yeah, fine. I get it." Masika bit her lip and winced when a horn blew, signaling the beginning of the combat. "Nobody's perfect."

"What?" Rainn drew himself up in mock indignation. "That's the *opposite* of what I said. You're kinda stupid, human."

"Shush." Masika's gaze flickered between Jarl Refur and Glauth as they circled one another. "We need to decide what we're going to do when one of these two spoiled children murders the other one. We can't go backwards, and we can't kill Morholt. Any ideas, or are we just making fun of me?"

"Can I challenge someone?" Rainn glanced around, settling on an elderly woman shouting bloody support for Glauth. "I bet I could take her for our freedom."

A gout of flame arrested everyone's attention on the fight. Jarl Refur frowned and pulled the burning wolf fur from his shoulders and threw it to the sand. He swung his sword in a wide arc in front of him and stepped forward.

The northmen cheered. Several of Glauth's people held their breaths.

Faster than Masika would have given the ancient fighter credit for, Jarl Refur dashed to Glauth's side of the island and swung a quick and heavy flat of the blade at Glauth's upper arm, intended to lift her bodily and throw her into the moat.

Masika gasped to see the fight ended so quickly.

But Glauth ducked the smashing blow, spun out from beneath it, and delivered a two-handed swing of her spear across his back to shove him into that same water.

She might as well have struck a mountain.

A low sword stroke forced Glauth to leap back, an intent smile plastered on her face. Her free hand wove a quick and intricate series of gestures, and a five-foot wall of flame sprang up between the two. She raised her hand and extended the arm, and as she did, the flame wall rushed across the ground at Jarl Refur, hemming him in and leaving him no place to go but the moat.

The citizenry of Knifewall thundered approval, and the northmen grumbled into their beards.

"Huh," Rainn muttered.

"What?" Masika asked, watching the flame race closer to Jarl Refur.

And Jarl Refur stepped through Glauth's fire wall and threw his sword at her head. His clothes caught fire, but he ignored it, smoking as he ran.

Glauth dodged to one side but left herself open to Jarl Refur's stone-fisted punch to her midsection, raising her from the ground before she fell and rolled onto her back.

A woman in the crowd screamed when the pommel of Jarl Refur's thrown sword glanced off her hip, prompting hooting laughter from Forbryttan. "I bet she wishes she was invulnerable!"

"Ask me later." Rainn's attention remained on the fight.

Almost gently, Jarl Refur scooped Glauth up on the iron toe of one foot and kicked her toward both water and victory. Glauth's grunt rose above the groans of Knifewall, and the northmen raised their arms and banged happily on their shields.

Once again Masika's eyes went round, watching the runecrafter spiral through the air, only to land on the downslope and arrest her roll with an outflung hand.

The sand beneath Jarl Refur's other foot glowed orange and shiny, and the big Hiimryker slipped and fell on his ass, flecks of molten glass splattering in every direction. He howled while the melting sand expanded beneath him, and he slid down the side of the mound into the moat with an explosively hissing gout of white steam.

After an instant of silence, Knifewall burst into joyous celebration.

"Looks like we move forward, not back." Heron cupped one hand and shouted to be heard. "Though I'm not certain how much better that is. We still need to keep Morholt alive."

The steam sputtered out and left a dark glass slide down the island's edge into the bubbling water. Glauth stood on the sand and laughed at Jarl Refur's fingertips, just cresting the surface and waving for help.

A pair of enormous Hiimrykers jumped in to lift Jarl Refur from the bottom. He came up with his back encased in a blob of brown and black glass nearly as big as he was.

The Jarl's own coughing laughter, not stunted in the least by his inability to stand up straight, eased Masika's worry. The Hiimrykers and the people of Knifewall picked it up and embraced each other.

Soon, they would all march to war together.

Rainn tapped Masika and Heron on the arm and led them away from the happy crowd. "In here," he said, and entered the first home he came to, a tidy house with plants by the front door and large glass windows.

Forbryttan hung off Rainn's shoulder and grinned a frightening grin into Masika's face. "I've never been in a *war* before. I can't imagine anything more fun!"

The sounds of the crowd withered as Rainn shut the door. "Right, that's better." They stood in a small sitting room with a round rug and a pair of rocking chairs. Embers glowed sedately in the decorated fireplace. "So what're our ideas? How do we march off to kill the very fucking guy we need to get outta this place?"

"We need to get out in front." Thoughts whirled in Masika's brain.

An impossible problem, sure, but that never stopped them before. "If we get to Morholt's castle or whatever first, we can escape with him before everyone else charges in behind us."

"If we can get in without Morholt's forces killing us." Heron picked a ceramic swan up from the mantle, turned it in her hand, and replaced it. "And if he can so easily escape, why would he even be there when we arrive?"

And how would they find their way to him without Inlittan?

"I think I have an idea there." Rainn showed his teeth in a tight, feral grin. "Glauth isn't the only runecrafter these people have. Heard about it over ales last night. She's been teaching others how to do it."

"And?" Masika found herself leaning forward to listen.

"And one of them makes storms."

"Oh." Masika rocked back on her heels. "That could change everything."

As the god of doing things out of doors in poor weather, Rainn typically displayed much less power than his more famous family members. But in a genuine storm, such as no area in the Undergates yet demonstrated, his strength, speed, and resilience jumped up to alarming degrees.

"I don't like relying solely on brute force for our plans, but that *is* a fortunate happenstance." This time Heron picked up a tiny straw doll of a farmer with a wide-brimmed hat, inspected it, and set it back down too. "We'll have to revisit any other ideas after we see what we're up against, but this's a good start."

"What about you, Heron?" Masika watched her run her long, tapered fingers over a pair of wooden owls. "Any luck remembering your magic?"

"A bit." Heron closed her eyes, and her perfect brow creased ever so slightly.

All at once, she became a dusk heron. Soft gray feathers, dark, daggerlike beak, and the same glittering emerald eyes.

Masika's heart leaped up into her throat. How long had Heron spent in this form, unable to resume her human shape?

And as if responding to Masika's worry, Heron became the beautiful woman with the soft gray hair again, her brown shirt fluttering out and tight leather pants hugging her hips.

"It's not much yet, but it's a start," she said.

"What about that burning light thing?" Masika remembered Heron scorching the tree branches that held her. "How does that work?"

"Inconsistently." Heron turned away from the mantle. "It seems to happen when I'm afraid, but I think I have some avenues to work with there. Nothing like Glauth though."

Not the news Masika was looking for, but a scout in the air could only help. "Rainn, you sounded like you figured something out during the fight. Anything helpful?"

"No, I don't think so." Rainn settled in the larger of the two chairs and rocked back and forth. "I like this. But I just figured out why we appeared in the Reaves instead of anywhere else in the Undergates."

"I just assumed everyone did." Masika sat next to Rainn. The chairs *were* nice.

"We never asked, but I don't think so." Rainn scratched his stubbled chin. I bet everyone goes where they belong. Andosh to Hiimryk, Darrish to Damah, Pavinn to the Untamed Paradise."

"And unbelievers?" Heron asked.

"Fuck if I know for sure," Rainn said, "but if I had to lay my dick on the table, I'd say they go to holes like this, in the Forests of Hell. Or that Hunter's Sweep place where they caught the soft foal. Babies don't believe in shit. But I bet that's why Glauth and Refur knew each other, because she appeared there first and left. That fight convinced me of that. They clearly weren't trying to hurt each other. Not for keeps, anyway."

"But why didn't the two of you appear in Hiimryk then?" Even as she asked the question, an unsettling answer formed in Masika's head. She pushed it aside. "And why didn't I go to Damah?"

Heron sat cross-legged on the rug. "I can guess at that. Rainn and I went to the Reaves, because Issta is the closest thing to our kind in the Undergates."

"Ugh. That's goddamn disturbing." Rainn scowled and gave a shiver.

"I know." Heron nodded at him. "And you, Masika, no longer believe in the truth of the P'tak. The only Darrish gods you've ever met tricked you into drinking poison and manipulated you. Why would you believe in that?"

"Never meet your heroes," Rainn observed.

"But I do believe in the two of you." It all made sense now. Masika's expected shame at losing her faith in the P'tak never materialized. Instead, she felt pride? "So wherever the two of you go is where I belong. I think that makes me happy."

Rainn laughed and clapped his hands. "May not be worth an asshole full of whale oil, but it's nice to hear."

With one hand over her mouth to hide it, Heron smiled. "Entirely repulsive. Hard to believe this is what an improved god looks like."

He winked at Masika. "There's always time for lube. You should see what they use in the Alireon. Takes three slaves and a cauldron of boiling lye to clean up after."

THIRTY-SIX

Killing your parents isn't as easy as people make it out to be, even in Hell. Sure they abused you and beat you and rented you and your sister out to their friends for kicks, nailed your feet to the floor and laughed when they ordered you to dance and you just stood there and cried, and then they had you sing "the Hymn of Short Jonn and His Mother's Giant Cock" in front of your whole school with a pissed-off razor-roach squirming around in your shorts, but ten is an awkward age for anyone, and it's still not an excuse for murking someone.

So instead, I just threw them in the same dungeon cell and ordered them given enough food and water to keep one or the other alive. Barely. Eventually they'll kill each other, and it won't be my fault at all.

Royal Handük Morholt the Red of Savach, Dan Tura Province, and Keeper of the Cognition Engine

W
ow." Rainn blew a low whistle. "I was not expecting that."

Masika agreed. Three weeks ago they marched out of Knifewall into the wastes of the Arrowwilds with fifty armed men and women, fierce soldiers all in their dark green and brown furs and leathers, as well as two hundred Hiimrykers in eight flying stone boats over their heads. Now they numbered over a thousand strong, as well as a monstrous lizard called a cave claw, at least sixty feet in length, despite its squat appearance and lack of a tail. The wide mouthed monster's green and black scales hissed as it moved with the voices of a thousand serpents.

"I know it's been me who was so free with the information before we got here," Heron said, one hand massaging the other to bleed off her nerves, "but I was just doing what my instincts told me to do. And my instincts are not telling me this is a good idea."

Behind Glauth's war wagon, a massive six-wheeled conveyance pulled by a team of twenty saurox, oversized oxen with two rows of high red horns and long muscled tails, Masika, Rainn, and Heron walked the broad road to Dan Tura, the province of Savach where Morholt the Red mercilessly ruled.

Or so Glauth insisted.

"You've said." Masika glanced over her shoulder at the cave claw, Glauth's mighty monster lizard-thing. Two hundred feet of marching soldiers separated them, yet every time Masika glimpsed it, the thing stared right at her and licked its four-foot fangs. They constantly had to rein Forbryttan in from challenging it to a fight. "But I disagree. And the sooner we tell her the better. Rainn, you have anything to add?"

"Nope." He gazed straight ahead as he marched. "I'm done arguing with you. Tired of looking stupid."

Abruptly, Forbryttan leaped from Rainn's shoulder in the direction of the mighty lizard. The jump carried him three full feet before Rainn snatched him by the tail and left him hanging in the air.

The trimpet kicked his feet against Rainn's wrist. "Aw . . ."

"Fine." Heron adjusted the collar of her shirt and tutted. "Let's get it over with then. But I'm coming with you."

The two women trotted ahead and waved to the soldiers at the rear of the wagon, who lowered a ladder to them. Heron went up first, followed by Masika, whose neck burned with the hungry gaze of the cave claw.

"This way." One of the soldiers walked them around to the front of the aft castle and opened the ornately carved door. Warmth and the smell of stew and ale wafted out.

"Hello!" Glauth stepped away from a big round table with miniature armies, castles, a long lake, and a tiny wooden cave claw on it. A dozen other people, including Jarl Refur but mostly elders of the Arrowwilds, frowned down at their plans. "Changed your minds about riding to war in style, I think. It's good to have you here. Our friend Jarl Refur isn't so sure we're bringing enough spears, yes? I think he's just cranky because he can't get all the glass bits out of his fussy old butt."

"You're new to the Undergates, woman." Jarl Refur squatted down to take a closer look at the mountain pass behind Dan Tura, shrugged, and raised his head. "Savach's got a reputation."

Glauth rolled her eyes and grimaced with one side of her face. "So will we when we kick Morholt in his pearly pink stones, yes? Now what is it you want to talk to me about, goddess Heron?"

"This one's all her." Heron pointed to Masika and stood aside. "I'm just here to watch."

"Maybe we can have a little privacy?" Masika asked. As a show of trust, she carefully lifted January's graver from her shoulder and leaned it against the wall.

"No." Arms crossed, Glauth stared down at Masika. "You can say whatever you want in front of all these people, is what I think. Yes? I trust them with, well, I trust them with *your* life, anyways."

"Yeah. Great." Masika swallowed and squared her shoulders. "You want Heron and Rainn's help, and according to Jarl Refur there, you're going to need it."

"This is true," Jarl Refur acceded.

"And what are you wanting in exchange for all of this godly help?" Glauth asked. Her gaze bored into Masika, making her feel both naked and small. "I assume you're here at this late hour to squeeze me for something, yes?"

"We need Morholt alive." Despite the glower from Glauth, Masika plunged ahead. "We need to return to the living world. Morholt knows how. And we need you to come with us."

Chuckles broke out across the map table, but Glauth only narrowed her gaze.

"Why do you think I should come with you?" Glauth asked. "Not that there is anywhere to be going."

"Ild wants you." Masika's words worked a change in Glauth, though it remained to be seen what that change meant. "He's angry you left him, and he wants to kill you himself. But we have your friends Catlia and Romi working on a way to protect you once you're back. I think you'll be safe."

She failed to mention that it would be Ild who intended to put Glauth's body back together enough for her soul to inhabit. Masika did not know exactly what this meant. Would Glauth's corpse be waiting for her in the far north where it fell, or would Ild have it? If the imp already possessed Glauth's body, instead of somehow mystically rejuvenating up in the Grim Pines, there would be no chance for anyone to protect her.

"There're more myths about doors to the living world than there are demons in the Undergates, girl," Jarl Refur said, kindness in his voice. "And they all got the same thing in common. They're all pigshit. Whatever you think it is Morholt can do for you, he can't."

"If what Jarl Refur says is true," Heron's silken voice floated across the humid chamber, "then you have nothing to lose by agreeing to our terms. We'll ask Morholt for help, he won't be able to give it, and you can murk him as much as you like. So do we have your promise, Glauth of the Arrowwilds?"

Glauth glanced down and back to Masika. "And if I were to give you this promise, how do you know I would keep my word?"

Although fully expecting the question, Masika had no answer for it.

Until this instant.

"Before I died and ended up here," Masika said, "my hero was the Hill Fury. We're friends now. I can call her Sarah."

Glauth's eyes narrowed further.

"I ran down every legend I could find about her. Studied any account of anyone she ever met. Anyone she"—Masika paused for Glauth's benefit—"killed. On purpose or not. Hey, Jarl Refur. Did Glauth here tell you the real reason she wants to kill Morholt?"

"I agree to your terms." Glauth spat in her hand and extended it to Masika, dirty anger in her glare.

Returning the gesture, Masika shook it.

"Don't really care why," Jarl Refur said with a shrug. "Though if the red fucker truly does have a way outta the Undergates and takes you lot with him, that's gonna ruin my day when I get home empty-handed."

"Then you shouldn't have taken it so easy on me in our fight, I think. Now the rest of you go." Glauth waved at the door and returned to the table, her back to Masika. "We have plans to make."

"WHAT NOW?" Rainn smiled wide as Masika's account neared its end. "I thought this was about Morholt raiding into the Arrowwilds and selling the captives to demons for slaves. That's not it?"

Restlessly, Forbryttan swung from Rainn's left shoulder to his right. "We're still gonna have a war, aren't we? You didn't talk her out of it, did you?"

"I don't think anything could talk Glauth out of her little war, Forby. The lady's determined," Heron said.

"Yay!"

Once again the little group walked behind the giant war wagon. Forbryttan amused himself by sprinting ahead of one of its massive rear wheels, letting it run him over and racing to do it all over again.

"I think Morholt's father was the slaver." Heron's vague smile showed her satisfaction with the way events played out in Glauth's war wagon. "But the son is supposed to be even worse? I don't know. It all seemed a bit nebulous to me."

"What's *nebulous* mean?" Rainn asked.

"Bullshitty," Heron answered.

"The real reason Glauth hates Morholt is because they were married." Masika stepped over a deep rut in the woodland road. "Or maybe they were boyfriend-girlfriend. I'm not entirely sure. She's a jilted ex. I figured there was no way she'd have confided that to anyone."

"That'd do it." A firm nod from Rainn indicated his opinion of those kind of relationships. "And if the rest of these fuckers found out, they'd likely turn tail and run. Can we use that?"

"No, because Glauth would just go with them. Anyway, that wasn't the important part." Masika scratched her head as she walked. She needed to wash her hair. Things like hair and grooming fell by the wayside when demons and monsters hounded your heels for months on end. "Sarah killed Glauth on accident with an arrow meant for Morholt, and instead of sticking to defend her, he ran away. I don't think she's ever forgiven him for it."

"Oh-ho!" Rainn slapped his thigh. "Liking this Morholt better all the time. He's my kinda jackass."

"Any jackass is." Heron nodded to Rainn and winked at Masika.

"But she's gonna do it?" he asked. "She agreed to go back with us?"

"Yeah." Masika glanced around them. "I think she is. Hey, it's lighter. I think we're leaving the forests."

The gigantic war wagon shuddered to a halt, and men shouted the end of the day's march. No one blew their horns.

The human nation of Savach lay just ahead.

"Good timing." Rainn rubbed his palm across the belly of the stained blue vest he wore. "I'm hungry."

The cave claw continued to stare at Masika.

THIRTY-SEVEN

I've never had particularly good luck with women. They always find some reason to hate my guts before the end, as if being mind-bogglingly hand-some and fucking them bowlegged weren't enough for any lucky lady. What more can any man do? Not rich enough for Selenna, not earthy enough for Romi, not crazy enough for Catlia, and all Glauth ever wanted was her own rune engine. Can you imagine that woman with even more power?

You know, in the end I think they all just hated my sister Raven. That makes a lot more sense.

Royal Handük Morholt the Red of Savach, Dan Tura Province, and Keeper of the Cognition Engine

---

She brought an army?" Morholt looked up from his plate and set down the golden fork. "Toad dicks. Can't the woman just talk these things out like a normal person?" He leaned on one hand and an errant lock of red hair fell into his face. "At least I leave an impression, I suppose."

Deep orange sunlight slanted across the well-appointed dining room through six tall windows. A fresh breeze smelling of flowering vines, evening fires, and the nearby loch blew in.

The servants left a while ago. Morholt trusted no one enough to listen in on his and his sister's conversations.

Still in her black leathers, Raven leaned against the mint green wall and sighted along the edge of one of her long bladed, curving daggers. "So much so that women want to kick the shit out of you even after they're dead." She aimed a flat stare at her brother. "You must be so proud." Pale as a corpse with an unruly mop of black hair, she resembled death in form as well as action. Morholt disliked how much use he had made of her talents since taking his father's seat.

"And we're sure she killed the envoy we sent her when she took over the Arrowwilds?" Morholt's fingers drummed against the short beard on his jawline.

Raven snorted and sheathed her dagger. "Not entirely. But I am sure that the cunt's parked fourteen hundred troops and a cave claw on the border between Dan Tura and her patch of trees. Thank fuck Venthria's already left for Murden. Her daddy wouldn't appreciate us for getting his baby monster killed." She snorted. "You do remember me telling you to murk Glauth when you pulled her in from Hiimryk? You know, like you ended up doing Reinar? Bad luck for him that he decided to lead one of Glauth's raids against the same guy who let him die back in the living world. I wonder how many people've been killed twice by the same asshole?"

He waved the comment off. Reinar had been a tragic misunderstanding after an equally tragic but unavoidable decision. And their family compound survived much worse assaults than a pack of savages from the Forests of Hell. Even if there were a lot of the wooden-dicked tree rats. "Fourteen hundred? We can take that many. They have the numbers, but we have height and better weapons. The only question is whether we can do it without murking anyone."

"No." Raven pushed off the wall and stalked, thin and whiplike, to stand beside her brother. "We can keep all of them alive by letting them murk all of us. Might happen anyway. We have four hundred of our parent's men we can't count on, and they have two hundred Hiimrykers in stone boats. So height doesn't mean—" Before ending her sentence, Raven whirled and both daggers jumped into her hands. She pointed them at an empty spot a few feet in front of Morholt. "And just who the arch-fuck are you?"

Luckily, Morholt didn't have long to wonder if Raven had finally lost it because a man with sandy yellow hair wearing a dark blue military jacket of the Reaves raised his hands. While the shimmer of his arrival faded from reality, the man said, "Hi! Wait. Please don't break me."

Eyes too wide, he grinned, glance shifting between Raven's daggers and Morholt's glower. "My name's Boridan, and I work for the Emissary of the Reaves." He waited for a response, and getting none, cleared his throat and started again. "The Reaves? Queen Issta? I'm a delegate."

"I know who your pecker-shriveling queen is, Boridan the delegate." Morholt sat back in his chair and clasped his hands over his narrow stomach. "Apparently, she's the one who likes to interrupt people's dinners without an appointment. Some might think of you dropping in this way as provocative. Raven, you think it'd send the right message if we tossed flappy here in the dungeons and sent an ear or two to that Emissary person? He's the one who's supposed to be diplomatting here anyway. Not that we've ever been important enough for him to drop by."

Raven slunk across the room and poked Boridan in the crotch with the point of a dagger. "Maybe not an *ear*."

"Oldam's great, granite gravy-stick." Nervous laughter trickled out of Boridan, and he wriggled in place. "I'm just here to make a request on behalf of the Reaves. I didn't do anything to you. King Veliel of Murden agreed to it too!"

The man's choice of expression irritated Morholt, reminiscent as it was of the kind of thing Keane the Usurper King might have said. Invoking Veliel irritated him more though. The Reaves was too far away to matter, but Morholt had made certain concessions to Murden to cement his place here with the Sovereign Council in Savach after deposing his parents, his wife Venthria among them. If the king of

Murden held any part of this Boridan's visit in his hand, Morholt had no choice but to listen.

Even as Glauth and her army readied for war.

"Yes?" Morholt's forced smile felt insincere, but Boridan reacted with obvious relief.

"Yes! Right." Boridan backed away from Raven a step, who watched him through narrowed eyes. "I come with news. Important news. The Emissary has asked me to tell you that Runecrafter Glauth of the Arrowwilds is marching to wage war on you even as we speak. He offers his help in eliminating the threat permanently in exchange for a singular concession."

Morholt glanced up at Raven, who smirked back at him. "And what concession would that be?"

"Three escaped slaves travel with Glauth." Boridan straightened, more at ease now that he mistakenly thought this meeting under his control. "You don't know them, but Queen Issta does. She wants them returned. All you need to do is sit by and allow my employer the Emissary to fetch them, and we'll take care of the rest of your problems. Does that sound good?"

This Boridan sounded extremely new to diplomacy. Morholt wondered if he could use that to his advantage. "Maybe," he said. He glanced at his cooling dinner and sighed inwardly. "Can your Emissary promise not to murk anyone while he's collecting his prizes? I already have all the crumpled-up bodies around here I need. Running outta places to bury the damn things."

Boridan became the picture of confusion. "Not murk? But Runecrafter Glauth wants to destroy you."

"My relationship with Glauth is complicated." Morholt pushed his distracting plate away. "And also none of your business. Can your master do it or not?"

"You like fucking crazy-assed cunts and now one of them wants to murk you. You want her alive because you *still* think she might fuck you again." Raven slunk behind Boridan and breathed in his ear, which turned bright red. "Simple," she whispered.

"Apparently my more lecherous relationships are neither complicated nor private." Morholt glared at Raven and tried to look mean.

Trying to keep Morholt's gaze and look over his shoulder at Raven left Boridan flustered and off balance. He cupped one hand over his ear and Raven blew on the other one instead. "I don't know. I'll have to . . . Can you stop that? I'll have to ask."

"Yeah, dignitary dickless. Go do that." Morholt had a battle to prepare for. "Go home and . . ." he trailed off. "Does the Emissary even have a cock for you to suck? He's a Standards demon, right? Nothing pokey down there? Well, go do whatever it is you do for him and get back to me when I'm not trying to eat dinner. You're seriously inconvenient. Tell him if he can keep everyone alive, he's got a deal. Otherwise he can fuck right off. I don't need any more variables up my ass right now. Got it? Great."

"That's just a myth. He has a cock." And Boridan shimmered away, carried on a windblown lake of magic.

"That's a good trick," Morholt observed.

"Easy to murk people with." Raven stepped forward and dragged a foot across the brown stone floor where Boridan recently stood.

"You're a hard person to love. Anyone ever tell you that?" Morholt shoved his chair back and stood. His back hurt.

She smiled at him. "Not twice."

CHAPTER

THIRTY-EIGHT

The Sovereign Council of Savach. Buncha withered old sacks is what they are. The only sort of entertaining thing about them is that they can't keep their crotches out of each other's faces. It's like they think they're the only ones good enough to squirt on.

Mom and Dad fit right in.

What I didn't know before was how much of their cruelty was mandated by the council. The raids into the forests, the third-child collections, all to keep the demons of Murden happy and Savach subservient. I even have a demon wife now to spy on me and make sure I stay in line.

Course she rolls my eyes back up into my head every night, and what she can do with that tongue is absolutely obscene, *so, you know, pros and cons.*

Royal Handük Morholt the Red of Savach, Dan Tura Province, and Keeper of the Cognition Engine

---

The horns blew.

Lightning exploded across the cloud-choked sky, detonating pockets of thunderhead in staccato bursts of light and fury.

Ahead of the onrushing force, the hilltop compound of Morholt the Red shuddered in the blue-white glow and grimly prepared her defenses.

"No, Rainn. Stay with the group." Masika held the god by the shoulders, fully aware that all of Glauth's army would be insufficient to hold him if he decided to go anyway. "I know you could take them all yourself. But we need you here to protect us." The war chants of thousands of years of northern fighters danced behind Rainn's eyes. Eyes that flashed with the lightning.

The two of them rode at the bow of Glauth's gigantic war wagon, looking down from its crenellated forecastle. Arrowwilds's soldiers held their bows at the ready around them.

"Heron got to go." Rainn's shirt ripped across his chest in time with a fierce lightning strike. Dense muscle expanded his arms, legs, chest, and back.

"Heron's a bird. She's scouting." Masika stared up six inches higher than before into Rainn's face. "We're part of the army. We're armying."

All around them, under swirling black and orange clouds, the army of Glauth ran through an empty town at the walled fortification atop the hill on the other side. The compound glared down the hill at them, the upper story of the central building and the top half of a pair of wide towers poked over a heavy wall across which soldiers scurried.

To port, the cave claw pounded forward, rough green and black plated skin bouncing under the force of its charge. For once, it focused on where it went and not on Masika.

Glauth's horns sounded constantly. Men and women roared, and stone squareboats raced ahead through the sky.

A black cloud lifted from those distant walls and scudded with speed at the lead squareboat. As the Hiimrykers entered it, the cloud solidified into a tightly grasping net that pressed the northmen against their vessel and left it flying in a vague, upward curve.

Seven stone boats separated and peeled off as their vanguard picked up speed and left the field of combat, its pinned Hiimryker crew shouting threats and deprecations behind them.

"Think this one's big enough?" Rainn held up a two-handed blade he'd taken from the war wagon's weapons locker. It moved in his hand as if made of feathers. "Maybe I should check if they have anything else."

"Could be bigger." Forbryttan slid down the blade onto the ground and licked it.

A headache formed behind Masika's eyes. "Forby, don't stress Rainn out any more than he already is."

"Could be *sharper* too." The little trimpet jumped back onto Rainn and stuck his tongue out at Masika.

"I'm getting another one. I've got two hands, why did I think I only needed one sword?" Rainn tried to move away toward the weapons locker.

"Rainn, that thing's a foot taller than I am." She continued to grip his wrist and felt the vibrations of his eagerness. The high horn blew, signaling the advance troops to assay the hillside road. "Just wait until . . . Oh, I guess that's us."

Masika and Rainn clambered down and joined Glauth and her team of runecrafters, as well as another fifty fighters of Knifewall.

"Ready to carve your names on the history of the Undergates?" Glauth shouted. "I'll be carving mine on Morholt's wicked backside before the day is out, I think. Everyone, after me!"

A broad road cut a meandering switchback up the hill to the mouth of Morholt's compound. All around its base, the homes and buildings of a small town lay empty, frightened skeletons of human habitation. Glauth charged up the road, Masika and Rainn hot on her heels.

"Oh ho!" From the roof of a small stone block fortification a quarter of the way up, another of the dark clouds reached out toward their group. Glauth waved a hand, and it caught alight, smoky tendrils of iron netting flailing within in its flames. "This will take no time at all, yes? I hope you're ready for an early lunch."

To the distant left, the cave claw clambered up the side of the hill, snarling, spitting, and gouging great furrows in the rock with gigantic talons.

From the short cliffside to the right, Heron flew to Masika and transformed into her human shape. "Three soldiers each to those forward installations, which you've just discovered." She pointed at the square walls nestled among a cluster of shopfronts to one side of the road. "Five of those along the way, and more nastiness at the top. How are you doing?"

"Not at all worried about what other weapons a nation ruled by runecrafters might devise. You?" Masika unlimbered the graver. The same weapon January cracked a Hiimryker solid stone squareboat with. She lifted it and pointed it at the fortification.

Strong. Clear-headed.

"Heron." Masika squinted out over the graver's sights, wishing Inlittan were there to guide her through her new friend. "Did you see any civilians anywhere on the hillside? Anywhere at all?"

"Neither saw nor heard nor smelled." Heron gazed up the long, twisting road. "But there were plenty behind the compound walls up top. Looked to me like they'd been evacuated there at some speed."

"Really?" Masika glanced at Heron over the top of the graver. "That seems un-evil. Maybe he knows we won't drag the place down if it's full of innocents?" Already the heightened sensations the graver instilled receded, now a comfortable presence in her chest and belly.

"Then he knows wrong." Eyes flashing orange, Glauth grinned wildly up the hill. "But first things first. And that"—she pointed at the fortification where a pair of soldiers worked to heft some new weapon of shining silver and smoky glass curves and points into place—"is first. I don't want to know what that silver bat-thing does, and I think you don't either."

The graver's first shot flew over the top of the square walls and exploded against the hill's cliffside. Debris rained down on the two blue-clad soldiers, but rather than distract them, it only served to speed them up. Masika had accounted for the fall of an arrow in flight, but a graver loosed differently. She adjusted and triggered it again.

Atop the walls, the silver weapon, the size of a man and superficially resembling a bat with wings spread, hummed and blurred the air around it.

The graver fired. Everything flew apart with a thundering peal of sound and fire. A thrill ran through Masika.

"Amazing." Glauth's grin touched her ears. "How many bullets do you have left? We have four more of those things to get through."

"Bullets?" Masika held the graver at arm's length, inspecting it. "It's not a sling. Wait. The pink stones?" She recalled the glimpse of a projectile Inlittan showed her when January used the weapon. "I don't know. How do you check?" Unlike Inlittan, the graver displayed no real purpose, no intelligence. It wanted use, perhaps, and a hand to caress its trigger arm, but that was it.

"Gravers aren't from here," Glauth answered, "so how would I know? They shoot graverstones. Pink gypsum. But we'll take whatever we can get, yes? Kerra, how're you holding up back there?"

A soft-bodied woman with short black hair, one of Glauth's runecrafters, drew slow patterns in the air and nodded. "Going strong."

They advanced up the road, close to the smoking hole of the forward fortification.

The sky boomed above them, eliciting an ecstatic groan from the vibrating Rainn, while Heron watched the woman named Kerra. "How very interesting. She is crafting channels of magical power and sending them to the others. They can keep this up much longer than I'd thought. Calling the power is tiring, but the arrangement is much more efficient this way."

Boomp. Boomp. Boomp. A trio of barrels flew over their heads from the compound walls and crashed amongst the main force of Glauth's army. Expanding rings of dirty yellow cloud wafted out from the impact points among the empty buildings, knocking soldiers to the ground wherever one intersected with the other.

"We need wind, now!" Glauth gripped the arms of one of her runecrafters, bearded, older—the one making the storm—and faced him toward the greasy clouds. His eyes fixed ahead, he sent a gale that picked at the heavy edges of the yellow clouds, dissipating the stubborn gasses into the sky.

Hundreds lay still wherever it touched.

"Halt. Damn." Closer to the ruined fortification, Glauth hid them all behind the abandoned surrounding buildings. "Way the road switches back, we're about to walk under three more of those weapons forts, all at once." She chewed her lip and pointed. "I'd hoped to save this but, Brandr, show that one some stars."

An attractive young man, broad shouldered with lanky black hair, closed his eyes and mumbled the runes of a spell beneath his breath. He reached up and twisted his fingers into unrecognizable shapes.

In the swirling sky above, Masika saw a single point of blue-white light illuminate the clouds from behind. At once, brilliant as any star in the night, the light burned a hole through those clouds and fell, rushing so fast as to become a single long streak, directly onto the middle—and closest—fortification over them.

The brilliance grew as it hit. When Masika could see once again, the stone installation was simply gone.

Brandr fell, brown face ashen, his pronounced cheekbones taking on a skeletal cast.

One of the other soldiers, minders to the smaller band of runecrafters, caught him and eased him to the ground.

"Takes it out of him, yes? But nothing's ever left. Kerra can't channel for him, or she'll go down too. Good job, boy." Glauth patted the unconscious young man on the shoulder. "We'll see you when it's all over."

Hiimrykers roared above as five of their stone boats finally made it to the hilltop compound's walls and descended, howling, into it. Screams and shouts followed.

"Oh no. That's not good." Heron pointed ahead on the road at the figure of Rainn, racing in front of the group, Forbryttan screaming joyously from his shoulders.

Before she considered the action, Masika took off after him. What she might do if she caught up to him never occurred to her.

At the same time, Heron launched herself forward, thinning and darkening, a blue-gray bird once again. Out of place on a field of battle, she stunned with her grace and beauty.

Rainn hit the bend in the road and turned left, barreling toward the next fortification, Forbryttan bouncing on his back. They loosed black nets at the pair. Rainn chopped them in half with the six-foot blade he carried in one hand. He jumped over a vast slick created when the desperate soldiers aimed their humming silver bat-shaped weapon at the ground in front of him, turning it to mud. Such a weapon became all the more threatening on a slanted road cut into the face of a cliff.

Pushing herself against the hillside, Masika picked her way through the slippery mud after her friend. Heron called to her as a bird from above. Unlike gods and sorcerers, Masika had no idea what Heron might be saying, but it sounded encouraging.

More screams. Blood dripped down the side of the fortification, and Rainn leaped ahead, leaving the building dead in his wake. Forbryttan slipped down to Rainn's calf and clambered back up his back when they landed.

Glauth and her retinue cheered, echoed immediately by the army behind them, snaking up the road and pooled at the bottom of the hill among the empty town.

Above, the cave claw reached the top and crested the compound's forty-foot wall, only to find its face snapped shut by a half-dozen misty black nets.

Masika cleared the slick mud and ran past the gore-filled weapons fort. The sky boomed and churned, but no rain fell. Not yet. She cast about her for something to point the graver at, but her enemies stayed stubbornly out of sight, over the top of the next turn in the road.

The soft gray feathers of Heron turned to a beautiful mass of soft gray hair, and the goddess ran beside her. Together they came to a thirty-foot across, fifteen deep, clean-walled bowl in the ground where the next fortification once sat. The one erased by Brandr's star. They ran around it and followed Rainn as best they could.

"None of the weapons Morholt's using seem designed to kill," Heron said as they ran. "It's occurring to me that everything we know about this situation is from Glauth, and she doesn't seem like the most objective voice in the room, you know?"

With hot liquid running out of her knee apparatus down her shin,

Masika jumped over a crack in the street. She recognized it as being caused by her marvelous graver when she missed her first shot at the fortification on the lower bend.

"I'm worried we're fighting on the wrong side," Heron shouted.

They ran through a widening in the road where more shops, an empty stable, and another Rainn-visited weapons fort splashed crimson on the dirt in front of its broken walls.

The graver clicked in Masika's hands—out of graverstones, and no chance now to get more. Just as well. She pitched it away and pulled her bow. "I think it's time for a weapon with a little more control."

"Never liked that thing." Heron peered over the side of the road while Masika gulped air. "Kinda evil. You good to keep going? We can just sit back and let Rainn murder everyone if you want. Though maybe someone ought to go tell him we're probably the bad guys here."

"Thank you." Masika grabbed Heron's arm and pulled herself erect. She nodded, and they ran. She felt she ought to be exhausted by now, but her nerves felt as if they were on fire.

So much had changed for Heron since she arrived, frightened and shivering, in the Undergates. Masika wanted to tell her how much Heron inspired her, how grand a being she continued to become. How much the goddess meant to her.

But no words came.

They ran together.

The final fortification had apparently dispensed with the non-lethal weaponry and loosed ballista bolts at Rainn, keeping him pinned behind an outcropping in the side of the hill at a place where the road, nearly at the hilltop, stretched to its thinnest. A pair of the giant crossbows cranked at an unrealistic pace, manned by the three defenders in blue tabards. Wherever the bolts hit, they sundered and flew apart into thousands of jagged shards. Rainn already bled from numerous wounds inflicted by one or more near misses.

She needed to get to him before he murked any more of Morholt's soldiers. How could she control the bloodshed taking place all around her?

Screams and bellows sounded from within the compound walls. Acrid smoke stung her nose, and a cold wind blew down the hillside.

Thinking furiously, Masika examined her options. She was too far away for her bow and would never get close enough to use it against those doubtlessly runecrafted ballistae.

"My turn." Heron ran and dove from the road, wheeling low on transformed wings. Heart in her mouth, Masika watched the goddess fly past the weapons fort, bank hard to the left, and drop on top where the ballistae launched volley after volley. As Heron flew, Masika raced up the roadway until she was within earshot of Rainn.

A single shout of alarm rang out, and the ballistae stopped flinging their deadly bolts.

Heron popped up over the top of the wall and waved, smiling.

"Let's go!" Masika shouted to Rainn, and they closed on the final, and silent, weapons fort.

As they grew close, Rainn's face wrinkled up, and he turned his head. He pointed to her knee. "That is the worst that thing has *ever* smelled. You keeping dead river eels in there? Might be better if we just chop the whole shitting mess off now. Throw it over the wall at the bad guys. I bet that'd kill anyone left."

His voice rang out too loudly, and every tendon in his body stretched against his need for violence. Even Forbryttan panted wildly. She needed to distract him.

"That reminds me," Masika said, not wanting to admit to herself how horrifying the smell truly was, "Heron thinks we might be the bad guys in this one." She slowed and peered over the edge at the mass of Arrowwilders below, spearheaded by Glauth and her runecrafters. At most, they were three minutes behind. "We need to figure out how to stop this."

A ground shaking roar sent Masika to her knees, and both she and Rainn clutched at their ears. Repeated crashes shook the hill as the cave claw, its head and shoulders covered in joyously popping blue flames, went bouncing down the side. Rainn grabbed Masika by the upper arm and dragged her away from the edge of the road, instants before a twenty-foot section dropped off onto the army below.

"Hahahaha! That'll teach you, you giant fucknose! War is the *best!*" Forbryttan danced on Rainn's shoulder at the cave claw's misfortune.

"Everyone all right?" Heron shouted.

Pulling on Rainn's hand to drag herself to her feet, Masika waved back. "Nope. Sorry to disagree with Forby, but I don't like war," she said to him. "Too dangerous. Even when you're already dead."

"The soldiers at the last bunker are unconscious and tied up with their own pants legs," Heron told them as she rejoined the group. "What? I can hit people too."

They gained the final bend in the road and stared at the walled compound. Sounds of the Hiimrykers fighting Morholt's soldiers continued within, and one of the big stone squareboats protruded from the front wall, lodged where it crashed.

Rainn leaned toward Heron and grinned. "Took off all their pants, did you? I knew you were a filthy girl."

CHAPTER

THIRTY-NINE

I only have one real philosophy concerning large scale violent conflict, and it's the same as my view on small scale fighting as well. Be somewhere else.

But sometimes the fight comes looking for you and seems determined to follow wherever you go. In that event, there is only one tactic left to use.

Hide and pretend to be somewhere else.

Royal Handük Morholt the Red of Savach, Dan Tura Province, and Keeper of the Cognition Engine

---

"Amazing job clearing the way," Glauth said, arms wide. "Now stand aside and we'll finish the job."

"We need to talk about—" was all Masika got out before lightning struck the compound gates. In truth she never really expected to sway Glauth at the enemy's wall, but the spirit of her papa's teachings demanded she try.

Half a sentence was still a little disappointing though.

Lightning continued to strike the gates and front walls over and over, throwing chunks of glowing stone in all directions. The sound was unbelievable, and the light grew so intense that even facing the opposite direction, Masika saw bones through the hands she kept pressed over her face.

Beside Masika, Kerra the runecrafter, who Heron identified as powering the others, fell unconscious to the dirt, followed seconds later by the bearded man who created the storm. Instantly the lightning stopped. The final bits of debris pattered to the ground, and Masika witnessed the ruin of the compound wall, shattered beyond hope of repair.

A dull boom from far above announced the start of the rain.

Two minders each dragged the downed runecrafters out of the way with speed, though Glauth did not wait for them.

She raised a spear above her head and bellowed, "Charge!"

Masika, Rainn, and Heron ran to stay in front.

"Now this is some properly crappy weather!" Rainn shouted over the rushing army. "Fucking clouds felt like they were holding their breath."

"Glad you're happy," Masika yelled back. They jumped over rubble and into the central courtyard where a scene of crowded carnage greeted them. A few felled soldiers of Savach lay here and there, bleeding out onto the dirt, but many more twitching parts of Hiimrykers, metal, stone, wood, and flesh, jittered around the ground. Were these bloody limbs and other less identifiable parts looking for the rest of their bodies?

Instinctively, Masika dodged left, keeping her back to the thick wall they had just climbed through. A massive melee took place in the center of the courtyard, with a determined knot of northmen battling nine-foot-tall men of metal, spinning bands of glowing runes worked here and there into their armor. Along the wall tops, Morholt's archers feathered the Hiimrykers, adding to their misery.

Where were all the evacuated civilians? Had Morholt invited them into his keep? Did he genuinely care about their lives? Masika's misgivings returned. She needed to get ahead of this battle, and fast.

Unbidden, thoughts of Masika's age entered her mind. She found Rainn and Heron when she was sixteen and turned seventeen while on the road to Mount P'takkin. Not that she told anyone. How long ago was that? What were seventeen-year-old girls supposed to be doing? Not fighting wars in the Undergates.

What was she doing here? Maybe she would worry about that later.

Stone squareboats floated unattended over the courtyard, trailing lines the Hiimrykers used to slide down into the fight. Masika deflected a sword stroke by an exhausted soldier, and Forbryttan leaped from Rainn, bounced off the soldier's forehead, and landed back on the god.

Rainn took advantage of the soldier's temporary daze to punch him in the jaw.

He fell, his jawline now taking on a new angle he would not later appreciate.

"Sorry." Rainn shrugged and ran past the unconscious man. This alone was remarkable, that in the center of the storm, Rainn retained the presence of mind to show mercy.

At that moment Glauth and her forces poured through the breach, adding flame and a strange buzzing to the fracas. Masika saw one of the Arrowwilds runecrafters go all blurry, and one of Morholt's men fell apart in a splattery pile in front of her.

"Mother Love's fortune, we need to get *there*." Masika pointed at the top of the fatter tower on the opposite side of the yard. More of the huge metal men ringed its base. The best defended, Morholt certainly waited at its summit. "But we'll never get past all that now."

Rainn swept the legs out from under one of Morholt's blue-tabarded soldiers with his huge blade, wielding it like a club in its scabbard. "I could make a lane, if you stick tight. Be just like chopping a path through the woods of Tyrrane—if all the trees and bushes were filled with blood and screaming."

"Better idea. Follow me." Masika dashed forward, dodged another blue tabard and elbowed the man in the back of the head. She sheathed her sword, leaped up, and caught the bottom end of a thick rope that dangled from one of the Hiimryker's abandoned stone boats.

Heron and Rainn scurried up behind her, while Forbryttan scrambled up over everyone else. "We can crash it better than this!" he shouted.

"Any idea how this thing works?" Heron ran to the squared bow of the boat, head down, trying to keep the rows of short benches between her and the archers on the compound walls above them. "We need some height!"

Masika moved aft and found a raised pillar, three feet high, where a ship's wheel might be on a regular craft. A brass disk with a handle sat in the middle, a lever extended to the right of it, and a row of three glowing blue runes ran up the left. Not knowing what else to do, she grabbed the disk's handle, then the lever and pulled, but both were locked in place. If only Inlittan were still with her, she could show Masika what to do.

Closing her eyes, Masika jabbed the top rune with an outstretched finger.

The rune briefly went dark, then illuminated yellow. This time when Masika shoved the wide lever, it moved with a satisfying amount of resistance, and the boat lurched forward. "Denari clear the fog, we're gonna make it!"

"Woo hoo!" Glauth yelled as she pulled herself up over the side. "For just a little bit I was thinking maybe you didn't know how to fly this thing, yes? But I knew I made the right decision to follow you up here. Now we're—look out!"

The stone boat struck the interior compound wall and rebounded from it, spinning and listing to port. Masika gave an involuntary shriek and spun the disk, drawing a finger up across the middle rune in hopes of stopping them. The squareboat reeled away from the wall, accelerated, and pointed upward.

Straight at the top of Morholt's best defended tower.

"Yikes!" Heron ran aft and ducked behind a bench, gripping it tight. Rainn and Glauth were already there.

Masika closed her eyes, smiled, and gripped the disk with all her might. That tower was the goal, after all.

CHAPTER

FORTY

---

*Everyone loves their home. They decorate it, make it comfortable for them-
selves and their family, and defend it against intruders that threaten it.
Unless home is Hell, in which case you begrudgingly try to keep everyone
alive and wish you were from somewhere else.*

Royal Handük Morholt the Red of Savach, Dan Tura Province,
and Keeper of the Cognition Engine

The boat crunched into the tower, which crumbled under its
speeding weight. The impact was not as bad as Masika
expected, given that the solid stone boat's impact was cushioned by the thinner, and collapsing, tower walls. Wooden beams and
the platforms they supported on the tower roof fell in over the bow,
and a sinister-looking war engine the size of a trebuchet but adorned
with smoky glass blades went with it. The device turned and rolled
backward down the length of the boat.

"Fuck!" Rainn grabbed Heron and dived to one side, leaving
Glauth behind. The wiry woman dodged opposite, and the bench she
abandoned was scraped entirely away.

The bronze and glass machine of war, as well as a half-dozen benches and a considerable amount of gouged rock, hurtled toward Masika. With no time to run, she stayed where she was, watched the catastrophe hurtling toward her, and ducked a fraction to her left.

The machine bounced, passed inches by her head to the right, and fell on the heads of Morholt's metal defenders below.

Straining, the four of them ran up the incline and jumped off the bow into the tower's top floor, Forbryttan clinging to Rainn and bouncing on his back, his toothy maw full of laughter.

Thirty feet across, this top floor comprised a single round room, sporadically lit by lightning through both windows and the gaping hole in the wall and ceiling they just created. Debris covered fine rugs and a wide table with a replica of the hill and compound on it. Rock dust swirled in the air.

At first Masika thought the room empty, but a red haired and bearded figure stepped out from behind a beautifully carved wardrobe and cleared his throat.

"There were a lot less expensive ways of talking to me than blowing up my whole life," he said, patting the dust from his worn green leathers. "I sent you an invitation, Glauth." He glanced at the others. "I don't know you. I'm Morholt. Handük of this broken dildo of a tower and everything you can see from it. Which is easier now with your renovations, thanks."

A musty smell of rain blew through the room, and thunder boomed. Though the runecrafter who brought the weather was unconscious, the storm he set in motion raged on.

Glauth pointed her spear at him. "You took me from Hiimryk, yes? You *informed* me I would become another of your wives, and you *still* wouldn't give me a shitting rune engine! Oldam's spear, Holt. This is exactly what you should expect, I think. And then you married a demon! Is that what you do when you can't find a human woman to get on her knees for you?"

"What's a rune engine?" Masika asked.

"Channels magic for runecrafters. No effort, no exhaustion. And I didn't make one for you," Morholt addressed Glauth, "because you're as nutty as a sack of squirrel turds. You'd burn the whole Undergates down for a night's entertainment. I simply didn't—hey. Cut that out."

Glauth extended her wiry arms at Morholt, describing fiery runes in the air. A cage of flame erupted from the floor around him, stabbing inward with glowing yellow spikes.

Morholt rolled his eyes.

"All this fighting is because this skinny little ginger fuck jilted you?" Rainn shook his head and chuckled. "Humans are just as stupid dead as they are alive."

In an amazingly accurate imitation of Rainn's expression, Forbryttan rolled his eyes, too, and nodded agreement.

"I don't care what he thinks," Glauth ground out between clenched teeth. "I never loved him. But I deserve his respect."

"Not from where I sit," Rainn said.

"Not human." Morholt cocked an eyebrow at Rainn. "Now I know who you people are. You need to get out of here. Someone's coming for you."

What did he say? Did Morholt know about the Emissary? Was the Emissary coming?

Oh crap.

"We were kinda hoping you could help us with that, Handük Morholt. If maybe everyone could stop breaking each other for a minute?" Hands open and empty, Masika extended her arms to Morholt in as non-threatening a gesture as she knew.

But Glauth shrieked, and lines of blood welled from cuts in her arms. The flaming cage went out, leaving Morholt unburned. Glauth whirled her spear, naked rage on her face. "Where are you, you black-souled bitch? Face me."

An audible *bonk*! sounded above the distant noise of fighting from the courtyard, and Glauth fell forward to the floor, stunned and writhing. A moment later, consciousness slipped away, and she fell still, an angry grimace still on her face.

As quiet as possible, Masika slid her slender blade from its sheath and backed into the closest wall. Whoever knocked Glauth out moved with both stealth and real invisibility, but her footsteps were easy enough to see in all the rock dust on the floor. Masika brought the blade up at the unseen attacker.

Inlittan would have been proud.

"We need you, Morholt." Masika moved the blade, keeping it pointed at the footsteps, which stopped. "People are in danger in the living world, and we need you to help us get there. All of us, Glauth too. We'll take her off your hands for a while. Until she dies again, anyway."

"He's not truly here." Heron stepped behind the image of Morholt and extended her hand through his neck as if through smoke. "I believe we're being stalled while the real Morholt flees."

Instantly, Forbryttan jumped through the image, disrupting the center as he left a hole in the colored smoke that filled in behind him. The trimpet jumped back and forth, squealing with glee as he sent swirling clouds of Morholt through the space.

The invisible attacker's footprints slid sideways, and Heron grunted and bent over, holding her middle. Before Masika could react, Rainn leaped to Heron's side and swung that huge blade—now out of its sheath—in a wide arc over Heron's head, hitting nothing.

Lines of godsblood arced through the air from wounds carved into Rainn's biceps by invisible knives. The god roared and brought his sword crashing down through the wooden floor, again missing his unseeable target, and receiving a pair of slashes in an X across his chest.

"The footprints, Rainn!" Masika dared not get too close to Rainn's wildly swinging sword, but she could at least tell him where to swing it. "Aim at the footprints!"

But Rainn was too far gone, consumed by rage and pain, as well as his protectiveness for Heron.

"Hey, stop." The illusory Morholt held up his hands and backed away. "Raven, cut it out. They're not hurting anything." He glanced at the ruined wall and sundered floor. "They're not hurting *me*."

While Rainn flailed, still collecting slashes that stained his clothing crimson, Forbryttan abandoned the illusory Morholt, found the foot-prints dancing in the rock dust, and launched himself at the air above them.

Snarling, the tiny demon wrapped his limbs around an invisible head and bit into it, yanking and straining with his teeth.

A woman shrieked.

Masika dove forward, carrying them both to the ground, except that part of the floor next to Rainn's previous attack gave way, and Masika, the invisible woman, and Forbryttan fell through to the floor below.

"Please, everyone stop." A second Morholt reached out and closed his fist, and the woman beneath Masika appeared. Rail thin, dusty black leathers, and a pair of long curving daggers still in her fists, she shoved at Masika and attempted to dislodge Forbryttan, who violently bit at her black hair. "Raven! No more fighting." This Morholt's voice reverberated down Masika's spine, louder than the thunder outside.

She rolled off Raven, and even Forbryttan stopped and looked up, the skinny woman's black hair trailing out of his mouth.

Details of the room filtered in. A bed stood to one side of this smaller room, partially covered in fallen timber. A blue pitcher and washbasin sat on a small table beside it.

"If you can get Glauth to call off the attack, I'll send you anywhere you want to go." Morholt took a dagger from his belt and laid it on the floor in front of him. He seemed to forget he also wore a short sword. "But we have to move fast. You don't understand who's coming up your ass."

"Oh, we've met," came a voice from the shimmering air beside the basin, "though it's been trying to have a decent conversation with them." A man of medium height and slight build, gray curls arranged neatly above amused eyes, stepped through the shimmer, his dark red and blue robes swirling. The Emissary had arrived. "The late Baron Stolas's palace, I believe? In case you're worried, I assure you I'm not interested in your asses."

"Rainn? You all right up there?" Masika stared through the hole in the ceiling, ignoring the Emissary. "How's Heron?"

"I'm fine." Heron poked her head over the hole. "Rainn's pretty cut up, but the storm's healing him. I trust that's the real Morholt? Oh. And him." Her brows drew down when she saw the Emissary.

"And a handsome devil that Morholt is too." Behind Heron, the illusion of Morholt stepped into view and smiled. "You know, goddess, you could do a lot worse. Got a good job and he's hung like a gold-tip bear."

Morholt waved and the illusion dissipated, a surprised expression on its face.

"What?" Heron looked across the opening and frowned. "Excuse me." She moved out of sight, and Masika made out snatches of conversation between peals of thunder.

"Thank you for keeping up your end of the bargain, Handük Morholt." The Emissary gave a short bow. "And now it's time for me to keep mine. Do you prefer Glauth and her minions in boxes or urns?"

"Bargain?" Though she did not yet understand the details, Masika felt anger rising in her cheeks. "What kind of deal did you make, Morholt?"

"That's *Your Excellency*, to you, young lady." The Emissary wagged his finger at Masika. "And he agreed to hand over you and your two pet Alir in exchange for me removing Glauth as a threat once and for all. Perhaps Morholt will prove wiser than poor, *late* Baron Stolas?" The finger stilled, and he raised it next to his ear. The thunder paused, and the sounds of fighting turned to terrified screams and the laughter of demons. "Ah, there's the tune I was listening for."

"I never agreed to this. I told your messenger no murkings, and judging from the sounds outside, you've already fucked the deal." Morholt's jaw clenched as he spoke. A dim orange light and a whirring noise came from his right wrist. "Go home, errand boy. You can't have any more people."

Whatever arrangement might or might not have existed before, Morholt obviously no longer wanted any part of it. Masika decided to consider him an ally. For now.

"It's Emissary, not errand boy, though I understand how you might miss the distinction." He turned his back to the room and poured water into a basin. "I want you to think carefully about things, Handük. Murking all your people is just me making the point that you're not in charge here, and hey, it's fun for me too. So that's happening anyway. But this is an important matter to Queen Issta. Important enough to go to war over. *Real* war. Do you think Savach would survive something like that?"

"Guess we'll find out," Morholt said, placing his left hand on his right wrist and turning a copper bracer there.

Even without Inlittan's help, Masika could see the fear behind his bravado. Morholt was terrified. Above the Emissary, Rainn crept into view. His bleeding stopped, he flexed his powerful hands and waited.

"Hang on." Masika picked her blade up from where it fell when she'd tumbled through the ceiling and sheathed it. "You made the same threat to Baron Stolas. We're not going with you regardless of your bargain with Morholt, so there's no sense in going to war with him over it."

"I had a feeling you might take that position." The air shimmered next to the Emissary, and he reached his arm into it. "So I arranged a little inducement. Is this anyone you remember?"

The arm came out, dragging a bound and gagged man who fell to his knees. He was thin and filthy, with a torn and stained slave tunic, hair and ragged beard gone gray, and pained eyes.

Allz's wounds—no!

"Papa!" Masika ran to him, gathering up his emaciated frame in her arms. She pulled the gag from his mouth, his lips pale and cracked. "What happened to you? Why are you here?"

Tennat Oburn, Masika's father whom she left behind in the living world, burst into tears and moaned.

The Emissary rolled his eyes. "That's what the gag was for. Tennat can't talk, just makes those horrible sounds all day. As I understand it, your older sister was afraid that he might convince your uncle, the emperor—good on you, by the way, *princess*—to forgive him and imprison her, so she had his tongue cut out. Can you even imagine your own daughter doing that to you? Now that is simply horrid.

Anyway, after the tongue-thing he stopped eating, which I imagine hurts to do with a bloody stump in your mouth. Though now that I think on it, plenty of humans survive getting un-tongued. We have tens of thousands in the Reaves. Of course they're already mirrors. I guess dear old papa might have been a little down-in-the-mouth about the whole thing, and just wasted away in sadness. Probably gave up wondering when *you* were going to come rescue him, princess. Showed up a week ago in the acid pits, so I had him brought to me. One demon's flaming pile of excrement is another demon's bartering leverage, I always say."

With her papa's terrified bones shaking in her arms, Masika swallowed her rage just enough to speak. "Do it."

The Emissary crunched against the floorboards under Rainn's falling boots. Forbryttan leaped from Raven's skull and yanked off one of the Emissary's hard-heeled shoes and smashed his toes with it.

Raven rose to a crouch and crept to the wall, daggers at the ready.

"Ah, toad dicks." Morholt held a hand to Masika. "We got to run. This is about to turn bad faster than an orgy full of rabid badgers. Come on!"

Lifting the dazed Emissary from the floor, Rainn smashed his face again and again with a fist that fell like the hammer of Hagrim's divine forge.

"Heron, we're leaving!" Masika shouted. She pulled her papa tighter, trying not to think about what his presence signified.

"She's already gone," Forbryttan said, pausing from destroying the Emissary's instep. "She went with Boridan. Said not to worry."

She *what*?

Rainn smashed a fist into the Emissary's smiling pulp of a face with a wet crunch, punctuating every few words with bloody violence. "But we're . . . fucking worried enough . . . to get kinda irrational . . . about it."

On the narrow wall of the room, Raven opened a brass-fitted door and peered over into a central spiral stairway that descended into darkness. Whatever she saw or heard that way caused her to scowl down the stair.

How could Heron have left them? Where had she gone? Masika stuffed her worries down. Now was not the time.

The Emissary spluttered, laughter creaking from his ruined visage.

"You're not nearly dead enough." Frowning, Rainn dropped the Emissary to the ground. "Hey, I got this guy's brains on my fists, and he doesn't seem to care. Is he getting bigger?"

CHAPTER

FORTY-ONE

Eventually, when your fields are salted and your towers are sundered, when your people's stock have been driven off or killed, and all hope seems lost, there comes a time when a man must summon the final reserves of his courage and stand against the tide of evil.

That's the guy I want covering my ass while I'm running away.

Royal Handük Morholt the Red of Savach, Dan Tura Province, and Keeper of the Cognition Engine

---

L et's go." Masika ran past Raven to the stairway, pulling her papa behind her. But instead of heading down, she scrambled up to the top floor. The hatchway proved unlocked, and Masika sprinted to Glauth's prostrate form and dragged her with her free arm toward the bow of the stone boat, still lodged in the tower wall. "Get in," she told Tennat.

He did.

If they escaped the thing growing underneath them, the thing Masika saw destroy Baron Stolas's palace, they could then track down Heron and deal with Boridan. Judging by the deepening laughter she heard from below, that was a bigger *if* than Masika was willing to think about.

Morholt grabbed Glauth by the armpit and helped Masika drag her. Rainn followed on their heels, and Raven leaped up through the hole in the floor. By now the Emissary's laughter rattled Masika's spine, and she heard wood splintering beneath his increasing mass.

"Give her to me." Morholt hopped into the boat, and Masika pushed Glauth into his hands. Rainn set himself in place and pushed on the boat to free it from the tower, Forbryttan on his shoulder shouting encouragements.

"You could try helping," Rainn grunted at his blue-furred friend.

Even as Masika lifted a leg to climb aboard, the tower shuddered, and the wall and part of the floor fell away, taking Masika with it. She shrieked, falling into wind and rain, hundreds of howling demons below playing in the fluids of the soldiers of both sides.

"Whoof!" Masika jerked to a stop, and Rainn hauled her over the side of the boat.

"No time to fuck around with those guys," he admonished her. "Get to the steering thing and get us the hell outta here!"

She nodded and gained her feet, heading down the sloping deck. Damn. The entire steering platform had been scraped away by the huge glass and bronze war machine when they initially struck the tower. Denari clear the fog, how would they escape now? It seemed as though the entire Undergates were arrayed against them.

At the thought, a swelling arm, the rough appearance of dark scales shifting across its dim gold surface, broke through the cut stone blocks of the tower wall just below their boat. The tip of one gigantic claw brushed the vessel, setting it spinning crazily. Masika gripped a partially destroyed bench, while Morholt screamed and held the flopping Glauth.

Head down, Tennat curled around the metal legs of a missing bench.

"I'd suggest we let the cunt fall and distract all those demons with the eating of her," Raven said to her brother as the two of them clung to Glauth. "Though she probably tastes like old piss."

"What're you saying?" Morholt raised his face to the rain, looking offended. "She tastes amazing. Why do you think I can't get over her?"

Raven pretended to retch into Glauth's unconscious face.

The tower crumbled and cast a monstrous plume of dust and smoke into the stormy sky. But not so monstrous as to hide the horror of the Emissary, who straightened to his full height and gazed down at the top of their craft.

He stopped their spin between thumb and forefinger of one hand. Dark gold scales repelled the water and wavered under Masika's sight, and the claws dug into the boat's stone sides. It stood like a hundred-foot-tall human, though reptilian. Muscles rippled beneath its shifting skin.

Terrified screams rose afresh from below. The Emissary's demons had broken into the big central keep of Morholt's compound, where the citizens of the town of Dan Tura huddled in fear.

"You know," the Emissary said with a slow, razor-fanged smile, his voice that of falling mountains, "I haven't had this much trouble with a job in over eight hundred years. Not since I had to convince the Grand Emperor of Damah that the Darrish weren't the only ones here in the afterlife." He chuckled, and the impact of his laughter rattled the stone vessel. "Those people really love a walled neighborhood."

Masika forced herself to her feet. She was the proud daughter of Tennat Oburn, and she would not cower in the face of tyrants. This enemy could not be defeated, but perhaps it might be reasoned with.

Movement caught her eye over the scarred outer wall of the compound.

Or perhaps something even better than reason might come up.

"Before you try"—the Emissary released the craft, which hung in space, a slow rotation bringing Masika even closer to the Emissary's dead white eye—"you should know you can't talk your way out of this. This is about the Standards. Issta has demanded your return, and I *am* the Standards. I don't really have a choice in the matter. Of course, if I did, you'd already be dead, so it's an open question as to whether that'd be better or not."

Reacting at the last instant to the monster behind the Emissary, Masika dove aside. She gripped the rounded rail atop the craft's wales as hard as she could and dug her toes into the scuppers.

Unbelievably silent, Glauth's massive cave claw launched itself at the Emissary's back and bore it to the courtyard ground, claws digging into golden scales and tearing huge rents across mighty ribs stronger than stone. As they fell together, Masika watched the monstrous lizard turn its head to bite into the Emissary's neck. The din shook Masika, but she chanced a peek anyway.

Rivers of bile-black blood poured from great slashes in the Emissary's shifting gold hide, carrying the stench of disease everywhere. The cave claw raked into him and tore his body with its teeth. But already, Masika saw that the huge creature held no chance of winning.

Dark gold hands settled on the cave claw's black and green plated shoulders and dug in, taloned fingers bringing huge spurts of gore splattering over the battlefield. Humans and demons alike screamed as they fled. The Emissary grimaced, strained, and an unearthly howl erupted from the cave claw as the Emissary tore its forelimbs bodily from it.

The Emissary was implacable. It would never stop. Could not even *be* stopped. This was all a waste of lives, and Masika and her friends would be taken anyway. A cold ball of terror formed in Masika's stomach, working its way through her and robbing her strength.

Her mother was wrong about her. Masika *could* be afraid of the right things.

That dead white eye fixed on Masika. "You are beginning to test my patience, Miss Oburn." The Emissary tossed the dying cave claw to one side. "Issta asked for all three of you, but she only needs the Alir. I bet she'd give you to me if I asked. I'm really very good at . . . Oh you're fucking kidding me."

"Jump on, now!" Jarl Refur, covered in bright red blood, brought his own Hiimryker squareboat astern of Masika's and waved them aboard with vigor. Two other northmen, massive with their replacement parts whirring and wheezing, helped pull Glauth and Tennat over.

"Sit down and hold on," Jarl Refur yelled. "This is gonna make one hell of a poem!"

The boat lurched forward and pressed Masika back into her bench. Behind them the Emissary stood, threw back his head, and erupted in a senses-shattering howl that sent a crack down the middle of Jarl Refur's boat.

But it did not stop them.

CHAPTER

FORTY-TWO

I love my family. Noble Kohmose, smiling and steadfast Djephan, even Mama, who scowls whenever I walk into a room. But I don't think I'll ever be closer to anyone than I am to Papa. He raised me up, taught me to be my own person, and invited me to be a part of his life. Enthusiastically and joyously. I have never had need to ask more of Mother Love's fortune than when he stood by my side.

Meritities? The woman who jailed my papa and took his tongue? Who left him to perish in squalor? No. I do not love her. Meritities is no family to me.

Princess Masika Oburn, niece to Holy Emperor Khasek V of Egren

---

After a week of travel at speed through the skies of the Undergates, Jarl Refur's stone vessel finally came to ground amongst the snowy peaks of Hiimryk. After poor food and sour stores of water, the feasting halls of the northmen felt almost like being alive again.

Almost. The trip back had been tense. Rainn's anger at losing

Heron left him eager to vent his rage at the most convenient target. Even the burly northmen learned to keep well clear.

But other blessings accrued from the Hiimrykers. The Andosh dead's hatred of Issta and her demon legions abated not a whit during Masika's absence, and they made themselves ready to raid into the Reaves to recover Heron the instant Rainn and Masika were prepared to go.

Masika, anyway. Rainn wanted to wade in rivers of demon blood without delay.

"Try it now." A Hiimryk woman in a gray, cowled robe sat back on her stool in the round, thatch-roofed hut, nodding to Tennat Oburn. "Go on. Say something."

"La-la-lahlalala!" Tennat grinned, his raggedly bearded face lighting up. "Lahamila! It works." He stuck out his new tongue of jointed hollow steel. "Incredible. How is this even possible?"

A relieved smile, though not an entirely happy one, crossed Masika's face. She ran her hand over her own new knee, which took up a portion of her lower thigh and upper shin. Its iron surface felt hot, and she had been assured it required no maintenance.

"Yours isn't the first tongue we've had to replace, Darrish." The cowled healer clipped Tennat on the side of the head. "Now eat something or I'll replace your stomach with a flap I can throw my trash into. You got me?"

Tennat grinned at her. "Understood, ma'am. Thank you for your work and attention." His voice carried a slight tinniness, but it was still him. "I appreciate it more than I can say."

"Hmph." The healer stood and moved to the door. "See that he eats," she told Masika. "A mirror of a man may not be able to die of starvation, but he can sure as Issta's drooping dugs suffer enough to wish he could." And with that, she quit the tiny hut.

Father and daughter sat in silence for a time, neither wanting to bring noise into their private space. From the moment Masika saw the Emissary bring her papa out of that shimmering window of air, they had been in the company of others. And now that they sat alone, she no longer had any idea what to say.

None of this was fair. Ild the imp, for whom they were bringing back Glauth, said he would prepare her body to receive her soul, though Masika did not understand what that meant at the time. Now she knew it meant that Glauth would have a working body to return to when she came back to the living world, and she still did not know if Glauth's corpse would suddenly be ready for her soul where it lay frozen with one of Sarah's arrows through it, or if the imp would make a new one for her where he was back in the tavern in Treaty Hill.

And perhaps Masika could make another deal with the creature. Have him prepare her papa's body in the same way, whatever that did mean. She resolved to keep the idea to herself for now.

Another deal. But if they succeeded in saving Glauth from the imp's wrath, how would there be any chance of it helping them again? And what about Heron? What more would she have to give to see her returned to Rainn?

"Lahamila . . ." Tennat began, stopping when he saw his daughter burst into tears. He stood with some difficulty and limped to her side, sat down, and put his arm around her.

She clung to him, lost at sea. Her papa was dead.

Eventually the tears subsided. Masika sniffed and wiped her shining brown nose on her cloak, wiped her eyes, and faced him. "I have to go back. I have to find Heron and take them both back to the living world."

"I know you do, my brave girl." Tennat pulled wet strands of hair from her cheeks and pushed them behind her ear. "Life isn't done with you yet."

"What happened?" Masika found she dreaded the answer to that question but had to know regardless. "How did you end up here? Was what he said true?"

"Yes, inasmuch as it went. The Emissary told the truth." Tennat put his hands on his knees and stared at the floor. "But as you might imagine, it wasn't the *whole* truth. Your sister—"

"She is *not* my sister," Masika growled with unaccustomed vehemence. "Not anymore. Meritities is no family of mine."

An expression of profound sadness clouded Tennat's features. He nodded and went on. "Meritities leveraged my capture and your presumed death to become closer to the emperor. He has much affection for her. But my brother is old and married, so he decreed that Meritities should marry the Divine Prince Majada instead. To keep her close to him."

"The emperor's son? He's ten." Masika had only seen the young emperor once before at a diplomatic event arranged by her papa, and the boy hid behind his mother's skirts the whole time.

"Twelve now," Tennat said. "But I believe your sis, *Meritities,* will not be satisfied being the eventual empress under her husband's thumb. I ignored her nature for too long, Lahamila. I pretended she was no different from your mother. But she's so much worse."

"You think she's intending to kill the emperor." Even here, a life and a realm away, Masika whispered the words lest some stray ear overhear them.

"And his wife. I tried to reach out to my brother to tell him of my fears, and Meritities arrived in my cell with the Saraph Jais instead. The emperor's soldiers cut out my tongue while she watched."

Masika's blood boiled in her chest, and she stifled a scream of rage. The woman who had once been her sister would pay for what she had done, and she would pay dearly.

"That was when I knew, the only thing left to me was to reach you before you returned." Tennat sighed and rubbed his hands against his thighs. "To let you know what you'd be facing when you went back. Give you some kind of chance against her."

"You let yourself die just to talk to me?" Masika's tears returned, and she savagely fought them back. A blissfully distracting thought occurred to her. "That's why you appeared in the acid pits too. Instead of Damah where you belong. You were looking for me."

"I didn't know that was a thing, but yes. I was looking for you." He shrugged and smiled. "And look at us. I found you. The Emissary did exactly as I planned."

Masika rolled her eyes and shook her head. "Where will you go now? High King Ivarr said you can stay here as an honored guest for all of time. There might be something to that."

"No." Tennat put his hand on Masika's shoulder, soft and warm. "I'll travel the mountains to Damah and wait for your mother. She'll already be irritated at me for getting there ahead of her. No cause to make things worse."

At that Masika let herself giggle. Her mother's pique never failed to get a rise out of her. "And I still need to go." Their conversation came full circle. "The Emissary won't give up as long as we're in the Undergates, and now we understand what that really means. I wish you could come."

"I have no body to return to, but you do. Denari's magic poison, right? It's all going to be fine, Lahamila." He smiled warmly and patted her cheek. "I'll be waiting here for you too."

An alarmed shout from outside saved Masika from responding—*Rainn's* alarmed shout. She sprang across the room—not even a click from this new knee—and flung open the door.

CHAPTER

FORTY-THREE

Princess Masika Oburn, niece to Holy Emperor Khasek V of Egren

---

Rainn stood in the center of the busy thoroughfare, six feet of honed steel raised above his head. Andosh raiders scattered in the crisp, cold breeze, dropping goods to the dirt in their haste to be out of the god's way.

"Heron?" Masika blinked, unbelieving, but the goddess remained. She stood in front of Rainn, one hand lifted to ward him off, the other hand behind her clutching Boridan. Relief and joy flooded Masika's body such that she could barely breathe. Tears of happiness filled her eyes.

Wiping her arm across her face, Masika bolted from the hut, her slender sword whispering free of its sheath.

"Will everyone put away their cocks and let me talk?" Though her voice spoke to exasperation, a tiny smile of pride lit Heron's features.

322

"Thank you both for wanting to defend me, but it's not necessary. Boridan brought me to you on his own. We should be thanking him, not chopping him to bits."

Boridan's eyes widened in alarm. His irises, Masika saw, were silver, reflective. Instead of seeing into his eyes, Masika only saw herself. He looked empty, as if whatever there was inside of him was no more than what happened to stand in his gaze.

Fist tightening around the grip of his two-hander, Rainn looked from Heron to Masika and back. "I'd really rather kill him. Can someone just tell me what to do here?"

"Put away the sword." Heron's smile turned to outright amusement, and she touched Rainn's upthrust sword hand. "Honestly, it's perfectly all right."

Scowling, Rainn sheathed the huge weapon. But Masika could see the redness in his eyes.

She left her sword in her hand.

"Why?" Masika stepped toward the three of them and Boridan flinched. "After everything you went through to take her, why just give her back? If this is another ploy of your master's—"

"No!" Boridan stepped away from Heron's protection, his hands raised to Masika. Once again she saw herself disquietingly reflected in his stare. "No. Oldam's pendulous marble pecker, Masika, the Emissary doesn't know anything about this. He promised me I could keep her forever, like *forever*-forever." His face contorted into a mask of misery.

"But just the idea of that. The very thought of keeping someone I love so much against her will made me want to die." He choked on the last word and hung his head. Masika had never seen another human being in such wretched despair. "So instead, I brought her to you. I've been looking for you for days now. You need to get away. I'll stay here. I want to be Heron's priest here in the Undergates. I don't know exactly what that'll mean, but it seems like the best thing to do with my love for her."

Masika sheathed her blade, but her hand never strayed far from the pommel. As far as she knew, the Alir did not have priests. "Kinda gross, but it's Heron's call. You want him representing you to all the underworld?"

By way of answer, or perhaps without regard at all to Masika's question, Heron gathered Boridan to her and, one final time, kissed him as she had before. He hung in her embrace, and tears rolled down his cheeks. Eventually he pushed away from her.

Howling winds and lightning crashed behind Rainn's black look.

"Please," Boridan said and wiped his nose. "Not now. Maybe come back when I'm worthy of you? Normal people aren't meant to be in the company of gods. It's overwhelming. I feel like it's killing me." The tears appeared out of place coming from the alien silver eyes. What happened to him out there?

Heron touched Boridan on the nose with a single fingertip. "That's how true worship always begins, Boridan of Tyrrane."

Speaking in a rough growl, Rainn squinted into Boridan's face. "What's up with this fucker's eyes? He looks like he's hiding behind his own eyeballs."

"I don't know." Boridan stared at the ground and shrugged. "Something bit me, I guess. It looked like a silver spider."

He hesitated before continuing. "I haven't known who I was for a long time now. When the Hill Fury replaced my personality with King Keane's, I think it made me happier. Less grim. But when I died, I couldn't tell whose soul I was. What I was supposed to be doing. Was I a brave man or a frightened follower? Being a mirror of a man isn't easy when you can't tell what you're supposed to reflect."

As Boridan spoke, Rainn moved closer to Heron. She took his hand.

Boridan continued, "I wasn't ready to love. I couldn't understand it. I had to figure out who I really was first. I had to smash the pieces of the mirror and put them back into something new. Something whole. Something me."

"And have you done that, Boridan?" Masika asked.

"I don't know." He answered her with a shrug and a smile. "I think what I've learned is that I'm not ready. Two personalities, maybe two souls, makes less than a man. But I know what I want now. I want to be worthy of the thing I'll never have. I want to be worthy of being loved."

An intense frown contorted Rainn's face. "Every human is worthy of being loved, Boridan. It's one of the ways you're better than the fucking gods. I mean, you'll never be worthy of Heron, but eventually your standards'll drop low enough, and on that day you'll find your love."

"Don't be such a turd, Rainn," Masika said. "Boridan, where will you go?"

"I don't know. Hopefully someplace they appreciate waterfowl." He grinned and winked at Masika.

A flap opened in the tent behind Masika, and Tennat emerged. He looked around at the faces and nodded to himself, making up his mind about something. "I hate to bring this up, but if Boridan could figure out where you three were, it's a safe assumption that the Emissary can too. It's time."

"Tennat?" Heron's brow rose in surprise. "Oh no, I'm sorry."

He waved her off. "I was destined to end up here eventually, this was just a little sooner than I'd planned. I imagine that's true for most of us though."

Masika struggled for breath. Her chest tightened, and she lost her speech. How could she go back now? Meritities was inches from the emperor's throne, her family was ripped apart, and her papa would not be there.

She pushed the thought away, concentrating on Boridan. A hollow shell of a man's soul, with only a veneer of someone else's personality imprinted onto him by Sarah. No wonder he remained so steeped in misery.

But Masika saw something else in Boridan too. She saw his love for Heron, a tiny, brilliant spark of it, utterly separate from the thin crust that lay over him. Something entirely his. Something he could build a new self around.

The idea brought to mind the vision Inlittan showed Masika of herself, even as Taywilah the sorceress cut Inlittan out of her head—a vision of Masika beneath the doubts. A true friend, a loyal daughter, and a woman of honor. Loving. Determined. She possessed the strength for this.

She had to.

Masika nodded. "Let's find Morholt."

CHAPTER

FORTY-FOUR

What is greater than respect? Wealth? Power? Family that loves you and does whatever you tell them to?

I don't know. That all sounds good to me.

Princess Masika Oburn, niece to Holy Emperor Khasek V of Egren

---

N o, it makes me sick." Raven's angry outburst guided Masika and the others through the snow-covered pines. "They don't need you; you just can't stand being away from *vagina of fire* here."

Stepping out of the trees, Masika frowned at Raven, dark and angry, Glauth, thin-faced and smirking, and Morholt, pale skin flushed, standing in front of a tall outcropping of boulders. The stones made a flat wall on which Morholt painted runes in a variety of sizes and circular patterns, and which also provided a bit of shelter from the snow.

"Don't give me crap about wanting some companionship. You have your dagger handles to keep you company. Who have I got?" He waved his hands in frustration. "Are you going to stay and keep an eye on things or not? Either way I'm going with them."

"You have *four wives* back home, asshole. It's not my fault they're all dumb as a full diaper. And yes, I'm staying. I sure as fuck don't want to watch what the two of you'll be doing." Raven stood stiff-backed. Threatening. "But we just got done taking Dan Tura from our goddamned parents. You leave now and how long do you think it'll be before someone figures out where we put them and lets them back out? Huh? A week? A day? Have you even thought about what'll happen when your demon wife, Venthria, gets back and you're not there? Do you know what a craptastic spectacle that'll be?"

"I like this woman," Rainn whispered to Masika, a sly grin creeping over his face. His hand remained in Heron's.

Masika patted him fondly on the shoulder. "You're a pig."

"Hey"—Rainn inclined his head to her, brow lowered in genuine concern—"I been meaning to ask, are you all right about the whole Sarah thing? I know you wanted to meet the fucking woman, but she kinda threw you in the latrines."

"I'm fine." And Masika meant it. "Sarah knew what she was doing. If she hadn't ordered the Hiimrykers to hold us captive, they would never have sent Jarl Refur after us. They don't like to leave their own borders, remember? And without Refur, we would've died fighting the Emissary at Dan Tura. If I'm meant to meet Sarah, I will. In the meantime, I'll settle for thanking her in my own heart."

Rainn's frown deepened. "Sounds kinda nebulous to me." He leaned in and lowered his voice. "That means bullshitty."

"By the way," Glauth said to Heron, interrupting Morholt and Raven's argument, "Ild lied to you, I think. I made him. No way he can sneak you into the Alireon under High King Oldam's nose. He can't actually affect the real world at all. Only convince others to do what he says. I know you changed your minds about going back home anyway, but I thought you should know, yes?"

"Thank you." Heron nodded to Glauth. "It was trusting of you to reveal that. And we'll still be beside you when you confront the imp."

"See, Raven?" Arms spread, Morholt cocked his head, the very picture of frustrated aggrievement. "Glauth didn't have to say any of that. She's a good person. You just can't see it because you shat out your heart in the crib and it got thrown out with the rest of your crap. Not like Mom or Dad would've seen the value in—"

"Stop." At Raven's dangerous-sounding hiss, silence blanketed the group. "One more word and I won't have to stab her when she gets you killed. Because I'll stab you myself."

Tennat stepped around Masika and up to Morholt and Raven. "If I may, it sounds as if you have a diplomatic problem. I intended to head straight to Damah when the rest left, but if you'd have me, I could travel back with you and help you sort out your problems first. I am considered to be something of an expert in these sorts of things."

"What?" Morholt stared at Tennat as if seeing him for the first time.

"My daughter isn't the only one who needs help here." Tennat smiled and clapped Morholt on the arm. "Now, as I understand things from what I gleaned on the trip here, Savach's Sovereign Council is pressuring you to raise armies and spend your own blood protecting Savach, while Murden pushes for so many concessions you might as well turn over your handükdom to the demons. Is that right?"

"Yes?" Morholt said, one brow going up.

Tennat squeezed Morholt's arm. "I faced a similar situation during my time as the Holy Emperor's chief diplomat, and we resolved that to everyone's satisfaction. Played both sides against the other and got their full-throated thanks for the privilege. I'd like to tell you about it."

"All right." Morholt turned away from Raven, seemingly forgetting their argument.

"But first," Tennat said, "my daughter and her friends need to go. You can always follow later after your affairs are straightened out, I suppose."

"Yeah, that's fine, I guess." Morholt nodded, his gaze far away.

"Your father's a marvel," Heron said. "I shouldn't wonder that he'll make Morholt king of the Undergates before the year's out."

"Can't believe the fucking imp lied to us about getting us home," Rainn said.

"Of course he lied." Heron put a hand on Rainn's forearm and squeezed. "You're just mad because you believed it."

"We ready?" Masika asked, stomping on the butterflies in her stomach.

"Almost." Face tight, Morholt nodded to Raven. "Glauth, will the Arrowwilds keep murking all my dignitaries? I've been trying to make peace, but no one would talk to me."

"You should've sent stronger dignitaries, I think." Glauth laughed at him. "But yes. I sent word the instant we landed in Hiimryk. It is maybe possible that we should've talked to you from the first, yes? But, to be fair, dignitaries and assassins look very much alike when you strip them and lay them out on a rack for flaying."

"Kinky," Morholt said. He indicated the runes drawn on the wall. "I've got this leg of the journey. You think you can handle the return trip?"

"Sounds like Ild is planning on handling that for me. But yes. I understand how you make the thing. We should be fine." Glauth smiled and grasped Morholt by the back of the neck. "You were adequate in bed, I think. But overall terrible as a boyfriend. Don't let the council or the demons beat you." She clapped his cheek. "And you promised me a rune engine, yes? I'll be expecting it."

Masika remained surprised that Glauth stayed true to her word to accompany them back to the living world. She and the Alir did keep up their end of the bargain, marching off to war against Dan Tura with the armies of the Arrowwilds, but it seemed to Masika as if there must be more to it. Perhaps Glauth was nobler than she seemed. Perhaps she even felt responsible for Ild's evils and wanted to be the one to rectify them.

Or maybe she just wanted to live a little more.

"Yes!" Morholt raised his arms and let them drop to his sides. "I'll make you a rune engine as soon as we get to Dan Tura. A tiny one." With that he drew a line with his finger down through one of the smaller painted rings of runes and set it spinning. "This one first. It's the fulcrum for the rest."

"I'm not blind you know." Glauth gave a little snort. "I can see which is the fulcrum. Making the gate is not so hard as knowing where it goes, yes? And you already told me that."

"Heron? Rainn? Are the two of you still resolved not to return to the Alireon after all?" Masika's emotions swirled, nebulous and unfathomable even to herself. She smiled. Nebulous. Bullshitty.

"What?" Tennat asked, flummoxed. "The imp can't be the only way. You're not planning to go back at all?"

Rainn put his hands on his hips and breathed in deep, filling his lungs with cold mountain air. "Yeah, the other gods are all fuckheads. Issta's an Alir, and she sent that emissary of hers to murk everyone and drag us back. That cut it for me. At first we wanted to go back because we thought they were our family. But none of them came for us when Angrim snatched us, and to be perfectly honest, they always treated us like trash anyway."

"And you, dear Masika, never have. You're the only family we need." Heron drifted closer and pulled Masika to her.

Masika pushed against Heron enough to look her in the eye. "But what about what Angrim did to you? He crippled you with the tattoos he put on your living bodies and robbed you of your godly power. When we go back, you'll be crippled again. Morholt said Taywilah lied when she told you you'd be fine. And you'll be stuck as a bird. What will you do?" Masika left it unsaid that the longer Heron spent in the form of a bird, unable to transform back, the more likely it was that she would forget herself and remain that way. An immortal heron flying the coastlines of Andos.

"And I'll get to be a sword again! It's about fuck time." Forbryttan yawned as he rolled over on Rainn's broad shoulder and grinned, his frightening tusks jutting out of his face.

Rainn rolled his eyes and chuckled. "*Fucking* time. Fuck time means something else."

Heron inclined her head to Masika. "I do not believe that I will be stuck in my other self. Before we came here, I could not recall how to affect the transformation. Now, obviously, I do."

"That's great news, Heron. That was really worrying me. I should have asked. But still, I feel like we're starting over again from the beginning." The thought rang bleak in Masika's ears.

"No, see, we got a plan." Rainn winked at Raven, who rolled her eyes and turned away. "Your girl Raven there knows of a person called Gak'inlon."

"Not a person," Raven said, examining the blade of one of her daggers. "He's a carpet. Or he's *in* a carpet. Something like that."

"Yeah, fine." Rainn waved his hand. "He's a rug. Not the important part."

"Raven believes that this Ga'Kinlon can help us find Fulnir-Einvald," Heron breathed.

Masika had no idea who that was.

"Einvald the Foul?" Tennat asked, his chin thrust forward. "Why would you want to find him? Why would anyone want to find him?"

"What am I missing here?" Masika asked.

"Einvald used to be Angrim's apprentice, back when the big Anger Under the Mountain caught us and threw us in the dark." Rainn smiled grimly as he said it. "First one, I think. What fuckery Angrim did to us was Einvald's idea. He knows how it works. And if he likes all his fingers on the ends of his hands where they're supposed to be, he'll unfuck it."

"Swords can chop off fingers," Forbryttan said brightly. "It's fuck time."

Rainn chuckled. "That's not what that . . . Ah, fuck time is close enough."

"Or we can just ask," Heron said.

"I'll ask. I'll ask nice." Rainn made a breaking motion with his hands and a nod to Forbryttan.

"I don't like this." Tennat frowned up at Rainn. "If you find him, it'll be a terrible risk. And how do you even know he's still alive?"

"He's not the sort who would go unnoticed in a place like this."

Heron twirled a graceful finger to encompass all of the Undergates. "And no one's mentioned anything about him."

"That's not really conclusive," Morholt muttered, "but then I haven't heard of a Foul Einvald either, and those're the sorts of circles my family traveled in."

"Raven, how do you know this Gak'inlon?" Masika needed to ask everything now, before they left.

"I was trained by the Khamsen," Raven answered. "Your people."

"The emperor's assassins aren't exactly my people," Masika said. "I don't even understand how that could happen. You're not Darrish. You're, well, you look Andosh." The Khamsen were the emperor's Desert Wind. Such a thing must be impossible.

"Long story, and beside the point." Raven flicked a glance at the wall of boulders, where the runes all spun at different speeds. "Gak'inlon's like a god but not. Not really. He helps those that would walk unseen, find things unfound. So naturally the Khamsen worshipped him. Because they're idiots. No offense."

"None taken." Masika felt she might ought to be offended but was not certain exactly why. They were not her assassins.

"Anyway, that'll be your guy." Raven nodded toward the Alir. "Those two already know my best guess for finding him."

Forbryttan sat up straight on Rainn's shoulder. "This was a lot of fun, but I can't wait to be myself again. I miss chopping bits off of people, chopping all the way through other people. Mostly I miss all the chopping."

"Have some standards. You a sword or an axe?" Rainn smirked at his faded blue friend as he said it.

Forbryttan's mouth dropped open, his small eyes as wide as they would go. "You take that back."

"So first we bring Glauth to Ild and hope Catlia and Romi have an idea to protect her," Masika counted items on her fingers, "and we save the heroes Ild's holding over our heads. Then we find somebody in a carpet who can tell us where Angrim's first apprentice is and hope *he* doesn't want to kill us for it, and lastly we beg *that* guy to undo what he and the worst monster the living world has ever known did to the two of you. Does that cover everything?"

And if Catlia and Romi failed to protect Glauth and the imp got what he was after, Masika would pretend that was her plan all along and bargain with Ild to make her papa a new body too.

"Sounds like it to me." Rainn rubbed his hands together and shared a nod with Heron. "Tennat, been good seeing you again. You and the ginger fuck try not to turn the place on its ear while we're gone, right?"

"And you keep my daughter safe." Tennat placed his hands on Rainn's shoulders. "I don't want to see her again until she's an old woman."

"You got it." Rainn hugged him.

"If we're all done?" Glauth gestured to the spinning rings of runes. "This thing only works if we step through it." She grinned. "And I gotta pee."

One by one, Masika, Heron, and Rainn locked gazes, took each other's hands, and walked to the runecrafted portal.

"I love you, Papa," Masika said, swallowing her grief. "I'll be back before you know it."

"I love you too, Lahamila." Tears welled in Tennat's eyes. "But don't be in such a hurry. Live a life first. I've got forever."

They stepped through.

FORTY-FIVE

I chased my sister to Mount P'takkin to save my family the embarrassment of her bringing a pair of horrible Andosh beast-gods to the most holy of all places, the Darrish House of the Gods. I think, deep down, I wanted to kill her, despite wishing to save our papa and mama the grief.

Later, it occurred to me that Masika only wanted to go to the Undergates anyway, and that was what waited for her at the top of that mountain after all. I really shouldn't have bothered.

Princess Meritities Oburn, niece to Holy Emperor Khasek V of Egren

---

Masika awoke to the sounds of muted conversation and breezes rushing through stone windows. She pushed herself up from the dirt and lifted the empty piece of jewelry that once was Inlittan. It sat heavy and lifeless around her wrist, its spinning bands of runes still and dark.

The spinning confused her. Was Inlittan dead or merely quiet?

In the next room she saw Heron and Rainn conversing next to the throne of Denari the Clear Eyed. They sat close to one another, their noses almost touching, eyes locked on each other.

But the throne room looked different than last time, dimmer. The divine luster replaced by bare walls of brown rock. Denari's grand Long Window of stained glass that used to display the entire universe sat empty, showing nothing more than the indirect light of an overcast sky.

But that still meant they were in the House of the Gods atop Mount P'takkin.

They had made it.

Masika dragged herself erect. Her body felt sluggish and unresponsive. As if she had overslept after too much berry wine. She stumbled into the throne room.

"Go slow," Heron hurried to Masika's side and supported here with an arm. "The poison Denari gave us takes a while to recede." She smiled. "But I'm happy you made it regardless."

Seized by a sudden yawn, Masika bent over, wiped her eyes, and glanced about herself. At Heron. "You're not a bird!"

"I'm not. Though I believe I told you I would not be. Still, I'd be lying if I said there was no anxiety there. I am grateful to be myself for certain." Heron's warm smile comforted Masika to the tips of her toes.

Looking around, Masika spotted a pile of blankets laid out across Denari Clear-Eyed's throne. The bedclothes were in a tangle. "Uh, how long have I been asleep?"

"Not long," Rainn responded with a completely straight face.

"Overnight. We wanted to let you sleep." Why was Heron not meeting Masika's gaze as she answered? Why had no one given her a blanket to sleep under?

Forbryttan—the sword—rested in its sheath, leaning up against the throne. One of the bronze rings set into the grip twinkled at her.

A frown touched Heron's mouth, pulling her delicate brows down with it. "Something occurred to me while we waited. Ild claimed he would restore Glauth's body so her soul would have somewhere to go to when we brought her back."

The expression highlighted the flush in Heron's cheeks, the red that ran down her neck, as if she had been moving furniture in the House of the Gods.

"That's right," Masika said. "That was our deal with him. He wanted to kill Glauth himself."

Heron gave a slight shake of her head. "But we already know he lied when he told us he could get us back to the Alireon. Glauth said he can't affect the real world at all. Just influence others. What if he lied about recreating Glauth's body too? What if he never could?"

"Why would he do that?" The first stirrings of anger ignited in Masika's stomach.

"Because he didn't just wanna kill her." Rainn's voice was low. Serious. "He wanted us to bring her back without a body to go back to. Little fucker wanted to *murk* her." He glanced down and spun away, adjusting his clothing.

Masika looked from Rainn to Heron and back again. They had to get off of this mountain. Find a way back to Treaty Hill. See if Romi and Catlia knew where Glauth might be and make sure they were all right too. If they tried to move against Ild before Masika returned, the imp could make them kill themselves with their own daggers. There was no time to waste.

All at once Masika's arm whipped out, her finger pointing from Heron's florid face to Rainn's disheveled clothing, and to the pile of tangled blankets on the throne.

"Denari clear the fog, you two just had sex! With me right there!"

The scarlet rose to the top of Heron's forehead, and she turned her face away.

Rainn grinned like a dog caught with his face in the roast duck. "Oh, better than that. I'm pretty sure the way this place works is that we can't see the real House of the Gods without drinking Denari's special poison, but everyone here, all the Darrish gods we can't see, they can all see us just fine. The grand P'tak just watched Heron and me consecrate that throne in the name of the Alir."

Soft gray hair fanning about her head, Heron's face whipped back around to stare at Rainn, open-mouthed horror creeping over her features. "You're . . . I can't . . ." She dropped her face into one hand, a tight smile peeking out.

"Sorry, we're leaving now, Blessings of the Alir on you!" And giggling, Heron grabbed Rainn in the crook of one arm, Masika in the other, and snatching Forbryttan from the throne, all four of them sprinted for the door.

Rainn burst into laughter as they ran out into the sunlit courtyard atop might Mount P'takkin. He held up his sword and spoke directly to it. "Yeah, Forby, you're right. That finally *was* fuck time."

Acknowledgments

I feel a little silly always acknowledging the same people, yet they continue to be the most important to me and what I do, and to putting these books into your hands. So here they are once again . . . with a few additions here and there.

First is Lena, my wife, who has *just* finished sacrificing yet another of her weekends to help me sign books and meet fans at Ancient City Con. She is amazing, patient, thoughtful, and brilliant. She is my best friend and my teammate, and I could not do any of this without her.

There have been at least a dozen industry people over the course of my career who, if you were to pluck any one of them out of my life, would result in my having no books written, no career at all, and no fulfillment of my lifetime's dream.

Among the first of these is Eric Flynt, in whose memory I would like to dedicate this novel. Eric gave the impression of being a gruff old crank, but in truth he was the most caring and generous of souls. He genuinely gave a shit about the people coming up in his industry and actively moved to help them. To help me.

Eric critiqued my work, helped me out with the rough patches, and helped me find my voice. He reviewed my contracts and gave me practical, professional advice on how not only to behave myself, but also how to expect others to behave and how to gently ensure that I was never taken advantage of by anyone. This advice led me to recognize and celebrate Cursed Dragon Ship as the best publishing company I could ever find.

Next is the crew at Cursed Dragon Ship, the owners Kelly and Kevin Colby, who work tirelessly to bring new books to the world and who I would simply exhaust myself trying to list everything they do for me. And also my editors, Kelly, Birdee, and Shannon, who improve these works far more than anyone will ever truly understand, and all from behind the scenes without any fanfare or public acknowledgment beyond what little I can provide them.

Lastly, I *have* to talk about my fellow *Misplaced Adventures* authors (in alphabetical order), Jen Bair, Ethan A. Cooper, William LJ Galaini, Jessica Raney, and C.M. McGuire. These people jumped on our (cursed dragon) ship with both feet, spinning astounding stories in previously unexplored corners of what is now *our* world. It has been one of the most profound honors of my life to read their works, discuss stories, and see my map expand in ways I could never have expected or accomplished without them.

Thank you. Thank you all.

And of course, you, the reader. I hope that you continue to stick with us and enjoy the adventures of Masika and the gang, and to perhaps take a look at what the other *Misplaced Adventures* authors are doing too. They are well worth your time.

—Kevin

ABOUT THE AUTHOR

Kevin Pettway hails from Jacksonville, Florida, and is the author of the Misplaced Mercenaries books, a funny adult fantasy series that was awarded by the NYC Big Book Club, a finalist in the 2022 Imadjinn Awards, and has received several professional write-ups in Kirkus Magazine for which the author did not even have to pay. He has published a modest number of short stories, both within and without the Mercenaries world, with more on the way. Most excitingly, Kevin's publisher, Cursed Dragon Ship Publishing, has threatened encouraged him to open his world to other authors, creating the Misplaced Adventures Shared Universe. There are currently six authors toiling away to bring even more humor, fun, and backstabbing murder into the world, with plans to add even more in the next few years.

Although the old stereotype about writers just wanting to be locked away in a darkened room with a typewriter is as true of Kevin as it is anyone else, the other thing he enjoys tremendously is going to conventions and meeting new people. (In writing, two opposing motivations in the same person are often used to create tension and conflict and engage reader interest. Now that you know his conflicting motivations you understand just how deep and fascinating Kevin is!)

He regularly attends a large number of popular culture conventions, selling books and telling stories to people who haven't heard them before while his wife Lena tries to ignore him. Feel free to walk up and say hi. Nothing makes him happier. (You might also express condolences to Lena, who has heard all the stories.)

River and Book, Kevin and Lena's two dogs, also love meeting people, but hotels rarely love meeting dogs, so they stay behind at the puppy resort. Canine fan-mail will be accepted and forwarded to the appropriate addressee.

Kevin thinks Strange New Worlds is the best Trek series, nudging The Orville off that top spot, and is enjoying the Tolkeinesque comedy The Rings of Power more than he thought he would. His favorite new author is Tamsyn Muir, and his favorite old author is Roger Zelazny. (He may be dead, but he's still selling!) He is also developing an obsession for kayaking, having discovered it late in life and is unable to get enough.

Despite being from Florida, Kevin still has all his own teeth and has never had a restraining order placed against him.

Make sure to join Kevin's newsletter from his website: https://kevinpettway.com.

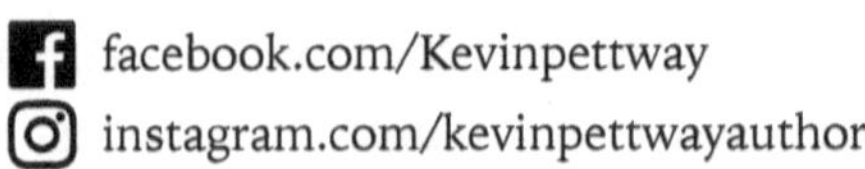

facebook.com/Kevinpettway

instagram.com/kevinpettwayauthor

JOIN THE CURSED DRAGON SHIP NEWSLETTER

Love what you just read? Want more just like it? Sign up for our newsletter so you don't miss out on the adventure. You'll get:

- A free book for signing up
- Advanced notice of new releases
- First word of books on sale
- Opportunities for free books
- Most up-to-date information on author appearances.

We're busy and know you are too. We won't send more than one newsletter a month.

Register below.

CHECK OUT THE ANTHOLOGY FEATURING CHARACTERS FROM EACH MA SERIES

A card cursed with self-awareness seeks a hero to retrieve his creator from the afterlife. Nothing could possibly go wrong.

CHECK OUT THE SERIES THAT STARTED IT ALL

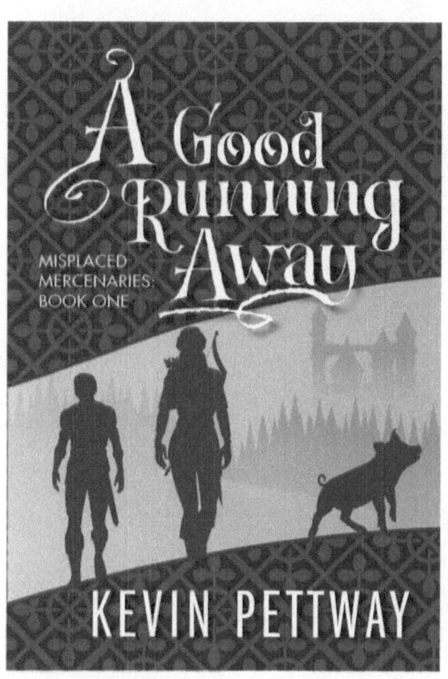

*Stealing the cash box of your mercenary unit as you run away
probably isn't wise, but it sure is funny.*